Praise for the works of Cheryl Sawyer

The Code of Love

"Once you're caught in the tangled web of this delicious, multitextured romance, you'll find it impossible to put down." —*Romantic Times*

"Offers romance and adventure on a grand scale, a story you'll want to read again and again." —BookLoons

"Beautifully written, wonderfully researched, and with a poignant love story . . . a must read and a Perfect 10." —Romance Reviews Today

"A commanding historical entwined with espionage and a celestial romance that will have you sitting on the edge of your seat." —Romance Junkies

"Splendid! Rich in history, romance and intrigue, *The Code of Love* brilliantly interweaves a thrilling tale of espionage with a captivating love story, when Cheryl Sawyer entangles two deeply compelling characters in a passionate struggle to find happiness against almost overwhelming odds. The result is a lavishly atmospheric and believable tale that's guaranteed to keep readers enthralled until the very last page. Highly recommended!"
—Julia Ross, RITA Award winner and bestselling author of *Night of Sin*

continued . . .

D0089612

The Chase

"[W]ill have readers enthralled with its complex characters, intricate plot, and richly detailed setting."   —*Booklist*

"Fine Regency romantic suspense starring an intrepid heroine . . . a tense historical intrigue."   —The Best Reviews

"Never before have I envisioned the whole tapestry as I do with *The Chase*. . . . It's one you want to plunge deeply into, immerse yourself into Sophia's emotions, and let the atmosphere sink into your pores."
                                            —Romance Reviews Today

"A powerful love story that will leave you breathless. Cheryl Sawyer has outdone herself again with an authentic historical woven with mystery, vivid imagery, and an intense passion that will have you turning the sizzling pages one after another. . . . *The Chase* will go on my keeper shelf along with her other novels."   —Romance Junkies

"Three-dimensional characters, deeply emotional storyline, and rich historical detail."   —*Romantic Times* (4 ½ stars, Top Pick)

"Sublime."   —Fresh Fiction

"A big, juicy, complex novel."   —All About Romance

Siren

"With its lavish use of history, boldly passionate story, and vividly detailed settings, Australian author Sawyer's American debut is a grand and glorious delight for fans of the classic love stories of Kathleen Woodiwiss and Rosemary Rogers." —*Booklist*

"[A] sweeping epic tale . . . wonderfully brings to life a bygone era."
—*Midwest Book Review*

"From the very first pages of this impressive novel, the reader is treated to a colorful tapestry of sights and impressions set amongst the vivid streets of New Orleans to the colorful beaches of the Caribbean. . . . A high-seas adventure." —Historical Romance Writers

"[Sawyer] infuses historical events with color, passion, and thrilling escapades. With impeccable detail and larger-than-life characters, this debut will be on historical fiction readers' must-have list." —*Romantic Times*

"All the scenes in this marvelous epic tale are intense. A fabulous historical read . . . and one that I highly recommend." —Romance Reviews Today

"I loved sinking into this rich and complex novel. . . . Sawyer's historical descriptions and rich prose are compulsively readable."
—All About Romance

"Cheryl Sawyer's rich narrative and brilliant characterization light up a neglected era in America's history. . . . A beautifully researched novel with a powerful love story." —RITA Award Winner Isolde Martyn

"Cheryl Sawyer's sensual and romantic historical epics will captivate readers. Sawyer creates lush tapestries woven with vivid images, rich prose, and historic authenticity." —National bestselling author Madeline Hunter

"A gloriously textured and crafted tale of history as well as a timeless, seductive love story." —*New York Times* bestselling author Bertrice Small

The Winter Prince

CHERYL SAWYER

A SIGNET ECLIPSE BOOK

SIGNET ECLIPSE
Published by New American Library, a division of
Penguin Group (USA) Inc., 375 Hudson Street,
New York, New York 10014, USA
Penguin Group (Canada), 90 Eglinton Avenue East, Toronto,
Ontario M4P 2Y3, Canada (a division of Pearson Penguin Canada Inc.)
Penguin Books Ltd., 80 Strand, London WC2R 0RL, England
Penguin Ireland, 25 St. Stephen's Green, Dublin 2,
Ireland (a division of Penguin Books Ltd.)
Penguin Group (Australia), 250 Camberwell Road, Camberwell, Victoria 3124,
Australia (a division of Pearson Australia Group Pty. Ltd.)
Penguin Books India Pvt. Ltd., 11 Community Centre, Panchsheel Park,
New Delhi - 110 017, India
Penguin Group (NZ), 67 Apollo Drive, Mairangi Bay,
Auckland 1311, New Zealand (a division of Pearson New Zealand Ltd.)
Penguin Books (South Africa) (Pty.) Ltd., 24 Sturdee Avenue,
Rosebank, Johannesburg 2196, South Africa

Penguin Books Ltd., Registered Offices: 80 Strand, London WC2R 0RL, England

First published by Signet Eclipse, an imprint of New American Library,
a division of Penguin Group (USA) Inc.

First Printing, April 2007
10   9   8   7   6   5   4   3   2   1

Cover painting of woman: *Queen Henriette Maria (1606–69)* by Sir Peter Lely. Musée Condé, Chantilly, France. Giraudon/The Bridgeman Art Library. Cover painting of man: *Wanderer Above the Sea of Fog* by Caspar David Friedrich. © Archivo Iconografico, S.A./Corbis.

SIGNET ECLIPSE and logo are trademarks of Penguin Group (USA) Inc.

LIBRARY OF CONGRESS CATALOGING-IN-PUBLICATION DATA:
Sawyer, Cheryl.
The winter prince / by Cheryl Sawyer.
p. cm.
ISBN-13: 978-0-451-22044-8
ISBN-10: 0-451-22044-7
1. Ephelia, fl. 1679—Fiction. 2. Rupert, Prince, Count Palatine, 1619–1682. 3. Charles I, King of England, 1600–1649—Fiction. 4. Great Britain—History—Civil War, 1642–1649—Fiction. I. Title.
PR9639.4.S29W56 2007
823'.92—dc22   2006029897

Set in New Baskerville
Designed by Spring Hoteling

Printed in the United States of America

To our summer prince, Arthur Samuel Hingley

Before my passion struck my reason blind,
Such generosity dwelt in my mind,
I cared for none, and yet to all was kind.

—EPHELIA

Rupert and Mary's England, 1642-44

✗ *Rupert's battles in this period*

SCOTLAND

Glasgow ○ Edinburgh ○

Tynemouth ○
Newcastle ○

○ Whitby

○ Bridlington

Irish Sea

Marston Moor ✗ ○ York

○ Preston

✗ *Bolton*

Liverpool ✗

North

ENGLAND

Sea

○ Chester

○ Lincoln

Newark ○ ✗
○ Nottingham

Ashby ○

Shrewsbury ○

✗ *Lichfield*

Bridgnorth ○

✗ *Birmingham*

Bewdley ○

Stratford-upon-Avon ○

WALES

Worcester ○

○ Cropredy

Powick ✗ ✗ *Edgehill* ✗ ○ Banbury

Gloucester ○

○ Woodstock

○ Aylesbury

Abingdon ○ ○ Oxford

LONDON

Cirencester ○ ✗

○ Wallingford

Cardiff ○

○

✗ *Bristol*

○ Reading

Cobham ○

○ Margate

○ Bath

✗ *Newbury*

Dover ○

○ Bideford

Exeter ○

○ Lyme

Weymouth ○

Plymouth ○

| 0 | SCALE | 100 |
Miles

Falmouth ○

The Winter Prince

"Prince Rupert is coming!" Snow was falling on Whitehall, turning the maze of rooftops, chimneys and courtyards into a glittering puzzle, as intricate as one of the sugared centerpieces with which the royal confectioner liked to grace the king's table. When the news stole through the palace, it made some military gentlemen frown and some ladies turn aside to conceal pink cheeks as though they had just taken a walk in the winter air.

King Charles the First made no secret of his joy. To him, Rupert was the most energetic soldier he could ever call to his side, the most devoted and the least ambitious, unless it were for service and glory. Some courtiers wondered, not without ambitious stirrings themselves, that a monarch in his forties should think of advancing a commander in his twenties, but Charles had no reservations. This was the son of his spectacular sister Elizabeth, a consummate soldier from early youth, and the prince who had just spent three years in an Austrian prison for making war on the Holy Roman Emperor.

Rupert had scarcely returned to Holland from captivity before he sent to say he was taking ship for England. His word was steel: in the new year of 1642 he would be in London.

"Prince Rupert is coming, *Dieu merci*." The queen said it with a smile that lifted her pretty top lip over her prominent teeth and gave her the air of an eager child. Her ladies-in-waiting exclaimed with well-rehearsed surprise and relief, except for Mary Villiers, Duchess of Richmond, who was at the window watching the snow drift down.

Mary remained with her back to the room, thinking of the gifted boy she had first heard of from Holland, whose sense of mischief had earned him his childhood nickname: *Rupert le diable*. And later, on his visit to London, the improbably tall young man with the rare, wicked smile who charmed wherever he pleased and deeply pleased those whom he charmed, or so rumor said.

A snowflake tumbled against a diamond-shaped pane and remained there. Mary turned to find the queen observing her.

Queen Henrietta-Maria said in French, "You are not amazed, madam?"

Mary smiled. "No, delighted for you. I know how you have hoped for this."

Henrietta-Maria said, "My hopes are for England. If Rupert brings comfort to my husband I am more than content." She sighed. "To have the prince answer so readily, so fondly . . . in this time of need . . ."

The queen's eyes were sparkling with tears, which always had their effect on Mary. She moved forward, took a stool near her knee and continued speaking in French, for it was Henrietta-Maria's language and the one she used among her ladies when she sought sympathy. It was also the language in which Mary could often make the queen laugh, though they were far from mirth today. "He brings no army? Just himself and his many talents?"

"I think he has a small company who fought with him in Europe. There are English and Scots amongst them. The king's men will welcome their experience."

Mary rather doubted it; the guards at Whitehall, whom Charles had greatly increased and put under a new commander, were much more likely to be jealous of Prince Rupert. She wondered how he would deal with that—at once, if he were still as arrogant as before. "He may be much altered, after all these years at war. And in prison."

The queen's eyes were still gleaming. "You remember him well?"

"Oh yes. I remember him."

Part One

And yet this friendship doth so fast improve,
I dread lest it in time should grow to love.

—EPHELIA

Chapter 1

ON THE COLD JANUARY day when King Charles decided to arrest five members of his Parliament, James Stuart, Duke of Richmond and Lennox, ignoring all other business in that crowded afternoon, paid a visit to his wife.

Entering the great hall of his London house, he had her summoned, but her tiring woman said that her mistress respectfully wished to receive him in her private chamber. As he walked through to his wife's apartments the duke wondered if she were unwell, which would not suit his purpose. Her health was ever delicate; perhaps she was lying down in the bedchamber beyond. But when he went into the first chamber, alone, he found her dressed and drying her hair before the fire.

"Your servant, madam. Must you do that every other day?"

"Yes, my lord." She straightened and the hair sailed back and settled over her shoulders, glinting with sparks reflected from the fire.

"Why court such danger?"

She shrugged, the movement tightening her gown across her white breasts. "It gives me the itch, otherwise." Her voice, with its light, amused timbre, made the answer sound like a special intimacy. He looked at her—at the tangled red-gold hair, the tolerant smile in her dark blue eyes—and it struck him that no other man in England could have just this view of the Duchess of Richmond. Of such covert pleasures was his life with her made up.

He gestured to a chair by the hearth, but she stepped forward. "Meat, drink—what shall I command?"

"There is no time. Please sit."

There was a crisp rustle as she took a stool beside the table in the middle of the room. She was dressed sumptuously as usual, in satin and pearls.

He said, "Tomorrow, when His Majesty attends Parliament, he

will arrive with a guard and arrest Pym, Hampden, Holles, Strode and Haselrig."

She drew in a soft breath and sat back. "Who proposed *that*?"

He shook his head. "No one. The decision is his."

"He has already asked Parliament to impeach them, and the House of Lords to try them. Why this?"

"The Lords have set up a committee, but he will not wait for their verdict on his right to arraign them."

She spoke slowly. "He will bring arms into the Commons."

He nodded. "I need not discuss the enormity of it. No sovereign of England has ever acted thus! But our objections have met a wall of granite."

He saw a shiver of alarm. "In what manner did you oppose him?"

"My good self?" He gave her a hard smile. "With all the tact I could muster. And as little success."

"What has brought him to this? Some new offense?" She caught his look. "No. This Parliament has been an affront to him ever since he called it. But if he removes such men as these, what makes him think the rest will bend at once to his will?"

"I fear he has gone beyond reason on the matter. He wants them in the Tower and he will have them there tomorrow afternoon."

She caught her hair up behind her head, turned her face aside, and he could see the concentration in her profile, rosy against her pale arm. She was never altogether still; her slender body seemed to crave movement. Then she glanced at him sidelong. "Can none persuade him otherwise?"

"You might. All the wisest, the closest, have tried. Except you."

Her eyes widened. It was the first favor he had ever asked of her. It was the only time he had ever let her imagine him vulnerable in the great arena within which each of them had been raised— the labyrinthine court of the Stuarts. She had no right to say him nay. But if she consented and lent him her aid, it would give her a power in his affairs that he had so far denied her. James Stuart held no high government office and he had no need to, for he stood at the king's right hand. Charles always turned to him for counsel, and he had never required his wife's voice to make himself heard. This one case, however, was perilously different.

She lowered her hands to her lap, and took a moment to answer. The fine skin around her eyes quivered as she looked down. Only in the bedchamber did he ever see this vulnerability—the flicker of shock, the hasty summoning of her defenses. But her voice was resilient. "I am flattered you think I might go the breach where others have fallen. But not convinced. If you think him beyond reason . . ."

"Though not necessarily beyond persuasion, especially where his trust is absolute. He loves you, therefore he will listen to you."

She put her head on one side, a touch of humor in her eyes. "I see. I am to appeal not to the mental parts but to the affections. The wall still stands, however—he may love me, but he hates Pym and all his stiff-necked company."

"Do not be tempted into discussing them. Draw him instead on his actions, his schemes." He leaned toward her, placing both hands flat on the tabletop with a force that jarred his arms. "Ask him at least what he expects to gain by this. For by God's wounds I cannot see it."

His vehemence seemed to create a contradictory calmness in her. "My influence, such as I have, is with the queen. If I approach him with this, she will see me as meddling behind her back."

He straightened. "But if you broach it with her first, she may well forbid you to take it up with the king. She wants these arrests as much as he, indeed more."

"That doesn't surprise me."

"He will be quite unprepared for you. Go to him with some personal concern so that he'll be willing to speak to you alone. Then bring up Pym and the Parliament. Try him on three arguments—"

She rose, so quickly he took a step back. "My lord, do not put words into my mouth, or he will know they come from you. This is for me to contrive."

So she would do it. Suddenly he felt afraid: he had never wanted her near the inner councils of the king, but here he was providing her with an opening. Ladies-in-waiting could wield significant political power at court, and they were always besieged with petitions, bribes and pleas by people seeking lucrative appointments. But Mary was incorruptible—it was beneath her dignity to beg for anyone's advantage with the queen or the king. Hence Charles and Henrietta-Maria trusted her absolutely. What if she startled Charles by this new approach? She might walk away with a sharp rebuff, and worse—as she feared—with a reputation for meddling.

She was but a foot away from him and the blue gaze was steady. "I understand what you demand of me. I consent, with this to say: it may well be—it is most probable—that I shall not gain our point with His Majesty. We may win little from this meeting. But I shall do my utmost to ensure we lose nothing."

We. Already, this issue was binding them together in a novel way, and the acknowledgment gave him a secret frisson. But if it was a wifely answer, it was also a clever one. Already, she was seeing beyond him—through him—to the possible consequences. He had been right to enlist her.

He thanked her, took his leave, and went to the door.

On the threshold he turned. "I forgot to give you the latest word. Prince Rupert's arrival is now sure for next month."

She gave a little laugh. "Really. How bracing."

"You don't share the enthusiasm?"

"I can't share the *fuss*. It's many, many days since I tired of hearing about him."

The duke was rather pleased at this rejoinder. The prince in his youth had turned ladies' heads; it was nice to know the Duchess of Richmond was immune. He said, "I saw nothing of his military side last time he was here. But by reputation, the prince is everything he should be. A good soldier; a leader. We are not so rich in such men that I could speak of his arrival with scorn." There was a pause, during which she did not reply; then he said, "What is your opinion of him?"

She shrugged. "You surely recall; he was here over a year." She continued brightly, "Very well: to answer you in the feminine, I suppose he is as fair as any mother's son—though he has not the Queen of Bohemia's fiery coloring, being black-avised. He is well made—*too* well made, for there is a great deal of him. He is monstrous tall, and for all I know growing taller—"

"Six feet and four."

"You see! Even you drown in detail concerning this prince. Do not chide me for trying to keep my head above water!"

He smiled. "Let us at once, then, to the masculine answer."

"He has a will, and he makes it felt. He has pride. He will be absolutely loyal to the Stuarts; he believes himself as much an English prince as a German. But he is not inclined to talk much about this will or this pride. When he comes, there will be those at court who find him stubborn. And some who fear him."

The duke gazed at his new creation, the fragile woman of dazzling mind who was about to take on the king. "And how should I find Prince Rupert?"

She lifted the perfect arcs of her eyebrows. "You will admire him. All the world does."

Before she went to the king, Mary felt sick, and had to sit down and pretend her hair needed doing again. Her tiring woman was not deceived, but silently complied: she pulled out the combs, unwound the seed pearls, ran her fingers through the curls to loosen them and then fastened up the whole elaboration in just the same way as she had before.

Mary paid no attention to the glass. She breathed shallowly, looking down at the rosewood under her fingertips and feeling angry with herself. This was not one of her usual weaknesses, though it was just as hard to combat and conceal. This was fear. Fear of failure—for she could never be afraid of Charles himself. To soothe her stomach, she thought of him; the man who had given her the love and protection of a father when her own father was murdered. She thought of the king's face when there was a softness in the brown eyes that for years now had also contained care and sorrow. She was his protégée, and she had never abused the kindness he showed her; moreover, she proved her gratitude every day by devoting herself to his queen.

She closed her eyes and kept her breathing regular. She could go to him as a daughter. She could discuss anything with him. . . .

She opened her eyes again. There was no denying the danger of this move. Her father, the great Duke of Buckingham, had been the most favored, the wealthiest, the most celebrated courtier in England, and the most hated. When he was assassinated, and Mary's world shattered around her, she made a vow never to seek the pitiless battleground of power that had cost her father his life. She had been six years old, and she had worshipped him. Even now, fourteen years later, despite having been taught the flamboyant catalog of his faults, she still did. Because they loved each other, he had shared with her as a tiny girl his grand journeys, his embassies abroad, the exalted courts that recognized him as the beloved of King James of England and then as no less a favorite of King Charles. She had walked a glorious road with the Duke of Buckingham, but when he fell, she faltered, for that road led to death.

She was enough like her father to see in herself the qualities that needed redirection. Secure in the heart of the court because of her place in Charles's affections and her marriage to Richmond, who was related to the king, she was informed on every point and loved to talk on the highest matters, but no one ever heard her press her own advantage or that of her husband. People spoke to her of plots and plotters, the more frankly because she was never part of any conspiracy. If some were wary with her, it was because she was married to the king's most trusted councillor, and for no other cause. When she and the duke received, the guests came for the pleasure of her company, not for hopes of advancement. And so, until now, she had pleased herself too, commenting on her peers with remarkable freedom, laughing at them and with them when she felt like it, and doing great harm to no one.

She spread her hands on the shiny surface of the dresser as the tiring woman inserted the last comb in her hair. Must she take on this task, after all her endeavors to ignore the nets of intrigue that hung about the court? Did Richmond have the right to embroil her now and violate the tacit agreement that had kept her out of his political activities during nearly five years of marriage?

Yes. For this was crucial. This touched all their lives. If the king took his armed guards into Parliament tomorrow, he would be declaring open war upon his subjects. Or Parliament would make sure it was viewed that way. He must not be allowed to do it. Mary shivered: how in the name of heaven could she say that to her king?

She felt the tiring woman's careful hands smoothing down the fine Delft lace that sat over her shoulders and fastening across her breasts the rope of pearls that was looped over the tops of her sleeves. Mary looked up at the square, dependable face in the glass, and said, "If you please, give it to me in plain words—how cordially is His Majesty hated in London?"

The gray eyes that looked back at her were startled. Mary's tiring woman had been with her three years and was a Londoner, the member of a large, respectable family whom she saw often. She prided herself on her Quaker sagacity and had never been a niggard with news or advice, but this question surprised her into silence.

Mary, seeing why, gave a low laugh. "Yes, of course, one may deduce that for oneself, over these past months. Witness New Year alone, with two hundred swords and staves battering at the palace gates."

"You don't apprehend danger again, my lady? Mayhap you should not attend just now—"

"No. Wait. Let me put it the other way. How well do they love King Pym?"

The woman smiled grimly at her mistress's use of the sobriquet. "John Pym, my lady, is a prodigious speaker. The Parliament can listen to him for two hours at a stretch, and so they have, their mouths open like fledglings eager for food, many a time."

A fine contrast to a king with a stammer, thought Mary. "What of the people who do not hear him?"

"They read him, my lady, and they hear him repeated. There cannot be another such city for readers and preachers as London. What John Pym says on the bishops, and pure religion, and the army plots—"

"I know what he says. To the last tedious syllable." Mary's stomach knotted. "Tell me: what would happen to their love for Pym if he led Parliament to impeach the queen?"

Her woman stared at her. "I've *never* heard tell of that!"

"Well, the queen has. A knave's tale, perhaps, but a costly one." She rose. "I shall wear the sables. Have the chair brought."

It was useless to put off going, though she had not a shred of an argument to take with her. If Charles could be made to expect total, outright revolt when he arrested Pym and the rest, she might stand a chance of dissuading him. But instinct told her that London was not ready to rise. Mobs of rioters prowling the streets, even at the gates of the palace, did not make a rebellion. Pym was a dangerous man, and many of the disturbances could be laid at his door, but in his speeches he was not a rabble-rouser; on the contrary, he was lucid, compelling, and called constantly on the rule of law. If she tried to put Charles into even more panic than he felt now, it would be a dishonest act. *Now* was not the issue. The future was the issue, and she had to somehow make him look ahead, and recognize the path he was about to tread.

Later that afternoon, when King Charles put business aside for a moment and strolled out amongst his intimates to be entertained, he found little enjoyment in the assembly. The men were oversolemn and the women subdued by the absence of the queen, who he suspected was bustling through her apartments, deciding whether to unwrap her plate again or to add things to the piles of valuables she had had packed for weeks in case they must flee Whitehall. It was perturbing and unhelpful, until the Duchess of Richmond arrived and ignited a spark amongst them that spread into a promising warmth.

When she put off her furs, he noticed she was wearing a gown of a pale purple lake color, similar to that in the superb portrait Van Dyck had painted of her five years before; the one that also showed her dwarf page, standing before her and holding up a pair of gloves. He remembered the painting perfectly—who could not recall every stroke of a Van Dyck?—and it tickled him to see Mary now and contrast her quicksilver animation with the haughty poise the artist had captured in the painting: the smooth oval of the face given distinctive character by arched eyebrows and slightly hooded eyes, the straight nose with its strong bridge, and the mouth, made to seem smaller than it really was because she had kept it composed, as though to conceal an entertaining thought not to be shared with the viewer. She had been fifteen, but held herself like a princess.

Meanwhile, throughout her sparkling merriment with the others, she threw him looks that told him she must want to speak to him alone. He was certain, because she had not brought her dwarf page to attend on her—she never did for a private audience, as she liked to have him to herself with no listeners. And he also knew why she had come: for reassurance, which he had always been able to give her and would not deny her now.

He began to look preoccupied, which was not difficult, and the others took the hint and looked ready to withdraw. Finally he thanked them and invited Mary to come with him and look at a new acquisition. "Someone has unearthed another little piece by Holbein," he said, cupping one of her elbows to steer her toward the doorway. "I haven't had it hung yet, but it's in . . . in the room with the others."

She went out with him, her hand on his arm, and nodded over her shoulder to the crowd. She gave them the sunny smile she always did, which to him never seemed to show the self-satisfaction of a favorite—it was universal, like an uncalculated gift.

"A portrait?" she asked as they walked along the first gallery.

"No, that's the charm of it." With Mary, when they talked of things they both relished, his stammer seldom bothered him. "It's a sketch in oils that he must have made in his youth. A simple scene from a window—you almost feel he was leaning on the sill, with a brush in one hand and a cup of wine in the other. It's a rare delight, a rare peace that it offers. I've been to look at it ten times today, and it's like stepping into a garden."

When she saw it herself she fell silent. It was on the large marquetry table near the tall windows, but not so near that the white winter light could harm it, and she leaned over, her hands moving along the gilded frame in slow, light strokes. Eventually she said, "You are right. Look at this path, disappearing. It might lead to paradise—a paradise quite within our reach." She raised her head, a teasing glint in her eyes, her fingers still caressing the frame. "It is unsigned. Sire, the subject is so unlike . . . You are sure—"

"That it's Holbein?" He smiled. "I think I know Holbein, madam."

"Where shall you hang it? Perhaps where you can see it at first light every day, instead of having to walk vast acres to view it?"

"I'll ration its effects. I don't wish to wear it out so soon."

She looked down again, slowly took her hands away and clasped them at the waist over the full, gleaming gown. "It will stand wear, sire. Far better than ourselves."

He took it up there. "Mall, are you afraid?"

Her hands tightened, and her voice. "Yes."

"You came well guarded today, I hope?"

"Of course. Richmond and I are always prepared."

"And so is all the palace." He gave her a stern look. When she was a girl, playing around his knee with little Charles, sternness had always worked with them both—it made them feel protected. "Sir John Byron fulfills his command to a fault. He was tested these last few days and proved worthy—his musketeers did not hesitate to fire on the mob. I have every confidence in him and shall increase his force if necessary."

Before answering, Mary opened her hands and laid one on the tabletop beside her, the polished surface cool under her fingertips. She summoned her audacity. "It is possible to fear Parliament more than the mob."

His expression of dignified gloom did not alter. "Indeed. There too I have taken measures—I may tell you that six men will be arrested tomorrow."

"Six!"

"You know of the impeachment of John Pym and the others in the Commons? I have just added a noble name to the list: Viscount Mandeville."

Mary took a breath, looked down at the painting without seeing it, then up at the chilly windowpanes. "They are a threat in themselves, certainly."

"A *threat?* One is used to . . . to *threats*, from all quarters. But this Parliament . . . what . . . what they have said, in the House, before me, is treasonous. They cannot be allowed to continue uttering treason."

"Toward the monarch?"

"Toward England. They are arraigned for traitorously endeavoring to subvert the fundamental laws and government of this kingdom. There are seven accusations. One of them concerns the monarch, yes: they are accused of alienating the affections of the people by their foul aspersions on their sovereign."

There was no stammer in this trenchant speech, Mary noticed—it was as though he had rehearsed it, as no doubt he had. How clever of him, to claim that it was all Parliament who set the people against him, and not his own actions! Telling him how loathed he was in London would merely cement his purpose. So she turned the subject to her own.

"London is flooded with their commentaries. But the rest of the country, which Parliament represents—do you deem it treacherous? I may tremble sometimes in this city, sire"—she gave a self-deprecating smile—"but when I think of the loyalty my sovereign receives from the great and little of the realm in general, I can have no fears for the king's peace."

The point in the center of his top lip drew down over the lower as he considered her. He could not quite see where she was leading, and thus remained silent. She tried not to find this intimidating.

She continued, "The signals that this parliamentary faction send to London are dangerous. But what sort of signal will it send to your devoted subjects elsewhere if you arrest their representatives?"

"It will send the signal that I will brook no attacks on the fundamental government of the kingdom. Madam—" Then he stopped, and frowned deeply. She could see he was not about to explain himself to her, and worse, disliked being put in that position.

"Sire," she said, "*I* have been afraid, but I could *never* conceive you to be. Yet what may the members of your Parliament think when you take up arms against them tomorrow? I should *hate* them to think you afraid, when I know your courage, your boundless courage." She had overflowed; there were tears in her eyes.

He was moved, for his voice shook as he said, "*Take up arms?* Drawing a few hundred guards around me, as I have done of . . . of necessity these months past . . . This is my right, and . . . and none can in reason protest at it. They did object to Lunsford, unjustly, as being impetuous and unruly—and I put Sir John Byron over him." He laid his hand, light and warm, on her bare forearm. "My cavaliers, as they call them, are not the matter. The matter will be abundantly clear tomorrow. You will know, and so will my Parliament, that the word of a king is stronger than a thousand men at arms, mightier than any army. I do not take up arms against them; I proceed, as their sovereign, for stable government and the rule of law."

He patted her arm and gave it a little squeeze, and she looked down, her eyes still brimming. She had lost the argument but not his heart. He was hardly aware that it had been an argument, so intent was he on setting her at her ease.

When she got home, however, she was ill, and the servants helped her to lie down. Richmond, returning, came in and stood by her bed. It seemed to her, in a glance, that he must be as pale as she.

"I stayed out of the way," he said, "so I've not heard. What happened?"

She shook her head carefully. "I can't speak. But be assured: we gained nothing . . . we lost nothing. There is no change."

He remained standing beside her and there was a moment

when she thought he was about to put a hand on her in comfort. Inwardly she shrank, and her stomach tightened. But in the end he turned and went quietly out. She was grateful for his restraint.

She lay with her eyes closed and gradually her head stopped spinning. When she came to rest she realized that, contrary to her own words, everything had changed. Henceforth she was committed to an untried path—out of gratitude, and her deepest affections, and Charles's gentle, paternal touch on her arm. England had need of him. She could not watch him lose his country's trust.

Chapter 2

JUST BEFORE MIDNIGHT ON the third of January 1642, a woman and a child braved the curfew to walk down a wide, unpaved London street toward the townhouse of Robert Devereux, Earl of Essex—once lieutenant general of the English army, now Lord Chamberlain, and one of the great Puritan peers of England. The night was frigid, the street was combed by a vicious wind and the woman held tight to her companion's hand, making sure hood and cloak were wrapped securely, and pulling her own thick mantle close across her face and body as they struggled on.

The air was clear but with no moon, and the melted snows of the new year still moistened the uneven surface of the street, muffling the sounds of the walkers' shoes amongst stones, dung and refuse. They kept to their way, two black forms hardly visible in the deep shadows cast by the upper stories of the houses that leaned out over them as though frowning at what went on in the wealthy, silent quarter after dark.

When they reached the house and knocked at the vast street doors, the porter could be heard grumbling and slipping as he approached across the cobbled yard within. "Who goes there?"

"Friend," replied a soft voice, but loud enough for him to hear through the crack, into which his lantern threw a feeble gleam revealing nothing about the visitor. "One woman and a little maid, sirrah. I think you might open to such as us."

It might have been the timbre of her voice, or the use of the word "Friend," that worked the trick—at any rate he opened the doors just enough, let them in, dropped the bar with a bang and then stumped before them back across the yard to the servants' entrance, where a household man stood holding a candlestick from which the candle shed a brighter flame. The petitioners remained bundled in their garments, however, and the porter could only see the gleaming eyes of the woman when he demanded, "Business?"

"An audience with the earl."

He laughed. "Thou? What dost think he—"

"Five minutes. I know this house. I know him. His light is on above and he will see me. Give him this and go ask him, if you please."

The porter was startled into taking what she held out—a white piece of paper no bigger than a playing card, folded twice. Nothing on the outside, and the inside hardly big enough to contain a signature, let alone a message.

"Well it won't take the earl long to read!" the other man said. "Give it here; I'll take it to the secretary and he can decide—it will wake him up. If we've got to keep watch the whole blessed night, he might as well join us."

The young secretary, once he had shaken off the approach of sleep, was indecisive. The woman was probably no better than she should be, or so said the fools below stairs. But they had not examined her and there was the oddity of the child—what if this was more complicated than a doxy plying a tawdry midnight trade, some touchy matter that the earl would prefer to remain private? It seemed best to give him the paper and receive his orders.

The Earl of Essex was in shirt, fawn breeches and heavy turned-down boots, sitting with his chin in his hand and his gingery goatee jutting toward the hearth, just as he had been for the last couple of hours. Except for the white lace-trimmed boot hose that the light from the fire turned a ruddy hue, he might have been one of his own harquebusiers off duty.

"Well?" he said at the secretary's deferential approach, and looked up.

The secretary could never quite throw off the impression of being on parade when his master addressed him. Essex had a strong figure and a powerful head. His meager fringe of fair hair did not conceal the squareness of his forehead, short locks on each side framed high-colored cheeks, and his mustache formed a broad horizontal line across them as though it drew a barrier against slackness. The secretary made his report clear but succinct, and bore with fortitude the earl's irritation and finally scorn.

"I can scarce believe you, lad. What a farrago to foist on a gentleman in the middle of the night! Hand me the paper."

He unfolded it, looked at it by the light of the fire, and the reddish mustache twitched once in surprise. Then there was a confused silence, much longer than the secretary expected. Eventually the earl bade him fetch the woman and child; then he was to close the door and stay near enough to be summoned.

Essex, alone, examined the paper again. There was nothing upon it but the deft sketch of a butterfly done in fine red chalk. Was someone sending him this woman as a joke? His cheeks grew hot with anger. A woman with a child in hand: if this was mockery of his principles she would suffer for it—and more than she, which was why he was letting her up here. He would be wisest to know who she was, and who had sent her.

The butterfly. A clue to her identity? He shook his head: impossible. The one woman he knew of called Butterfly—and that only by her intimates, of whom he most surely was not one—was the Duchess of Richmond, who could not be crawling the streets like a beggar in the dark, and least of all to his door.

When they were shown in, he rose without a word and gave them his coldest stare. As soon as the door closed behind the child, it scuttled into the farthest corner and crouched there with hands folded over its knees. The woman stood with her hood drawn across her face like a witch in a play, and her invisible hands, which manifestly held no weapon, fluttered within her mantle as she kept it close about her. It struck him that she was listening while the secretary's steps faded beyond the door.

"Enough of this charade. Take that off."

She obeyed, whipping the mantle away with a single gesture so that it whirled onto the boards beside her, held by one white hand. She was shivering but her eyes threw him a challenge.

For a moment he was dazzled, as if by an apparition, for her pale face and shoulders stood out starkly from the deep tones of the wood paneling behind her head and the rich black of her gown. Then he recognized her. The Duchess of Richmond.

His chin lifted in bafflement, and in the dark blue eyes he saw a flicker of irony as she said, "Thank you for seeing me."

He knew the light, pleasing voice, but tonight it sounded thin, as though on the edge of exhaustion. "My lady, you astonish me." He stepped forward, gestured: "Will you take a seat, near the fire. Allow me to relieve you of—" He took the mantle and placed it awkwardly over the leather back of the chair as she sat down, then he burst out: "You came through the night, alone?"

She turned her head, but instead of answering him, spoke to the person in the corner. "Anne, draw near the fire if you are cold."

The girl shook her head, and the movement revealed a square, scowling face that caused the Earl of Essex another start of surprise. She was not a child but a dwarf.

At his helpless look the duchess smiled, nodded to the crouching figure, then tilted her head to Essex. "I was not alone, as you see. Mrs. Gibson was with me, so that if anything happened on the way, she could run home and tell them. No one knows I am absent. Only Mrs. Gibson. She is to be trusted."

The earl sat down heavily in his chair, then rose again. "I have offered you nothing. Let me—"

"Thank you, I do not have long. I wish to talk."

"You will take some wine. I insist." He went to the buffet and poured it himself, the decanter ringing against the fine rim of the wine cup.

She took a sip at once, still shivering, her gaze on the fire. The gown, sewn all over with beads of silver and jet, winked at him as he bent and picked up her butterfly drawing from the floor between them.

She looked at him as he sat down. "I beg you to forgive the subterfuge. You will understand when you hear what I have to say." But she did not say it at once. Instead she took more wine, and he could see in the way she swallowed and sat straight, and laid the other hand in her lap, fingers slightly curled, that she was disciplining her body into stillness.

Finally she said, "You are a patron of John Pym."

The name dropped, cool and clear, into the warmth of the room, and the earl sat back.

She continued, "Be advised that tomorrow, when His Majesty attends at Westminster, he will arrest Pym, Holles, Strode, Hampden and Haselrig on the spot. Viscount Mandeville is also arraigned. I have no information about whether or where he is to be arrested."

He managed, like her, to stay motionless, until he realized he was not breathing. After a gasp of air he said, "Why do you tell me this?"

"Because it may become your view, or that of John Pym, that he and the other four members should not sit in the House tomorrow afternoon." She rose, quite steadily, and replaced the wine cup on the buffet.

Essex gazed at her from his chair. "No. Why do *you* tell me this?"

"That is a matter for my own conscience."

He rose, and the dwarf in the corner gave a jump of fright. "Forgive me, your grace, but you cannot come here in secret, at this hour, at the risk of exposing yourself and me, without telling me your intentions."

She considered this, then spoke with deliberation. "My lord Essex, you are a true and honorable servant of His Majesty. I am such another, and shall be for my lifetime. I do this out of duty. I believe that if my king"—here her voice failed her for a moment, but she recovered—"that if His Majesty puts members of Parliament in the Tower, without waiting for the Lords' legal permission to arraign them, he may forfeit some of the trust of his subjects." The challenge was in her eyes again. "It is a trust he deserves to have. I would wish their loyalty to be as untainted as yours and mine, for it is his by right."

"No one else knows you are here?"

"I come to you of my choice alone. On my conscience be it."

"You may find it weighs heavy in time. You may wish to share the burden."

"Never."

He believed her. At least, he knew that the Buckinghams and the Stuarts, her unreliable and devious families, would never hear of it.

She beckoned the dwarf, who rose and came to her side. She said coolly, "Of course, I am aware that this conversation may be quite unnecessary. If you know of the arrests already, my visit is pointless." She held his eye—"Indeed it may as well never have happened."

He would pay her the tribute of taking her cue. He said levelly, "I already knew. It did not happen." Then he stepped to the hearth and threw the scrap of paper into the flames, where it took fire at once, twisted in the air, and darted out of sight on the updraft.

He came back toward her but she herself put on the mantle, wrapped it around her as before and took the dwarf by the hand.

He said, "My lady, I cannot permit you to make your way back alone."

"You permitted me to see you, and I am grateful. It is all I shall ever ask of you, please God. Now I must go."

So he let her leave, on her terms, simply enjoining on the secretary that she was not to be molested on departure. And not be given any more alms—she had already begged enough of him.

When she was gone, it was hard to believe she had been in the room at all; it seemed like a hectic waking dream, caused by too many sleepless nights. He would not sleep tonight, either, for many hours.

Before he did what he had to do, he sat on for a while, looking into the fire. *Butterfly*. She had been ready to get her wings scorched, and not for herself or for Richmond. He had seen courage where to date he had noticed only the fine natural beauty, the quick wit, and the weaknesses endowed on her by privilege, luxury and princely indulgence. He wondered who else knew that she was not as frivolous as her nickname.

When Charles walked to Westminster next day he took with him Prince Rupert's elder brother, who was the heir to the Rhine Palatinate—if he could ever wrest it back from the Austrians. Prince Charles-Louis was a fit companion for a show of strength in the face of Parliament: personable and with natural dignity, he had been at his uncle's court for some time, an ever-present sign of the Queen of Bohemia's continued devotion to her royal brother and as well-regarded by the people as Elizabeth herself, whose image had never faded from their minds despite her long absence in Europe.

Charles-Louis had suggested they go the short distance on horseback, which amused Charles, because he fancied his nephew was tactfully wishing to increase his stature in public. In fact Charles cared not a whit about how short he was, for a monarch of five foot four was still a monarch and if he could magically change anything about the horror of his existence at the moment it would not be his height.

Taking Charles-Louis served an important purpose: it hinted at the range of foreign support on which the king might draw if Parliament continued to debate on their own grievances rather than voting him the funds needed to strengthen the English army. After ruling without Parliament for eleven years, and then calling and dismissing another last year, he had summoned this one for precisely that purpose, and if they would not provide for the troops required to keep the rebel Scottish Covenanters from the border, they must expect him to look elsewhere. Indeed, they were constantly promoting rumors that he was going to bring an army over from Ireland, which he had no intention of doing; it was too inflammatory, and a last resort.

He and the prince advanced to Westminster surrounded by three hundred of the palace guard, fully armed. Charles had also taken the precaution of sending a message to the Lord Mayor the night before, letting him know he would not permit the city troops to protect the House, but he would expect them to fire on rioters should any demonstrations in the street get out of hand. The walk, however, was not impeded by the crowds. He had been told that Pym, Hampden, Holles, Strode and Haselrig had all taken their seats in the House in the morning, so victory awaited him.

Charles left most of his escort outside but brought eighty men into the lobby with their pistols and swords still about them as a salutary hint to the Parliamentarians who could see them through the open door. At last, justice was about to be done.

When he entered the House, however, beneath the stiffness and ceremony he suddenly felt swamped by bitterness. This long, high chamber had hosted many harrowing scenes, and in this moment he could only feel them as humiliations. He slowly paced the distance to the Speaker's Chair with Charles-Louis, and instead of searching for the miscreant members' faces in the throng he found himself counting the abominations of the recent past. The day Pym claimed before the Commons that the king was bringing over an army from France, funded by Henrietta-Maria's family. The bill they passed, in his presence, condemning Strafford to death, the Lord Lieutenant to whom he had entrusted Ireland. The acts they made him sign for the abolition of the Star Chamber and the Court of High Commission. Their triumph: the decree that this Parliament could only be dissolved with its own consent.

The wintry light from the immense bank of windows at the end of the chamber hurt his eyes as he mounted the steps. He turned, took his seat and arranged his ermine-lined cloak so that it draped on either side of his knees, while Charles-Louis remained standing on the floor below.

Above Charles stretched the chairback, more than twice his height and shaped, he had always thought, like a town clock, with the painted and gilded lion and unicorn supporting the royal arms. Beneath the Speaker's Chair was the vast timber platform that filled the center of the room, the only items upon it being the table and the chairs used by the recorders, who sat with their backs to him. Far at the end he could see the mace, held visible to confirm his presence in the House. And around the platform he could see the usual bewildering parade of knees, for the place was filled with ranks of members right back to the walls, and those who sat in the center were crowded close to the platform, where they could look up at him from under their hat brims with piercing eyes.

He spoke, and spoke well. It came out as he had rehearsed it: slow, majestic, and without a stammer. He began to observe the room, pausing now and then, searching for the Five. He could see none of them, but perhaps they were in the area behind him, avoiding his eye. He would not demean himself by looking around for them—the time had come to summon them by name.

"I call upon John Pym. Let him come forth." Silence. "I call upon Denzil Holles. Let him come forth."

Silence. Not a movement, not a whisper. The upturned faces did not even bend toward one another in surprise or speculation. The Five were gone.

They could not do this. They must hand them over. Bitterness rose in his throat and he said more loudly: "Mister Speaker, I charge you to tell me, where are the members I have named?"

There was a murmur as the mild and unassuming William Lenthall came obediently forward. Then another hush, as he fell on one knee. "May it please Your Majesty, I have neither eyes to see nor tongue to speak in this place but as this House is pleased to direct me, whose servant I am here."

It took a moment for Charles to believe what he had heard. He leaped to his feet, then just prevented himself from falling down the steps by grabbing the heavy armrest with both hands. He shouted something incoherent, words he didn't even understand himself, as Lenthall continued to apologize.

Charles descended, all the bile of his anger spilling over the

Speaker's head, his gaze raking the packed House like ordnance ready to spit fire. Charles-Louis said something he did not hear and he walked out, his legs pumping as though he could march a hundred miles, his head bursting with curses on all their treacherous heads.

"Privilege! Privilege!" they shouted as he went, and hands and feet thumped the floor and the platform.

He walked past his cavaliers and white light hit him as he went out through the great doors. He closed his eyes and watched the blood surge behind his eyelids.

They were all one, and that One his enemy.

Chapter 3

THE CLIFFS OF DOVER beckoned like smooth white arms, and Prince Rupert leaned on the rail, alone in the bow, and willed the clumsy ship toward them. On leaving the coast of Holland he had spent hours debating with the officers and sailors about what was wrong with the hull of the *Expedition* and what sort of trim might correct its failings, but he had had to resign himself in the end to a slow voyage—nothing like his breakneck ride home from Vienna after his imprisonment, when he had arrived in the Hague on the same day as the courier bringing the news of his release. He smiled inwardly at the amazement he had caused at his mother's little court.

There would be no such astonishment at that of King Charles, but there would be a more splendid welcome. He would rather take horse at once for Whitehall, but there would probably be some ridiculous reception at Dover, drummed up when the local aristocrats and the mayor got word of his ship's banner. After that, however, he could rattle away to meet the king at his own favorite pace.

Impatience kept his uncle's court clear and bright in his mind. He wanted to step into Whitehall—or Hampton Court, perhaps, or Windsor—and feel that unique atmosphere descend on his shoulders like an elegant, feather-light cloak. It was his easy acceptance by his uncle's family that had first touched him when he lived amongst them as a seventeen-year-old. Everything had flowed from that: the heady days out riding in the English countryside with Charles, the only man he knew who hunted as much as he; the long, shimmering hours spent strolling about the palaces and grounds, never alone but always with someone agreeable. He had needed to make no special effort to please—there was a general assumption that he belonged in that warm, refined environment. He had invented games in the gardens for his cousins the royal children; he had been introduced to the wit and the teasing indulgence of Henrietta-Maria and her coterie, and to all the circles of clever, cultivated women. No other time in his existence could compare with the benign education he had received in the best of English habits, manners, arts and conversation.

Rupert thought of it with nostalgia, because it could never be the same again; a few days of that charmed inaction were all he could allow himself. Charles-Louis might still be stuck in it like a drone in honey, turning this way and that to look for support, but now was exactly the wrong time for begging yet more funds from Charles, to win back the Palatinate or for any other purpose. Charles had already done wonders with fierce diplomatic efforts to persuade the Holy Roman Emperor to release Rupert after three years as a prisoner of war. He was not here with his hand out; he was here to say thank you. He would refresh himself in their sincere affection—and then he would set out across the country to raise the finest army England had seen.

He was heading for Dover because on his first landing, at Margate, the ship's captain had learned that the king had left London and headed southeast. These tidings disturbed Rupert and he hoped there would be no unpleasant surprises awaiting him in Dover, from whence he expected to move inland to rendezvous with the king. He arrived without hindrance: the wind was in the right quarter, the captain had no trouble getting them into the harbor, and then they were near enough for Rupert to discern it— the royal standard, flying from the keep of Dover Castle, high on the headland above. He was with his officers in the stern, and they all turned to him as he looked up through a spyglass and frowned. For a moment he thought the king might have sent little Charles, Prince of Wales, down with a ceremonial escort to greet him, but he dismissed that—the standard could only mean that the king or queen were present. It seemed an impossible time for the king to leave London, for Parliament was still in session as far as he knew, and when last he heard it had not yet granted Charles the army funds. He lowered the spyglass. Despite the gratified glances of his escort he felt a jolt of foreboding, which he hid by going below to change his clothes.

There was a press of people at the wharves by the time the ship docked, and as the gangplank was lowered Rupert scanned their ranks for the cavalcade of reception. At that very moment the crowd parted and the party came into view, on foot, a stream of courtiers richly dressed and flanked by a troop of guards. All were male except a golden-haired lady in front, who was taking delicate steps across the flagstones of the dock, one gloved hand bunching her full skirt to keep it out of the dirt. She raised her eyes as the gentleman beside her lifted his arm and the party came to a halt. Rupert registered the ultramarine blue of her gaze, and a split second later recognized the gentleman also.

There were Stuarts indeed to welcome him—the Duke and Duchess of Richmond.

He descended and there were cheers from the crowd, which made him grin and caused them to cheer the more. The Richmonds remained in formal pose, the others tidily disposed behind them. Beyond, banners flapped in the sea breeze, and in the middle distance, over the heads of the multitude he could see a group of horses waiting, saddled and bridled.

The duke and duchess bowed and Rupert extended his hands, one to each, and gave them greeting.

The duke was as he remembered him: of medium height, square-shouldered and fair with regular, freckled features and an alert air. His rounded voice made itself heard without effort. "Your Royal Highness, Prince Rupert of Bohemia, Count Palatine of the Rhine: His Most Gracious Majesty King Charles of England and Scotland has great joy of your coming. As Lord Warden of the Cinque Ports and Constable of Dover Castle I am charged to bid you his most fond welcome to England. He enjoins upon his subjects that as you honor us with your august presence you will enjoy in every part of this kingdom the exalted respect and admiration of his loyal people." There was another cheer from the bystanders, and under cover of it the duke said more sensibly, "I trust Your Highness is well and traveled safely. How did you sustain your journey?"

"Well, I thank you. His Majesty is in Dover?"

"The king and queen are in residence in the castle with the royal household. It is my honor and privilege to convey Your Highness into their presence."

"Why Dover?"

Seeing her husband balk slightly at this abrupt question, the duchess answered, "The court has left Whitehall. We moved out of

London on the tenth of last month and spent some time at Hampton Court and Windsor. Then we took ship from Greenwich to come here."

He looked at her without replying. There was an expression of faint distaste on her beautiful face, but he could not tell whether it was caused by her reaction to him or to the retreat from Whitehall.

"His Majesty," the duke continued, "awaits you with fond anticipation, and he will acquaint you with all his concerns." There was movement behind the duke and he turned, sweeping his hand toward the escort. "It is also His Majesty's pleasure to bestow on you this gift, trusting that it will be acceptable to his illustrious nephew."

The courtiers parted to make way for two grooms and a powerful black horse, expensively caparisoned, that pranced toward him with its great polished hooves crashing on the flagstones. He took it in with a glance: it was a stallion, the right height and weight for him, with a deep chest and strong, solid legs. The dark liquid eyes rolled toward him as though he were being sized up in his turn, and at his soft chuckle the horse snapped its nose forward, causing one groom to stagger as the rein jerked in his hand.

Rupert nodded to the grooms to step aside, walked up to take the reins, then swept off his hat to address the crowd. The long feathers drooping over the brim brushed the stallion's gleaming coat, and the skin beneath twitched once and was still.

"I thank His Gracious Majesty for this magnificent gift. Almighty God has called me to serve my uncle, King Charles of England and Scotland. Whenever I raise my arm in this country I do so in his royal service, and by the same token do I pledge myself to faithfully serve his loyal subjects." He raised the hat high and there was a roar, such as he had never heard before, welcoming him to England.

When he caught the eye of the duchess again, the distaste was gone and her expression was open and receptive, as clear as her marvelously pale skin. He gestured for the couple to turn and precede him, to spare them any mischief the stallion might do with its heels, and walked behind them through the other ranks, giving a swift, frank greeting as he went to those whom he remembered. There were many, which was both heartening and a puzzle. What were they doing in Dover?

When they reached the horses they mounted up and wound in procession through the streets, still flanked by the guards, who bore halberds and were also equipped, he noted, with wheel-lock pistols. He was placed at the head and took his direction from the duke and duchess, who rode at a walk on each side. He towered over them on the stallion, the route was noisy and they were not always abreast of him, so talk was difficult, otherwise he might have asked more questions of the duchess, since she had been ready enough to answer him.

Rupert had some liking for Richmond, but on his previous visit to Charles's court he had spent very little time in the company of the then fourteen-year-old Mary Villiers. To begin with there was an old scheme of Mary's vainglorious father, the Duke of Buckingham: during one of his embassies to Elizabeth of Bohemia's court, he had once assiduously promoted a marriage between Rupert's elder brother, heir to the Palatinate, and his little daughter. Rupert's mother, though responding in her usual tolerant way to Buckingham's notorious charm, had not given the proposal a second's consideration. Rupert had presumed Mary Villiers was aware of the duke's extraordinary presumption, and finding the thing an embarrassment he had avoided her as much as possible. And then there was her attitude to him. He was made a great fuss of when he first arrived, and some of the very young ladies felt free to tease him, as they might a pet to be doted on. He certainly minded none of this, but in Mary Villiers's clever glance he thought he saw something satirical, and he detected a mocking edge in her voice that he did not hear elsewhere.

Time had passed, however, and the woman beside him, riding expertly astride, had no power, and certainly showed no disposition, to make him uncomfortable. Instead she looked at the bystanders in the streets and he sometimes saw her smile—with a radiance that transformed her dark figure, in purple riding gown and sable furs, into a golden being whose hair and face ravished the eye like a queen in an old fresco. She dazzled him, but in a different way from before. She was married now; a woman complete. He could be near her without anyone's assuming he wished to woo or impress her. The closeness tempted him, and he gave in to it without the least thought of danger.

As they broached the road that wound up to the castle and left some of the spectators behind, he leaned down toward her and said, "You are content in Dover, madam?"

"I hate it." On this passionate exclamation the smile disappeared and she bit her lip. Astonished, he watched her struggle for control. Then she said, "I cry you mercy, Your Highness. You may very soon understand what I mean. And if you do not, please grant me the favor of forgetting what I just said."

"I doubt if I can. May we talk of this again?"

There was a long pause while he looked at her half-averted face and then, though she did not speak, she reluctantly bent her head in assent. They rode on without another word.

With her husband the Duke of Richmond, constable of the castle, Mary was present when Prince Rupert had his audience with Charles and Henrietta-Maria in the great hall. It was an emotional reunion; he fell on one knee before them but was raised and embraced, and both king and queen shed tears. Precisely how Prince Rupert reacted at first, Mary could not see; as he bent to them his face was hidden by the thick, tumbling waves of his dark hair, which reached to just below his shoulders. After that she listened rather than watched; her eyes were somehow dazzled, and she did not dare to look at him for long in case someone could read her face.

She had felt absurdly overwhelmed from the moment he stepped from the ship—all her self-possession vanished and it was like being suddenly drunk on one sip of wine. She had never before felt that in any man's presence; not the handsomest of any country or race, not the most seductive of any visitor to the court, had ever had this effect on her. He was too much for her to take in.

She had hidden this folly from her husband and please God from the prince, but she could not overcome it. In Dover, while he had stood before her or ridden beside her, it had seemed quite impossible to command her voice. Yet on both occasions when he addressed her she had answered him at once, in irresistible response.

Charles's audiences were always coldly formal and when he received delegations or strangers to the court he usually expected to be the only one seated; when each visitor got his turn to speak he had to fall on one knee and rise when he had said his piece. But this was a family reunion and the queen, the king and his nephew were all seated as they began the eager round of conversation.

For Mary, it was touching to see the little dark-haired king and queen gaze up at the prince with affection and trust, but she tried to avoid looking at Prince Rupert, lest the tall lean form, the straight shoulders, the poise and balance of his strong frame increase whatever magic had her in its grip. The fine clothes, evidently chosen with care but worn with lofty carelessness, emphasized his natural grace. The long, well-shaped hand that he had extended to her when they met held no rings and he wore no other jewelry. He was not seeking to impress but to be what he was—the traveler returning to a friendly port, the soldier prince whose help the king had long looked for. Well, he was here, and he should make no more difference to her than the sensitive young man of years before, whose beauty and charm she had been able to withstand simply because everyone else made too much of him.

The talk was of family matters: his mother, Elizabeth; his brothers and sisters; the Stuart children, where they were housed and who was looking after them. His deep voice sounded sincere and his replies were direct and deferential. His accent was more German than she remembered, and she was surprised: besides his father's tongue and his mother's he spoke French from childhood and also Dutch, Spanish and Italian, and she had recalled his way of speech as almost neutral. Today, it sometimes made him sound solemn, a quirk she was sure she would have made fun of at an earlier age. She would soon be over this foolishness and able to laugh at him again. The terrible thing was that she had no will to break the strange spell. It was too new and reached too deep for her to yet find ways to escape.

Meanwhile, at every moment Mary could feel the prince wanting to ask why the court was not in London. Charles, in his hospitable, magnanimous way, skirted the issue for some time; then with occasional outbursts from the queen he gave Prince Rupert the story of Parliament's defiance and his decision to remove his family from Whitehall.

When it came to this, Mary could not help watching. For one thing, everyone else's eyes were riveted on the speakers and no one was observing her, not even her husband. For another, some of the exchanges seemed like an extension of the dialogue between herself and the prince on the way up to the castle. She felt like crying out, "I told you! You see what they have done? You see what they have thrown away?"

Once the subject was fairly broached, Prince Rupert held his long upper body bent forward in his seat, one leg extended and a hand on the thigh, his fingers curled inward across the supple leather of his high boot. All his questions drove toward the same point, and Mary was astonished that Charles did not see it and stand on his dignity.

"I wish to understand," said Prince Rupert. "In the first week of January, there was a possibility of an impeachment of the queen. What was the accusation by Parliament?"

"There was a base rumor," the queen said loudly, "that I was encouraging Catholics to revolt in Ireland!" In her indignation she looked on the point of tears again.

The prince nodded but looked at Charles. "And was a bill of impeachment brought against my dear aunt?"

"No. I forestalled Parliament by arraigning the seditious members."

"And were they arraigned?"

"The Lords were determined to put obstacles in the way—I decided to arrest them."

And were they arrested? To Mary's mind, that question hung in the air like a challenge, and she could almost see it forming on the prince's lips.

"But at midday," Charles went on, "before I attended the House, unbeknown to me the five members got into a city barge and escaped by the Thames. The moment I heard that, I knew my family could never with safety inhabit the city of London while Parliament was present."

The prince sat straighter. She could feel this hit him, as it had hit her when her husband came to tell her that they must scour Whitehall and strip it of everything portable, and that the old, rambling warren of beautiful dwellings was no longer to be the palace of kings. Henceforth, everything in it and about it would be disposed of by Westminster.

"Parliament was in session when you left?"

"Yes," the king said.

Prince Rupert's deep brown eyes were hooded as he made

the next pronouncement, so no one could see to whom it was addressed. "Then they have London."

The public audience over, the king took Prince Rupert to his apartments for a private talk, after which the prince was to visit the queen in hers. Henrietta-Maria took her ladies back up to the rooms that the lieutenant of the castle had had furnished for her, and only Mary remained in the great chamber. The others were asked to gather in another, some distance along a gallery, that they had christened the blue room. Once alone with the queen, Mary heard the overflow of feeling that the prince's coming inspired. Then Henrietta-Maria retired into her bedchamber to kneel at her prie-dieu and give thanks for his safety and for the succor he brought the king, leaving Mary in the sumptuous room.

It was the most comfortable in the massive castle, for it was crammed, indeed bulging, with an eclectic set of furnishings gleaned from its finest corners. To fulfill his high office as Lord Warden of the Cinque Ports, the Duke of Richmond had often been in Dover over the past year to hold court at Saint James's Church near the castle. His office was soon to pass to another, however, as the king required his constant advice in council, so the duke had had to largely depend on the lieutenant of the castle to ready it for the king's household after the flight from Whitehall.

The lieutenant had lavished great attention on the queen's accommodation. Her main chamber, positioned on the ocean side and with a vast outlook over the harbor and the Channel far below, was hung with tapestries on the inner walls, which almost totally masked the chilly, ancient stonework. All the scenes depicted woods or verdant landscapes, and standing at the window was like viewing the sea from a forest glade on a mountaintop. With this vantage, Henrietta-Maria could have followed the morning's cavalcade as it breasted the high ground and passed under Constable's Gate to enter the castle precincts. With a soft shock of regret, Mary suddenly wished she could go back and repeat that slow ascent, and drink in to the full the nearness of the man who had ridden beside her, for there were gaps in the event, during which she had been too dazed under this new experience to do anything but force her eyes away and pretend to take in what passed elsewhere.

She must have astonished Prince Rupert with her outburst

about Dover just after her husband had mentioned that he was constable. It had certainly made the prince curious—and she was not quite sure how to give him an explanation if he brought it up again.

The queen soon returned, making no mention of her devotions. In their dealings together she was discreet about her religion, and the public, vulgar accusations of rabid Catholicism that were thrown at this susceptible and sincere woman often made Mary angry. The queen espoused no fell conspiracy to undermine the staunch Protestantism of the king or his kingdom and her only missions of conversion were directed at intimates of the family, who bore her fond persistence with good humor. Mary could even make the queen laugh at herself when she achieved no results.

Henrietta-Maria smoothed the creased satin of her nacre-colored gown with delicate hands as she stood in the center of the room, smiling quizzically. "Now, where shall we be seated? There are chairs for a multitude—I can never decide."

A great fire roared within the tall, carved chimneypiece at the end of the room but Mary knew the queen disliked intense heat. "You have chosen well where you are, madam, I think. The chairs at that table are of the highest quality. I believe the dear lieutenant had them carried all the way from the armor room."

"You're right; very fine." The queen sat facing the door and gestured for Mary to join her at a small polished table of indeterminate origin supported on stout oak legs. "I have asked the ladies to wait in the blue room," she went on, "because I have something to explain to you."

Mary had a swift, terrible sensation that her reaction to Prince Rupert had attracted notice.

The queen put out a hand. "You look stricken. Know that I shall never ask of you anything you do not feel fit to perform. Richmond has generously given his assent to your going. But the sacrifice—if you should consider it so—you are free to refuse."

Mary whispered, "Sacrifice? Where am I to go?"

"Ah." Henrietta-Maria put her hands to her cheeks for a moment and looked an apology. "The king and I have discussed it so long, I imagined everyone knew, more or less. They usually *do*," she said with a smile. Then she composed her lips with great seriousness. "The king cannot live with his anxiety on my behalf. *I* cannot live in England while my presence is considered a reproach to its monarch and a danger to his sovereignty. For the love of my husband and children, I choose to leave for Europe."

Mary exclaimed, but Henrietta-Maria put out her hand again, the intricate lace of her full cuff drifting across the tabletop. "Not for long, perhaps, but I must be prepared to wait out this crisis. And I shall not be idle. My crusade," she said, her expressive eyes glowing, "will be to enlist the support of all the rulers of state sympathetic to His Majesty's cause. I shall not return empty-handed." She put both hands on the table and leaned forward, her eyes bright. "Will you come, Mall? May I beg you to accompany me on this great journey? I shall be lonely, heaven knows, but lonelier still without you to encourage me and keep me strong."

Mary had to swallow hard and put a hand to her bare throat to stop from crying out. So this was how the day of Prince Rupert's coming ended. Just as he arrived in England to stay, she was to go. The king, the queen and Richmond were in league for it; there was no hope of reprieve. She fumbled for words. "Could you think for a moment, madam, that I would refuse you in your troubles?"

The queen looked at her shrewdly; it was not quite the reply she had expected. Then she resorted to emotion. "You of all people must know how it hurts me to go." She gave a tragic smile. "But whilst I remain, I am considered a provocation to Parliament."

"I thought that the king still hoped for reconciliation?"

"He does. Hence the wisdom—and the agony—of my departure. By the grace of God, the removal of all provocations that *can* be removed will promote that reconciliation between the king and his Parliament." The queen leaned forward again. "I sail first for Holland, to the Queen of Bohemia. We go to the dearest friends; you will be quite safe with me." Without waiting for a reply the queen rose, arms raised from the elbows and her hands open toward Mary, as though in plea or benediction. "I must not press you. I must allow you to think on this, in your fond heart." And without waiting for Mary to rise, she glided from the room and closed the door behind her.

"Oh!" Mary's pent-up breath expelled the sound into the room. She rose and the chair teetered behind her as the legs caught on the rush matting beneath. She moved away, her gown brushing the floor, but she heard only the roar of the fire and a loud pulse in her ears. They had wrenched her from Whitehall and her house, and now they wanted to send her from these temporary quarters, this cold mockery of a home, to lodge with a queen in exile. Her quick steps took her to the other side of the room and she put her palms flat on the tapestry there, pressing the green and white threadwork to the wall and her forehead to her crossed hands.

This was no plan to get her away from the court. Her fleeting weakness over Prince Rupert was her secret, and this showed how mad she was to have thought otherwise, even for a second. They did it without thought and without malice. It was simply fitting for the Duchess of Richmond, Lady of the Bedchamber, to take ship with her queen.

She went to the window the farthest from the fire, and standing in the curtained embrasure she looked down at the sea. It was gunmetal gray under a lowering sky and France was not visible. Why not France first? But she knew why: Charles was wary of the changeable policies of Cardinal Richelieu. And if Henrietta-Maria went to a Catholic court, even though it was that of her birth, it would seal the enmity against her in England.

Mary's hands crept up the curtain at her side, her fingers gripping it as though seeking a lifeline. She bent her head into the thick fabric, her face still turned to the windowpanes but her eyes closed. Yes, she hated Dover, because it was not London. But she hated still more to leave it now.

She heard the door open but did not look over or step back into the room; she was fighting for composure.

Then it shut with a crash. *"Gott!"*

She looked, and started. Prince Rupert stood with his back to the door, his weight still forcefully against it, his hands lifted to the level of his shoulders and clenched in front of him.

"Tonnerre de Dieu!" The second exclamation was less carrying but more vehement, uttered between his teeth, and his face was twisted by a fury that Mary had never seen on anyone's countenance. He had not noticed her; he thought the queen's room empty. He was staring blindly before him, his brows knotted, his lips curled in anger and bitterness, his eyes burning with a devilish light.

He took a step into the room, hardly aware what he was doing, and with the movement half turned his back to her, which brought him closer to the fire and a pace from the chair in which the queen had been sitting a few minutes before.

He stood there, oblivious of everything around him, his shoulders rising and falling as though he needed deep breaths simply to stand under the crushing weight of his wrath, and then he came out with a string of curses in French and German too fast for her to recognize, and lashed out with his boot, sending the chair flying like a missile against the chimneypiece.

There was a splintering crash and the chair, in two pieces, fell onto the hearth.

Mary stepped straight out into the room and instinctively he turned.

She gazed at him and a coldness stole through her stomach as she looked at his contorted face. Anger and violence did this to her—where others might shrink, Mary was without fear; instead she felt disdain. A field of ice formed around her and collided with the surge of temper to which the other had basely given way.

She said in clear, wintry tones, "That, Your Highness, is the queen's favorite chair."

He glared at her, the anger still blazing in his eyes, then marched to the hearth and picked up the heaviest piece to swing it backhanded over his shoulder. It thundered into the immense grate in a storm of sparks. A second time he lifted and swung, and the rest shattered against the bricks at the back of the chimney, sending the fire leaping in a gout of flames and flying soot. "Now it's firewood." And like a whirlwind he strode out.

She stayed where she was while the coldness crept up through her breast to her neck and face. She felt as obdurate as a statue. Even when a door opened farther off, and there was a bustle of excited questions and nervous exclamations underscored by a rustle of skirts coming her way, she remained still, looking at the fire.

The queen appeared in the doorway, backed by her ladies, the same avid astonishment on every face. "*Bon Dieu*, what in heaven is going on?"

Mary raised a steady hand toward the fireplace, and the queen stepped inside to look. "Prince Rupert found fault with the furniture."

The queen gave a gasp, took a faltering step and collapsed onto the remaining chair by the table in the center of the room.

Then, caught at the climax of this long, momentous and trying day, she gave way to hiccups, and to wild peals of laughter so near hysteria that the others crowded in to kneel around her.

Mary surveyed them, her face revealing nothing. She had regained her composure.

Chapter 4

Three days later, at eleven o'clock on the night of Friday, February 20, the Duke of Richmond knocked at his wife's bedchamber door. She opened it at once, and looking over at her curtained bed he could see that she was not yet thinking of sleep.

He thanked her and entered, his gaze traveling over her body as he stepped past into the warm space—warmer than his own, for he had not been in it for hours and the day's business was only just over. She wore a nightgown with two layers, the top one of which, silk or some such, shifted under his fingers as he slid his hand slowly over her waist and hip in passing. It was his signal, long established.

He spoke, before the gradual pursuit across the room began. "The *Lion* is nearly ready. She sails on Monday. I must warn you, the king does not really hope to see the queen again in years."

"I know. Perhaps ever." Her voice was light and distant.

"I want you to know that I opposed your going. As far as I could."

"My lord, I shall return."

He knew she was thinking of the court, her lifetime milieu. But there was always the far-off, scarcely to be contemplated idea that she might sometimes think of him. Whichever, it was a promise, and Mary always kept her promises.

The desire that this impelled in him shortened some of the stages by which the act was accomplished. He plunged his hands into her hair, not with the impulsiveness that had taken him on her wedding night, when he first startled her with his swift approach, but with a smoothness that drowned his hands in her unresisting curls before she moved away. They had the habit of talking as they circled the room, about things he could never remember afterward. But tonight she was silent, and he had an odd impression that when she stretched herself out on the top of the bed and he untied his breeches and leaned over her, she was seeking shelter in the shadow he threw across her.

Her fingers entangled themselves in his as he drew the night-dress to her hips, and a powerful sensation coursed through him that she was about to hold him; but soon her hands opened and she laid them at her sides on the counterpane. He stopped seeing her then, except for the exquisitely offered parts of her that she allowed him to touch. He did not kiss her lips, for though smooth and soft they never moved or opened to his. He pressed his mouth to her cheeks, her neck, he explored the svelte hollow above her collarbone, and his hands molded themselves to her breasts. The loose nightdress, as he moved, alternately covered and then released the soft nipples into his palms.

He parted her slender thighs and lost himself, but when he looked down for her now and then it seemed as if her closed eyes and face accompanied him, this time, in a rhythm that drew them forward as in a strong current, which shook them both over rapids and deposited them, gasping, on a new, strange shore.

Then he moved back and sat sideways on the end of the bed, and by the time he had tied the damp breeches across, and leaned forward with straight arms and his hands flat on the edge of the counterpane, she was as still as before, and he had no way of knowing how she had made the journey to this tense, familiar place.

She said nothing, her eyes open, her hands discreetly rearranging the nightgown over her legs.

He bent his head, looked down at his still trembling thighs and said without thinking, "How was it, with you and Herbert?"

Her hands stilled, but after a moment she pushed herself back and sat up, the small of her back against the bolster and the embroidered hem of her gown hiding her drawn-up knees. There was surprise in her voice but no defensiveness. "I was thirteen and he sixteen. We were raw and tender children when we married. We fumbled a great deal, and laughed. . . ." She looked not at him but toward the green hanging on the opposite wall, as though she spoke the words into a clearing amongst dim trees. "It was a game, for a year. Then he was gone. No more games."

Sir Charles Herbert, heir to the earldom of Pembroke, had died of smallpox in 1637. James married Mary when he was twenty-five, not so very long afterward, and whenever he had asked questions about her first husband she had avoided answering, so he had stopped.

He stood up, walked around the bed away from the light of the fire and went to the window. Mary had seemed to him so practiced and refined when the king gave her to him in marriage, and her clever, teasing wit had lent her such a polish that he had imagined the expert pleasures of their first encounter with an intensity that had kept the preceding nights ablaze with lust. It had not been his fault. But looking at her now, sidelong, he could still see in her pale face the vestiges of wonder and youthful eagerness that her first husband had enjoyed, and that with her own strange kind of innocence she had brought to her second. If he had ever felt he harmed her by his approaches, he would have ceased them, despite his yearning for an heir. But in a strange way he knew this would distress her, however unenthusiastically she accepted them. Neither had ever been able to discuss the subject—until now. Which struck him as somewhat late in the day.

Her voice sounded small within the vast canopy of the bed. "My lord, do I not satisfy you?"

There was an unbearable silence as he looked at the black windowpanes. "I have no words, madam, to express what you do to me."

Silence again, and he felt her shrink back.

She would be wanting to cleanse herself, in that absurd, fastidious way that so frequently exposed her to the dangers of water, despite every warning.

He went to the bed—not sitting upon it, in case he spotted her counterpane—took one hand and, bending, brought it to his lips. "God keep you from all harm, my lady."

She put up the other to touch his cheek and then in a rare gesture curled it around the back of his neck, under his hair, and left it there.

He froze, blinded with hope and regret, and then she took it away.

He straightened and went to the door. "Prince Rupert will also accompany the queen to the Netherlands. It was confirmed this evening."

She clenched her hands and her eyes grew wide. "So *that* is why I saw him vent his spleen in such spectacular fashion!"

"Quite possibly. At any rate, Prince Rupert's presence here

sends a very strong message of opposition to Parliament. He was so eager to serve the king, and he came here with such a will, that London will be ringing with the news and full of fears about what will happen once he rides at the head of an army. His Majesty has changed his mind—he deems war far too great a risk at this moment and he has convinced himself it is wisest if the prince goes home. I wouldn't speculate on the outburst you witnessed; Prince Rupert professes himself honored to escort the queen to his mother's court."

"Does he indeed?" The elasticity was returning to her voice. "Well, now that he is reconciled to it, I hope he apologized to you in some fashion for reducing your chair to kindling—he certainly didn't offer any excuses to me!"

"He may have said something; I brushed it aside."

"I'm surprised you have any regard for him at all."

"Whatever his temper may be, I hear more sense from him than from ten others combined, and I am thoroughly sorry he goes. I know your opinion of him, but I hope you may so far overcome it as to do what you can for his return. Before many months have passed, I predict we will have need of him as never before."

He could see the reluctance from across the dark room, but she spoke with her usual irony. "Consider it done. Or if I cannot compass it, I strongly suspect he will take it upon himself."

On the day Henrietta-Maria sailed, Charles felt an oppression that he thought would sink him to the ground, and it was impossible for him to summon any words of cheer. So he spoke his heart to the farewell party that rode down to Dover, something of which he hoped never to be ashamed.

As they gathered on the shore, he reflected with acute pain that there was scarcely an element of this departure not forced by Parliament. His dear little nine-year-old Princess Mary, married last May in a chaste ceremony to Prince William of Orange, had been forbidden to leave the country with her consort when he went home—because Parliament maintained that Henrietta-Maria, who had wished to take her daughter to the Hague, was bent on plotting abroad. Now they had changed their tune and given their consent, perhaps believing he would be more cooperative with Parliament once his "warring" queen was removed from his side.

Henrietta-Maria could not even take leave of their two small-est children, six-year-old Princess Elizabeth and Henry, the infant Duke of Gloucester, whom Charles had thought best to leave under close care and guard in Saint James's Palace in London rather than to expose them to the uncertainties of travel.

With desolate eyes Charles watched the fleet being made ready, thinking of his two elder boys, the Prince of Wales and the Duke of York, left behind him under the protection of their governor. He wondered what scars this desperate struggle with Parliament had already caused in their young minds, though these would be as nothing to the sorrow of being parted from their mother.

He looked around him. Prince Rupert, whose coming had awakened a new hope and courage in his breast, he must part with, lest the blackguard Pym consider him poised for an instant inva-sion of London. Mall Villiers, whose smile once had the power to brighten his deepest melancholy, he and Richmond must sacrifice to the queen's cause. He watched her taking leave of her house-hold, all of whom must have trudged down to the harbor to bid her farewell, there were so many. When she spoke to a tall, square-faced woman in plain Quaker dress, who was wiping her eyes on her apron, Mary leaned forward to embrace her and slipped some-thing into her hand.

"You know where to take this," he heard her say, and the woman nodded. Mary turned to her dwarf page, and said, "I hope you never regret, Anne, that you choose to go while others stay."

"I little thought these little legs would carry me so far, my lady," the dwarf said in a quaint, high voice, "but you give me little enough to carry away," and she patted a leather glove case that she held under her arm.

Mary laughed, then looked up to see Charles gazing at her, and left the group and ran into his arms. They stood swaying to-gether as though the ground beneath them were the deck of an unsteady ship.

She drew away and put her hands to her eyes. "Where shall we meet again?" She gulped, lowered her arms. "When we do, I pray the Prince of Wales and the Duke of York will be with you. I shall have stories from the Hague to tell the boys. And all Prin-cess Mary's news. And Dutch gifts to bring." She looked at Charles, blinking back tears. "I have taken leave of my lord. It is time for me to go on board. I must go, and allow you to . . ." She threaded her way through the crowd and he lost sight of her.

And so it was time to embrace his own little Mary, and when he burst out that he might never see his daughter again, she screamed with grief.

Then he walked up and down the shore with Henrietta-Maria, and as many times as they turned to the waiting boat they swung around and walked away again, and he could feel his people wondering if he could ever let her go, and he was sure he wondered the same. When at last they parted, their faces were streaming with tears, and later when he mounted and rode up to the castle he galloped up and down along the clifftops, waving his hat until there were only smudges on the horizon to wave to.

On the next day the Duchess of Richmond's former tiring woman set off to London to rejoin her family on a journey paid for by the duchess, carrying hidden in her apron pocket a note for the Earl of Essex. Written in rounded, childlike letters in red chalk, it began with a rather comical sketch of a devil's head. *R sure to return, perhaps within months. Essential that reconciliation be sealed before then.* It closed with a butterfly.

Chapter 5

꩜

RUPERT WAS SITTING AT the chart table in the captain's cabin of the *Lion*, trying to teach Dutch to Princess Mary. They were hours out from England but neither her mother nor the Duchess of Richmond had been seen outside their cabins. Princess Mary, with the resilience of a child, had soon come to scramble about the vessel with him, explore all the decks and learn why the *Lion* was much more shipshape than the tub on which he had arrived in England. When he got talking to the sailors, however, he sent her back to her quarters, presuming that her mother, like his own, had a lifetime aversion to young royal persons conversing with the lower ranks of blunt, open, knowledgeable men who built and sailed their ships, forged their weapons and fought their wars for them.

The princess's curiosity about Dutch was much less active than her interest in seafaring, but he persevered. "Your husband, William, speaks some English, and you can be sure he learned it in your honor. You'll find him ready to teach you Dutch in return— why not let me give you a start?" Her little forehead was high, which made her face look long and in this instance rather mulish, for her pretty mouth was disagreeably pursed. He said, "My mother and father, you know, met in London to be married, like you and William, but neither of them knew how to say a word to each other in their own language. Can you imagine not even being able to say hello to your husband? Or, No, thank you, I don't want pickled tripe today"? He had her attention now. "However, my parents both knew French, so when they were affianced in the Great Banqueting Hall, someone translated the ceremony out loud from the Book of Common Prayer. But the poor gentleman's French accent was so bad that my mother and father took one look at each other and burst into a fit of the giggles."

Mary opened her mouth to smile, then said, "But they did get married, though?" When he nodded in amusement, she said, "The

Bishop of Ely married *us*. And I wore silver tissue and pearls, and William wore velvet, and he gave me this gold ring. And we used the Book of Common Prayer. Therefore my mother could not come."

"You are lucky that you and William share the same beliefs. Share your languages, and you may live as happily as my mother and father did."

"*Ma mère* says your late father was the King of Bohemia?"

"My father was Palsgrave of . . ." Then he dismissed this with a gesture and said, "Yes, briefly."

"So are you going back to Bohemia when we get to the Netherlands?"

He laughed, but she looked disconcerted, so he put aside the papers in front of him and leaned forward. "A long time ago my father was invited to Bohemia by the people, and so he went to Prague and he and my mother were crowned king and queen. But the Austrians were extremely angry and made war on my parents and drove them out. They were not in Bohemia for much more than one winter. That's why people call my mother the Winter Queen."

He smiled. "Now we're going to play a guessing game. When my parents, the king and queen, were rushing to escape from Hradschin Palace, they had to pile everything in as many carts and coaches as they could find. At last they were all ready, and my mother and father were about to drive away, and meanwhile servants went running this way and that to look for anything precious that might get left behind. One of them came upon something all by itself on the floor in one of the rooms—small and round and wrapped up in white linen. So he grabbed it and ran downstairs and threw it into one of the coaches as it rattled away. Can you guess what was in that bundle?"

Mary considered, her elbow on the table and the tip of one finger in her mouth. Rupert sensed movement behind him and turned to see the Duchess of Richmond leaning in the doorway, on her feet but not quite with the usual color in her lips. He began to rise but she waved him down.

"On no account," she said. "I can join in perfectly from here, if the Princess Mary will let me."

"Very well," cried the princess, "but I have first guess. Was it the crown?"

"No."

"A basin of goulash?" said the duchess's light voice behind him, and he shook his head as Mary gave a peal of laughter.

"The scepter?" said the child, her eyes glowing.

"No." He shifted his chair to include the duchess, but she remained where she was.

"A ruby necklace!" shouted Princess Mary, drowning out another contribution from the duchess.

He shook his head. "Neither of you will ever get it, though you," he said with an approving nod at the princess, "are by far the nearest. No. When that bundle was thrown into the coach, it landed with an enormous thud, and bounced about quite a lot, and wriggled and twisted, and then it let out the worst-tempered howl you ever—"

"*A puppy!*" shrieked the princess, beside herself.

"No, a baby. Me."

Mary ceased jiggling up and down on her chair and said, wide-eyed, "No, it wasn't. That's not fair. You're cogging."

"It was me."

There was a soft exclamation from the doorway and he looked sternly at the duchess. "The truth, upon my honor."

"You mean you *remember* it?" she said in horror, but he shook his head.

Princess Mary's mind was now moving rapidly. "Are you the Winter Prince, then?"

"No. I am a snowball."

They both laughed, and he scooped the pages with his drawings and labels in Dutch back toward him. The princess reacted quickly: "Can we have another guessing game?"

"Certainly, if you first recite the harbors of the Netherlands."

"This I must hear," said the duchess, and came to sit at the table.

"Rotterdam," said the child confidently, then stumbled through them until she came to the port where they would end the voyage. "Halvenius."

"Hmmn," said Rupert. "I hope the captain doesn't take us there instead."

"Herrenslush."

"You're floundering. Come: it starts with Hel."

"Oh dear," said the duchess.

The princess began giggling and could not go on.

"Helvoetsluys," he said as severely as he could, but a catch in his throat destroyed the effect.

"No, truly?" said the duchess. "What sort of a name is that? Hel—" Then she gave up and said breathily, "I wish someone had warned me. I very much doubt I'd have come."

Little Mary jumped down off her chair. "I'm going to make my own game. I'm going to wrap something up and *you* have to guess what it is." And she ran out of the cabin.

There was a pause, while he looked across the table at the duchess and she at him. He realized now that it was not so much her satirical tongue that had intimidated him in the past—it was her beauty. Today he was simply grateful for it, no matter what she thought of him, for the sunlight of her presence filled the space where they sat enclosed together. She had lately treated him with a coolness close to dislike, but now this seemed somewhat mitigated, either by his efforts with Mary or because she was weak from sickness. He said, "I hope you are feeling better, madam?"

"I think I have my sea legs now. I was given an odd remedy that did wonders—a bowl of rice with lemon juice squeezed over it."

"Yes, not everyone knows of it, but the purser and cook did, so I told them to give it a try."

"You?"

He bowed slightly. "There's the added advantage that the rice can be cooked to disguise the weevils."

She gave a scandalized laugh. "Oh no, do not make me queasy again!"

"Never," he said. "Though Princess Mary found it most interesting that they—"

"No!" she cried again, lifting her hands in front of her face. "Now I don't know whether to thank you or run away."

"A dilemma shared by my uncle."

It sounded more bitter and sarcastic than he had meant, and he would not have blamed her for taking her chance of retreat, but she sat very still for a moment and then changed the subject. "It was well-meaning of you to give the child another story of a family in flight."

"Was it? I was halfway through before it even occurred to me."

"Whatever your impulses, the point is that the princess now knows you have come through a quite remarkable—indeed *lurid*—event and lived to tell the tale."

He considered her. She was here, and temporarily in the mood for talk, so he might as well ask her the one question that mattered. "How much does the queen expect to raise?"

She was so taken aback she went pale, and he felt sorry for her. "I really . . . Well. We carry the crown jewels, including the most precious white diamond in existence, the Grand Sancy—not to mention the Cité, the Rose of England and the Mirror of Portugal. There are jeweled crosses, priceless gold collars that belonged to Elizabeth I and Henry VIII. And vast articles of plate that the queen intends to sell or raise money on. She has all these treasures, along with a voice in Europe that I believe will . . . carry weight."

"So how much does she hope to raise?"

She looked surprised, then annoyed, at his repetition of the question, and did not at once reply. He hoped that the pause allowed her to see that if there was no precise view of the result to be achieved, and no plan, there might be no point in their whole endeavor. At last she said, "She is a queen. That is an incalculable advantage."

"So is my mother," he said pleasantly, "and since my father lost the Palatinate she has been a queen in exile, dependent on the hospitality of another nation. The United Provinces have been kind to us, but the allowance they pay her is modest. For my whole lifetime my mother has had to turn this way and that for her income, to the other states that are allied against the Austrians. And, I'm sure you know, to the King of England, who despite his love for her has never been in a position to send her a great deal."

She said briskly, "He supplied ten thousand pounds to help you and your brothers when you tried to win back the Palatinate!" She was better informed—or had a better memory for figures—than he had thought. She continued in the same tone, "Are you saying we shall be received unhandsomely by the Queen of Bohemia?"

"Do not wilfully misunderstand me, madam. My mother is devoted to King Charles—your welcome will be generous and sincere."

"Thank you. And I have every confidence in the queen's reception by the United Provinces and any other state she may approach."

She still did not realize. "Madam, our republic, the principalities and other countries of which you speak have one vital element in common. Most are Calvinist, like my family. Others are Lutheran, or follow other doctrines within the reformed church. In other words, they are all Protestant."

She stared at him resentfully. "What you mean is—Henrietta-Maria is Catholic."

He nodded. "There is the incalculable point that you mentioned."

She looked at her hands. She was running her fingers over his drawings, as though simply by being within reach they belonged to her, and she had the right to know them again by touch, to repossess them. Then she stacked them, lined up the sides of the pages, put them down squarely between him and her—and he realized she had not seen them at all.

She raised her eyes and gave him a brilliant, instructive smile. "Your Highness, just remember, my queen is not alone." Then she got up and left.

He half rose to his feet to see her out of the room but she was too quick for him, and he sat down heavily. She made him look as if he was somehow set to hinder his aunt in her bold campaign to raise funds for Charles, whereas from everyone's point of view, the more specie she could lay her hands on, the better. He would not hinder her; he would do everything possible, but this could not include riding around hat in hand to the rulers of northern Europe and spending weeks in their reception halls dripping with elaborate courtesies and false cheer. Henrietta-Maria knew him well enough not to expect that of him. They all did, especially the Duchess of Richmond—he remembered the disdain on her face when she caught him cursing like a Hun and fit to break one of the rooms apart at Dover. He would supply escort and guard if they asked for it, wherever they wanted, and then leave them to it and go hunting. Since that was all that his uncle had given him the freedom to do.

The longer he sat idle in the captain's cabin the darker his temper grew, but he was not in the mood to ramble about the ship in search of company. He did not take the scowl off his face until Princess Mary came back, and did not smile until faced with her glee when he failed to guess that the object voluminously wrapped in some of her mother's packing material was a single grain of rice.

Henrietta-Maria claimed that she never had any luck when she traveled by sea, and Mary was inclined to believe her, for shortly after the queen recovered from her queasiness the *Lion* ran into a storm that scattered the little fleet. It was unnerving to see sails disappear ahead of them over the horizon, since the queen's other ladies-in-waiting and much of her precious cargo were divided up amongst the other ships.

The storm abated, but everyone except Prince Rupert remained below. He preferred to be on deck, which Mary could well comprehend, since with his immense height there was not a space within the ship, even the captain's cabin, where he could stand upright.

He was still somehow too much for her to take in. When he returned from the brisk air outside, clad in an enormous cloak and with his long hair swinging about his face as he ducked low to get in the doorway, he billowed like a dark ship in sail himself. If the captain was present the prince would start talking to him at once while he let the cloak fall over a chair and flicked his hair back behind his shoulders with both hands. She would turn away and engage the queen in lively conversation or read amusing pieces from the books, French or English, that they had brought with them.

The prince had explained to Princess Mary that on board a ship, the captain's orders took precedence even over queens and princesses, and he adhered to this himself, but in fact Mary could see that the officers and crew were completely under his spell. He was a natural leader, and Mary could tell that if her relations with him were different he might expect her to bend just as everyone else did before his boundless energy, enthusiasm and passion for activity. As it was, she preferred not to go on deck when he was there, and thus saw him mainly at table, where he loomed opposite, talking affectionately to his aunt and little cousin, and pleasantly to Mary herself, though she could sometimes see in the corners of his large dark eyes a gleam of amusement at her wariness.

She was certainly wary; the memory of his fit of rage in Dover Castle had not faded from her mind. At that crucial moment it had turned her from him, and given her a defense against him that she sorely needed. When they happened to be together she was never comfortable looking directly at him. He dressed plainly in calfskin breeches, boots and a padded doublet over a soft linen shirt, but the wings of the doublet, which extended beyond the gathered tops of his full sleeves, gave such emphasis to his shoulders that Mary remained absurdly conscious of his strength and lived in his presence with an insidious sense of threat.

On their last afternoon on board, in quieter weather, most of the dinner things had been cleared away and Prince Rupert, the queen and Mary were still at the table. Princess Mary had been escorted up on deck by a lieutenant whom the prince trusted, and the queen had assented, without giving much thought to the matter, for she was sleepy and soon dozed off in her chair. It was high-backed, and when the queen's dwarf page, Jeffrey Hudson, decided to put a cushion under his mistress's feet and another behind her head, she looked comfortable enough for Mary not to interfere. She and the prince exchanged an involuntary smile across the table as Jeffrey tiptoed out.

After a moment the prince said, "You said something when I came to Dover. What did you mean?"

Mary started and could feel herself looking conscious, so it was silly to pretend she could not remember the intense moment on the ride up to the castle. She glanced at the queen, who was asleep. "It's simple; I held Dover in hatred because it was not London."

"You think the king should not have abandoned Whitehall?"

"It's not up to me to question his decisions, but no. It . . ." She paused, but it was such a luxury to discuss this with someone, even if that someone was ready for a quarrel, that she continued, "It made him look afraid."

He shrugged. "That is a courtier's view. How he *looks* is not as important as what he does."

"Why do I suspect I am about to hear the common soldier's view, Your Highness?"

He took this seriously. "Because in one sense you have hit it: leaving Whitehall was a retreat. And retreat is a very dangerous first move in any conflict."

"The Roman emperor Fabian," she said with a smile, "would have disagreed with you."

He nodded. "But his problem was different; he was trying to outfox a powerful invader. Look." He took the half-empty fruit dish and placed it before Mary, then scooped up an array of knives and arranged them in a fan with their points toward her, halfway across the table between them. "You retreat," he said, "while your opponent's army is divided or disoriented or taken by surprise or otherwise unfit for battle." With his long hands flat upon the arsenal of knives, he pulled it in formation toward him. "The enemy makes an incautious advance"—and he moved the fruit dish away from Mary toward himself—"you surround his force and dispatch it." Mary winced as with a knife in each hand he impaled two apples. He glanced up, caught her look and said, "Would you care for one?" She shook her head.

He lifted the nearest apple from the dish, pulled the knife out and began peeling it. "None of that applies to the king's situation. For a start, Parliament may be unprepared, but they have the sense to know their own infirmity. There was little risk of their attacking His Majesty in London, and none of their pursuing him out of it, so retreat was the wrong tactic."

"If they had, however, we should have been safe at Dover."

"The castle is built to resist invasion from the sea, and from there it's impressive. But I shouldn't like it to face a force by land. Your husband invited me on an interesting ride around the fortifications when I arrived and as I regretfully told him, in their present state I wouldn't give them three days."

After a moment she said, "Never think I don't appreciate the martial lesson, but isn't it perhaps a little early? Are we at war? We still have the opportunity to treat with Parliament."

He cored the apple with the narrow blade of the knife and quartered it. His careful silence made her think he might be reluctant to quarrel with her after all, but eventually he said, "What else did he deliver to Parliament on the fourth of January but a declaration of war?" He looked up, reached over and slipped the knife back onto the fruit plate. "Therefore there is but one strategy. Raise an army with all speed, strike first, and take London. Then treat with Parliament. If they remain in session, even if they are still led by Pym, my uncle will find they think very differently from before. If they have disbanded themselves, the king should at once call another Parliament and the same applies." He caught her gaze, which perhaps expressed some shock, and said grimly, "Beat your enemy before you talk. Any other course is a waste of time and men."

She was about to reply when from above, on deck, there came the high-pitched scream of a child. Mary was transfixed but the prince leaped to his feet and was gone in seconds. Mary jumped up, threw a glance at the sleeping queen, hesitated, but then the sound of Prince Rupert thundering up the companionway roused her and she ran after him, scooping her skirts about her as she flew up the steep steps, the princess's cries ringing in her ears.

When Mary burst onto the poop deck, a stiff wind whipped her hair about her face and made her eyes water. She did not see the captain step to her side, but she felt his arm under her elbow and turned to where he was directing her. By the rail Prince Rupert stood with the lieutenant, and sprawled on the deck, her arms wound around the calf of one of the prince's boots, was Princess Mary. "I won't look, I won't!" the child wailed.

Mary exclaimed in bewilderment and advanced as the prince stooped and lifted the girl to her feet. "Stop shrieking." The princess at once did so. He put one hand on her shoulder. "Look there, Mistress Mariner, and report what you see."

The princess gave a ragged sob. "It's sinking!" She saw Mary and cried, "Our ship is sinking!"

Mary looked frantically around the *Lion*, her hands to her mouth. Meanwhile the prince took both the princess's hands, clamped them to the rail and then knelt behind her so that his calm, deep voice resounded in her ear. Mary reached them, took hold of a piece of rigging and put the other hand around the princess's tiny wrist.

Prince Rupert said to the princess, "The ship is about a mile away, so you need to look carefully. How does it sit in the water?"

Mary looked where he pointed. Land was in sight—a long skyline and the entrance to a bay. There was more than one ship in view, most of them being vessels of the royal flotilla, but Mary saw at once the ship that had caused the princess such a fright. It was listing, its sails flapped uselessly and it was making no headway.

"It's on its side!" the princess sobbed.

"*Goed*. And can you see what is in the sea around it?" The prince pulled a spyglass from the front of his doublet and adjusted it for the girl's eye. She said at last, "Boats! They are letting down boats. And there are people in them!"

"*Heel goed*. You see, the storm has been worse for them than for us. This harbor is Helvoetsluys, and I know it well—the ship has hit a sandbank. Your ladies-in-waiting and the crew are taking to the boats. Now, how far from them is the land at the end of the bay?"

Mary concentrated. "Two miles?"

"*Nog beter.*"

"But how can they go so far?"

He chuckled. "Come. If the big brave sailors from the *Lion* were rowing you to shore from here, don't you think they would get you to safety?"

Princess Mary gave a shy, rather ashamed glance at the lieutenant beside her, then nodded and handed back the spyglass to Prince Rupert, who rose to his feet and continued observing the ship. At that moment the queen burst onto the deck and rushed toward them, her hands stretched out in panic.

"Madam, fear not!" cried Mary, taking both her hands as the ship lurched beneath them. The wind freshened and she had to raise her voice. "Fear not—one of your ships is in danger but everyone seems to be safe."

The queen gave Mary a wild look, broke free, rushed upon her daughter and flung her arms around the child's head. "Oh, *juste ciel*, what shall we do?"

Mary struggled forward, reached the rail and looked on helplessly, knowing that in this kind of crisis the queen needed to vent her feelings without hindrance, though her daughter must be suffocating in her embrace. But the prince put away the spyglass, gently extracted the princess from her mother's arms and winked at her. "Perhaps we should have gone to Halvenius after all?" Which to Mary's astonishment made the child laugh.

The queen looked up at Rupert and wailed, "What can we *do*?"

"It's too perilous for us to go near and pick up survivors, but all the boats are in the sea and making good way. For the ship we can do nothing, because she is foundering. I recognize her build: she is the *White Hind*. Whom did you have on board?"

The queen staggered, gripped the rail and cried, "Ah, *que Dieu nous aide*! All the gold and silver plate from my chapel!"

Mary, a little surprised by such an answer, took a pace or two away from the family group, and with her hands gripping the ratlines mouthed a prayer for the safety of her own aunt, her father's sister: Susan Villiers, Countess of Denbigh.

The queen was in tears, and as they all looked out toward the far-off scene on the dark green, heaving sea, the prince put one arm around his aunt's shoulders and pressed her to his side, while on the other he held the princess's hand.

Mary, unwanted and unnoticed, stepped away. She looked back at the group before she went below: the statuesque man holding the slight, trusting woman and the little girl. For that moment, she felt excluded and bereft.

In her cabin, she lay down on the hard cot and stretched out to try for some rest before the work and bustle of disembarkation. The short voyage was nearly over; it was unlikely that she would ever again be alone with the prince. She had promised her husband that she would encourage Prince Rupert to return to England as soon as possible, but James Stuart, Duke of Richmond, seemed very far away.

She lay there feeling like the army that the prince had described—divided, disoriented and unfit for battle. What if this path she had chosen proved more solitary than she could bear? It came to her now that the court of the kings of England had been her one true home, both before and since her father's death. While she was away from it, she was deprived of the vitality and warmth that had nourished her all her life. Moreover, she suffered the dread of not being able to return. Or of returning to find it changed forever.

She was still haunted by her attempt to protect the king from his own illegal actions—the arrest of the Five Members in January. As it happened, another lady-in-waiting, the Countess of Carlisle, had also gone to Essex with warning of the arrest—at what exact time, Mary did not know, but it seemed to have been on the very morning of 4 January. Thus in one fateful day the countess had banished herself from court and declared herself for the Puritan cause—a betrayal that had cost Henrietta-Maria spasms of fury and tears. Through the furor that followed the king's failure to arrest the Five, Mary had wavered many times over whether to confess that she too had leaked his intentions to the Earl of Essex. But in the end she could see no purpose in doing so; she had not changed loyalties like the Countess of Carlisle, she loved the king and queen no less, and though her own stealth and secrecy might shame her, she could not yet feel sorry that the Five had escaped.

If she confessed, her king and queen would turn on her. She would lose their love, her place at court and perhaps her freedom, for Charles might not stop at banishing both her and her husband—he might accuse her of treason. She would never tell anyone what she had done.

These thoughts tortured her too much for her to lie still, and she swung her feet to the floor and sat on the edge of the cot, her elbows on her knees and her chin in her hands. So, she was alone. But she must never imagine that she could turn to any gentleman for comfort, not even her husband. And she could expect no help from such a man as Prince Rupert. He had worlds to conquer, while she had but one to fight for—the enchanted circle about the throne of England.

Chapter 6

It was late June, and Rupert was in the province of Utrecht, hunting wild boar in the forest near his family's country house at Rhenen, with Thomas Howard, Lord Arundel. The new ferns and saplings under the trees had grown thick in the warm days of early summer, and the hounds nearby could be heard rather than seen, plunging about and hallooing to one another in their search for a fresh scent. He and Arundel kept their horses on a broad track with good visibility, and he told the rest of the party—two of Arundel's men and three of his own, also on horseback and bearing the weapons—to keep alert, for with boar hunting a peaceful clearing could turn into a field of blood in seconds.

In the emerald screen of foliage ahead, a busy white shape appeared now and then, and a woolly head with long, soft ears poked out to ensure Rupert was still there, before vanishing again in a flurry of leaves.

"I'm glad to see you still have Boy," Arundel remarked, nodding down the ride. "Never tell me you've been able to make a pig dog of him?"

Rupert laughed. "No. But he makes a fine scout—if you see a streak of lightning go past us, it means the others have found a boar."

"You take him everywhere?"

"I left him behind in February—it seemed wrong to take a poodle to war. But I was sorry to part with him. So from now on, yes, he goes everywhere, including England. Maybe he'll bring me luck this time. If and when I'm called back."

A new tone suddenly came into the barking of the hounds in the underbrush, and on a piercing note Rupert whistled Boy out. He saw a smile on Arundel's hatchet face as the poodle raced toward them, his ears bobbing and his tongue floating in happiness; it was Arundel who had given him Boy as a puppy, when the earl

was on an English embassy to Vienna and Rupert was spending the
first miserable year of his imprisonment in the castle of Linz. Boy
ran once around Rupert's hunter and came to a stop, panting, on
the ground between himself and Arundel.

"Do you happen to know whether the king still has the black
stallion he gave me in Dover? I was sorry to part with that, too."

"Why not bring it over?"

Rupert shook his head. "I don't like transporting horses by
sea—it knocks them about too much. Does His Majesty have it in
York? When Charles-Louis came over he couldn't tell me."

"I'll ask for you, when I return." Arundel gave him a quizzical
look, and Rupert could tell he was wondering why he inquired
about an animal when there were armies to discuss. But it hurt and
angered him to listen to endless talk without being able to act. The
news of Charles's preparations, constantly brought in by gentlemen like Arundel, were in a state to sicken Rupert of the whole
subject. Parliament was by all accounts arming and training faster
than the king, and when Charles had gone north to secure his
largest arsenal, at Hull, he had found it already guarded by parliamentary forces. Meanwhile neither side would publicly admit that
civil war was now inevitable.

Suddenly the baying began, deep and heartfelt from the larger
hounds, and with a high, wailing overtone from the brown bitch
that was Rupert's boldest when it came to latching on to a boar.

"That's a warning—the prey is big. They haven't closed and it
hasn't bolted—see the ferns waving under the oak? They have it
surrounded."

Arundel looked skeptical. "Can't see a thing. Let's get
nearer."

"Not unless you want that nice piece of horseflesh cut down
at the hocks. Ten to one it's a tusker, and you know how fast they
move. Wait—we must see where it charges."

While he could not view the situation his hounds had created,
Rupert hesitated to give the whistle for them to close in, and meanwhile the boar made up its mind and went for freedom. There was
a deep, sinister grunt, a terrible thrashing of leaves and a frantic
chorus from the hounds, then the boar burst from the thicket onto
the ride, at right angles to the hunters, two of the hounds snapping
too late at its heels, the brown bitch hanging on to one ear and the

youngest dog biting at its shoulder. Rupert cursed—with a flick of its head the boar could gut the youngster with its tusk and the brown bitch would be all alone, inches from death.

The boar, meanwhile, a huge beast with a long snout and curled yellow tusks, acted as though the hounds did not exist. It halted, turned, took one baleful look at the waiting hunters and charged straight toward them.

"Ausgezeichnet!" Rupert cried, and sprang from his horse. As he ran past one of his men he said, "Richard!" and put up his hand. Once clear of the horses, he stood with legs apart, balanced a spear in both hands, and watched the beast thunder headlong toward him, the faithful bitch slipping, scrambling and dragging at its side, her eyes rolling and her teeth clamped clean through the boar's right ear. She did not let go, and her tenacity slowed the boar just enough for Rupert to accomplish what he needed to do.

The spear came high, the seconds flashed by in his head, he calculated the number of paces that divided him from the battering ram that hurtled toward him, and at the last moment he drove the point of the spear down and forward through the ribs into the heart. The shock wrenched his arms but he took it, nimbly adjusting his weight so he moved back without losing his balance, and exerted all his strength as the boar faltered, skidded toward him and fell in a squealing mass, its sharp trotters scrabbling right at his feet. The bitch was trapped for a moment but Rupert could not let her out until the boar was dead, which took some time, sweat and effort on his part. Then she slid out, shook herself and came to lick his hands. He could feel them trembling as he handed the spear back to his friend Richard Crane, who like everyone else had now dismounted.

"Good God," said Arundel at his shoulder. "That's the only time I'll hear a man shout 'Excellent!' in a fix like that! And I've never seen that done."

Rupert shrugged. "It all depends on the hounds." He looked down and laughed at Boy, who had come to sniff at the boar but did not dare to touch it with his nose.

They left two of the men behind to attend to the kill and rode back in the direction of the house, the dogs trotting unharmed at the horses' heels. Rupert was content. "You see why I said the hunting is good up here. Can I tempt you out hawking tomorrow?"

"I deeply regret, Your Highness, duty calls me to ride down to the Hague again." Arundel risked one of his dark, sardonic glances. "And what about yourself?"

Rupert smiled grimly. Arundel was a powerful lord and a consummate politician but he was capable of plain speech and Rupert had always liked him for that, besides the man's kindness when he was in prison. "Damn the Hague. I should like to go where I'm of use. Pawning the crown jewels is not my forte—I leave that to the queen. And to some of her ladies-in-waiting, who show a gift for accounts that I cannot match." Arundel grinned at this sarcasm, but Rupert did not reveal the person he thought of instantly in that connection—the brilliant Duchess of Richmond. Mary Villiers was proving a clever and persuasive commander in the queen's high campaign for funds. "The other half of the mission I complete with a will: the purchase of arms. We garner money and we spend it. I should just like to be sure the ordnance and weapons I buy will be put to use."

"The queen is crying for war, am I right?"

"Indeed. She wrote to my uncle recently to tell him that unless he agrees to read Parliament a lesson she will retire into a nunnery." He laughed, albeit with a bitter taste in his throat. "I can just see my aunt in a convent!"

"Then she must be burning for you to join His Majesty."

"No. She says she needs me here."

Arundel thought for a moment as the group of horses cantered easily beneath the trees along a path dappled by sunlight. "Your Highness, you have a multitude of voices with King Charles, mine included. Richmond, now: he has the king's ear always—and he told me that he has asked his magnificent wife to do all she can to promote your return. There are few who can withstand Mary Villiers, and our king is not one of them. Nor is the queen, who adores her. May I suggest you woo the Duchess of Richmond, if you have not done so already?"

Rupert did not reply. This news struck him disagreeably, and the longer he thought about it, the more puzzled and disturbed he felt. The Duke of Richmond, the king's devoted kin and valued adviser, had poured vast sums of his considerable personal fortune into Charles's coffers to prosecute the war, and Rupert knew he had Richmond's support. But could he count on Mary Villiers to stand as his friend alongside the powerful Duke of Richmond? No, by thunder, for she had said nothing about her husband's championship of him. On the contrary, every time they met she let him see how lukewarm she was about the king's taking up arms. The duchess served the queen faithfully but when it came to the prospect of war itself she was all for delay and compromise. She had never given a hint that she would encourage his own cause with either the king or the queen.

Arundel was musing aloud. "To woo Mary Villiers. Now there is a mission I envy any young blood." He caught Rupert's eye and said, "I speak tactically, of course. Otherwise, she is invulnerable. The most beautiful woman in England, the most captivating and the most chaste. She is untouchable—first married at thirteen and since then never a whisper of . . ." When Rupert still did not reply, Arundel gave a sigh of romantic regret and lapsed into silence.

Rupert did not smile. He was working out how quickly he could cover the sixty-odd miles back to his mother's court and tackle the Duchess of Richmond.

Mary was in a large reception room with the two queens, Prince Charles-Louis and a little crowd of ladies and gentlemen, mostly English. The Wassenaer Hof, the Hague residence of the Winter Queen, glittered with life. It was a beautiful day, and the sun was throwing patterns of color through the stained portions of the handsome windows into the room, where they floated across the ladies' rich gowns and traced diamonds on the tiled floor amongst the men's elegantly heeled shoes. The most exquisite gentleman was George, Lord Digby, arrived from northern England only the day before and full of news, which he was directing just now at Prince Rupert's mother, at her request, while they sat together on the sunny side of the room. Standing on the edge of Henrietta-Maria's animated group of ladies, Mary had leisure to observe them.

Elizabeth Stuart, once heir to the throne of England—until the birth of the Prince of Wales—seemed to Mary to possess some of the fire the great and glorious Elizabeth the First must have had, with an added handsomeness of feature and the splendor of height, for she was six feet tall. No one seeing her alert, straight-backed figure, with the abundant red-gray hair setting off her blue eyes, would suspect that this was a woman who had had thirteen children, and through her legendary love of her husband had gone through battles, tribulations and exile by his side. She was resilient and decisive, she handled her position amongst the sober and cautious burghers of the Hague with diplomacy, and she showed a fine understanding of the predicament in which her beloved brother found himself in England. In many ways, Mary thought ruefully, she was in contrast to Queen Henrietta-Maria, who in private gave way to despair about her husband's plight and her own, and in public sometimes received humiliating slights, as when prominent Dutchmen and their wives rose from her presence and walked away without speaking to her, in a gesture of sympathy for the Puritan cause in England. Elizabeth in the Hof and Henrietta-Maria in the New Palace on Staedt-Strasse received each other in apparent harmony, but underneath neither had much affinity for the other.

Lord Digby was welcomed by both the royal women. Indeed, however complicated a political situation might be, Mary had every confidence in her friend's sliding through it and out the other side, dispensing apt opinions and soothing advice on the way, without the least cost or danger to his own strategy—which remained a secret that only he ever knew. He had previously been a stout supporter of Parliament's cause and was married to the daughter of a Puritan lord, the Earl of Bedford, but he now declared himself just as staunchly royalist, and the king trusted him. Digby, though ten years older than she, was one of her intimates, and it was impossible to decide what she valued most in him—his easy temper, the charm of his blond good looks and canny blue eyes, or his ability to make her laugh at herself and him, even in the worst of situations. He was enjoying his audience with the Winter Queen, who sat at an angle to him and with her head slightly bent to listen, while she stroked a tiny marmoset that she held in her lap. The queen possessed a huge array of pets, and several of her spaniels were also in the room, fussing at each other around the shoes of the guests. Digby, ignoring the menagerie, gave the queen his devoted attention and meanwhile managed to keep abreast of everything else that went on in the room, with a quick glance around him every now and then that always ended in a flashing smile at Mary.

Eventually the queen said kindly, "You must share some of this fascinating news with the Duchess of Richmond. My dear madam," she said, beckoning to Mary with one hand while clamping the marmoset in place with the other, "I know your loyal heart is in York with my brother. Pray join us as we speak of him."

With a bow of the head Mary stepped forward. Digby rose, handed her into his chair with a flourish, and remained standing. "I have the pleasure to inform you of His Majesty's recent appointments. He has named Lord Falkland Secretary of State, and Sir John Culpepper, Lord Keeper of the Great Seal, as Chancellor of the Exchequer."

Nearby, Mary saw Queen Henrietta-Maria's startled face turn toward them. Had Digby not given the queen these details the previous evening? Perhaps she had not asked—she had a tendency not to seek the full picture when she was being informed of events.

Digby, while aware of the interest from this quarter, went smoothly on, "And in York he has available to him the steady counsel of Sir Edward Hyde."

"Hyde and Culpepper," Henrietta-Maria said loudly, unable to contain herself, "were my husband's exigent critics during all the years when he declined to call Parliament. And they have scarcely been his warmest advocates within it!"

Digby bowed respectfully in her direction. "A great deal has happened since your departure from England, madam. In recent months Sir Edward Hyde has emerged in another light. He has in fact made it his business to put the king's view in Parliament. He has done it with some skill—and without alienating the obdurate Puritans in either house. His advocacy has gone a long way toward encouraging His Majesty's most influential subjects to leave London one by one and join him at York, as a demonstration of their fealty." Digby being one of them, he waited a second for a sign of gratitude from the queen. When it was not forthcoming, he risked a humorous look at Mary and continued, "If negotiation can be achieved"—he waved a deprecatory hand—"and who can say whether it can or not—it may well be reached through such gentlemen as Falkland and Hyde. Their high aim is to safeguard the privileges of the monarch without in the process destroying the legitimate rights of Parliament."

"Their aim is not to make war, you mean," the queen said sharply. "In that case they can be of no help to us."

Digby bowed again. "Others have shown themselves equally reluctant to promote civil war. I regret to inform you that when His Majesty called the Earl of Essex to him, he refused to come to York and join us."

"Essex?" Mary exclaimed.

Digby gave her a regretful look. "A great loss, I concede. Whichever side Essex may take, there is no denying that there goes a courageous and principled man."

Queen Elizabeth gave him an approving look at this speech, Queen Henrietta-Maria pouted, and Mary gazed at the floor, her shoulders drooping. It hurt that Essex had repudiated Charles. It hurt even more that this meant she had secretly treated with the enemy—twice. And she felt a tremor of anxiety. If war was declared soon between king and Parliament and her actions were discovered, they could now be judged as treason. No one would defend her or try to mitigate her actions before the king. Even James could not do so, for he would be tainted and mistrusted simply because he was her husband. And no friend, including Digby, could afford to stand up for her. The king was surrounded just now with constant fears of conspiracy, and thus by courtiers overanxious to prove their fidelity; Digby's own allegiances had swung to the royalist cause all too recently, so he had a reputation to defend—he could spare no support for her.

But would her king believe that she could be a traitor to his cause? Surely Charles knew her too well for that. He would be bitterly hurt, but he would listen to her reasons. And then banish her and her husband from court.

Mary shivered while Digby said to Queen Elizabeth: "The Earl of Essex is rather naturally dismissed from the office of Lord Chamberlain!"

At that moment Prince Rupert walked in. He had been away for a week, everyone had missed him, and they showed it in a general murmur of pleasure and greeting. Except for Digby, who was seeing him for the first time and was of course keen to take his measure.

Rupert looked splendid, and more like a prince than Mary had ever seen him. His clothes were in rich blue Spanish cloth, heavily worked in silver thread, and for once his boots were more suited to the court than to the field. They had low heels, but he loomed as usual.

He stepped further into the room, with a broad, friendly grin for everyone in it, and directed a special look across to his mother. Mary, in the line of sight, intercepted it with a jolt, and for a frightening second she thought it intended for her. Then she dropped her gaze, confused.

The Winter Queen, without waiting for him to approach, called out, "My darling, not that creature again—you know he worries Jack."

Mary looked up to see that a dog had followed the prince into the room. It was a large white poodle, clipped around the back and haunches in the normal manner for a water dog, but sporting a mane of woolly hair about the shoulders and head.

Prince Rupert grimaced at Jack, the marmoset, which showed no sign of alarm, and raised one eyebrow at the poodle, which gave him a smile full of very sharp teeth, shut its mouth with a snap and stepped straight across the room to flop down with a sigh over Mary's feet.

Everyone laughed at Mary's start of surprise and the prince said, "He read my mind."

His mother chuckled and said, "Very gallant, but I forbid you to lie at the Duchess of Richmond's feet—you take up quite enough room as it is."

He strode over, greeted his mother properly, then Henrietta-Maria, and returned to make his bow to Mary. He shifted the poodle away from her with a touch of his toe, took Mary's hand as she rose, and brought it to his lips. This distinguishing behavior was all too odd and disturbing for her to comprehend, and she felt she made a poor job of presenting Lord Digby. Digby was good enough not to be put off by this and began talking with the prince in his accomplished way. At one point he said, "May I know the name of your remarkable dog?"

"Boy."

Mary caught Digby's eye at this and could not help saying with a complicit smile, "How very original."

The prince looked at her sidelong. "If I'd cared to be original I'd have called him Girl. He's clever enough."

Digby laughed at this and bent to scratch Boy's head. The dog gave him an indifferent look, then sat on his haunches and gazed up at Mary, the tuft on the end of his tail moving slightly from side to side in expectation that she would sit down again. The prince, noticing this, drew Digby away to talk with the group around Lord Arundel, a few paces away, and Boy trotted after him and lay down at his feet, without so much as a glance at the little spaniels or Henrietta-Maria's lapdog Mitte, which eyed him from the safety of the queen's skirts.

Mary conversed with great aplomb for the next hour, but moved from group to group, arm in arm for a while with her elegant aunt, Countess of Denbigh, First Lady of the Bedchamber. She intended to avoid the prince, for he perplexed her and she did not like the feeling. But it was useless—she slipped up once, and once was enough. She was alone under the high leaded windows looking out at the courtyard below, when he suddenly appeared at her elbow and said in a deep murmur, "Madam, we must talk. When may I see you alone?"

She looked quickly from side to side and then turned to face him, her face calm and prepared, though her heart was thumping with a kind of fright. "If you will observe, we are alone."

"Here?" Scorn roughened his voice. "I beg you to accord me a few minutes. Tomorrow?"

She summoned her coolest demeanor. "I cannot imagine, Your Highness, what you may have to say to me that cannot be said before anyone in this room."

He reddened at once. He was unused to this—just as he was unaccustomed to handing out compliments, except for the sincere tributes of affection he paid to family and friends. But she was not his friend, and he must know that. She would certainly have thought he knew it well enough not to attempt an assignation!

"By my troth," he said, "I mean no disrespect. Do you walk the spaniels down there tomorrow morning?" He nodded his head toward the courtyard below.

"I do," she said with frost in her voice.

"Then allow me to speak with you at ten." And he was gone before she could withhold her consent—that is, if she could have got up the hardihood to refuse what amounted to a royal command.

She looked swiftly around the room, but no one's face indicated that they had seen the brief altercation. Digby, whose inquisitive eyes she feared the most, had his back turned.

She felt annoyed all afternoon and it took her hours to go to

sleep that night. She woke in the morning unrefreshed and unde-
cided, for nothing the prince had done the day before added up to
anything consistent with regard to her. If it was a sexual approach,
it was unbelievably uncouth; he knew full well he could not treat
her like one of his mistresses, supposing he had any such in the
Hague—no, in the first shock she had misinterpreted him there.
He had too much dignity to behave with anything less than the
princely courtesy on which he prided himself.

Yet why beg for a private meeting? He was a direct speaker and
no one lingered in the dark about his opinions, but he was rarely
abrupt and never rude, at least not with ladies. He was surely not
seeking a rendezvous just to say something disagreeable? Sometimes she could see the anger that had poured forth at Dover sim-
mering beneath the surface, but so far he had held it in. And she
had never, thank God, felt it directed toward herself.

What would he do if he ever learned of the note she had sent
to Essex about him? The devil's head . . . The warning . . . She
went cold at the thought, then shook her head. Essex would have
thrown the message in the fire, just as he did the first, and whatever
his conclusions he would have no motive to reveal its contents to
anyone, friend or foe.

So why did she fear this interview with Prince Rupert? The only
answer was that when he first said, "We must talk," it was as though
his whole being were engaged in the words. He was about to demand something of her—something difficult, dangerous?—and at
the same time offer something of himself. She had shrunk before
the unknown vibration in his voice and the mysterious supplica-
tion in his dark, glowing eyes, but she had not been able to rebuff
him.

Chapter 7

THE MORNING WAS BRIGHT and cheerful, roses were blooming in the flowerbeds in the middle of the courtyard and the sunlight painted the neat squares of grass a burnished emerald. This little sanctum in the Wassenaer Hof was surrounded by a colonnade, like a cloister, and the three diminutive spaniels that Mary had brought down with her liked to run here, their nails scratching on the flagstones as they skidded around the corners, and they raised the echoes with their yapping when they caught up with one another and lay in a heap against the old stone walls. Mary really came here to be alone, but the prince threatened to spoil her solitude this morning. Looking up, she could see the window against which she had stood when he made this appointment the previous afternoon. In fact, either of the queens or any of their companions could easily observe the encounter by looking out the same window at any time. It was silly of Mary to feel nervous of what the prince would say, but she felt it nonetheless.

Perhaps he felt it too, for when he walked into the courtyard and greeted her, he did so without the air of easy dominance that had hung about him the day before. His determined mouth, with its strong, chiseled lines, usually had an upward quirk at the corners that could make it look haughty or humorous depending on his mood. Today the corners were compressed into straight lines, as though he were thinking hard about his first words.

She spoke little, which did not make it simple for him. After a moment he chose a stone bench in the sunshine, the farthest away from the main door opening into the cloister, and gestured: "Will it please you to sit here? Unless you find the sun too much?"

She sat down without a word and arranged her gown about her, noticing that it was the same red color as a rose that rambled over the arch in the center of the garden. There was no room for him to sit beside her so he remained standing, his left hand against

a column and the other on his hip, with his left leg bent out sideways and his heel resting on the instep of the other boot. It was a
casual pose but his glance was far from casual.

At last he said, "Madam, I have been a soldier, and nothing else,
since the age of fourteen. My life is spent in action; I have no other
role and no other hope of contentment. Three years ago I was captured in battle and thrown into prison without provision for ransom.
There was no chance of release unless I converted to the Roman
Catholic faith and agreed to fight for the armies of the Holy Roman
Emperor, both of which I refused to do. Those first twelve months
were the worst of my existence. I have no words to express how utterly miserable I was." He said this with a desperate, gloomy earnestness, and she was so taken aback by this beginning that her eyes were
on his face the whole time. "Then someone took pity on me and
befriended me. She should have treated me with the utmost severity,
for she was the daughter of my jailer, the Count von Kuffstein. But
she became my friend, and I hers. I shall never forget her; she saved
my future. Through the efforts of others my plight was relieved and
I obtained my freedom last year. But she was the instigator; it was her
sweet influence, day by day, that first gave me hope and rescued me.
From her I learned the purest . . . friendship."

There was such a long pause before the last word that Mary
dropped her gaze, and a strange and desolate sensation swept
through her. If he had pronounced the word "love," she was aware
that this sensation would be jealousy. She kept her eyes down as
with her fingertips she created small knife-edge pleats in the crimson satin of her gown.

"Madam, you see me trapped in this country, when you know I
belong in England with my uncle. I have no need to tell you what
torture it is to be idle—it is as terrible as a prison to me. I have come
to the point where I must dare to ask a favor of you. If you cannot
perform it, then so be it, but . . . can you, out of your generosity—
that warmth and generosity which I see every day lavished on my
aunt—" He took a breath. "Can you consent to be my friend?"

She looked up in absolute amazement at this conclusion. He
flinched when he saw her face, abandoned his nonchalant pose,
so out of keeping with his sad recital, and stood straight as though
expecting a judgment. Before she could speak he said, "If I may
win your friendship, I beg you to tell me how."

"Your Highness," she said, floundering, "is friendship something to be won? Between two people—does it not develop? Or not, as the case may be."

"Ah," he said passionately, "then you do hate me. Why? What have I done? Whatever it is, will you allow me to make amends?" Seeing the shock in her face he said quickly, "There is a barrier between us—there always has been. If it cannot be removed, if your hatred is fixed, pray tell me and I'll importune you no more." He actually turned, ready to cross the garden and leave.

She put out a hand. "No! Your Highness, let me assure you, I do not hate you. I'm appalled that you should think so." With his brow furrowed he looked down at her outstretched hand and she took it back. The dialogue had strayed into extraordinary paths but she had the means to return it to civilized discourse. That is, if her quivering voice would obey her. "I blame my own comportment. I was not, I think, very agreeable to you when I was younger. I teased you, I remember—and I shall probably do so again. I tease everybody," she said in a lighter tone and with an attempt at a smile.

He said thoughtfully, "I was not mature enough to recognize that. I was afraid of you."

She gave a little laugh. "And lately I have been afraid of you."

He looked fierce. "That's not possible! Why?"

She made up her mind. "Your Highness, you have described yourself to me, though I'm sure that you don't for a moment believe that your sketch is complete. Allow me to do the same, with the same proviso." She said with self-mocking emphasis, "I am a very indulged, frivolous, luxurious, demanding being. I like to be happy—it is my observation that I like to be happy more than anyone I know. And I like to make others happy, in whatever way I can." Then her voice fell. "Since the beginning of this year, neither of those has been possible. I have not lost my purpose, but I have lost joy."

He shook his head. "I don't understand. Why does that make you afraid of me?"

"My world has changed for the worse, so much so that I hardly feel I have a place in it. But I cannot bear to see it destroyed. Forgive me, please forgive me, but you force me to speak my mind. If my king makes war on his own subjects, you will be the instrument. You are his one hope of victory, I see that plain. You will also be his agent of destruction."

She expected towering anger, a radical end to the conversation and his enmity forever. It hurt her to the soul, waiting for his wrath to fall upon her, but she watched his face, as though for the last time.

To her astonishment he dropped lithely to the ground and sat with one leg stretched out before him and an arm resting on the other raised knee. He was staring at the grass, thinking. The spaniels, sensing a change of mood and delighted to have him at their level, bounded from the shadows into the sun and took turns to lick his boots and jump at his dangling fingers.

He raised his head to look at her and his face, framed by the thick waves of hair, suddenly looked as clear and open as it had many years before when he came to court in his first youth. "Is that all? Now I know. You think me reckless, rash, headstrong, belligerent, ruthless, aggressive beyond measure—"

Despite herself a smile sprang to her lips, but she interrupted him firmly, "In a word, yes."

"That is my *reputation*. That is not *me*." He looked at her hopefully, as though this were a full and satisfactory explanation, then caught her expression, sighed and grew solemn. "Believe this, madam—and I am willing to swear it like a Catholic on the Gospels—I do not wish to join King Charles out of a lust for war. I do not wish to go because I am a trained professional, a veteran of many campaigns, an obsessed scholar of warfare, avid to take on any task because I have no idea what else to do with myself!" His voice dropped. "I do not even go for my uncle's sake. I go to save the kingdom of England." He held her eye. "I would say this to no one else. I would say this only to a friend. Will you help me to fulfill my destiny?"

It was grandiose, and youthful. It was trusting, yet said with the fire and vigor he put into everything he did.

She reached out her hand again, careless of any watchers in the queen's room above, and he took it at once and held it hard.

She said, "Give me time. I cannot say, yet. But I am no longer afraid of you."

Prince Rupert of the Rhine, Count Palatine, Knight of the Order of the Garter, third son of Elizabeth, Queen of Bohemia, hosted a great banquet in the Wassenaer Hof before his departure for

England. Everyone of importance was there, including the Stadholder, some members of the States General and many prominent burghers of the Hague. Those who had contributed to the coffers of Queen Henrietta-Maria and thus to the shipments of arms that the prince bought for England were distributed about the board amongst the nobility instead of all being placed at the lower end of the enormous table, which gave an unusually democratic flavor to the occasion.

On his right hand the prince placed his mother and on the left his aunt. Some of his brothers and sisters were also present, but it was observed with amusement that those of his siblings who approved of his command in England were placed nearer to him than the rest—which meant that Prince Charles-Louis, his mother's heir and also her clear favorite, was not amongst the highest. He had slipped away from England when things looked unpropitious for the king, and had no intention of returning. His mother was said to have been somewhat ashamed of this, and feared Charles-Louis's honor was "a little engaged in it," but in fact she did not encourage him to go back and had equally done all she could to prevent Prince Rupert from leaving—she was cautious about sending her sons to take up arms against Puritans. By contrast to Charles-Louis, Rupert's younger brother Maurice, a soldier like himself, held a high position and contributed much to the laughter and cheer at the top of the table.

Present also was Princess Mary of Orange, who had taken some months to fit into the public life of the Hague, but true to the injunctions of Prince William was always treated with the respect due to her rank. Placed near enough to join in the merriment roused by her host, she was accompanied by Baron Heenvliet, the Grand Superintendent of her household, and his wife, the English gentlewoman who was her governess.

Those burghers jealous of their own importance were surprised to find a scattering of plain military men about the board, amongst whom were a Scots engineer, an ammunitions expert and three cavalry officers, Richard Crane, Somerset Fox and Dan O'Neale.

There were toasts throughout. At one point there was one to the "Queen of Hearts," and Prince Rupert gave from memory a sonnet written many years before by Sir Henry Wotton in tribute to his mother, Elizabeth.

You meaner beauties of the night,
That poorly satisfy our eyes
More by your number than your light,
You common people of the skies;
What are you when the moon shall rise . . . ?

More than one person noticed that as he came to the end of the poem the prince's gaze was directed to the Duchess of Richmond, seated nearby—perhaps he, like others, felt that the bright-haired duchess was somewhat the picture of Elizabeth in her lissome youth.

Mary herself was happy, in great suspense and suffering from a fever, though she managed to conceal the last, counting on people to think her burning cheeks were due to enjoyment of the occasion. She was happy because over the last weeks her letters to her husband and the king, and her many earnest conversations with Henrietta-Maria, had helped to persuade Their Majesties that Prince Rupert belonged in England. The king had reached a decision and named his commanders. According to royal tradition he would lead the armies himself as Captain General. The Earl of Lindsay—in his sixties, if Mary remembered him aright—was Lord General, and Prince Rupert was appointed General of the Horse, commander of all the king's cavalry, reporting not to Lindsay but directly to the king. She was full of suspense for precisely the same causes—she could not know, until her friend proved himself in his service to Charles, whether he could achieve what he advocated: a quick, decisive victory and then a firm treaty with Parliament.

She was also in suspense because she had broken the rules of a lifetime when she used her influence with the king and queen for Rupert's advantage. Charles and Henrietta-Maria had now seen her champion someone else's cause, and this was an act she had never committed before, not even on her husband's account. Never in her life had her adoptive parents been given an excuse to imagine that she was capable of conniving, intrigue or conspiracy. She belonged in their trusted inner circle by birth, by virtue of their protection and because they believed she deserved that protection. She must continue to take great care that they saw her present support of Rupert as part of her commitment to the survival of the kingdom. No one must think that she was unduly swayed by Rupert himself.

She was happy that she and Rupert were friends—and confused by it. She had told him why she had been afraid of him politically; she had not told him that his presence still disturbed her, nor that the closeness of friendship was not an easy place in which to keep her equilibrium. Each day she too much looked forward to seeing him and was far too disappointed if he did not arrive. Today she regretted his going, and knew it, and reproached herself for it.

After he pronounced a toast to Henrietta-Maria, and it was indulgently received and the hubbub was dying down, the prince caught her eye and said to her along the table, "And to the Duchess of Richmond." The others around her smiled; her influence with the queen on his behalf was widely known, though it could hardly be a matter for a general toast. He raised his wine cup and smiled into her eyes. "Ever my friend."

She laughed softly and lifted her own cup. "I think everyone knows me better than that. *Lately* and truly your friend, Your Highness." She paused, feigned to take a sip and put the cup down. "Indeed, without the good offices of Lord Arundel, I might be sparring with you still."

He looked nervous. "Arundel?"

"Before he left here, he told me what he had suggested to you." Their companions looked extremely inquisitive at this, so she laughed again and said, "His Highness made me a very pretty speech about friendship—appealing of course to my feelings, the most volatile thing about me, as everyone knows." She smiled at him. "And won my friendship."

He frowned. "I am used to think that friendship is something that develops. Or not, as the case may be."

"But with cunning skill you persuaded me otherwise. There, you see, you have much more of the subtle courtier in you than you suppose." The others laughed but he looked uncertain, so she continued lightly, "Your Highness, I am teasing. Remember, I promised you I should?"

He laughed and the talk resumed, but she could see that underneath he was startled that she should refer in public to their overwhelming encounter. Well, now he realized that she knew he had worked on her emotions that day. And he had done it not from some irresistible impulse of his own, but because Arundel had told him to win her over.

Nonetheless, she could not resent his behavior, which showed just how vulnerable she was. She might tease him in order to maintain an essential distance between them, and make it clear to all that she had no secrets to conceal, but in reality what he had said and done in the sunlit garden brought her dangerously close to him, in a way he must not suspect.

When the banquet was over and the horde of guests had taken leave, Queen Henrietta-Maria invited the intimates to her private room in the New Palace to pledge a fond farewell to the prince. Mary had never seen the queen so joyful or sanguine about the future; she now considered her mission half accomplished if she could sponsor Rupert to England, and she looked on him as her personal champion.

Henrietta-Maria gazed around at them all with smiling eyes and said, "Tonight was a refulgent occasion. It needed nothing more to make it perfect; otherwise I should say, What a pity we are not in a country of sport and revels where we could dance the night away."

Mary said, "Even if Dutch restraint did not forbid it, we have not the room here, madam."

"Ah," the queen said nostalgically, "at the French court you would never hear anyone say so. There is a dance for every excuse and every corner. Rupert," she went on, "in your travels, you must have learned something new that you could show us. No one can object to your dancing, surely, supposing our secret trespasses ever came out. You are not so Calvinist as to deny us, I hope?"

Prince Rupert raised his eyebrows. "I met your compatriots only on campaign, aunt."

"I know. So what about Turenne? Turenne is a great ornament at court."

"He was a great ornament at the siege of Louvain too, but—" He paused, and Mary could see mischief in his eye. "Very well, there are some new steps I could demonstrate, but we need room."

The queen clapped her hands with pleasure and the ladies pressed their chairs against the sides of the chamber. Mary failed to catch the prince's eye at this point, which made her a little suspicious, but he began with perfect grace. He had a jeweled scarf across his shoulders that he unwound and opened out as he advanced into the middle of the room, his feet in their court shoes correctly turned out and gliding through the first long steps.

Then with a solemn expression of concentration on his face he raised his long arms so that they arched above his head, and wiggled his fingers in a way that reminded Mary of a wayward butterfly. With equal solemnity, and without moving from the spot, he brought his arms down, spread them wide and, bending from the hips extended one leg, resplendent in silver breeches and hose, out behind him. Everyone else was spellbound but he teetered a little, like an unsteady clothes horse, and Mary put up her hand to hide a smile.

Wobbling dangerously now, the prince brought the raised leg round on a spectacular angle and waggled his foot about in front of him, a fixed smile now on his face. Mary began to giggle. With a scandalized look at her he suddenly dropped his foot and executed two rapid pirouettes, flapping his hands and flicking the scarf across his face and tousled hair.

"Oh no," cried the queen in reproach, and began to laugh.

He spared no one. Quartering the room in high, ridiculous steps, he stared manically at each person in the audience, pausing inches away in a rigid, contorted pose, with the haughty mien of a Spanish matador, or a pompous official—or an absolute idiot. The Countess of Denbigh, who was in a wild fit of mirth, would not look at him when he arrived in front of her and sat with head bent, shaking it from side to side to avoid his eye. No one could have him near without collapsing into shrieks of laughter, and his brother Maurice begged him with tears in his eyes to leave off.

He finished with Mary, who by now was laughing so much she could scarcely breathe. With his eyes boring awfully into hers he executed a deep and elaborate bow containing so many flourishes that he whirled himself into a tangle of limbs on the floor at her feet. Hysterical applause broke out, and propping himself on one elbow he looked up into Mary's streaming eyes, put his hand into his breast and pulled out a lace handkerchief that he handed up to her, laughing.

With a ragged gasp of mirth, she took it, spread it in her hands and covered her face. She held it there, hiding her laughter and her tears. And knew she was in love.

*   *   *

Such was Prince Rupert's haste to fulfill his commission that he sailed with a very small retinue in the *Lion*, the ship that had brought him from Dover in February. The captain was the same but seemed of a different temper from before—when they struck a storm on the first day, he took fright and for the prince's safety insisted they should put ashore until it abated. Rupert was scornful and unwilling but could not prevail against this insane caution. He resigned himself, remained in the bow like a drenched and disconsolate figurehead all the way to land, and found quarters ashore where he could stay until morning and better weather.

But in the morning the *Lion* was gone—she had slipped away without him in the night. The rage that gripped him terrified everyone in sight and sent his small party into a panic. He was wild with himself for never guessing the captain's subterfuge, and ready to tear to pieces whoever had put the scoundrel up to it—except that he suspected, too late, that the person was his mother, probably aided and abetted by Charles-Louis.

Then a letter came. In his fury he ripped it roughly open, but a moment later he flattened it with his fingers and sat down to read.

It was from the Duchess of Richmond, and he was both surprised and glad to see her vigorous signature at the foot of the page. She had been unwell on the morning he left, closeted away and unable to take leave of him. This contact gratified him, in more ways than one.

> *May it please Your Highness,*
>> *Though this letter is in my hand, in effect you should consider it as a message from my gracious queen, who would have written to you herself but for the reverence, respect and tender gratitude she holds toward the Queen of Bohemia, and but for her natural wish never to displease or disturb your mother in any inadvertent or ill-judged manner, whether by word or deed.*
>> *On this understanding, Her Majesty allows me in this fashion to send you some information, which we are afraid, however, may not reach you before you sail. Forgive the delay if this is so—I overheard this information but an hour ago, and have only just conferred upon it with Her Majesty. It is this: we fear that the*

captain of the Lion *is not worthy of your trust. Indeed, he may have been given orders to prevent your sailing for England. If you should meet with difficulties of this kind—and may God preserve you from any more serious—my queen begs me to assure you that there is a ship, provided by the Stadholder, in port at your disposal. It is Her Majesty's fond wish that you look no further than herself for aid in the glorious mission you undertake for her sake, for her husband and for England.*

There was no subscription except the duchess's signature. He folded the letter, kissed it, put it inside his doublet and strode out to discover where the Stadholder's ship might be. He made his preparations with more thoroughness this time, sending out for everything and everyone he wanted, and when he left he took with him his brother Maurice, the military guests from the banquet, his dog Boy and a new pet monkey, all on board for the island of his dreams.

Chapter 8

HENCEFORTH MARY HAD NEWS of the prince only by letter, but he was frequently mentioned in those from her husband and the occasional witty missive from Lord Digby, who was now governor of Nottingham. James's epistles were of a logical, informative and sometimes nerve-racking kind. Reading them, Mary had to face the truth that in supporting Rupert's return to England, she had helped to place him in the utmost danger. Since his arrival the prince had spent his time hurtling about Yorkshire and the Midlands raising the king's horse and seizing any parliamentary troops or supplies in his way. To this end he had attacked a mansion in Warwickshire that was gallantly defended, only to discover on taking it that his opponent was the lady of the house. He left all her possessions untouched and marched on. Elsewhere, however, he was ruthless and exacting as he stripped the countryside for the king's good; and he always led his troops from the front, however formidable the opposing forces happened to be. The duke, with uncharacteristic relish, told her that the prince already had a reputation for invincibility that put the fear of the devil into those inclined toward the Parliament.

Digby's reports, though idiosyncratic, created clearer pictures. Prince Rupert when he first landed at Tynemouth had set out on horseback at once to join the king, but in the frosty darkness his borrowed horse had slipped and fallen on him, dislocating his shoulder. "How they found a bonesetter at that time of night I cannot conceive," Digby wrote, "supposing I should ever be unhandy enough to want one—at any rate, they put the shoulder back in and rode on. I heard the tale when he arrived in Nottingham—I roused His Highness from sleep the same night to inspect some new weaponry about which His Majesty hotly called for knowledge."

It was enough to make her feel she had been there. She saw Prince Rupert dragging himself back to consciousness as someone stood over his rumpled mattress, raising a pale, exhausted face to the inquiry, then compressing his mouth in silence, rising with an effort and buckling on whatever you buckled on at midnight, and walking out to do his duty.

The king raised the royal standard at Nottingham on August 22, Digby said, and then it blew down in the night. "It was considered an ill omen at the moment," her friend wrote, "but it is perhaps countered by the prince's putting two pistol shots through the tail of a weathercock on the steeple of St Mary's church, Stafford, these three days past. I am no expert in such things but for aught I know it was an auspicious sign. We are now at Shrewsbury, which we reached 22 September, and one eagerly awaits further prodigies."

The queen's money-raising meanwhile went on apace and gave Henrietta-Maria great satisfaction, though there were always other worries to beset her. She was concerned about her eldest boys, Charles and James, who were now with the king, but even more so about the two youngest children, who were still at Saint James's Palace in London. It was Parliament's responsibility to ensure that they were unmolested and well cared for, but Henrietta-Maria was never comfortable with that thought and Mary could hardly blame her. By one interpretation, little Elizabeth and Henry were hostages for their parents' conduct, and it chilled Mary to think of a six-year-old and an eighteen-month-old in that position. Parliament proved vigilant, however, and when the Countess of Roxburgh, the children's governess, applied directly to them for assistance, claiming the children were "in want of everything," as she wrote to the queen, Speaker Lenthall told the House their plight was shameful and eighty hundred pounds a month was allotted for their maintenance.

"I sometimes wonder," Henrietta-Maria said to Mary one day, "whether I could spare you to go to London and find out what is happening to my babies. You have no children, my dear, so you can have no motherly feelings to distract you—I need a frank account, and you are so good at describing things that I shall know at once how things go if you write me."

Mary looked down at her hands cradled in her lap, wondering if she presented a sufficiently unmaternal figure in that pose. Five years married and no children—how in the name of fortune did that result in people's thinking she did not want them? But somehow it did. If she were to be sent back to England, why should it be to London, when her true home was near the king, wherever he happened to be? Wherever James, Duke of Richmond, was lending his fortune, his support and his life to the royal cause. The place from which Prince Rupert of the Rhine led the king's horse forth against Parliament.

She raised her eyes. "I beg, madam, that if you think of sending me back to England you will give me a task that takes me close to my husband. Each time he writes I see his wish for my return in every line, yet he never says it in so many words."

Henrietta-Maria reached out and patted her hand in one of the sudden impulses of sympathy that so often disarmed Mary. "Forgive me—no, you shall not go to London. You shall stay with me. My little Mall, we are both made widows by this war. But we shall win it, and our joy will be the greater when love comes into our lives again."

The Earl of Essex was riding down a peaceful country road with short, woven hedges on each side that allowed him to see fields of stubble and the occasional meadow lined with thin coppices still in their summer green. But it was autumn, and he and Prince Rupert had not yet come to a meeting. By the grace of God, however, it must happen in the next few days. He knew where the prince was, roughly, and he knew with cold certainty what he wanted—London. Which was why he had first arrayed his own army—Parliament's army—of fifteen thousand men at Northampton, across the line of march the prince must take to reach his goal.

Essex had spent a diabolical summer pulling together men and equipment and getting them into some kind of shape. Despite the backbreaking labor, he had known nonetheless that the king's men had a worse job to do, and it gave him some satisfaction as the hot months ground by. Parliament, having brought in an Impressment Bill and Militia Ordnance in February, met no hindrance to raising troops. King Charles, in a conciliatory mood, had signed the Impressment Bill on the road to Dover, in addition to dropping the charges against the Five Members. When it came to the Militia Ordnance, however, he had delayed so long that Parliament finally passed it themselves—and these were the tools Essex needed. He had begun with London and its environs, taking over the Trained Bands of each town and building the basis of an army. Though "trained" was in his private view a somewhat facetious term.

The king, meanwhile, deprived of the very resource he had been fighting for over the last few years—namely, public money for his armies—had to raise troops by commission. The predictable nobles had rallied rapidly to this arrangement, and some unpredictable ones had already spent fortunes arming forces of their own for the king. Recruitment had not been easy for either side, but Essex could not help feeling that his own army must be larger than the king's and more united in spirit. The king's main force had lately been at Shrewsbury, but Essex had a good idea that his objective was Worcester, and there was thus every chance that King Charles and Prince Rupert were now heading south through the pretty countryside of the Wick toward him.

It was past time that he and Prince Rupert met, for more than one reason. Essex was annoyed about the exaggerated tales of the man that filtered into his own army by the day. Prince Rupert was reported to be in so many places within such short periods of time that the most superstitious declared him magical—able to divide himself so as to be in two localities at once, and never needing a wink of sleep. This was farcical—of course the prince was flying about the country like a demon, for with a captain general like King Charles he would be doing all the military coordination single-handed.

Many towns and cities in the region, aghast at the prospect of civil war, were voting themselves neutral—a tactic which Prince Rupert simply ignored, seizing what he could, where he could. Essex approved of this, since it was what he intended to do himself, but meanwhile it gave a savage and brutal aspect to the prince's activities.

At the same time, Essex did not fall into the trap of underestimating his opponent. He knew of the prince's style, from Englishmen like Lord Craven, who had served alongside him in Europe: fierce, dashing and unstoppable. And Prince Rupert had never been wounded, not by so much as a scratch. He had the luck of Lucifer: once in the thick of battle a cavalryman had fought his way right up to him and leveled a pistol at his head—but it did not go off. Time and again he had stared death in the face and come away scot-free. He had only been captured at Vlotho when, riding alone and with an Austrian troop after him, he put his horse at a high obstacle and the beast refused—no wonder, for surely few mounts could lift that giant over anything higher than a bramble hedge!

Essex also had every reason to know his methods, which could hardly be very different from the Dutch tactics he had learned himself early in his career, with Sir Horace Vere in the Palatinate, fighting in fact for the prince's father. So there would be nothing new in the coming engagement, except for his confronting Prince Rupert of the Rhine on the field, a notion that spurred him on.

He sent an advance guard of one thousand troopers out well before his main force to clear the Worcester environs immediately ahead and let him know whether the king had taken the city, and if so how he looked likely to defend it. If they happened to spot Prince Rupert's advance guard in the process they were to use all caution.

It was a fine day with no sign of any autumn rains, and the gently rolling country of the Wick would have given good visibility if the screens of trees drawn here and there across the landscape had not been in full leaf. As it was, there was no warning of what had occurred until he reached Pershore.

The bad news was delivered by Captain Nathaniel Fiennes, a member of Parliament and a man of sense and courage, and the earl took the brunt with grim attention.

"We have been through an engagement, my lord, and I regret to tell you, have come off the worse."

"Are you pursued?"

"No, my lord."

"Continue, then. Where, how and how many lost?"

"We got as far as Powick, my lord, not two miles southwest from Worcester. Colonel Sandys ascertained on the way that the king is not at Worcester, and Sir John Byron has been lately there but is gone off. This gave the colonel the view that the king's men we then spied in the fields were but a small force. They did not occupy the village, but low ground called Powick Ham. They were across the River Teme, around a bridge."

"The colonel gave the order to attack, I take it?"

"We—" Fiennes hesitated a moment, his exhausted brain clearly struggling over whether to say the next thing or not. "Three of the troop captains suggested not, my lord." He hesitated again, decided not to name himself among them, and went on, "The ground there is cut by the river, which is a narrow one with steep banks, and there's more than one gully—we had a poor sight on our enemy, but they appeared to be resting, dismounted and with no arms about them. We were near enough to come at them, and the colonel bade us do so, and the long and short of it is, my lord, a great many of us were trapped in a sort of defile and cut to pieces." Essex felt the officers around him flinch. Fiennes paused for a second, then went doggedly on. "Prince Rupert was there, my lord, and the moment he saw us he leaped to horse and they charged us. They caught others of us on the bridge and by the river. It's a strange sort of country bridge, narrow, and with pockets at the side of it where you can stand aside and let carts and horses go by—well, with us in there they played billiards with us."

"How many lost?"

"Colonel Sandys has taken mortal hurt. Fifteen officers are gone and I'm not sure how many men, but a hundred or more. And they've carted off the prisoners, about fivescore."

"He's *gone*? He rides roughshod over you and doesn't advance? What is going on, Captain?"

Fiennes looked suddenly close to tears. "What's going on, my lord, is that our lads are burying the dead, and all I can offer to do, by way of further information, is to ride back there and count them. If such is your order."

"I'll do so myself," Essex grunted, then relented and praised the man for his report and for keeping his head in the affray. He left Fiennes with the army, then took some defeated troopers as guides and proceeded with a group of officers at speed to Powick. It was just as Fiennes had described, therefore not pretty. Casting about for some picture of what the bastard Rupert was up to, his men came upon a churchman from Inkborough, Richard Baxter, who had viewed some of the battle and then taken shelter in Powick village.

He was, the earl could see, a sensitive man, shattered by the encounter and left with a deep impression of royalist brutality. The earl interviewed him in the church on top of the knoll, which seemed to give the young Church of England clergyman some reassurance. Essex also knew that his visit there would discourage any soldiers in his army who thought knocking the heads off church statues somehow constituted a tribute to the Almighty.

Baxter knew a lot about the royalist situation, no doubt from the news that flowed through Inkborough to his parishioners. Sir John Byron, one of the king's commanders, had apparently come down toward Worcester with a large baggage train of plate and treasure from Oxford, intended for the king's coffers. The king had sent Prince Rupert to meet up with Byron and occupy Worcester, but the prince, perhaps recognizing how imperfect the defenses were around the city, had decided not to occupy it, and had sent Byron and the train off to unite with the king at Shrewsbury. He had himself formed a rear guard carefully positioned to cover Byron's withdrawal—and, seeing Essex's men, had charged at once and driven all before him.

Since his departure the prince had sent back his own chaplain, the Reverend Lacy, to minister to the dying Colonel Sandys, who was not taken prisoner but allowed to be conveyed into Worcester.

The handsome, well-kept church was very quiet when Richard Baxter finished his recital—leaving unsaid, Essex noticed, much the same things that Fiennes had not brought himself to say. The earl sat sideways on the pew he occupied with the cleric at the rear of the nave, and watched motes of dust spinning in a last ray of light that penetrated the high windows.

"Have you thought of taking a commission as chaplain in the army?" He ignored Baxter's shudder and went on, "To their sorrow, our men will witness such acts as you have seen every day. It is a high calling to give them the measure of comfort that the Scripture affords, in their most need."

Baxter looked at him with such horror that Essex rose at once, thanked him, shook his hand and left. Outside, he prepared to ride down the hill again to devastated Powick Ham, and thence to Worcester. From here he could see the dark tower of its cathedral beckoning him on. Prince Rupert might not want the city but Essex would occupy it with pleasure, and next time his army met the prince's, he would himself be at the head, with sword, pistol or whatever it took to banish the triumph from that young, arrogant face.

"Anne," Mary said one cool September night, "I desire you to give me a poem about love."

"One of yours?" said Anne Gibson, who was sitting on the end of Mary's bed. Mary often had trouble sleeping, and so did Anne, so when their wakefulness coincided and Anne was spending the night in the household, Mary would sometimes call her in to talk. At home in London, James frowned on this because he never thought she took enough rest. Alone in the Hague, however, Mary did as she liked, knowing that Anne very much liked it too.

"One of mine?" She raised her eyebrows. "I write none, as well you know."

"Oh," Anne said with her head on one side, "your first poem about Lord Digby would do for a love sonnet. Provided you left out the quatrain about the way he curled his hair."

Mary laughed. "You know they are all too satirical. And no one is ever to read them except you and I. You have the glove case locked and safe, I trust?"

"Amongst your others, as always," Anne said, skidding to the edge of the bed. "Shall I . . . ?"

"No, thank you, leave it be." Mary sighed and clasped her hands tighter across her knees as she sat against the bed head, a woolen scarf close about her shoulders. "Can you recite me any love poems, Anne?"

The dwarf said in her thin, humorous voice, "I can recite you one about marriage, if you like." Mary remained silent, so Anne wrinkled her nose and thought carefully. It was Mary's guess that Anne was striving to remember all the words to a poem by Edmund Waller that he had written for the occasion of Anne's marriage many years ago to the gifted court painter Richard Gibson, also a dwarf. The marriage had been sponsored by the king and queen— the king had given Anne away and the queen had presented her with a diamond ring. Finally Anne chose to recite just six lines, with a glint of pride in her lively eyes:

Thrice happy is that humble pair,
Beneath the level of all care!
Over whose heads those arrows fly
Of sad distrust and jealousy;
Securèd in as high extreme,
As if the world held none but them.

"There! A fine hymn to marriage." Then she added slyly, "But what would a little body know about the poetry of love, mistress?"

Mary raised her eyebrows. She knew little about Anne's domestic life except that she and Gibson had children, all of normal size. "Don't tease me, I'm too tired. Oh, very well . . . If you say me nay, then you have but a little heart too."

"Yea, small enough to fit in a neat little locket. And J. H. might wear it around his neck, though he knows it not."

Mary sat up straight. "J. H. . . . ." The initials of the queen's dwarf page. She stared keenly at Anne's whimsical face, then whispered, terribly afraid of being gulled, *"Jeffrey Hudson?"*

Anne laughed enigmatically. Mary was tempted to ask why the locket should not hang around the neck of Dick Gibson. Then she realized Anne was playing games.

Anne went on, "But lately I cannot help setting my sights higher. And *taller* than any little woman has a right to aspire to! What do you say to P. R.?"

Mary raised her eyes toward the brocade bed curtains, hoping to give nothing away. "Don't you mean K of G?"

"King of . . . ? Oh no, I see, Knight of the Garter."

"Or W. P."

Anne considered, twisted her face around, then pouted. "No, too hard. I think very little of that one."

"The Winter Prince."

Anne clapped her hands. "Now *there* is a fit character for a squib!" She slid off the bed with a thump, ran to Mary's desk and returned with paper, ink and pen to sit on the floor, her favorite writing position. Anne, whose handwriting was unknown to the court, wrote out all Mary's poems—which meant that, if they were ever discovered, no one could possibly guess who had been wicked and devious enough to lampoon almost everyone of importance in England. But of course the hidden pieces never would be read by anyone else; it was just a midnight amusement.

"The Winter Prince," Anne said as she laid out her things on the floor. "Now, William Shakespeare wrote *The Tempest* for the wedding of Prince Rupert's mother. Might you do a little something with that—summer tempest, winter storms?"

Mary did not reply, and while Anne was trimming the quill

she sat with her head on her drawn-up knees and closed her eyes, imagining for one moment that she really could write about Prince Rupert. What a dangerous, intoxicating, delirious process that would be. Or *to* him. A stab of frightening pleasure went through her. Then, before the pause grew too long, she opened her eyes.

"I think we shall start with a tale that Lord Arundel told me. It is called the Ballad of Boy and the Boar."

There was the faintest glimmer of disappointment or disbelief in Anne's eyes, then she bent her head, ready to write.

Chapter 9

AT THE END OF October the Duke of Richmond was riding through the outskirts of Edgecote, a few miles out of Banbury, with three of his younger brothers—George, John and Bernard—and Prince Rupert. James's first favorable judgment of the prince had grown into a firm liking, and it seemed to be returned. The prince was impulsive in action but cautious in his relationships— yet with James, despite the seven years' difference in their ages, he relaxed into something very like friendship. Since the Stuart brothers had taken up their commands in the army, James had sometimes prevailed on Prince Rupert to take a meal with the four of them. It was not easy to get the prince to sit down even for an hour, however, so today they were accompanying him as he rode out of headquarters at Edgecote before making one of his wide-reaching tours of the army, which was at present quartered in the surrounding villages. With them rode the commander of the prince's life guard, the alert and doughty Sir Richard Crane, who had recently been knighted by the king, and another of the prince's friends, the competent lieutenant colonel of his cavalry regiment, Dan O'Neale.

The prince was full of good humor and the subjects they spoke of were cheerful, especially the hope that they could shortly smash Essex—who was known to be on the move from Worcester—and then take the high road to London. In the midst of these discussions they were skirting a village square at the trot, when the prince brought his tall black stallion to halt and stopped to watch a company of pikemen being drilled. The rest of the party also halted and saw with resignation that the prince was disposed for an inspection. He rode up to the young officer, who froze, as did his men, and said: "Good morning, Major. What company?"

"Third company, Lord Lindsay's Regiment of Foot, Your Highness." The prince had not introduced himself but that was superfluous, for there could not be a man in the army who did not recognize him.

"All right." The prince swung down from his horse. "Let's get a look at them."

The major hastened to draw the hundred or so men up on parade and the prince strode about, looking at them as much from the side as the front, James noted. He presumed the prince was checking the spacing between the ranks—an important matter when they carried eighteen-foot weapons with pikeheads of razor sharpness.

The prince seemed satisfied. "These pikes are the new issue?" he asked the major.

"Indeed, Your Highness—delivered Tuesday."

The prince nodded. "Not before time. Very well, let's witness one in action." Without waiting for the youthful major to choose his man, the prince stepped forward, tapped a young bear of a soldier on the shoulder and said, "We'll see the postures, if you please."

The soldier marched smartly forward, well clear of his comrades; James and the prince's party stayed at a safe distance; and the prince and the major withdrew to the far side. James motioned his own and his brothers' wolfhounds to the ground and the prince's dog, Boy, after a quick look at his master, joined them. The soldier meanwhile took the posture called Order Your Pike, the weapon towering over him while he waited for the word to commence.

"Now lad," the prince said in a carrying voice, "let's see how well you can impress the Duke of Richmond!"

Two hundred eyes turned James's way and he grinned and touched his hat brim, then set himself to observe. The Earl of Lindsay had outfitted this company well: their armor consisted of gorget at the neck, back and breast plates and helmet, with tassets to protect the thighs; they were equipped with swords, and every piece was highly polished. The pikeman glittered as he swung meticulously through the postures, executing the footwork with great care and consequently a certain grace, while the weapon swung and circled in his hands then settled for a split second in one of the classic positions before being spun into another. Except for the thump of the soldier's stout shoes on the packed earth there was silence in the square while the waiting company and the major willed their man to perfection. For a moment it seemed to James that he was watching not a preparation for war but an elaborate dance. He almost felt like applauding when it was over, but instead gave the pikeman an approving nod before the prince sent him back to his rank.

Prince Rupert patted the man's shoulder, said a few words that brought a smile to the soldier's face, then to James's surprise took the pike from him and walked out to face the company again.

His voice carried easily to the farthest rank. "A handsome demonstration. You've just seen Edward Pyne show us fifteen postures. But as your major knows, there are more than that in the full drill." James, watching the major's face, was none too sure of the officer's detailed experience on this point, and hoped the prince was not about to expose him before his company. Especially since the regiment was that of Lindsay, the Lord General.

"The major will now give you men a lesson in pike drill that he does not expect you to forget."

"Bugger," James said under his breath.

But the prince went on, "For your benefit, the major will count each of the postures out loud. Order Your Pike is number one." The prince took up the stance, planting the pike upright and just before his turned-out right foot, with his gloved left hand on his hip and the right holding the wooden shaft at the level of his eyes.

There was a startled pause, then the major came to his senses and roared, "One!"

Watching the prince, James found himself mouthing the numbers as the postures flickered before his eyes and the major's voice resounded about the square. The prince's height and his long arms gave the weapon a reach and compass that struck awe into the watchers. Seeing the vicious pikehead whirl through the air, James could almost feel the metal graze his skin. It was a dance all right, but this time an exquisite dance of death. He could not distinguish the new postures, so when the major's voice reached "Fifteen!" he had no idea how many more they were to see.

The drill finished at eighteen. The major visibly relaxed and the prince nodded to him, then leaned on the pike in a very unmilitary pose. "You'll see I'm out of breath," he said to the rapt soldiers. "I'm just as unused to this bloody exercise as you are!"

They laughed, accepting the insult with grins on their faces that mirrored the prince's own. "And I'll be back in two days so you can show me how it's done. Unless we meet the Roundheads first, in which case God save you."

In the cheer they gave as he handed the pike back to their comrade, James could hear the ring of worship. The prince drew the major aside and James heard him say, "You have Gheyns's *Exercise of Arms?*"

"I think so, Your Highness."

"There's a more recent manual with everything you need. You'll have it by tomorrow morning." He turned to Crane. "Sir Richard! You heard that?"

"I did indeed." Crane pulled out the notebook he carried with him everywhere and scratched in it with a pencil.

As their little cavalcade rode away, James said, "I have to tell you, I found that a remarkable feat."

His brothers, riding behind him, exclaimed in agreement, but the prince shook his head. "A mistake, also. It might have looked very foolish if I'd put my shoulder out again." He grinned at James. "Thank you for putting up with it—I wish I could afford you better entertainment than pike drill."

After a moment James said, "I hear from my wife that you also dance with great skill."

The prince glanced round at him, baffled. "I do not—" then his eyes widened and he said, "Ah, the duchess wrote to you about that evening, did she?" He gave a short sigh and looked away. "I have never laughed so much."

This was the prince's cue to ask after Mary, which normally he never failed to do, but he said nothing more, so James returned to his first point. "I imagine it will somewhat surprise Lord Lindsay to hear you have been drilling his troops."

The prince said, "It's of no consequence. It was random—like the talk I had with Lord Digby's lieutenant colonel of horse the other day."

James grimaced. "With *Digby's* lieutenant colonel?"

Rupert glanced at him keenly. "Is that a friendly warning?" He shrugged. "I had good reason. Lord Digby has no knowledge of war and his men know it. But he has courage—all he needs besides that is excellent officers. His lieutenant colonel is first-rate; I just noticed he needed a little help. I gave it and Digby ought to thank me for it."

Since they both knew this was beyond the realms of possibility, James dropped the subject. Right at the beginning of the prince's recruitment campaign, when he first arrived in Nottingham, Lord Digby had made a waspish comment about Prince Rupert's mixing with men below his station—probably in resentment at his spending more time with the regiments than at court—and the prince had flared up at once. Digby had had to make a humiliating apology, which the prince might have forgotten but which would still be burning in Digby's memory.

"And how is the Duchess of Richmond? Is she well? Have you had a letter from her lately?"

James smiled ironically to himself; the prince could never resist asking about Mary. In her letters, however, she showed no equal curiosity about the prince. "She and Her Majesty have had great success in applying to the King of Denmark. So yes, all goes well on that front and I hear from her faithfully. I do have some concerns, however. . . ." His voice trailed away. Mary hated anyone thinking she was not perfectly strong, and loathed it if he worried on her account.

But the prince was observing him. "About her health? She is unwell again?" Though James looked startled he persisted, "She was suffering from a fever the morning I quitted the Hague and I could not take my leave of her, much to my regret. You have given me good reports of her since; are they not true?"

This blunt question might have irritated James if it were not for the genuine anxiety in the prince's eyes. "You are very kind. She doesn't say so, but I have some fears that her duties, or the North Sea climate, or another influence that she does not confide to me, are exerting some strain on her health. I have discussed it with His Majesty—his physician has always attended her—and there is the possibility she may return to England in advance of the queen. If Her Majesty gives her gracious consent."

"And if she herself agrees to come, you mean," the prince said with his usual frankness. "I have seen her devotion to my aunt. If her duties exhaust her, the last person to complain of them would be the Duchess of Richmond. May I help in any way?"

"You are very good," James replied, with considerably less

warmth than the prince. "I shall ascertain her wishes first." It pained him not to be able to guess these, and it irked him to know that the people who had lately seen much more of his wife than he did—namely the queen and the prince—held more sway over her than he did himself.

It was Sunday, October 23, and King Charles was leading a council of war on the top of the precipitous ridge of Edgehill. It was an impregnable position, and the army, at Prince Rupert's urging, had been assembling since the early morning, for Essex's army had finally materialized around the town of Kineton. They were clearly visible from the top of the ridge, and on sighting the royalist presence had begun forming on the plain. Now that the moment had come, Charles felt confident and unafraid, which pleased him.

The council went well, and his officers showed as much respect for one another's opinions as they showed reverence for his demands. The Earl of Lindsay rose to the occasion as Lord General with a neat, conventional plan for the way the army should be drawn up—the horse on the wings for an initial assault upon Parliament's cavalry and then upon the flanks of its infantry, followed by a frontal infantry attack.

The old man pointed to his sketch of the battle plan, his finger falling on the infantry brigades across the center. "The regiments shall form in line abreast."

The king nodded. It was the usual Dutch formation and he expected the others to agree. But his field marshal, Patrick Ruthven, also an older man, said, "With respect, my lord, the foot will have more maneuverability if they form in a diamond shape."

Lindsay was not happy. "That may have worked in your day under Gustavus Adolphus," he said, and the king saw Ruthven frown—Ruthven was at least ten years older than Lindsay but the Swedish methods had as many adherents among modern armies as the Dutch. Lindsay went on, "But our troops are not sufficiently trained for them."

"Yes they are." It was Rupert who interrupted. "They can cope with the Swedish formation—I agree with the field marshal."

Charles studied him as he tried to make up his mind. Rupert was already in armor except for his helmet and stood in the center of the crowd like a fine statue in a rich setting, his hair drifting over the burnished steel on his shoulders, the red royalist sash tied in a wide swath across his long, lean waist. He looked what the older men in the army and the court sometimes insinuated to Charles—a picture of strong, impetuous youth. To the king, however, he looked like a conqueror.

Rupert reported directly to Charles, but he was general of the horse and this decision about the deployment of the foot was not his to make: the field marshal must come to an agreement with the Lord General. Charles glanced at the two old men, and saw that they were refusing to look at each other. They gazed instead at him, Lindsay's fine-skinned face drawn but firm and Ruthven's red about the high cheekbones.

Charles opened his mouth, shut it again, then drew himself up. "Our affair cries haste. The enemy is at hand. The field . . . the field marshal shall dispose the battle lines."

Lindsay stepped back from the table, bowed, and said in a steady voice, "Sire, if I may not be trusted to draw up the army as Lord General, permit me to return to my regiment and serve you henceforth only as its colonel." Then, without waiting for Charles to reply, he bowed again, very low, touching his sword as he did so, and retreated backward until he was on the very edge of the gathering.

It was a wounding moment, and Charles resented Lindsay's high-handedness. At the same time a stab of pity and regret made him wonder if the situation could be saved in some way. Then he said stiffly, "My gallant gentlemen, let us continue."

Rupert was ready. So was the parliamentary army, who began firing their artillery as soon as they saw the king and his two young sons ride the length of the royalist army to give encouragement to all. Both armies were on the plain; Essex had given no fight while they occupied the ridge, so Rupert had masterminded a maneuver down the steep slope, and they were now drawn up on the flat. It had been a risk, bringing more than fourteen thousand troops and a score of guns down the woodland tracks where they had been strung out and vulnerable, but the trees had given good cover and the men had done it with a speed that caused him satisfaction. The months of nonstop labor since Nottingham had paid off; they were an army now, and today Parliament would know it.

He looked behind him, up at the ridge they had just abandoned and to the knoll where the king would view the battle from amongst his reserve, surrounded by high courtiers like the Duke of Richmond. Rupert glanced toward the village of Radway, indicated by the hexagonal spire of the church above the trees. He had left Boy there in safety, with the Stuart brothers' wolfhounds. Then he looked straight across at the left wing of Essex's cavalry, toward which he would lead his own life guard, his regiment of horse and the cavalry of king's guard. These last had been mercilessly mocked by the rest of the army and named "the Troop of Show" because of the splendid gear they wore, and they had pleaded with Charles to let them take part in the first charge instead of staying with the reserve. Rupert smiled; if they wanted the gloss rubbed off them they would have the perfect chance shortly, for he had ordered all cavalry regiments in the first charge to forget about the conventional method of riding at a trot toward the enemy and then halting within range to fire pistols from the first rank—instead they were to ride straight into them at speed and put them to the sword.

The dragoons went first, to clear the sides of the area through which both cavalry wings would advance. They were doing a steady job amongst the enemy musketeers and dragoons when a horseman broke from Essex's side of the field and rode, alone and unmolested, straight up to the first rank of Rupert's cavalry. The horseman took only a few seconds to spy Rupert, and came up to him, disarmed and flanked now by two cavalrymen. His message was riveting: the moment the king's cavalry charged, a troop of Sir William Waller's regiment of horse would move forward, fire into the ground and join them.

As the rider was taken behind, Rupert laughed and said to Richard Crane at his side: "One way to recruit, *nicht wahr*?" Then he gave the signal to advance.

It was midafternoon, and light fell clear and bright on the fields, on the gleaming shoulders of the horses and the glitter of armor as the broad line of riders moved forward. The cannon spoke again ahead, earth and flesh flew high, but his front rank did not waver. The turncoat troop from Essex's side swung out to join them, tore off their orange sashes and melded their horses into line. When he was near enough for musket fire to whistle past, Rupert put his big stallion to a trot, then perhaps two hundred yards from Essex's motionless cavalry his own broke into a canter. With a shout he pointed forward, his sword flashed in front of him, and his mighty host swept into a gallop. It was so fast, his heart leaped as those of the incredulous watchers must have done. He could feel the phalanx tear the ground to pieces as they came ever closer to the bewildered enemy, then there was thunder in his ears and lightning in his eyes as his horsemen struck, roaring like a hurricane.

They plunged on, slashing their way through, then they used their pistols point-blank as he had ordered and there was the smell of smoke and blood in the air, and of the rank sweat of horses and men gripped by fear and wrath. Their own movement was so puissant that the enemy mounts began to turn and then run with them, and he and his men kept on pounding, smashing the horsemen aside and harrying them down the sides of their own infantry. Rupert twisted in the saddle at one point to see Sir John Byron's regiment charge on cue behind them, ready to turn inward and attack the enemy flanks, and beyond he saw the king's infantry advance in their massive drive at Essex's center. After that he was occupied, while Essex's cavalry resistance, such as they had been able to muster, turned into a bloody rout, and then he was chasing them toward Kineton, leaping hedges and ditches, cutting them down as they fled, and all at once they were near Essex's long, well-stocked, vulnerable baggage train.

It was too far. Turning, Rupert dashed amongst his flying men to bring them back to the center of the battle, but it was torrid work beating against the wave of riders. His temper rose, and he let out a stream of curses when he saw that most now were Byron's men, who should not have followed this far. But he bullied three troops of horse together and hurtled back in to the broad fields where the royalist and parliamentary foot were locked together under a pall of smoke.

It took until nightfall for the smoke to clear. It was a day of courage and impetuosity and blunders and near misses. The king, seeing his infantry under threat, moved forward with his group of courtiers, sent the princes to the rear and led his life guard of foot into attack, losing and then regaining the royal standard in the melee. Across the other side of the field the left wing of cavalry, against Rupert's orders, thundered far beyond the appointed position and only two hundred of them could be gathered and returned to the thick of the battle where they mattered most. It was a day of plunder, for Rupert's horse took most of Essex's baggage train and the king's army now possessed seven more cannon and a mountain of fresh weapons. And when the armies had fought themselves to a standstill, the king's men held the field. It was a day of death; one thousand Parliamentarians and five hundred royalists fell, among whom were the courageous old man, the Earl of Lindsay, mortally wounded; the king's standard bearer, Sir Edmund Verney, who died defending it; and George Stuart, Seigneur d'Aubigny, younger brother of the Duke of Richmond.

It was very cold and Rupert was momentarily alone, leaning against the trunk of a tree and looking down the slope across the bivouacs and cooking fires to the muffled plain below, where the burial parties had stopped working because the night was too black.

He was thinking of what they had done; what they might have done; what he would do tomorrow. They had blown open the road to London; they might have cost Essex more men if the light had not failed; and tomorrow he would harass and torment the earl's regiments in retreat and see if he could snatch more of the baggage train.

He was unscathed, and exhausted, and along with his raw regret for the men who had been killed a fierce glow of victory filled his chest.

He thought further on, to the king's triumphant return to Whitehall, to the homecoming of the queen, to peace with Parliament and the resumption of the cultivated court that gathered around the Stuart family, whose refinement and sweetness meant more to his future and his dreams than he would ever have conceived.

He thought about the Duchess of Richmond. In the courtyard of the Wassenaer Hof he had begged for her friendship, yet the moment she gave him her hand he realized he could never be her friend, except in name. Ever since, he had been wrestling with what this meant.

But he knew, tonight, how it would be. The Duchess of Richmond would return and walk into his life again, never to escape.

He could not touch her, he could not have her, because she was his friend's wife—and because she told her husband everything. And the world everything. But against all these odds he would conquer her and win her love. He would have her heart and soul, as she had his.

Part Two

> . . . *Then you conveyed*
> *Soft amorous tales into my listening ears,*
> *And gentle vows and well-becoming tears,*
> *Then deeper oaths, nor e'er your siege removed*
> *Till I confessed my flame and owned I loved.*
>
> —EPHELIA

Chapter 10

THE VALIANT PROTECTOR DELEGATED to bring home the Duchess of
Richmond was her younger brother, George Villiers, second Duke
of Buckingham, and this move was subtly arranged in correspondence by the Duke of Richmond. George Villiers, having lately
obtained his master's degree from Cambridge, had gone down to
reside in London, where the Earl of Northumberland, Algernon
Percy, had long taken a friendly interest in him. The earl was one
of the gentlemen nominated by the House of Lords to see that
the two royal children at Saint James's were well cared for, and he
could thus entrust to George Villiers reassuring news for the queen
in the Hague. In addition, Northumberland, once the king's commander in chief, had remained in London instead of declaring
for Charles, and though Church of England, he was showing clear
signs of sympathy with the Puritans' views and political purpose. He
thus had no trouble getting authority for the young duke to travel
to the Hague on a privately funded voyage—a desirable measure of
security, since Parliament now commanded the English navy.

The lively and good-looking Duke of Buckingham, accompanied by four of Northumberland's personal men at arms, was welcomed in the Hague—by the queen, avid for news of her babies,
and by his sister Mary. Mary learned that with his studies completed,
George had secretly joined the royalist army and was itching to report to headquarters on his return. It did not at all surprise her
that her husband, James, should have given him this responsibility,
for while it conferred a mission on him, it also delayed his entry
into the king's forces—George was but fourteen years old.

The visit was short, as Richmond and Northumberland both
had reasons for its being discreet. When the ship left the Hague
it did not return to London but sailed for the north of England,
where the Earl of Newcastle held the coast for the king and provided a secure landing for the Duchess of Richmond. Meanwhile

Mary was not known to be on board by either Elizabeth's court in the Hague or by the English navy. Queen Henrietta-Maria gave out that the duchess was unwell and then left on one of her funding drives, intending to announce the departure of her Lady of the Bedchamber when she returned, thereby giving Mary time to go safely to England.

Thus it happened that one bitter December day, George and Mary were sitting before a roaring fire in an apartment at the Black Bear Inn, in the Yorkshire port of Whitby.

George was looking into the hearth, his eyes and cheeks shining, and reflections from the flames danced in the glossy auburn hair that fell in a straight fringe over his forehead. He looked pleased with himself and awfully young, though in public his bearing often reminded Mary of that of their father—proud and self-assured.

"I'm still surprised the queen let you go, Moth." He considered this a witty pet name for Mary since it echoed Butterfly. "Every time she spoke to me when you were out of the room she would tell me how *she* is always considered *just* as prone to ill health and she did not know what she would do without you while you were come home to be cured. She said only the king's letters could have persuaded her. By the way, are you cured? You look it already."

"I don't know," Mary said, brushing this aside as she always did. "I'm far too cold. Remind me never to go anywhere near the North Sea again. How long will it take us to get to Oxford?"

"It depends. If you are fit enough to ride we shall get on fastest. The troop"—George always called his four men a troop, though he knew quite well that a troop of horse was supposed to contain seventy—"will conceal their weapons; they have enormous Dutch overcoats to hide them under. So we shouldn't be stopped by the military of either side. I think you should wear an overcoat too, and put your hair under a Montero hat and muffle yourself up, and no one will ever know you're in England until you burst on Oxford. It will be just like our masquerades of old." He grinned at her, as though the time that had divided them from each other was an age. "Have you written any masques lately?"

"In Holland? We could never perform them. Tell me, has Parliament closed the theaters in London yet?"

"Yes, did you not know? By decree, in September."

"Just as I feared. Oh, *why* could not the king have let Prince Rupert push on to London when they had the chance? I still don't understand it."

"Well, you know all I do on the matter. There were any number of debates but the king ended up siding with the gentlemen who were looking for compromise. Digby's father said Prince Rupert would raze London to the ground if he took it. Falkland and Hyde said they should approach agreement carefully instead of annihilating Essex. The king was miserable after the deaths at Edgehill, not least over Cousin George. Despite his great loss, Richmond was of Prince Rupert's opinion, but the king went against it. That's why he's set up the court at Oxford. Which the prince is busy fortifying at a rate of knots."

"He must be devastated."

"Who, the king, the prince or your husband?" George said with a shrewd look.

"Prince Rupert."

"No doubt. I should like a purse of sovereigns for every time you've mentioned him this voyage. I presume he has already cast himself at your feet?"

She considered. "Literally yes, emotionally no."

"Oh, a pity. It would have been interesting. What about Lord Digby then, the future Earl of Bristol—is he still swamping you with tides of sentiment?"

"No, dear, I teased him out of that long ago. I tease them all, and not one has been proof against that. Besides, need I remind you I have a husband?"

He looked at her with speculative eyes. "What a loyal heart you have, Moth. I wish I had a loyal heart; I'm sure it would do me the world of good."

"Does this mean the proctor's niece is out of your august favor?"

"That was not love," he said, "though I wrote her a score of sonnets liberally salted with the word. I now know what love is. And so does my new wicked angel . . . though she is five years my senior and due to be married after Christmas." Mary raised her eyebrows in eager curiosity but he sighed and said, "No, I shan't tell you her name unless I conquer her."

She laughed. "Then I shall never hear it!"

He gave her a brilliant smile and allowed a higher note to jump into his new manly voice. "Ah, I must tell you, I have the face of an archangel. You would be surprised how far youthful innocence will get you!"

"Tell me," Mary said ironically, "what did you do when the proctor's niece said nay in syllables you could understand?"

He looked at her in reproach and then laughed. "I cried for two days. Well, not quite two because a friend came around to play billiards. Then I wrote poetry for another two—in rather better vein than the first folio, but of course it was too late by that time. And then I forgot her; otherwise I could tell you *her* name. But don't think I'm misprized by the female race, Moth. Far from it. The married gentlewomen are the ones to watch." At Mary's mock frown he said lightly, "Just because you keep the dust on your wings doesn't mean others resist capture."

"You bid fair to make a very scandalous creature, George, in a few years' time."

He was pleased. "Do you think so? Well, one of us has to; it's the family tradition. With a father who was James the First's most exquisite bedfellow, we have a lot to live up to."

"Or down. So no woman will ever hold complete sway over you?"

"No one but you and Mam," he said, and the facetious smile disappeared.

Mary looked at him sadly. "You were so little, my dear, when the king took us away from her."

"What difference does that make?" George said. "What difference does it make that Mam's Catholic, or chose the cursed marriage to Antrim? What, you mean you changed allegiance the moment Charles brought us to court?"

"No, darling. I put her love for me, and mine for her, in a corner of my being, and I tried to make us a place where we could be happy."

"No one can *choose* to be happy," he said fiercely.

"No. I agree with you. Now."

He caught her eye and said in another tone, "What a sparkling little Mother Goose you were. Did I ever thank you?"

"You just have, *monsieur le duc*, by bringing me home."

He looked into the fire again and sighed. "Mam seems happy,

at any rate. She sends me things from Ireland. Ships me wolf-hounds, if you please, and I have to keep giving them away. Does she do that to James?"

"Yes, we're overrun with them. You'll see when we get to Oxford."

"Roll on," he said, his eyes bright once more. "Roll on."

Before Mary reached Oxford, on a sunny but freezing afternoon, George sent a messenger ahead with news of their coming. Approaching from the northeast, she was impatient to see the city, but each time they trotted briskly up a hill she was disappointed to find another looming in front of them, studded with bare trees or featuring another church spire tucked below the crown and surrounded by a neat village. Then they breasted a very long incline and from the ridge she could see Oxford on its long, gentle eminence. She pulled her mare to a halt.

"Look, George, how beautiful." The farmland immediately below stretched on to the dark lines of outer earthworks, and beyond were the meadows surrounding the colleges and the stout city walls, and within these the handsome buildings of town and university clustering upward, crowned by towers and spires pointing to the steely sky. "See the tallest steeple? What does that belong to?"

He grinned. "What else but Saint Mary's Church?"

"Is it the chapel of a college? And did it declare for the king when he marched here?"

"The church stands alone, at the top of High Street. As for the colleges, they all support the king except Merton. The Merton men, doctors, tutors and students all, are gone to Wales. His Majesty is readying Merton for the queen. You can't see it from here—it's very near the walls, to the south, close to Christ Church, where the king is housed."

When they resumed their ride toward the city, she felt a curious reluctance to arrive. She would find it so altered—the town of scholars and philosophers, home of precious libraries and ancient centers of learning, changed into a garrison. Already she could see from afar busy contingents of men toiling at the outer fortifications. Already, she and George had ridden through villages disfigured by the war—pretty and peaceful and rural only as they approached, but once penetrated, bristling with fell purpose on every street corner. Each time she saw a cartload of munitions, or a bunch of horsemen, or a group of soldiers lounging to talk with one another in the narrow lanes outside their billets, or a piece of ordnance lying like a huge muzzled beast in a town square, she thought of Rupert, and wondered whether he knew she was on her way, and whether she might meet him around the next bend in the road. And as her senses quickened at the thought, she felt ambushed by love and shaken by resentment. This was his war, and it was transforming the landscape of her memory and the very contours of the land itself into something terrible. She tried to push away the idea of their meeting. She tried to imagine James riding out to greet her, to bring her into the haven of their new home.

He met her at Holywell, riding a new chestnut horse, his hair pale gold in the cold sunlight as he swept off his hat and bowed to her with a long flourish from the saddle. As he approached she gloried in how English he looked, how noble in his steadfast way, and she appreciated as always how he clothed his concern for her in the perfect grace of his welcome. She was in tears by the time he touched her, and her first words to him were incoherent, muffled by his quick embrace after he swung her down from the mare. With her hands on his broad shoulders she leaned away a little to look at his face. "Who would have believed *this* is where I should come back to you?" Her voice was so weak it became a whisper. "What can I say to you about our dear brother that I have not already written? Where is he buried?" The sentence ended on a little sob.

He shook his head, to banish his own sorrow and hers. "Here, in Oxford. He might have wished for Cobham, but in these times . . . And you, how are you? All these weeks, the king and I have been lost to know whether the journey would do you more ill or good."

"I am well; how could I be otherwise, now I am home?" She let James go and stretched out one arm. "And here is George, whom I have to thank for it."

"I too. I too," said James, and embraced the young man.

After that he sent on a group of servants to meet up with Anne Gibson, Mary's servants and the baggage, all an hour or so behind on the road, and they headed toward the city.

Their cavalcade filed past Holywell Mill and along the well-kept

road that went between the lovely tree-lined meadows of Magdalen
Walks and Magdalen Grove, which was now the artillery park, and
joined up with the end of the East Bridge over the Cherwell. They
rode past Magdalen College and along a handsome street to the
towering East Gate, then James escorted her through the guards
and steeply uphill to Saint Mary's, where they wheeled left and
downhill again toward Christ Church, to their dwelling near the
king. There were groups of people on the way who stopped to stare,
and as their party progressed through the town there was curiosity
and recognition that brought cheers and shouts of greeting. Men
doffed their hats and some of the women waved their handkerchiefs. The news that George had sent ahead had penetrated the
city: the Duchess of Richmond and the young Duke of Buckingham had come to join the king and to brighten the winter for the
Duke of Richmond, who for almost a year had been in want of his
wife. Mary took off her hat and would have thrown her greatcoat to
George if James had permitted it. She was proud and grateful to be
home, and she smiled at everyone all the way down the hill.

When they reached their quarters, James wanted her to sit
down and rest but she persuaded him to take her through them
while George lounged in the great chamber. Their apartments
were all she could have wished and more, for James shared her
tastes and had indulged his own lavishly. Back in the great chamber she still did not sit, but drifted around the room, feeling it
close about her in a dark, friendly embrace. The walls were high
and paneled in oak with a linenfold pattern, stained so deep it was
almost black, and gleaming in the way she liked. The dressers and
cabinets along the walls had a warmer hue, and she trailed her
fingers over the carved surfaces—rose and lily, leaf fronds, and dai-
sies cut like stars—and James looked at her, amused and content,
from a settle by the great fireplace, where logs crackled, built high
and hot in her honor. She had never set foot in this place before
but she already felt she belonged. And she realized, rather to her
surprise, that in this moment she had no desire to be anywhere but
here, with James.

She came to the center of the room where George was seated,
and before sitting down she wound her fingers into the smooth
spiral at one side of the chairback and looked at the table where a
pile of rare fruit, nuts and cheeses, arranged as though in a Flemish

painting, glowed red, green and primrose yellow against a wide gold dish.

"Take some," James said. "Then I shall take you to the king."

At midday, when Rupert heard the Duchess of Richmond was expected in the afternoon, the temptation to intercept her by accident was so strong that to combat it he took horse at once, told no one where he was going and escaped, alone except for Boy, in the opposite direction, toward the castle and the West Gate.

He made himself stop at the castle, which housed the parliamentary prisoners, and check a story that had come to him about what they were being issued to buy food: they were supposed to get sixpence a week but the money seemed to be going somewhere else and they sometimes got as little as a penny halfpenny. The officer he talked to pretty much confirmed this, without any shame on his ratlike face, and Rupert was furious, which changed the other's expression at once to fearful humility.

Rupert dug at his waist for the purse he had with him and threw it on the table of the wardroom. "You'll distribute that, and they're to have bread at least, every day, whether they pay or not. *Donnerwetter*, Oxford is bulging with bakers and good bread—it's a sin for anyone in this city to go hungry. Look to it."

He rode out the West Gate, then through an area oddly named Paradise, and leaving it with a grim smile rode through Greyfriars and out into the country.

During the months of his separation from Mary Villiers he had asked about her past, discreetly probing everyone who might know except her husband. He had heard a great deal about her now, including why her circle called her Butterfly. When she was a lot younger, little Prince Charles had been looking out the window of one of the palaces one day and happened to see a creature fluttering through the gardens below, screened by flowering fruit trees. He called out to his servants, "Shoot that thing and bring it to me." So they went below to carry out his command, and found her instead, alone in the garden. When they explained, she thought quickly, and had them put her in a laundry basket and carry her to the prince. The child opened the lid to see his prey, and there she was curled into the basket and laughing up at him with her blue eyes full of mockery and mischief.

After that, sometimes when Rupert was with the clerk of the ordnance at New College watching deliveries of munitions roll in from Dudley or Stourbridge, he would look at the big timber cases of guns or grenades and imagine finding one that was gossamer light, and having it carried to the courtyard of the town clerk's house where he lodged, and coming there alone and tearing off the lid of the case to release her supple body into his arms. Which did nothing whatsoever for the mad resolution he had made never to touch her. But lately his fantasies had perished before the sure knowledge of her return.

He had found out all he could about her marriages, too, though the information was contradictory. Both unions had been arranged by the king. Some recalled the first as moderately happy; others claimed it was never consummated. This last was impossible, he knew—no one could be married five minutes to her without aching for consummation. Her second had produced no children, which some people thought of as a sign that it might in some way resemble the first, especially since the Stuarts as a race were demonstrably fertile. But that was impossible too. Despite the calm, almost detached way that Richmond spoke of her, only a cod's head could fail to notice how her husband looked forward to her return.

Thus, every day that brought her closer also brought on the night when Richmond would again enter her bed. With this prospect to torture Rupert, he no longer had the heady confidence that visited him after Edgehill—instead he felt jealous, guilty and powerless.

Thank the light of heaven that she thought of him as nothing more than a friend. It was the only thing that gave him the courage to meet her again.

Chapter 11

CHARLES HOSTED WHAT FOR him was a perfect meal on the night the Duchess of Richmond came to Oxford—or if it fell just short of perfection, that was only because his queen was absent. He had his two boys there, Charles and James, who loved Mary like a sister. The other guests were the dukes of Richmond and Buckingham and Prince Rupert, who came later because he had been out all day at the garrisons. The others meanwhile had had hours, in the kind of warm intimacy Charles loved, to talk of family and friends, get over the first tender stories of the men who had been lost since Mary was in England and move on to matters she had a genius for—what they would do at Christmastime, and how the King's Music—Charles's chamber orchestras and choirs—was being revived at Oxford.

The prince brought a soberer note, with his dignified and respectful greetings and his meticulous inquiries about the journey, his aunt, and his mother's court at the Hague. He was freshly dressed, and had shaved and combed his hair as though it were morning, but he looked worn out, though it never did any good to tell him so. He had the curious habit, if anyone was foolish enough to voice concern, of speaking of himself as though of an acquaintance: "Rupert is never tired."

Mary was radiant. Charles had feared the voyage would try her, but coming home seemed to have lent a bloom to her cheeks. On his insistence she had been visited by his physician already and Sir William Harvey had given him a cautiously optimistic report. Her maladies were feminine, so Charles could not discuss them with her and did not invade her privacy by probing Harvey either, but it appeared that the type of food she had been eating on her travels might have weakened her blood, and careful attention to this now that she was in England should be of benefit. It had given him a secret pleasure to make sure the meal was well planned for this evening, and even more to see her eat it without knowing how much thought had gone into it for her welfare.

Rupert had told him that he and Mary had come to a friendly understanding in the Hague, and he saw evidence of it as they sat at table, though their conversation with each other was a little subdued. He suspected this was due to a shyness caused by long separation, and hoped to see it dissipate in time. Rupert had a score of close and devoted friends amongst his own officers, but in the councils of war and the daily business at court, Charles sometimes thought he looked almost lonely, and certainly he was often remote. It was heartening therefore to know that he was always comfortable with the Duke of Richmond. Charles valued Richmond's many qualities and was glad to see friendship between the two; now that Mary was returned, their household might provide even more comradeship and support to his nephew. As a commander, Rupert stood in no such need—but as a young man burdened with great responsibilities, he could do with true friends from his own station in life, even if he was not aware of this himself.

At one point Mary said to Rupert, "Forgive me, I have not asked—where is Prince Maurice and how does he fare?"

"My brother shares my quarters and some of my duties. He is at Wolvercote tonight and tomorrow—we have a manufacture of swords there. May he call upon you to give you greeting, when he gets back?"

"That will afford me great joy." Mary gave a hesitant smile that contained a hint of mischief nonetheless. "And I shall now descend to bathos and make you think much the less of me—but where is Boy, and how does *he* fare?"

"He is downstairs."

"Why?" said Prince Charles at once. "Cannot he come up? Mall," he continued without waiting for an answer, "you must see Boy's tricks. He has learned a prodigious number, and I taught him one, all by myself, which I warrant will astonish you."

"If you are going to make him flop down all over my feet, I thank you, but he has already learned that one."

Rupert said, with the first glimmering of a smile, "He has grown more refined since. It is only one paw, and only if Cousin Charles says so."

"Then I think I must see these improvements and judge for myself."

Rupert raised one eyebrow at the king, who was happy to have the dog sent for. While he was awaited, young James said to Mary, "Cousin Rupert once had a hare that did tricks. In Austria."

"And what was the hare called?" she said with amusement.

"It had no name. It was given to me while I was in prison. I had a pretty good idea how much it must yearn for freedom, so after a while I let it go."

Then Boy bounded in with his usual enthusiasm and Mary skidded her feet back under her vivid green gown with a show of alarm.

Charles and James asked permission to leave the table, and the two lads got Boy to demonstrate his talents. The king, watching, felt how different his twelve-year-old eldest son was from himself at the same age—and he rejoiced in it. Young Charles was self-assured without being stiff, expressed himself well and clearly, and had a sense of fun that he liked to share. He could make one smile just to look at him. Young James meanwhile followed his lead and joined in without self-consciousness.

Boy performed well. He jumped wildly in the air on the prompt "Charles," which made everyone laugh, flopped down dead when ordered and jumped through James's arms on cue, though bringing him to the floor in the process. Then, after a certain amount of coaxing from the Duke of Buckingham, Mary advanced her foot far enough for the poodle to lie down, place his paw on it and look up at her with adoring attention. Whereupon the king fed Boy a few slices of capon under the table, as he usually did, and the talk resumed.

During the merriment, while Mary's eyes were on the young princes, the king saw Rupert give her a look of great earnestness. Perhaps he had noticed something that Charles himself had always been aware of—in the company of men, Mary could supply all the sweetness and charm of womankind in her person alone. They were six gentlemen and one lady in this room, yet there existed within it an effortless balance of light and shade, of ebullience and strength. He thanked providence that she had come back to them all.

Mary was surprised at how quickly she settled into Oxford, despite the changes that were tragically manifest in every corner of the city. She did all the things she had planned: with James, she visited the grave of George Stuart, Seigneur d'Aubigny; she expressed her deep sympathies to George's widow, Katherine Howard; she put the finishing touches to their dwelling that James had only awaited her coming to complete. She went with tradesmen of all kinds to Merton College to prepare the accommodation for the queen, imposing her selections of fabrics and furniture on them all in the sure knowledge of Henrietta-Maria's needs, and she had such items as the royal couple had gleaned from Whitehall placed to best advantage about the warden's quarters, which provided the queen's principal rooms. Mary also met often with her favorite amongst the masters of the King's Music, William Lawes, who to her consternation had volunteered as an officer in the army, but who nonetheless was often available, with Prince Rupert's permission, to consult on the preparations for the Christmas music at court.

She and James fell without difficulty into their old routines, which meant they spent most of the day apart because of his activities and hers, and he exercised his husbandly privilege from time to time, except when she was indisposed, and with his usual tact.

In her new state, made vulnerable by hidden passion, she sometimes wondered how it might have gone if she and James had been in love when they married. Might their bodies have met in a more open way, if she had been able to submit differently to his hands? He had modified his approach since, but her body had never ceased to shrink: the first impact on her was indelible. James's hands were hard, with broad palms and strong fingers. Predatory, somehow. The rest of his body, which she had never seen or cared to see, felt the same: raw-boned and insistent. Yet in the life they shared outside her bedchamber, she had a respect and gratitude toward him that never wavered. The king had given her a husband beyond compare; it was not his fault that she was secretly flawed.

As for Prince Rupert, however, it took her days to find some way of coping with his presence. She had been tense all through the king's dinner, for she was torn between the thrill of seeing him again and the fear that she would betray this to the company or, worst of all, to him. He had not helped; he looked neither relaxed nor animated, being settled instead into a seriousness that she could not dispel, however often she attempted lightness, wit or humor. He came next day with Prince Maurice, looking if possible more saturnine than before, but Maurice's wonderful good nature could not bear stiffness or restraint, and he soon had them talking as though little time had passed since they were all in the Hague. Even then, however, Rupert suggested he and his brother leave rather early, and she could not get over the feeling that he was looking for escape.

But James was convinced the three of them were destined to be friends, and the prince did not refuse his kind offices. Rupert might be absent every day and sometimes a night or two from Oxford, but his quarters were in the house of Oxford's town clerk, at no great distance from their own, and in the first week they dined together twice, with no formality—a note from James arrived each time during the day, forewarning Mary. So she commanded meals that could be eaten late if necessary, when both men dragged themselves away from their duties and arrived to eat in the comfortable private chamber, closeted away and eager to talk of other matters.

She was able to smile naturally and give Rupert a friend's greeting. He treated her with warmth and respect, and she found ways to tease him once more and make him smile in return. She had an excuse to spend hours in his company—did she have the right to yearn for more? And while he talked to James she had time to observe him. She found delight in letting her gaze travel over his face and body, as she might look at a dearly loved painting. Yet out of guilt, or discretion, or to assist a gratification of the senses that she had never known herself capable of, she rationed these effects. On his second visit, she chose to study one part of him alone. Irresistibly, it was his mouth.

It was chiseled and firm, with the upward tilt at the corners that she knew how to turn into a smile. Under the lower lip was a dint of shadow that made the whole shape of the mouth look willful, even arrogant. There was a cleft in his strong, determined chin, and although she could tell he shaved every morning, within the cleft the blue shadow that darkened on his face during the day grew deeper. She sat silent, with her gaze caressing his mouth, and imagined running one fingertip down over the contours of his lips, to the little hollow underneath and over his chin. While his eyes were turned away she could do this. She could touch him, as she had never wanted to touch a man before.

The fourth time he came to her home, she was there alone.

He was shown into the great chamber, and when she rose to greet him she felt confusion and a deep inner response. He seemed in too much haste, however, to notice her reaction. Clad in a buff coat and a black suit under an enormous greatcoat, with his sword buckled on and leather gauntlets on his hands, he was clearly on his way out to the garrisons and had no time to linger.

He bowed, smiled and said, "Forgive the intrusion. But I promised to drop this off for your husband." He held out a worn-looking book bound loosely in calf leather.

She took it, and instinctively held it to her without looking at it, her hands folding over it to clasp it to her midriff. Then she felt embarrassed, opened her hands and the book, and looked down. It was a battered copy of *Militarie Instructions for the Cavall'rie* by John Cruso. She looked up to find he was watching her intently. Mary was thinking only that with his book in her hands she now possessed one more item of his along with the handkerchief he had given her in the Hague. She could never let anyone know how she treasured it, least of all him.

Misinterpreting her silence, he said firmly, "It wasn't my idea; the duke asked if he could borrow a manual on the use of cavalry. He may keep it; as you may imagine, I know every line and picture." When she still did not reply he continued, "His interest is theoretical. I hope you do not think I would ever encourage him to take a command or to be involved in the army any more than he . . . You cannot think that of me?"

"No," she said. "No, never. That was not what I thought."

But he held out his hand, palm open. "Perhaps you would like me to take it back?"

"No!" Afraid of losing the book, she stepped away quickly and placed it on a dresser at the side of the room. "It is most kind of you. James is something of a student of strategy, as you know, but he is not versed in tactics. He will find this fascinating. And when would you like it returned?"

"As I said, he may keep it," he said softly. He stepped forward, and the expression in his dark eyes changed as he looked down at her. She felt the power of his gaze, as though until this moment, for all the time they had known each other, he had been keeping it in reserve.

She must protect herself. With an attempt at her usual tone

she said, "Do you have a large library of military books? Where on earth do you store them?"

"I have books of every kind, kept in several places, Oxford included." He smiled into her eyes. "I don't flatter myself I have anything that would interest your elevated mind. But if there is aught I can bring you—books or anything else—you have only to ask."

"Thank you," she said brightly, "I know your largesse. I already have something of yours, if you remember?"

By another change in his eyes she saw he did remember, in every detail. But he did not speak for a moment and neither could she. What had possessed her to mention the handkerchief? Now she must at all costs conceal the dangerous value it held for her.

She took a deep breath. "Of course, that too was a loan. You must tell me at once if you would like it back. Delft lace, if I recall, and the finest linen."

He looked at her as if she had done him an injury. He frowned, took a small step back and glanced at her sidelong. "Pray return it, madam, if that is important to you. For myself . . ." Then he bit his lip and looked at the floor.

She was lost; the conversation had gone beyond her horizon, and she must bring it back to a navigable channel. In the same playful tone she said, "Oh, I'm not sure I can part with it, when I recall the unique spirit in which it was given. You remember the moment—you had us all in fits. When you handed it to me, I was in tears of laughter. But let us agree: you may have it back when I provoke the same in you. Laughter, or tears, or both together."

His expression darkened still more and his voice took on a deeper note. Facing her, he said, "Laughter is ever your territory, madam. As for my tears—you command them at any time." Then he gave her a low bow and immediately left the room.

She remained looking after him, transfixed.

His tears? What did he mean? She shivered, and put a hand on the dresser to steady herself. There was only one interpretation, and with the intensity of his gaze he had meant her to know it. She stayed there for a moment longer, taking it in.

Then she went to the window and looked down, in time to see him emerge from the front. His officers were a little way up the street, mounted and in a group. Boy dashed over the cobbles toward him and the heads of the men turned, but Rupert ignored them and stopped in the roadway. His tall figure was a straight black line against the gray stones but his head was bent. He was thinking. She held on to the window frame, afraid that he would turn and look up but unable to move away. He regretted what he had said or done; or he wanted to make himself clearer—either way, she could tell he was debating whether to turn and come back. But suddenly he replaced his broad-brimmed hat, so she could not see his face, joined his men and mounted his horse, and they all clattered off down the street.

She sank onto the carved coffer under the window, faint with shock, and hung on to the sill with one hand. She commanded his feelings. He loved her.

Rupert spent the morning riding across fog-bound country to inspect the work at the watermills on the rivers, where gunpowder maker William Baber was setting up production. Talking with Baber in the dark expanse of the big Thames mill, standing on the riverside where coopers labored with timber and iron to make barrels for the powder, or riding east for miles through farmland and villages to the second mill, on the Isis, his mind kept coming back to what he had just said to Mary Villiers.

Thinking of it was like succumbing to vertigo. His campaign for her heart and soul had begun—but without any planning. Nothing could have been further from his intention when he paid her that fleeting visit; all he had wanted was an excuse to see her without Richmond by, to watch her face as she bestowed a smile of greeting on him alone. All he had wished for was a harmless, stolen pleasure to begin his day.

But she had given him an opening, and he had stepped straight into it. There was no going back; he had no desire to go back.

She had directed the conversation with her usual skill but there had been that flicker of alarm in her eyes over the handkerchief. She did not want to give it back to him; it was as though she was clasping it to her, just as she had held the book. In that moment of confusion and alarm she had retreated, and so had been forced to bring out her sharpest weapon—she had teased him. At once, without forethought, he had come out with his riposte.

It was all in the open now. The battle lines were drawn. She knew he loved her and she need not think he would try to conceal it any longer. Except from her husband and the world.

He had no idea about her feelings, for the altercation over the handkerchief was a trifle; it might mean nothing at all. He was not going to make the mistake of underestimating his opponent's powers of resistance. And at the very same time, at the thought of her, all his own defenses collapsed and desire overtook him so strongly that he could hardly see, or ride, or pick his way forward through the misty countryside.

Yes, his campaign had begun. She must not guess that she was at present the victor on all points.

Chapter 12

꙰

THE EARL OF ESSEX was at Windsor, his new headquarters, neck deep in horses and cavalry training. There was no lack of funds from the Parliament at present, so he was spending it as fast as he could get it—all his new captains of horse were entitled to 1,104 pounds to mount and equip their men, and the hunt for horses had spread out around London. Officers with high standards were prepared to pay up to ten pounds for a suitable beast—at least fifteen hands, strong and sound—and he knew there were many who did not buy them but obtained them by force from royalist supporters. He chose not to know that yet—Parliament was preparing a sequestration act for just these purposes, and he himself was formulating articles of war for the army to regulate such activities for all troops.

On a frigid December morning, he was seated on his horse under leafless trees in Windsor Park, watching a troop at exercise that was trampling great complicated circles of fresh green into the frost-covered grass. Observing the way they bungled every turn, he cursed under his breath and saw them in his mind's eye, presented—God forfend—with a charge like that of Prince Rupert's at Edgehill.

Training these recruits and their mounts took time, and he was not sure how much of that he could dispose of. It could take weeks just to accustom a horse to gunfire—letting off a musket closer and closer to him as he fed, then riding him into a mock volley. And even at the end of that, some horses couldn't stand it and had to be dropped. As for the men—except for the veterans of the European wars—their military understanding, even amongst the officers, was of the crudest. Their first thought about cavalry movements was to wheel the regiment—a maneuver so ponderous you could be at kingdom come before your men understood where you were trying to point them, or had the vaguest chance of completing the order. Close maneuvers, by contrast, involved facings, doublings and countermarchings, the kind of spinning-on-a-farthing tricks that the men before him were signally failing to grasp, even with the standard six feet between one horse and another. There was one close order that required every man's right knee to be locked under the next man's left ham—he could imagine it lasting about two minutes with this lot, who would end up lying stranded on their backs like lobsters, with the battle chargers stock-still and swinging their heads at one another in surmise.

One consolation, as he watched the jostling mass before him and listened to the clash of metal and the thunder of oaths, was that Prince Rupert would be struggling with the same problems. Indeed, his full-tilt charge at Edgehill had given Essex an illuminating idea of the royalist cavalry's lack of training. If you could not deploy a disciplined force, the only solution was to run them like a battering ram at the enemy and hope for the best.

He had no doubt about what Rupert was doing now; after skirmishing around London he was strengthening the garrison towns and fortifying Oxford itself while consolidating his armies. Let him look to it: London still belonged to Parliament—and Parliament could call on more certain supplies of men, materials and funds than the king. In addition, the Londoners who had marched out to Edgehill had done so as much for their homes and children and livelihood as they had for John Pym and the rest. Slaughter, rapine and pillage they understood—and they wanted none of that for their wives and families.

Soldiers were unpopular with both sides. Essex's own troops had been banished from the city into the countryside around him—they were too unruly in town. Their reputation had preceded them: he had not been able to prevent their desecrating Worcester Cathedral and other churches when the town was occupied, or despoiling the regions they passed through on their return to London. But they were good lads and true, if a little ragged around the edges. He could hold them together. And devil take the prince when they met up with him again.

Christmas came to Oxford, and despite a few puzzled protests from the men in her circle, Mary got everything she wanted with respect to the celebrations. She wished for no military fanfare, drums, bugles or marching, so instead of a church parade on Christmas Day there was to be a late service on Christmas Eve. There was some concern that this might look popish but she laughed it down—the king's preacher, Dr. Symmons, was already preparing his sermon. She had asked him, as a favor and encouragement to the ladies and children who came to worship, that he refer as little as possible to the stern demands of war and concentrate on the Good News brought by the angels to earth. She reminded him how sad it was that the two young princes were without their mother this Christmas, and how much family affection meant to the king. He seemed very struck, and by the time she left him to it she admitted to herself, with a laugh, that the dear man was very likely to have them all in tears on the night.

There were many advantages to an evening service, not the least being the time it gave for high-ranking gentlemen in the army to ride into Oxford from their garrisons. In addition she knew that the officers and functionaries in Oxford would be only too happy, when the service was over, to go back to their billets or homes, and wassail with their hosts, friends or families, knowing they could sleep in with great joy and contentment on Christmas morn.

Having talked about the music and left William Lawes to rehearse the king's musicians and the cathedral choir, she set her mind to decorating Christ Church. She was determined that the colleges of Oxford, which had all been subverted for some military purpose, should furbish the cathedral. The Law and Logic Schools now being granaries, she ordered some clean golden straw from them, to be strewn across the floor of a crib that she had had set up below the shrine of Saint Frideswide, where people most often came to pray during the day. Frowns appeared at her idea of a Holy Family being figured there (popish, again!) so she had to be content with a porcelain Christ child in a manger, swaddled to the eyes to conceal that it was one of her old dolls, Isabella, that had been found jumbled in with the young princes' possessions.

The Music and Astronomy Schools now stored cloth and cloaks, so she put them to work with white and green fabric to make banners striped in the Christmas colors. She also commandeered the ensigns from the regiments, against an objection from James.

"This is irregular. If the regiments were on church parade they could march them in and—"

"No, please, no squadrons of men forced to shiver and stamp

about the quadrangles in the freezing cold! It's Christmas. They will lend their colors to us very graciously, if it means they can gather around the garrison fire and drink a toast to the king instead."

"I don't know why you want them, then."

"The regiments are nearly all new, therefore so are their ensigns. They will look superb hanging down the sides of the nave."

"Madam, ensigns are carried to God's house to be blessed. An ensign is like the spirit of the regiment, and any soldier, to the lowest and meanest recruit, will die to protect it."

"I know. All the more reason for them to hang near His Majesty's precious standard that was lost and recovered at Edgehill. And the Prince of Wales's ensign and the Duke of York's. When they are all returned on Christmas Day, they will be welcomed back with reverence."

In the event, the splendid ensigns, six-and-a-half-foot squares of silk painted in rich colors, brought a dignity and significance to the service that even Mary had not foreseen. They were fixed high on the pillars at each side of the nave, and a glance upward revealed them suspended below the glorious intricacy of the vaulted ceiling, which was sculpted by light flung up from the massed candles below.

As Mary listened to the music, she rejoiced again at the familiar beauties of evensong. She closed her eyes while the choir sang, and saw behind her eyelids the Nunc Dimittis of Christopher Tye and the Magnificat of Hieronymus Praetorius speed to the vaults of heaven like flights of golden arrows.

She was surrounded by Stuarts, and as the service progressed and God was called upon to protect and redeem mankind, she could feel the men around her mourning in their prayers for those who were far away—and those who could never worship with them again. She only glimpsed Prince Rupert, who was across the aisle, when the gentleman beside him sat back and the prince was revealed still kneeling, his forehead pressed to his knotted fingers and his hair obscuring his face. And she looked away, pierced by guilt and regret.

This was the first Christmas since the king had divided himself from his subjects. The Stuarts and their supporters knelt now before God to beg his blessing for their cause—which was why Mary had striven to make this a flawless, uplifting occasion. How could she remain in the cathedral while her thoughts and her heart swayed toward Rupert—toward adultery and betrayal? Every prayer she uttered would be a lie before God; she would be putting into spiritual peril everything she had tried to achieve. When it came time to kneel once more, she clasped her hands and whispered, *"Forgive me, Oh Lord. And heal me."* Even James, close by her side, could not catch the words, for they were not meant for mortal ears.

The sermon was gentle and spoke of peace. If the young princes wept—and she hoped they did not, being manly souls both—she could not see it through her own tears. The sermon was followed by the Lamentations of Jeremiah, for which William Lawes had chosen the sublime music of Thomas Tallis. While Mary listened a mournful image of London came into her mind.

> *How doth the city sit solitary, that was full of people! how is she become as a widow! She that was great among the nations, and princess among the provinces, how is she become tributary! Jerusalem, Jerusalem, return to the Lord thy God.*

Then there were the final carols, and the heartfelt benedictions and responses, and the warm murmur of voices as the cathedral emptied.

Outside she was briefly alongside Prince Rupert; they both came to a standstill while others were filing past, drawing their cloaks about them and talking in cheerful tones.

The prince was silent, gazing down at her, until she looked up and wished him the blessings of the season in a clear, sad voice.

He returned them, then said with somber gravity, "For what did you pray, this night?"

"For the soul of George Stuart. For all our souls, Your Highness. And you?"

"I prayed not to love you. May the Lord hear my prayer." He walked on.

And let our cry come unto Thee. She bent her head. Scarcely any time had passed since Rupert had let her know that he loved her. Now he vowed before God to end it, before sin could destroy them both. In the sacred refuge of the cathedral, her own prayer had matched his. She marveled that in that house they should both have sought, at the same time, the same kind of peace. And sacrifice.

*   *   *

Rupert had made a resolution in Christ Church and what was more had told her of it. He therefore wondered whether he should join in the gift-giving that Charles's family indulged in at midnight, in the king's private chambers. But the pull of her presence was the same tonight as at any other time, and if he were to renounce her, as he had fervently told himself in the cathedral, then to avoid her at this first opportunity meant he had no faith in his own strength.

So he went, armed with the gifts he had assembled over the last week—and succumbed to the family's festive spirits the moment he stepped over the threshold. It was a relief to put aside high purpose and watch her second the king's welcome with a friendly smile. Looking at her radiant face, he could almost believe she had not heard his charged words outside the cathedral. She was following her dearest aim, making other people happy, and on such a night nothing should stand in her way.

The gifts were many, some extravagantly wrapped, for Mary Villiers had carried from Holland Christmas tokens from the queen and Princess Mary, which she had kept at home and now brought forth to great glee, especially on the part of Princess Mary's brothers. Charles and Henrietta-Maria always made a fuss of any kind of celebration, and delighted in presents; it was likely that there was more fun at Christmas in their household than in all the rest of Oxford put together. Sir William Harvey, the princes' governor as well as the king's physician, was given the scholarly task of supervising mulled wine at the fireside while the presents were carried back and forth across the warm room and placed in people's laps.

The king received his Christmas gift from the Duchess of Richmond, which was exactly what he requested each year—an affectionate kiss on each cheek. In return she received a square parcel that proved to contain a jewel-like painting from a window. She gasped, and held it to her midriff in the way she had, and her eyes danced as she looked at Charles. "This! Have you discovered it is not Holbein after all, so you pass it to me?" The king laughed outright as he received two more kisses, gentler and more emotional than the first. At this Prince Rupert looked at the floor.

It was revealed to the assembly that the Duke and Duchess of Richmond did not normally exchange gifts at Christmas. Instead they had an elaborate feast by themselves, which consisted not of traditional fare but instead of any kind of food that was difficult to obtain at the season. "Our table is always the silliest sight," the duchess confided. "Once my lord found me a pineapple—I still have no idea how or where. It costs us a fortune, of course, and it's shameful and sybaritic and produces the wildest melange you ever saw. Salmon and oysters and samphire and oranges . . . Anyway, since we are with you tonight we have forgone the cornucopia. So, husband, I had to rack my brains and purse to find you this."

It was clever and Richmond acknowledged it with a smile: a blue dish of Venetian glass, expertly blown so that large golden apples decorated the rim. "My lord's favorite fruit," she explained, as the duke sat admiring it in silence. "We are absurdly proud of the orchards at Cobham."

The duke's gift to the duchess proved, as the king wittily remarked, "the perfect pendant" to hers: a solid gold pineapple, a tiny forfeit on a fine chain, made by the renowned jeweler Jean Petitot. She gave a crow of delight and clutched it to her, laughing. There were no kisses, and husband and wife did not touch, but this coincidence of ideas between them cut the prince's heart as nothing else could have done.

What did she think of his announcement outside the cathedral? Did she even care whether he loved her or not? It was torture to watch her smile and laugh with seeming happiness. But there was just one clue that she might be hiding something of his own regret and loss—when her mood appeared brightest, she could not meet his eye.

Rupert distributed his gifts, which included a bunch of gold ribbons that he tied around the necks of Boy and then his uncle's spaniels, which dashed back and forth across the hearth trying to pull the bows off one another. Harvey, with a mock frown on his fire-reddened face, said it was time all small creatures went to bed, but the princes were oblivious.

For the Richmonds, Rupert had bought books. The duke received a crisp copy of Robert Ward's *Animadversions of Warre*, a recently published critical assessment of modern warfare, and the duchess a beautifully bound copy of the sonnets of William Shakespeare. "No doubt you have them already," he said. "But perhaps not in Oxford."

She expressed her gratitude with sincerity but without a kiss on each cheek. Her fingers lifted the gold-leafed vellum cover and fanned the pages. "I have read many of these, but not all." She eyed him speculatively. "I suppose you are aware that the poems devoted to a gentleman are suspected to have been addressed to a handsome rival of my late father?"

The love poems? On catching the sardonic eye of the present young Duke of Buckingham, Rupert received mute confirmation of this.

"Though no one has ever suggested," the Duchess of Richmond continued, "that the poems to 'A Dark Lady' were written for any rival of my mother's. Hers, I'm afraid, were all male."

He put his elbow on his knee and his hand on his forehead, with a helpless laugh that was more like a sigh. "Dear me. My literary education has been sadly neglected."

"You have only to apply to the Buckinghams," George Villiers said, "for spectacular improvement in that area."

They all laughed, and he with them, and he reflected that since she knew the poems she would be unlikely to open the book again, or thus pick up the nefarious way in which he had mined it with meaning. It was better so.

Her present to him was a fine handkerchief. He spread it over his knee and could not look up as she explained the gift to her family with her usual candor. "I had no need to rack my brains for this one. His Highness lent me his handkerchief one evening in the Hague, when we were all laughing with the queen. I have not given it back—so rather than trying to lay hands on it, I considered it only right to give him a new one. Inferior to his own, I fear, but I had no time to send to Delft or Utrecht for the lace."

He raised his head and smiled at her. "It is the thought that counts."

But what thoughts might be passing behind that Venetian blue gaze, he could not at that moment decipher. No doubt it was better so.

The queen had planned to arrive in England in January, and Mary was very occupied in preparations for her return. But storms arose in the North Sea and her boys, though worried, joked about "Mam's ill luck at sea," which was probably driving her ships back to the Netherlands. Henrietta-Maria was to land in Yorkshire, and

Mary felt constrained to go north and greet her, but James dissented; Newcastle still controlled the coast, but not as securely as when Mary had arrived. The queen must be well guarded on her progress and would be much more in need of a strong armed force than of another female attendant. Therefore Mary lingered in Oxford.

If she lingered for Prince Rupert—and she tried to convince herself she did not—she met with some disappointments. He came much less often to dine with them, and then only at James's insistence. He was overburdened by work, harrassed at one garrison town after another by questions of supply—and yet from every source she heard tales of his acumen, energy and genius for commanding solutions to the problems that beset the army.

Stories from the other side multiplied at the same rate and filtered through their own forces. At some time after Powick Bridge, Rupert was reputed to have disguised himself as a country gentleman to take a close look at Essex's troops in Worcester, and when enjoying food with a widow in her own house had agreed heartily when she told him that the bastard Rupert should have been strangled at birth. In addition, half the parliamentary army seemed to believe that Boy the poodle was his "familiar," privy to all his secrets and plans, and while he ran like a ghost beside Rupert's black horse in the forays across country and the lightning raids on Essex's troops, Boy could disappear at will and then reappear alongside his master to give him exact information on all the enemy's movements. The Roundheads feared Boy as they would a demon, and though they fired upon him whenever he was seen, they dreaded that he could never be killed.

Mary cringed when she heard this, and tried to imagine how Rupert would take the stories, but he never raised them with her. Eventually she learned that on receiving a crude pamphlet distributed to the troops that featured an ill-executed woodcut of himself on horseback and a bad rendition of Boy running alongside, he had tacked the paper low on a tree trunk and asked Boy to pee on it. Which he did, to much merriment.

When Rupert came to dine, however, nothing had changed between them. It was like stepping into an enchanted space carved from the chaos around them. There was always that first breathless moment when they met, as he came through the door or she stepped into the room where he was seated already, talking to James; and in his eyes, however decorously his voice and hands and body might behave, there was the fire of love, burning so fiercely that Mary wondered how it did not ignite the air between them and denounce him to the world.

For herself, the delectation was as covert and penetrating as before, and she felt sure he could not guess it. One night she was watching his hands as he talked to James about cavalry movements and shifted items around the table to demonstrate. His use of weapons and the hundred rough tasks of his daily life meant that he wore no rings on his long fingers, his palms were callused and his nails ragged, though usually clean. This evening he came straight from a long foray to the east that had kept him away three days. He and his officers did not wear armor for these expeditions, trusting to the protection of buff coats of thick leather and sometimes helmets, but Mary noticed deep red marks on his left wrist and across the back of his hand. He must have had on a bridle gauntlet all day—a piece of armor designed to protect whichever hand held the reins, for during an attack it was a common enemy ploy to try to sever that hand and make the rider lose control of his horse. When this sank in, she felt sick, but could not drag her gaze away from his hands. He noticed, glanced down and took them from the table, looking apologetic. She felt like crying.

The conversation about tactics continued, however, and the prince seemed pleased to learn that the duke had finished the military books by Cruso and Ward and was looking for others. Rupert grinned. "There are certainly more where they came from!" He turned to Mary. "Tell me, have you read the sonnets I gave you, or are they quite beneath your notice?"

She could not tell him how she had pored over the book. "Some, but not all." James gave her a reproving look at this coolness. The Stuarts were all very sentimental about presents, and he had praised the prince's gift to her at Christmas.

Rupert said, "I wish you would. I should like to discuss them with you." His eyes sent a shaft into her own that James could not detect, and she knew at once that despite the prince's resolution at Christ Church and his restraint since, there was a hidden message in the sonnets that he now longed for her to see—and he would return without fail for her reaction.

Later, alone in her chamber, she sat on her bed and reexamined the book by the light of a candle. Everyone had seen and approved of the dedication on the first page, laughing at the extravagant way he had elevated her rank: "To the Most Excellent Princess Mary, Duchess of Richmond and Lennox. With everlasting respect and esteem, Rupert." On the rest of the pages were printed more than a hundred and fifty sonnets. Not a pencil mark, not an ink blot, not a scratch or a tear beside the lines, not a turned-over page corner, not a ribbon or marker of any kind betrayed the purpose of the giver, supposing there was one. The book was as pure as if it were still hot from the press.

She looked through it yet again, frustration and a kind of miserable urgency making her hands shake. Wondering if there might be a very small slip of paper jammed into the crease between two pages, she held it in the light and fanned the uneven pages rapidly. Nothing fell out. But she saw something. She fanned them again, then stopped at a telltale page and held it closer to the candle flame. On the level of one of the lines in Sonnet 17, in the outside margin, there was a minute pinprick. She fanned the book again. There were more, flickering like tiny sparks that went out as the book closed.

At once she guessed it: there would be fourteen of them.

It was not just her hands that trembled now—her whole body buzzed with an excitement that made the space around the candle flame warp and shimmer. She would not mark the book any more than he had done. Instead she took pen and paper, moved to the floor with the candle as Anne was wont to do and leafed through the book from the beginning. At each line designated by a pinprick she stopped and wrote out the words.

She was right. There were fourteen lines, selected in order throughout the poems, the last being from Sonnet 123.

If I could write the beauty of your eyes—
So long as men can breathe and eyes can see—
To find where your true image pictured lies,
Then may I dare to boast how I do love thee.
With my love's picture then my eye doth feast,
Thou best of dearest, and mine only care;
Within the gentle closure of my breast,

Against that Time do I ensconce me here.
In all external grace you have some part,
Whilst I, my sovereign, watch the clock for you;
It is so grounded inward in my heart—
O, know, sweet love, I always write of you:
*   Beyond all date, even to eternity,*
*   This I do vow, and this shall ever be.*

She read it again and again. How many long hours had it taken him to contrive this? How much care had gone into reading and rereading the poems in sequence, on freezing nights in bivouacs and billets, protecting the book from candle grease and the filthy surfaces on which he might rest it, and from the dirt on his own hands, and then sealing it up by day to carry it unscathed into a dozen dangerous encounters?

Her eyes blurred; she could read it no more. She took it up from the floor and held it against her, and knelt weeping for him and the love she could never repay.

Next evening Prince Rupert and the army rode through a mighty thunderstorm toward Burford to meet up with the Marquess of Hertford, the king's lieutenant general in the west, in a campaign to take Cirencester and open the way to the western counties. Hertford and his forces did not make the rendezvous, but snow prevented parliamentary forces from reinforcing the town, so Prince Rupert returned two weeks later and took Cirencester in a fierce and terrifying assault, thereby handing over most of Gloucestershire to the king.

Chapter 13

AS THE DAYLIGHT DIED on a gloomy February day, Prince Rupert was seated on horseback between Sir Jacob Astley, commander of the foot, and cavalry commander Henry Wilmot, as they watched musketeers at drill. Rupert had an easy understanding with Astley, whom he had known since childhood; the old soldier had been his first military tutor and since then they had fought together in the wars in Europe.

Suddenly Rupert felt movement around the back of his neck and Astley started. "By heaven, what's that?"

Rupert looked toward his shoulder in exasperation. His pet squirrel monkey, having hidden all day behind his neck, under his hair, had decided to emerge. "She escaped from quarters and ran after me this morning. She does that now and then, and I can never figure out how. She rode on Boy's back once; he didn't like it one whit."

Astley shook his head and looked at Rupert in amusement, then said, "Does your mother the queen still refer to me as her Monkey?"

Rupert grinned. His mother preferred her menagerie to her children, and had always kept the one at court and the others at a palace called the Prinzenhof, ten miles away in Leiden, where they were attended by a host of tutors. "You are still a fast favorite with her. In her letters, she never fails to ask about you."

At this point the monkey wound her black-tipped tail around Rupert's neck, swung onto the other shoulder and bared her teeth at Wilmot, who looked away, not a little surprised by her and by the conversation.

"Your Highness—," said Astley, but was drowned out by a roar from Rupert.

"You there! That man there—direct your weapon away from your comrade's head or I'll have yours!"

Astley watched the man start, fumble even more perilously with the weapon and then obey. He bent a stern glance on the soldier, then went on, "Do you still recall the thirty-six postures of a musketeer? I remember, when you were eight years old you could perform them without fail."

Rupert shrugged. "I'd need a weapon in my hands before I could tell. I can do the pike drill, but it's shorter."

"What do you think of this lot, then?" said Astley in his blunt way.

"Better than average," Rupert said, then laid his hand on the older man's shoulder. "I want to see them with new muskets. Strode and Wandesford have the order—I shall beat at their door until they produce them."

"Then I thank Your Highness in advance," Astley said with a smile. "They're as good as delivered."

When it got too dark to see what anyone was doing, Rupert rode back to Oxford. He did not go to his quarters; he had given the Duchess of Richmond quite enough time to understand the significance of the Shakespeare sonnets and he could not wait a moment longer to confront her—otherwise his nerve would fail.

He arrived to find Richmond not yet at home. This he had counted on. What he had not counted on was that the duchess was entertaining Lord Digby and a covey of ladies in the great chamber. He ground his teeth. Perfect. He would walk in with a monkey draped over his shoulder and be faced with Digby and company.

He entered, the duchess smiled at him and he melted, then he greeted the others and felt himself solidifying again like lead in a bullet mold. A great fuss was made of the monkey, which looked from one guest to the other with round, attentive eyes. The perfect white mask on its face, its black cap and soft reddish fur were much admired. Rupert was asked why he had kept it away from court and he felt bound to explain that it sometimes bit. Hope stirred in his breast in connection with Digby, but the little creature remained on his shoulder.

Questioned, he explained that it was female and had no name.

"Ooh," said Digby, "I see the symmetry. Boy is a dog and the monkey is a bitch!"

There was laughter. Everyone always laughed at Digby's jokes so Rupert had no need to join in.

The ladies approached, but the monkey took a liking to no one except the Duchess of Richmond—unbidden, it suddenly skipped across two chair backs and a table, ran up her arm and slipped a sly little hand into her bodice. Everyone shrieked with laughter, the duchess turned pale in shock and Rupert stepped forward.

He extended his hand. *"Liebchen,"* he said softly, and his pet returned to him at once. The duchess was shivering. "I cry you mercy. You don't like monkeys—I remember, from the Hague. I never meant to bring it, it was with me today and I've had no time—"

She recovered and laughed, moving away. "I perceive it does have a name, however?"

"No." He sought the word. "I use—"

"Endearments?" said Digby. "Charming."

Rupert took the monkey to the side of the room and placed it rather more savagely than he had meant in a bookcase. He gave it a curt order and it whimpered, ran into a corner behind a stack of volumes and put its little hands over its face. He turned back to the room to find himself less popular than before.

A tedious hour followed, redeemed for Rupert only because Richmond still did not return. He ignored Digby as usual but he did converse, replying to each of the ladies as they advanced in their turn and asked courteous questions.

The duchess and Digby indulged in their usual convoluted dialogue and everything revolved around them, while Rupert avoided being drawn in and hung about waiting for them all to go. At one point he noticed that the Shakespeare volume he had given the duchess was lying on a side table, and his heart lurched to see it there in full view. Eventually Digby swept the ladies away, after a careless remark that the king wanted him at Christ Church to talk about the cavalry, at which Rupert gave a curl of the lip but bade him a proper farewell.

So they were alone. Except for the monkey, which had cried itself to sleep in the bookcase.

Mary Villiers was standing near the fire, smoothing the green skirt of her gown. She was wearing something else over her shoulders, black and shiny and slashed with white where her sleeves showed through, and which left her forearms free. Her wrists were wound about with pearls—they looked accidental, as though she had dipped into a deep coffer and they had clung to her as she pulled her hands out.

He was about to speak but she got in first. "As a friend, may I suggest you avoid giving unnecessary offense to Lord Digby?"

"He's an ass."

She raised her head and said without undue emphasis, "I find him very agreeable."

"Of course you do."

She flashed back, "May I also suggest that in company you deign to clarify what you mean?"

"It's obvious."

"No," she said, "innuendo never is."

He was suddenly angry. "What I meant was that Digby is a flatterer. Flattery works with most people. It paves the way. It makes things easy—meaningless, but easy. One uses the word 'agreeable' about such people, as you have just done. There—was that worth explaining?"

"Oh yes," she said, her eyes glittering. "Otherwise I might have thought you meant I risked making a spectacle of myself over a secret infatuation!"

Ach, so *he* was the spectacle! He stepped to one side, swept up his hat and struggled to get the words out. "You want me to leave?"

"No. I should prefer you to talk. I thought that was what you came for."

After a second's hesitation he strode forward, yanked out one of the chairs, sat down, clapped his hat on the table and put his hands on his thighs.

She sat down opposite, drifting into position with her usual lightness and resting her hands on the table so she could lean toward him.

His fury vanished and his voice came back. "Have you read the book?"

"Yes."

"And understood it?"

"I believe so."

He put out his hand and took hers. She pulled her fingers free at once and sprang from the table. He gave a groan. "You are my happiness. Don't take it away."

She walked across to the other side of the room and then circled around him, one hand brushing the walls. She was not looking at him, so eventually he leaned on the tabletop, shading his eyes.

He felt the softest touch on his shoulder, too fleeting for him to do anything in reply but raise his head, and she slid into the chair opposite once more. "I am your friend," she said.

The worst beginning.

"Do you agree that friends may sometimes catechize each other?"

He nodded miserably.

"Then I may ask you: have you ever seen any sign, or heard any suggestion, or met anyone who has the slightest suspicion that I might be unfaithful to my husband?"

"No! How can you—?"

She put a finger to her lips, then took it away. "Then do you agree that there could be no greater injury, to my lord and to me, than to have anyone—anyone at all—say such a thing of me?"

He hated leading questions. He knew their power; he used them himself. "That is not *it*," he said. "I love you. I would never harm you or your husband. All I ask, all I implore you, is to let me tell you that I love you. What, do you forbid me your—?" He stopped, just in time. If he said "house," "company," "friendship," she could annihilate him with one syllable.

"Oh!" she said, and her voice changed. "I beg you not to make my life impossible."

Something had altered. He searched her eyes and saw a reversal. There was anguish in the blue depths; she was no longer on the attack, but assembling her defenses. The temptation to sweep through them was almost overpowering, but he forced himself to rise, take his hat and make her a deep bow.

"I would rather die than make you unhappy. You command me. Tell me what I must do."

"Be my friend. My true friend." Her face was white and she did not rise. "I am so afraid that I have more need of you than you of me."

"How can that be? I love you." He took her hand and kissed her fingers, then turned them and kissed the palm, and walked out the door. He left her, when he might have taken her in his arms and felt her trembling like a bird against him. He left her, knowing that if he pressed her now, he would come back tomorrow to find she had closed all the doors against him. He left her in that moment of vulnerability, without threats or promises.

He left her without knowing whether she loved him. He had not even asked.

Just as the servant was closing the street door behind him, a spiderball of fur scampered up his boots and body and onto his shoulder again, and there was a shriek behind him as the door was slammed to.

He leaned his head toward a little nose that nestled against his cheek, and felt tiny arms wind in under his collar. *"Liebchen,"* he said, as he lifted his cloak and placed it gently across his shoulder. *"Ma vie. Mi amor."* The words penetrated him like liquor. He would say them to her. He would say everything.

In the first months of 1643 the steady friendship of Prince Rupert and the Richmonds became an accepted fact, and everyone could see the advantages it afforded to each person in the triangle. For Prince Rupert, who was by no means in high favor with everyone at court, it cemented the support of Richmond, who was a man of ability—the duke handled the factions around the king with ease, was not quarrelsome, and when he gave opinions or advice he always made excellent sense. The duchess was useful to the prince in a different way—her warmth, wit and savoir faire softened his demeanor in good company. He had always been charming when he wished to be—now he was doubly so, for he smiled more often. As the genius of the king's army the prince led a punishing life, and few could begrudge him this friendship, which offered him the rewards of refined conversation, affection, laughter and comfort whenever he sought them. For the Richmonds, this closeness strengthened the inner circle of the royal court, soon to be increased by the return of the queen.

During these months, in between the prince's many absences from Oxford, there were occasions when the three needed one another's consolation. The queen reached the northern coast in February but she landed at Bridlington Bay, which was promptly bombarded by the parliamentary fleet. "Being in the open when they began," she wrote to Mary, "I was obliged to take shelter in a ditch! I hope soon to descend to safety in York." From there she would march to Oxford with thousands of fresh troops gathered from the north, and a great baggage train of ordnance, munitions and funds brought from Europe—but Newcastle had yet to feel certain that he could provide a strong enough escort. So Mary must wait longer to see the queen, and Prince Rupert must curb his impatience to receive the much-needed arms.

Meanwhile all three were sometimes in despair over the king's policies for an end to the war. John Pym did not at the moment have total ascendancy over the House, and a peace party within it was advocating a treaty with Charles so that he could return to the capital and rule in conjunction with Parliament. The Commons and the Lords had approved this plan, the treaty was being drawn up, and Parliament's commissioners came to Oxford in mid-March to discuss it. Mary was interested to note that amongst them was the poet Edmund Waller, who had once written a poem to celebrate the "royal" wedding of her little page Anne to Richard Gibson.

At first the king seemed encouraged by the commissioners' overtures, but then Richmond began to sense uncertainty. Every evening when he came home to Mary he had a different story to tell of the king's mood, outlook and projects. Meanwhile the royalist armies were growing stronger—Newcastle's in the north, the king's own in Oxford, and a powerful force in the southwest under the Marquess of Hertford.

One night, after a late meal in the Richmonds' great chamber, the duke sat silent for much of the time as the others talked. Mary was telling Rupert about the plans she had for entertainment once the queen was installed in Merton College. With much laughter, she was teasing him with the idea of his performing another ridiculous, creative dance, and he was firmly refusing. All of a sudden James, who had not been listening to a word, said into a lull, "I have heard something that I must tell you. It has been oppressing me all day. I know if I share it with you both it will go no further."

Mary and Rupert stayed silent, gazing at him in suspense. Mary had seldom seen James so cast down. At last he said, "The king has lent himself . . ." He shook his head, leaned his forearms on the table and looked at the books and sheets of poems and plays that Mary had gathered. His narrow face beneath the loose fringe of golden hair looked pale and tired. "Seventeen secret commissions have been given out to His Majesty's loyal supporters in London. The chief of them is . . . a former Lord Mayor."

"*Commissions?*" Rupert said.

"Yes. At the right time—yet to be named—they are to mount an armed uprising and seize Parliament and London for His Majesty."

"What?" said Mary. "I don't believe you. Seventeen men, to raise an army from the streets; my God, what is this madness? With no support from elsewhere?"

"None that I can confide to you."

"They will go to their deaths," Rupert said. "Nothing is surer. Meanwhile he has three armies gathered to do him service. . . ." His voice roughened with anger and he got to his feet. "Why? Why was I not told?"

James looked up at him and said dryly, "Because you would have spoken and looked as you do now." He put out a hand and gripped Rupert's wrist. "Sit down, Your Highness, sit down. Do not distress yourself. The commissions have not been activated. I shall do all I can to make sure they never are! I only tell you because there are times . . ." He took his hand back and leaned his forehead on it. "There are times when His Majesty will listen to no counsel but his own. He is capable of agreeing to a course of action in the morning and then countermanding it in the afternoon—and without consulting anyone in between but his own thoughts. I can only hope that his best thoughts will dissuade him from this unfortunate project."

"Unfortunate?" Mary said. "Oh, husband, with the commissioners here in Oxford—it is dishonorable."

Rupert looked hard at them both, sat down and remained silent. He never criticized the king. His own honor demanded unswerving loyalty and he gave it. If Charles went against his advice in council, he bowed to the decisions, then without question or comment hastened to carry them out.

James sighed. "I'm sorry—I should not be burdening you. There is nothing any of us can do but hope the conspiracy will stay dormant. I am too weary to talk about it more." With an attempt at a smile he reached forward and tapped the pile of papers before Mary. "What is this—another masque? You have not written one for a long time."

"Some poems to share with the queen. None of them mine.

Except—" Her throat went dry as she pulled one handwritten sheet from beneath the rest, and she had to fight to regain her voice. "I have one that might please Her Majesty. It is on friendship." She could not look at Rupert; she kept her eyes on James, who took the sheet from her fingers and glanced at the beginning before turning it over.

"Not too long," he said. "That's good." His eye fell on one of the last stanzas. "Ah, a ditty from a bashful shepherdess to her swain, I see?"

"Heavens no! Not a *swain*; she wishes him to be her friend." By this time Rupert was staring so hard at the side of her face that she almost put up a hand to shield herself.

James grinned. "Phylocles and Ephelia—fit names, I'm sure. May I read it another time? I confess I am about to fall over. I leave you to literature." He rose and laid a hand on Rupert's shoulder. "Do not let her tire you with a whole flock of Strephons and Phyllidas and Celadons—there will be enough of that when the queen comes home."

They said their good nights and James left the room.

Mary was trembling inside. She and Rupert were never alone; this was the first time since his ill-judged visit after she had read his sonnet, for she had always contrived that they should meet only in company. Rupert had submitted to this, letting her know by stolen glances, by his look at greeting and farewell, by the attention he gave to her every word and gesture, that all his happiness depended on her. He let her know that he was grateful that she allowed him near—but she could see that his passion was undiminished. Once, while taking his leave, out of James's hearing he had said in a broken whisper, "This is torture."

Now he sat on the opposite side of the table, the paper untouched between them, and gave her a dark look of longing and apprehension. "You wish me to read this?"

"I should like your opinion of it."

He looked down at it as though it were about to shoot out flames and scorch him. "I see no title. Does it have one?"

" 'To Phylocles, inviting him to Friendship.' "

"Do you mock me, madam?"

She shook her head. "How can you think so? You once gave me a poem; this is my gift in return."

"I did, but in words not my own. And there was nothing in those words to inflict what this will inflict on me."

Tears filled her eyes. "I wrote it for you. And you will not even read it?"

He saw the tears and his expression altered, but he growled, "You showed it to your husband first! Everything you do is public—I cannot claim one word or action that belongs to me."

She shook her head to banish the tears. "Do you not understand me yet? Do you not realize yet—if something is to lie hidden, it is often best to place it in plain view?"

"Ah," he said in a low tone, "you will always be too subtle for me." Then he looked down, put out his hand and took the paper. His fingers shook, so he put it on the table and fixed it there with his thumb across the upper corner.

She watched, breathless, as he silently read each line. *Best of thy sex!* It began. Surely there was no hatred in that? But he gave a sardonic smile when further down he read: *In a strict league, together we'll combine, And friendship's bright and best example shine.* He turned the page and the smile faded. He read with fearful attention, which changed suddenly at the second-to-last stanza, when she saw color steal along his cheekbones.

> *Why do I vainly talk of what we'll do?*
> *We'll mix our souls, you shall be me, I you;*
> *And both so one, it shall be hard to say,*
> *Which is Phylocles, which Ephelia.*

She watched his face intently as he bent his gaze further to read the final stanza, and so she saw the most radical alteration in his expression. He stabbed at the poem with his forefinger. "With this word, *purity,* you shut me out. *Forgotten friendship . . . to its native purity we will refine.* I understand; pure friendship is all you can bear to offer me. You might as well say you never want to see me again." He put both hands to the paper and she thought he was about to rip it up.

She felt such rejection it made her voice shake. "Do I mean nothing to you? I have been wasting my kindness and my time. Certainly *this* means nothing to you!" And she rose, tore it from his hands, crossed the room and threw it into the fire.

"No!" He was behind her, then beside her, like a whirlwind. At the very moment when the paper hit the flames and ignited, he snatched it back. She shrank away, he dropped it on the hearth and extinguished it with his boot.

She stayed a few paces off as he stood before the fire, his face contorted with despair and anger; he was panting, unable to speak. For a moment he frightened her. Then he shifted his foot and looked down, gave a muffled exclamation and bent to pick up the paper, which was blackened across the bottom where some was burnt away.

He turned it toward her and, holding it by the top, stepped toward her. "The last verse is gone. There is no purity in our friendship. There never has been. Now this reads as it should."

He was a foot from her, strong and unstoppable, so she did not move away. She watched his face as he folded the poem and put it in the breast of his doublet, then she tilted toward him and he kissed her. He did not touch her otherwise than with his lips, which crushed hers, then parted and opened them, firm and tender at once. With a hand on his chest, she could feel him tremble with the restraint he exercised not to take hold of her, not to pull her to him.

He did not resist when she stepped away. She moved toward the table, looking at him over her shoulder, filled with joy and pain. The house breathed and creaked around her, the fire crackled, warm air shimmered over the hearth behind him, but he seemed very still and remote, fixed like a dark figure in a painting.

He said, "Good night, *ma vie*," and left the room.

Chapter 14

PRINCE RUPERT AND LORD Digby left Oxford in the last week of March with a force of around 1,900 men and some cannon, with which to capture Parliament-held Birmingham. The garrison there was weak but its commanders were not disposed to let the prince ride in and take over, especially as they had a healthy manufacture of swords in operation for the parliamentary armies. They split their forces in two for defense and blocked the main entrances to the town, so the prince had some outer houses put to the torch and in the confusion his cavalry were able to skirt around through fields and enter by gardens and between buildings. In a short and bloody time it was over, and the prince accepted the town's surrender and had the fires put out. As his forces moved on to Lichfield next day, some of his soldiers lit more fires by way of farewell. The prince was angry, and said to Digby, "Here comes another parliamentary pamphlet, I warrant you. You'll figure with me on this one!"

"Oh, I'd as soon leave that privilege to Boy," Digby remarked dryly.

As they approached Lichfield, their next objective, Rupert learned that Essex was ready to go on the move up through the Thames Valley if peace negotiations broke down at Oxford, which left him no time for a well-conducted siege of Lichfield—he would have to get this over and rejoin the king as fast as possible.

The worst drawback was his artillery, which was too light to make much impression on the thick stone walls of the town's cathedral close, into which the garrison had withdrawn. The solution he found had never been tried in England—he set the men to draining the moat around the close and bridging it; they would then cross and undermine the wall so a breach could be blown in it, through which he could pour his forces. Local miners were rounded up to do most of the digging. To Rupert's surprise, Digby was intrigued by the idea and labored valiantly under the walls, fired upon from the garrison and up to his waist in mud, until he was shot through the thigh.

On the mild spring night of April 19, Rupert paid a late visit to his wounded colonel of cavalry and found Digby in his billet, stretched on his mattress and attempting to read by the light of a flickering candle. Digby made to sit up but Rupert waved him down and went to the door to shout for a lamp and some wine.

"How goes it?" said Digby painfully.

"The miners have stopped mining; they're packing in the barrels of gunpowder. We'll blow it tomorrow. Once we have our breach, we'll fire the cannon through to soften them up and then we'll be in."

"Are you going to give them quarter?" Digby said. "I heard a murderous string of curses from you when they hanged one of our prisoners from the wall the other day. You're not hankering to be lampooned as the Butcher of Lichfield, by any chance?"

"The king has written and asked me to show clemency. They'll walk out with the honors of war. If they surrender at once."

Digby propped himself on his side, winced, and raised the wine cup that Rupert handed him. "I have a sharp sensation they will. Here's to a bloody great bang."

Prince Rupert's regiment of horse was quartered at Abingdon on the Thames, but Charles chose to meet him with his homecoming forces on April 25 farther downstream at Wallingford, which was closer to recent disasters that the king had been trying to contain. He and Rupert sat in the king's lodging in the royalist garrison town and went over the last few days.

"Whom have you left in charge of Lichfield?" the king asked.

"Richard Bagot is appointed governor."

The king nodded. "And the town is intact?"

"Apart from the breach in the wall, yes. No fires broke out and all the industry there remains as it was—unless we make it better. We now have more gunpowder manufacturers and foundries. And the food stocks are considerable."

The king said quietly, "It is one of your greatest triumphs, nephew, to take a town like that with a small force and such meager artillery." Rupert bowed his head but did not reply, so after a moment Charles said, "How is Lord Digby?"

"Well enough to be moved, so he is on his way to Oxford."

"What is your opinion of him?"

"As a soldier? A brave man. But he intends to resign his commission."

The king started. "Surely not?"

"He's in most profound earnest. No doubt you will shortly hear his reasons, sire. He tried to explain them to me but they made no sense. Even when he was wounded he seemed to approve of the campaign, but soon after he began bickering about it. In the end I refused to listen—I had urgent things to do. I'm sorry, but I doubt if he can be persuaded to take up his command again, and I shall not be the one to try it."

The king gave a sigh, then said, "And the young Duke of Buckingham—how is he faring with your forces?"

"He acquitted himself well; I happened to speak to him yesterday and he sends his respects, to Your Majesties and to his sister."

"Thank you. Mall will be pleased; he can be lax about keeping his family informed of his doings. I don't like her to worry. She is already distressed enough about the Earl of Denbigh."

Rupert nodded but made no remark. Denbigh, fatally wounded at Birmingham, was the husband of Susan Villiers, aunt of Mary and George, and one of the queen's closest friends. The Denbighs' son Basil, who would now inherit the title, was fighting for Parliament. The king already had Rupert's written report of those killed and wounded in the campaign, but the prince hated losing men and the king knew he would not go into Denbigh's fate in this meeting. Instead Rupert asked, "And the parliamentary commissioners?"

"Gone back to London. With my blessing—there was nothing more to be said."

Rupert stared at him, then at the table, then at the wall, his mouth set. He was often clean-shaven, but today wore a narrow mustache. Charles reflected that if he let it grow thick like most courtiers, he would look like a bandito; even as it was, his appearance today was more aggressive than usual and he looked disappointed, almost angry, at Charles's answer.

The king said, "I expected to see you keen to prosecute the war at this stage. You are carrying all before you!"

Rupert clenched his hands on the table. "Sire, Parliament has printed any number of calumnies labeling me a warmonger. They know no better—but it is not a reputation I covet as general of Your Majesty's horse."

"You are much more than that, and well you know it," the king said. "I depend upon you." He took a breath and spoke again, beginning in a tone of resentment but modifying it to dignity: "Parliament drew up a series of . . . of conditions, of such a nature and in such a manner that I could not have acceded to a single one and cleared it with my . . . my conscience or my honor. In fact I am in little doubt that they expected this response before they even sent the commissioners, in which case they wasted my . . . my time and theirs. They went back ten days ago and already Essex has laid siege to Reading."

He could see from Rupert's face that he knew this already, but the prince still asked a series of careful questions to ascertain the picture. It was not attractive: Charles's governor in the city had been injured and it was defended by a brave commander who had fought at Edgehill, Richard Feilding; but, the king explained, "He has agreed to terms of surrender—he considers his troops insufficient and we cannot reinforce him. We cannot get across the Thames to him at Caversham Bridge; the parliamentary forces there are too powerful."

"Can Feilding hold out a fraction longer? If he can, we can get help to him."

"He appears to have accepted the terms."

"Then let him send Essex another billet-doux declining them," Rupert said, rising to his feet. "Will you permit me to talk to Feilding if I can?"

The king looked up, startled. "My dear Rupert, you have not been out of the saddle for days. Is this haste and risk necessary? What chance do you have of getting anywhere near Reading?"

"I shan't know until I try, sire." He cocked an eyebrow. "Will it help if I promise not to swim the Thames?"

"How do I know you won't?"

The prince frowned. "Rupert keeps his promises." After a moment he said, "May I ask what is so amusing?"

The king said, "Go . . . just go. And God keep you."

Rupert was in the Prince of Wales's reception room in Christ Church, and sun was streaming through the windows onto the floor, covered in good Norfolk matting, where young Prince Charles sat pulling Boy's ears and plunging his fingers into his woolly mane to give him a scratch. The lad was listening carefully, though, to what Rupert told him.

Rupert, seated by the window, laid his arm along the sill and looked out into a quadrangle brilliant with new grass. "I couldn't get to Feilding but I managed to sneak through to a place by the Thames where I could hail him, and we shouted across the river to each other. I asked him what he had to say about the surrender and he said he could not compromise himself by going back on it—he had accepted the terms. You understand the phrase 'with the honors of war'?"

"Yes, of course." Prince Charles lifted his dark head, his round face composed and earnest. "You may march out without being taken prisoner and you are unharmed."

"*Bien.* That is what Feilding had agreed to, and I allowed him to keep his word and approved his decision. So in a sense, if you blame him for what happened afterward, you might as well blame me also."

"That is not what my father says," Charles said, his hands still caressing Boy. "He says—"

"Allow me to continue. Feilding kept his word, but the parliamentary forces did not keep theirs—some of our soldiers and the baggage train were attacked when they marched out of the town. When he came back here to Oxford, Feilding was stripped of his commission, court-martialed and condemned to death. Why must he die, in your view?"

Charles looked rather fearful on being asked for his judgment, and Rupert wondered whether this was the wrong tack. But after a moment the boy sat straight and thought hard. "Because he surrendered the town."

"Sometimes these decisions have to be made: it is a matter of strategy. Do you allow your forces to be pounded into nothing or do you preserve their lives so they may fight another day?"

"All right then," Charles said seriously. "Because he did not protect their safety in the event."

"Well considered. But was it his fault that the enemy did not keep their word?" After a pause, Rupert said, "Richard Feilding fought for you bravely, Your Highness, at the Battle of Edgehill.

Think of Sir Edmund Verney, who also fought there, and died defending the royal standard. Do we execrate his memory because he lost it?"

"No," Charles said with a shudder. Rupert had never been sure whether the two boys should have been witnesses to hundreds of men dying in the field for their cause, and he knew their governor, Sir William Harvey, had been very anxious for them to be taken back out of sight if not sound of the battle. Hiding under a hedge as the big guns sent cannonballs flying by, Harvey had even tried to read aloud to them from the book he had with him! But perhaps it was as well that Charles should come to face the realities of his position. The boy looked solemn. "You think my father should show mercy to Richard Feilding?"

"Your Highness, if he does not, no one else can. No commoner, no court or judge, no great lord, can pardon a man once he has been condemned. Mercy is the prerogative of princes. It is a grave responsibility; for without the action of princes, mercy cannot exist."

"If I speak to my father and I tell him I do not think Richard Feilding deserves to die, will he listen to me?"

Rupert rose and Boy sprang to his feet. Rupert bent to ruffle the prince's hair in a swift caress. "I leave you to consider that. But I think you know the answer."

For Mary, the welcome home and the meal that evening were the best she and James had ever offered Prince Rupert. He had been two days in Oxford but unable to accept their invitations; tonight, however, he came, and with happy news—the king had been moved by an appeal from the Prince of Wales and Richard Feilding would lose neither his life nor his liberty. Mary looked across the empty hearth at Rupert as they sat in comfortable chairs long after dinner, and she inwardly rejoiced, with a fierceness that made her face glow as though she had drunk too much wine. Here he was, back once more unscathed from campaigning, relaxed and ready to talk about anything but the war once the first inevitable subjects were gone by. He answered their anxious inquiries about Lord Digby, who was making a good recovery, relayed news of the Duke of Buckingham and mentioned with respect and regret the Earl of Denbigh, dead of his wounds after Birmingham. Denbigh's son, a Parliamentarian, had been allowed under a flag of truce to visit his dying father, but he had come too late. Mary had seen the letter that her aunt Susan Villiers subsequently sent to him. Part of it read:

> *O my dear Jesus! Put it into my dear son's heart to leave that merciless company that was the death of his father; for now I think of this party with horror, before with sorrow. This is the time that God and nature claim it from you. Before, you were carried away by error; now it seems hideous and monstrous. The last words your dear father spoke, was to forgive you and to touch your heart. Let your dear father and unfortunate mother make your heart relent—let my great sorrow receive some comfort.*

But such comfort as Susan Villiers received came only from those who mourned with her at court.

On this evening of mixed emotions, James told the prince ironical stories about the parliamentary commissioners' stay in Oxford, and Rupert listened with an alert look and a quick glance now and then at Mary.

Suddenly James leaned forward and said, "My dear friend, you are bleeding!"

"Nonsense! No, I'm not."

"But you are! My lady, we must call someone."

Mary sprang up and went closer to Rupert as he put a hand to his forehead. "My apologies; it was healing yesterday. I thought it had stopped." Mary gazed in sick apprehension at a trickle of blood descending from under his hair. He looked up and said quietly, "There is nothing amiss. If you would just give me one of the napkins from the table . . ."

She brought it to him and he pressed it to his forehead, then took it away. "There, it's over."

"Oh no," she said, "I insist on looking." She took the cloth from his hands and standing in front of him parted his hair to examine the top of his head. Her fingers shook: she was overwhelmed by touching him at last, nervous of James as he watched from behind her, longing for the touch of the prince's hands in return and desolate at this impossibility. His thick dark hair felt silky under her fingers. "Oh," she murmured, "you have a bruise and a gash here that must hurt like . . . I can't possibly press on it. Let me just remove the blood from your hairline. There, it has stopped."

"Thank you," he said, and took the cloth from her fingers again. "I beg you to sit down."

She withdrew and sat down, trembling inside, as James said, "How did it happen?"

"It was nothing; it was on the march back from Reading. A stray shot, courtesy of a scout for Essex, perhaps; the life guard went looking but found no one."

"Could you not wear something under your hat?" Mary exclaimed. "There is a cap for that purpose, made of steel, and it has a strange name. . . ."

"It's called a secret," he said. "I don't know—secrets may sometimes do more harm than good. One grows careless." With a hollow heart Mary searched the meaning of this and meanwhile he went on, "The bullet only annoyed me for one reason; this is the first scratch I've ever sustained. Oh, plenty of wrenches and dents and bruises and marks—but no one had drawn my blood."

"And yet you've held arms since you were a boy," James said in wonder. "And you were as reckless then as you are now, I'll be bound."

Rupert considered this with a subtle smile directed at Mary. "Yes, I have been accused of recklessness."

"But have you never known fear?" James persisted.

"Of course. And you are right, I first recognized it when I was a child. At least, I suppose it must be called fear, I don't know. With me it was a shrinking of the flesh, when you stand ready but your whole body is expecting a blow—how do I explain it?" He smiled. "It was quarterstaves and I was preparing to fight another boy. So I looked at him and I said to myself, 'That staff of his will smash into my head and knock me to the ground, and it will hurt like ten thousand devils and they will take me unconscious—or awake and cursing, I forget which—to my room in the Prinzenhof.' And after I had said that, my body ceased to shrink—because it was going to happen, you know?—and I went forward and . . . vanquished him," he concluded, meeting Mary's horrified glance too late.

"And your first battle?" James said, oblivious.

The prince answered James. "The same. I said to myself, 'This is the day God chooses for me to die,' and I went forth and at once

I stopped thinking about it." The reminiscent smile faded from his face. "My profession is to kill God's creatures. One day, when one of God's creatures puts an end to me, it is by His will. Because of this I do not pray on such matters—all is in His hands." He looked at Mary and said, coaxing her to smile, "I could not match Sir Jacob Astley's prayer at Edgehill: 'My God, thou knowest how busy I shall be this day. If I forget Thee, do not Thou forget me. March on, boys!' "

James turned to her then and saw her face. "Your Highness," he said, "my wife is not used to hear such melancholy matters spoken of. If I ever do so, all her fires go out, one by one," and with a rare gesture James stretched out his hand and touched her hair.

"I'm sorry," the prince murmured, his eyes on the boot that he had extended across the hearth.

James said to Mary, "You had no sleep last night. You are overtired. Why not withdraw? His Highness will be good enough to forgive you—you look pale."

She rose, because she knew James would not let her do otherwise, and looked at Rupert. She thought he might be mortified by James's remarks, but instead, while her body shielded him from her husband's eye, he gazed at her with all his love showing in his face. He was moved by her terror for him, and could not conceal it. She said, commanding her voice, "Very well, but I shall not depart without fixing our next dinner, a week hence. I have reason to believe you will be in Oxford."

He rose and bowed. "I will do everything in my power—"

"Wife," said James behind her, "cease and go."

"And you have not told me whether you prefer the pigeon pie or the capons. When you come—"

James said in mock wrath, "Go!"

"Anything," Rupert said, and kissed her hand.

"Until next week, then." Out of the corner of her eye she saw James half rise and point to the door, and she pulled her hand from Rupert's fingers, just touched James on the wrist as she went to the door, and closed it behind her.

She stood outside it, dizzy for a moment and unable to move.

Within, she heard Rupert say in a low voice, "Forgive me. I have driven her away."

"Do not concern yourself, Your Highness. My wife is like the sun—she likes to bring warmth. If she cannot do so today, tomorrow she will rise again and beam forth as dazzling as before. She's in need of rest, that's all."

In her chamber she went through her bedtime rituals with great care, then climbed into bed and sent her tiring woman away. The bedroom closed around her, and because there were no embers in the grate and no light from elsewhere, the darkness was complete and full of menace.

How terrifying Rupert's religion was—he had surrendered himself to death at the age of fourteen, if God so willed it. Calvin taught that a soul was chosen by God—no virtues or selfless deeds could save a person already damned. No man could know whether he would be received among the chosen: he was a creature under the knife.

All along, without knowing it, she had believed in the aura of invincibility that surrounded Rupert. She had feared for him, but not in this cold, griping way that twisted her stomach as she lay in the hollow middle of the night. He was flesh and blood. And there was nothing to protect him, not even his own vigilance, for he felt no fear.

Chapter 15

IN LATE MAY, THE Duke of Richmond's worst alarm for the royalist cause in London was justified. A conspiracy of seventeen men, including former Lord Mayor Gardiner, was exposed before the plotters could do any harm to Parliament or its citizens, but the panic and reaction to it were fierce. All the conspirators were arrested and two were hanged at once in the street before their own houses. One of the plotters was Edmund Waller, who had been a commissioner for Parliament in Oxford in March. At his arrest Waller informed on the others, which did nothing for his own cause—he was condemned to death and sent to the Tower.

In June, Queen Henrietta-Maria, announcing herself as Her She-Majesty Generalissima, at last began a slow progress down the country with several thousand troops. The huge shipment of munitions she had brought from Europe went with her in convoy, including two demi-cannon nicknamed Gog and Magog, thirty-two guns, ten thousand small arms and seventy-eight barrels of powder.

Prince Rupert, meanwhile, galled by the loss of Reading, was trying to ensure that Essex could obtain no further hold over the country around Oxford. In a raid that lasted just twenty-four hours, he penetrated the enemy forces from west to east and back again, capturing one hundred men and killing more, and with a series of lightning charges in farmland near Chalgrove scattered the parliamentary horse, mortally wounding an officer, John Hampden, one of the members of Parliament whom King Charles had once tried to arrest. Rupert returned to Oxford with his prisoners on June 18, having lost but twelve men.

Mary sometimes wondered whether Merton College, which was now ready for the queen, was in the most secure position for Henrietta-Maria's safety, since it was right against the city walls, beyond which meadows shaded by trees stretched away to the outer fortifications. But the prince reassured her; the queen had after all her own life guard, led by the very competent Lord Jermyn, and she and her ladies would be well protected.

"I shall see you less," he said once in a regretful murmur. "My aunt will want you near her morning and night."

The conversation was occurring at court within others' hearing and Mary could not show her disappointment freely. Yet she did not look forward to the future any more than he—Henrietta-Maria's return and her own resumption of duties would crowd into her life and drive her keenest pleasures out of it. She said, "But you will often visit her at Merton?"

"I shall escort Her Majesty back, but she will have many to attend on her once she settles in. She will be surrounded and I shall only see you in a crowd. I don't know whether I can bear that."

She whispered, "Don't say so. Don't torment me."

"By heaven," he said, "what do you think you do to me?" It was an outburst that he could not control, and Mary looked around to see if it had been overheard. Apparently it had not, but he saw her anxiety, bit his lip and with a muffled exclamation moved away. She did not see him again that day.

On the next she was at Merton again, clad in warm clothes and with a mission in mind. She was still worried about the safety of the college, because a rumor had it that in earlier times a tunnel had been dug from the foundations. It was said that it might go as far as Christ Church; it might have been a hiding place during times of unrest; it might have served as a means of communication with enemies beyond the walls. No one shared Mary's curiosity about this and James joked about it: "Merton was built in 1264—ten to one the tunnel fell in centuries ago, if it ever existed. And if it's there, I'll warrant it's a passage cut from somewhere in town so the scholars could bring in secret supplies of drink."

She was determined to find it, nonetheless, but without letting on to James, who would laugh and think her fanciful or frown at the risk. She took Anne Gibson with her and was escorted by two of their own guards to the college. She left them at the gatehouse and led Anne through the building, where they came across members of the small staff that was keeping the place dusted and aired for the queen's coming. There were fewer servants in the area of the main kitchen, sculleries and storerooms where she expected to find the tunnel. In the last few rooms at that level she found but one man, who was putting up shelves in a windowless pantry, standing on a ladder and whistling as he worked. He nearly fell off the ladder when he caught sight of the figures behind him in the gloom, but when he had descended and recovered his wits, he proved to be just the help Mary needed.

On being questioned, he pointed across the narrow passage. "Well, your grace, there is a door in the drying room over there that opens onto nowt. It's pitch-dark and none of us has had cause or time to seek beyond. But the cook heard tell it leads to one of the cellars."

"Show me, if you please."

The door was set into the far wall of another windowless room that backed onto a kitchen. It would be warm by day and night, and was hung with racks for drying clothes when the weather was wet. The door was plain for all to see, but hard to open, and the workman had need of his brawny strength to wrench it wide into the room, with a squeal of old, dry wood against the flagstones and a windfall of dust that eddied around his feet. Beyond was darkness, as he had said.

"Would you bring me one of your lanterns?"

He gave an inquiring, nervous look at Anne, who cocked her head to one side and whispered up to him, "Even a little light would much improve our day."

He escaped and came back with the lantern. "You wish me to have a look, your grace?"

"No, I shall go. And Anne will stay here and make sure no one shuts this door against me."

He gaped. "Alone, your grace?"

"I shall not go far," she lied. Why should it be necessary to lie, even to a servant, to have an hour by herself?

"Then I have but one word to say, your grace. Rats."

Anne gasped but Mary laughed. "At the merest squeak I shall be back here at the run."

So she went alone. After a yard or two there were steps going down, roughly made but solid, for the ancient masonry did not crumble when she stepped on it. The floor was of stone and so were the walls and ceiling—the tunnel was quarried out of solid rock. Quite soon she did find a door set into one side of the tunnel, and although she could neither open it nor see through cracks around it, she deduced this must be an alternative entrance to the cellars.

All surfaces were coated in gray dust, and here and there dampness seeped down the walls, but as she went higher—for the floor sloped gently upward again—the air grew dryer and less stifling. She thought there must be other doors or openings farther on, or holes in the floor or ceiling, for although there was no draft down the chilly space before her, it was eventually possible to breathe as easily as if she were walking in the woods beyond the walls. She had worked out the direction, however: this tunnel led not outside Oxford but up the hill toward the heart of the town. It thus posed no threat to the security of Merton.

She hit her toe against an irregularity in the floor and stopped, and it was at this point that she admitted to herself she was afraid. The darkness closed in around her circle of light, and back where she had left Anne she could see no difference in the gloom—she had perhaps turned a slight corner, or the first flight of steps had cut the gray rectangle of the open doorway from view. She knew that if she called, however, Anne would send people pounding along the tunnel to her aid.

She looked into the blackness ahead and tried to make up her mind. If she saw rat droppings or footprints of any kind on the floor, she would turn back, but so far there were none—it was as though this tunnel had been forgotten by earthly creatures for centuries. No, what she feared were ghosts. People must have crept along this subterranean corridor in the past, ferrying their secrets from one part of the ancient city to the other, or hiding down here while slaughter or plague raged above. There might be souls trapped here still: lost, unshriven, searching for the peace and rest that they had been denied by history. She smiled to herself, to banish her fear. If she met an unquiet spirit, she would have much to share with it.

She wore a gown of fine Flanders wool, so she was not cold, though the tunnel was at a lower temperature than the sunny June day above. Her shoes were the pair she had worn through the streets to see the Earl of Essex in the previous new year—she would throw them away after this, for the two wearings alone would be enough to ruin them. Her greatest fear, apart from ghosts, was coming upon a hole in the floor and stepping into it by mistake, but the tunnel was well constructed and showed no signs of cave-ins. To her surprise there were no other doors, but she passed through little bays now and then, with curved benches carved from the rock where people could sit and rest, out of sight of anyone moving down the tunnel.

She was just leaving one of these bays when the ghost appeared. Far ahead there was a moving light—white or silver, faintly glowing with a fire she knew to be not of man's making. She swung her lantern behind her skirts, held her free hand against her lips and peered into the darkness, her heart thumping. The apparition was growing, bouncing and zigzagging toward her like a swift, erratic ball of Saint Elmo's fire.

She did not scream—her heart stopped and she froze. Then panic jolted her and she gasped and backed into the bay, out of the ghost's path. She stumbled against the bench and her lantern, swinging in her hand, hit the stone beside her and went out.

"Diable!" A man's voice roared down the tunnel. *"Halte!"*

She jumped and shrank back further, but nothing reached her or passed by. The spirit had obeyed the man's command! She sat shivering in the dark, straining with eyes and ears, and detected the scratching of something hard and sharp on the floor a few yards up the tunnel to her right, then the sound of hollow panting, hoarse and regular. And suddenly, flickering along the walls from that direction came fingers of lantern light; the man had turned a corner farther on and was descending toward her.

"Boy," said the voice clearly, *"petit diable, qu'est-ce qu'il y a?"* There were a couple of curses, this time in German, as he picked his way noisily down the tunnel, and then he said in English, "All right, carry on then. What is it, rats?"

She stepped out, bent and held out her hands, and Boy the poodle ran to her at once and buried his nose in her open palms. *"C'est moi,"* she said to the tall, black, stooping shadow beyond.

He staggered and hit his head and shoulders against ceiling and wall, the lantern jumping in his hand.

"Don't drop it," she pleaded. "Mine's gone out already."

He stayed there for a second, leaning breathless against the wall, then held his lantern high and came forward, incredulity and delight flooding his face. With his free hand he rubbed his head and flicked the hair out of his eyes. *"Mon dieu.* This is a miracle."

"Where in heaven's name have you come from?"

"The Blue Boar." He pointed back the way he had come, rather unnecessarily she thought. "And you? Not *Merton!*" When she nodded he said, "Richmond told me your fantastical notion, but I never dreamed . . ." He stepped past her as he spoke, and bent to light her lantern from his, crouching in the dust, his dark head bent. She could tell from his voice that the rapturous smile still transformed his face. "I got the clue to this place from some of my men who are billeted in Saint Aldates. When I was drinking with them last at the Blue Boar they said there's a secret passage there where the innkeeper stores barrels. Some kind of contraband, I thought. There." He put her lantern at one end of the bench and his on the floor in the center of the tunnel. "I closed the door back at the inn. If another opens anywhere, the air will make that flicker. Boy"—he pointed—"stay." Boy flopped down and dropped his head on his paws, his nose pointing in the direction from which Mary had come.

Rupert took off the riding cloak that he wore over one shoulder and cast it on the bench. "Pray be seated, madam."

She did so and looked up at him. "Won't you?" He could not stand straight in the tunnel; he had to bend from the waist.

"No, I want to look at you. I never can." He was pulling off his gauntlets and gazing at her, his eyes still full of incredulous joy. "I bullied my way past the innkeeper to see what else he had down here. Barrels of gunpowder stacked under the streets would not have made a pretty picture. But instead I find you. This is a miracle—it's fate." He caught her look and said suddenly, "You are not afraid?"

"No." It amazed her, but she was not. "Meeting a man and his familiar in Stygian gloom under a hill is not something I normally do, but I feel . . . almost comfortable. I shall be more so if you sit down."

He obeyed, throwing his gloves on the floor and sitting on them in the same attitude that he had adopted a year before in the cloister garden of the Wassenaer Hof. As before she extended her hand and he took it and held it hard.

"I love you and I can never tell you. It kills me. Sometimes I think that if I could be alone with you for one second every day, and say it to you each time, I could die happy. But then—"

"You are not to talk of dying!"

He kissed her fingers. "I'm sorry."

"And also, every time you go on campaign, you have to come and say good-bye to me."

"*Mi amor*," he said, "I don't always know—"

She took her fingers away and put her hands on each side of his face. "Promise."

He freed himself by getting up from the floor and sitting beside her. Then he put his arms around her and pulled her to him with a force that almost drove the breath from her body. He bent over her and his piercing whisper stirred her hair. "Why are you not mine?"

She clung to him, buried in his embrace, her face against his chest. He took a deep breath, gave a husky sigh and released her, smoothing her hair, her face and neck with light caresses. "Why could we not have married when we were very young? We might have done. You could have been mine. If only you had married me instead of Pembroke. I was sixteen, I was ready—I knew everything by then."

She looked at him, stunned. "I always thought you were an arrogant boy!"

"I mean, about women. I would have made you so happy."

"And an equally arrogant man. Heaven knows why I love you."

His hands stilled. "You love me?"

She put up one finger and placed it on his top lip, then drew it slowly down over his mouth and chin. He watched her face, his large eyes glowing within the dark lashes as though her words had lit something in him that could never be quenched.

"I love you," she said.

For Rupert it was a moment of astonishment and glory. He possessed her heart, and he could never have imagined that she would declare it at such a moment. This exquisite woman, who belonged in the world of elegance and high luxury where he had dreamed of conquering her, was with him in this tunnel, as dank as a prison, where the only comfort he could offer her was the protection of his arms. Yet she was oblivious of the contrast, and as her finger softly traced the contours of his lips he felt a potent sweetness steal into his body that eclipsed the memories of every woman he had known. And at the same time, watching her face as she completed the gesture, he saw something he had not noticed or felt before in her—something trusting; something very close to innocence. A new, poignant wonder coursed through him. Was it possible that he was not only her love, but her first love? But his jealousy of her union with Richmond was so deep-rooted that he could not bring his mind to bear on this idea, and her eyes beckoned with such ardor that he could not resist kissing her, banishing all thought.

Her lips parted under his as they had before, soft and yielding. This time he could touch her, winding his arms around her supple waist and pulling her against him. She abandoned herself to him, her eyes closed and her mouth questing as though she were about to demand everything he had to give. Her breathing changed, her eyelids fluttered against her cheeks, and he deepened the kiss, until all at once he felt her body go taut in a movement of doubt or resistance. He did not let her go; after a moment he released her lips but kept her in his embrace, holding her head against his shoulder.

He waited in silence, his heart pounding heavily, then murmured, "Imagine if we had married in the Hague. I would have thrown everyone out of the Prinzenhof for a week—or a month or however long you wanted. And piled all the fires high because you like to be warm." He tightened his arms. "And we would have walked hand in hand, naked, through all the rooms."

"Naked?" Her voice was muffled within her hair. He put his fingers across to gather it back from her face.

"And we would make love before each of the fires, until the embers burned low. At night I would cover you in fine linen, and in the morning when we awoke I would turn to you." He moved her gently so that she was facing him, and placed his hands on the smooth sides of her neck. "And I would slide the sheets slowly down over your throat, and your shoulders and your breasts. . . ." His hands moved with the words, brushing her skin with the utmost tenderness, and though a torrent of desire filled him, he made himself feel her reaction also. By the time his hands came to rest on the soft swell of her breasts, he had heard her breathing change and watched her eyelids flicker over her deep blue eyes. "And then we would lie naked in each other's arms all day. You would be mine."

"Naked?" she whispered.

He bent his head and kissed the white skin that his hands had touched.

Suddenly there was a scratching sound as Boy got to his feet. Rupert looked over to see the dog rigid and alert, his nose pointing down the tunnel from which Mary had come.

"They are coming to look for you," he said softly. "You must go back." Mary was like someone waking from a dream. He brushed her lips with his. "Come. Stand up, take the lantern and go."

He helped her to her feet, put his own lantern next to the stone bench and threw his cloak over it. Then he motioned Boy to him so that they were both out of sight. "I'll wait here in the dark until you're safe."

She stood looking at him, her face pale in the golden light of the lantern. At the far end of the tunnel he could hear the faint sounds of feet approaching.

He had the painful apprehension that she might not walk away in time, or that she might say something to him and perhaps betray them both. But she simply held his gaze for a long moment, then turned her head, raised the lantern before her and stepped out of sight.

He sank onto the bench, put his hand on Boy's head to quiet him, and listened. He heard the sound of her going, and eventually voices, but he could make out no words, though her own lilting tones reached him unerringly. Then there was the distant closing of a door and silence.

He took the cloak off the lantern before it could get scorched, and Boy got to his feet. But Rupert stayed sitting on the bench with his elbows on his knees for a long time. This dark, dusty, cool alcove underground was the place where he had conquered and held her. He had no idea whether he ever would again.

That night when James came to her, Mary sensed that he had a greater need for her than usual. At dinner he had confided his anxiety and alarm about Charles's latest plots—it worried him that the catastrophe of the royalist conspiracy in London had taught their king very little; he and the queen had some underhand scheme going in Ireland, which even seemed to involve Mary's stepfather, the Catholic Earl of Antrim.

Tonight, Mary could do nothing to relieve her husband's mind, but she tried to receive his body with sensitivity. Physically, she had been in a daze since she had told Rupert she loved him. His tantalizing touch and the things he had said had given her a new vision of how she might respond to a man. In time, gradually, if she could allow the tenderness Rupert had shown her to awaken her body, she dreamed that perhaps one day it might bring her to wholeness.

When James came to her bedchamber she spoke to him with sympathy, and when she lay down she tried to prepare herself to relish his hands and the strength of his need. She would not think of Rupert; she would not sin to that pitch. And she could not have, anyway, for her husband moved too swiftly. The act brought its usual awkwardness, confusion and shame on her part. When James sat on the edge of the bed afterward she had to shield her eyes because there were tears in them.

She said, "I'm so sorry."

He sighed, stretched one hand round and patted her knee. "So am I. But what can we do? I only hope His Majesty acknowledges the London plot for the mortifying mischief it was, and takes stock accordingly."

Chapter 16

꩜

IN EARLY JULY, WHEN Prince Rupert took a force out of Oxford to meet the queen, the Duke and Duchess of Richmond went with it. Prince Rupert was reluctant at first, for he and his men were on the march to ensure that the queen's route was free from detachments of Essex's troops, and if they met any they would be fully engaged in driving them off. But the duchess wanted to go to meet the queen, and the duke said he would not let her go alone, and the king gave his eager consent. So in the end the prince agreed, provided they stayed at a safe distance behind his advance guard.

Thus Mary saw hardly anything of him, for he was a whole advance guard in himself. She sometimes caught glimpses of him during the day, riding ahead or on the flanks of his troopers on the great black stallion, but never in the evening, for he lodged and slept—if he slept—some way ahead, though he sent word back each night to James about where he was to be found, and wherever they lodged they always discovered that every preparation had been made for them by his order.

James was pleased to get out of Oxford for a while and appreciated seeing the prince in action, as he put it. Mary, who never saw enough of Rupert, was silent on this point. And when they did see him, she found him different. He was alert, energetic and vigilant. When he approached like thunder from somewhere and wheeled the big horse around to ride with them, his eyes would signal her a secret greeting if James was looking the other way, but his attention never left what was going on with his troops and in the countryside around. If he were only within earshot ahead of her, she often heard a roar of command, or a burst of laughter from the men. He was part of them; they followed his every gesture and responded to every tone of his voice. His friend and officer Sir Richard Crane told James that at Buckingham, on their route, Rupert had been shaving in the morning when a cavalryman came rushing up to say that there were groups of the enemy in the fields, forming to attack. Without finishing his shave, Rupert was on horseback in seconds and calling everyone out after him. When his troops charged, the enemy scattered like chaff. "And you'll notice we haven't seen a shred of them since," Crane said with a grin.

Once, when by rare dispensation Rupert was riding with them, she said, "Do you ever think of your friends and loved ones before a battle?"

"No." He withdrew his gaze from the hilltop village they were approaching and stared at her.

"What do you think of, then?"

"Madam," said James beside her, "will you leave His Highness—?"

"The enemy," Rupert said.

"And in battle?"

"The same."

When he had gone like lightning, James said, "For an intelligent woman, you do ask some irrelevant questions at times."

"For an intelligent man, you do come up with irrelevant interruptions. I was just about to ask why he very evidently had not shaved this morning. Now we shall never know."

He burst out laughing as they rode on.

Except for being able to snatch the occasional hour of Mary's sunny company, Rupert hated taking her to meet the queen, for two reasons: having her and Richmond with the military party was a constant concern to him; and the nearer they drew to the meeting, the more hollow he felt at the thought of what it would mean in terms of Mary's time and preoccupations. He came close to resenting Henrietta-Maria for her return.

But in the event, the reunion at Stratford-upon-Avon was spectacularly joyful. He had never seen the queen so blooming and happy, and when he told her that the king planned to meet her on the battlefield at Edgehill, where he himself would take her as soon as she pleased, she blushed and her eyes shone with proud affection. He teased her a little about her title of Generalissima, but she pouted and looked hurt, so he turned instead to the engrossing catalog of the armaments she had brought and she beamed with gratification.

They held a veritable little court in the pretty old town, where the queen was received by William Shakespeare's one surviving daughter at New Place. The queen put Mary Villiers through an interrogation about the home that awaited her at Merton and was delighted with the sound of the college. Her eyes lit up when Mary said she had someone looking at the ancient tennis court across Merton Street. Mary explained, "It is the only one in England apart from yours at Hampton Court and I thought we shouldn't neglect it. The roof still leaks, so one can only play on fine days, but the surface beneath is in good condition."

"I am so glad I arrive in summer. Much better than gloomy January after all. And can we take walks outdoors? Are there gardens?"

"There are several little rectangles of green called quads," Rupert said. "Even the Duchess of Richmond cannot turn them into gardens. But you might stroll in the meadows, with Lord Jermyn and his lads to escort you."

"Or we could keep within the walls and take a walk up Magpie Lane on market days," Mary said. The queen raised her eyebrows and looked quite startled. "You will see, we are small in Oxford, madam. But I think we can make the most of what it has to offer if we are not too nice. I have already worn out several pairs of shoes on the cobbles of Oxford town, and I don't regret them one whit."

Henrietta-Maria gave a pretty frown. "I shall reserve judgment. But I warn you, I didn't come all this way to be *rustic.*"

"Oh, that is a pity. We have a quaint little pony and trap to take you around the walls to Magdalen Grove and back, perhaps even to the river, and Lord Jermyn has already told me he'll teach you to drive it. I shall give instructions for it to be sold to some deserving rustics."

The queen laughed. "Why have I so missed your raillery, my dear madam? But I have. You make me feel I am truly come home."

When the queen finally did come home, on July 15, it was a time of festivity that required a mountain of organization, which Mary took over as best she could. Oxford responded ebulliently to the queen. Underneath, Mary knew, it was a town divided—it had become the king's new capital by force; nearly all the silver and gold plate from the colleges had long been melted down to be turned into coin in his new mint; and Charles had decreed that every male citizen between the ages of sixteen and sixty must work one day a month on the wide system of earthworks that surrounded the city or pay the fine of a shilling each time. Few could afford such a sum and thus worked cursing by day, some of them even creeping back at night to tear down what they had built. Many citizens of town and gown who bowed to royal command in their daily lives did so with sympathy for Parliament in their beliefs and their hopes. But when Henrietta-Maria came home to the king, Oxford threw off care and celebrated.

The king held a long dinner of state in the banqueting hall of Christ Church followed by superlative music, and there was a thanksgiving service in the cathedral, which Henrietta-Maria could not attend but spent in prayer in a Catholic chapel. There was a brilliant reception in the king's apartments at Christ Church and a more intimate one at Merton. At all these, Mary saw little of Prince Rupert and then only in a crowd. This would have been cruel, but for the memory of the minutes they had spent alone in the tunnel that lay between Merton and the Blue Boar Inn. Now that the college kitchens and sculleries were packed with servants, Mary had no chance of venturing into the place again, so its dark refuge was closed to her. Indeed, whenever she thought of it, it seemed unreal, like a land of the shades that she had been summoned to just once, to meet the prince of the underworld and hear him demand her soul. But then with quickened breath she would recall the touch of Rupert's hands and the sound of his voice—real, alive and compelling.

On the second night she spent hours opposite him at a dinner in the Dining Hall, hosted by Charles and Henrietta-Maria, whose elation at being together was obvious to all the guests as they looked along the vast, splendid edifice to the high table. Rupert asked Mary about some of the old portraits hanging below the high windows, but conversation across the board was almost impossible against the talk going on around them. Above Rupert hung a more recent portrait of Sir Edmund Verney; she could never look at that proud face, with the long nose and dark blue eyes, without a wrench of the heart at the thought of his death at

Edgehill. Belasyse, one of Rupert's commanders, was also shown, resplendent in red trimmed with silver. She could look at the artist's rendition of Belasyse's small, determined mouth, lazy-lidded eyes and delicate hands, and then glance down the table to compare them with the original, who was pulling a chicken leg apart and laughing at a witticism from her cousin Lady Ann Dalkeith, Countess of Morton, another of the queen's ladies-in-waiting. There was also a picture, mercifully behind Mary, of James's late brother, George Stuart, Seigneur d'Aubigny, which she did not turn to view. During the awkward conversation she saw Rupert look above her, flinch slightly and drop his eyes without posing another question.

Later, when they all left, there was a dense crowd on the stairs. The king and queen were standing almost at the bottom conversing with a group and everyone had come to a standstill. Mary was above the king and queen, at the top of the first flight of the elegantly proportioned stone stairway, and Rupert was nearly at the bottom of the upper flight, facing in the opposite direction from her. She could not look at him. The loneliness and deprivation of the past days overwhelmed her in this moment when he was only feet away, and all at once she felt faint. She was next to the broad stair rail and for support she put out a hand and hooked her fingers into the elaborate stonework below it. A moment later she felt his touch. He had pushed one finger into the narrow opening between two whorls of carving next to hers.

If they did not look at each other, no one in the crowd would notice the profound message of love that traveled from hand to hand through the stone. With a new weakness invading her limbs, Mary stood in silence, looking down the stairs while all around them people chatted on, oblivious. Suddenly, under the power of this most tenuous of contacts, she understood to the core what it would mean to be his.

On the third night after their return to Oxford, James Stuart was surprised to receive a very late visit from Prince Rupert. He and Mary were fully dressed and playing backgammon in his private chamber, and they went out together into the great chamber to welcome the prince.

He was still in court clothes so they did not at first guess why he had come unannounced. But he bowed to them both and apologized to James: "Some time ago I received from your lady wife very strict instructions to take my leave whenever I go on campaign. I regret I shall have no time tomorrow, so I am reporting now." He saluted Mary, who could not quite return his smile.

Mary hated leave-takings. To spare her, James said, "And where do you go, Your Highness?"

"Bristol."

James nodded. The king had been talking of nothing but Bristol since the queen got back. "With what force?"

"Fourteen regiments of foot, some companies of dragoons and the horse, plus siege cannons—but," he said unhappily to Mary, "you cannot wish for such details. I should tell you, Lord Grandison commands one of my brigades."

William Villiers, Viscount Grandison, was an Irish cousin of Mary's who had fought at Edgehill. She saw little of him and he was better known to the Duke of Buckingham and Prince Rupert than herself—indeed the prince valued him as a friend.

"On the contrary we shall welcome your details," James said; then he added to cheer them both up, "Now, my wife will not be able to issue your instructions unless you tell us what you are going to achieve. Sit down, if it is your pleasure, and before you go we would like a view of your projects."

After a second the prince complied, but said he needed paper and something to draw with, so Mary went off to fetch her best artist's chalk and a large sheet of paper.

While she was gone, James said, "Tell me frankly, has His Majesty granted you enough men and equipment to take to Bristol?"

"I can't answer that. Five thousand five hundred troops, more or less . . . but my brother Maurice joins me with his Cornishmen on the way. We shall see."

Then Mary came back and the prince's fingers sped over the paper with the sharpened stick of red chalk; James had heard he was a fine engraver, which was one of the improbable skills he had learned in prison. As he sketched, the prince said, "We must have Bristol. We cannot leave the second greatest port in this country to Parliament any longer, for our armies of the west need support and supplies, and we must prevent Parliament's navy landing troops there. You see where the city lies, inland from the Severn estuary and between the Avon and the Frome Rivers, so unfortunately it has a natural moat."

"We heard what you did with the moat at Lichfield," James put in.

The prince gave a short laugh. "Would that I could . . . There is an outer line of defense around the city wherever the natural defenses fail—ditches, earthworks and forts. I can't tell what Maurice and I may do until we take a look from the high ground, here, where one can approach by land. But artillery is useful from this vantage." He looked up from the paper. "The commander defending Bristol is Nathaniel Fiennes—apparently I met him at Powick Bridge. This meeting will be a little more protracted; I suspect that we can only take the city by attacking on several sides."

James would have posed a few more questions and ordered some sherry, to which the prince was partial, but he could feel the man's tension and knew he was desperate to go. Prince Rupert embraced him, which softened James almost to tears. He mastered them, then stood aside to let his wife make her farewells. She had said almost nothing since Prince Rupert arrived, which was rare with her, but she rallied enough to talk brightly of when he would return, and what a reception the king and queen would give him, and how Oxford would be filled with victorious soldiers. Her voice was very strained and James could not help thinking it an odd, artificial way to farewell a man who might be going to his death.

When Prince Rupert bowed over her hand at the last she put the other up to cover his for an instant. They were by the door, so James did not hear her murmured words before the prince departed.

He sat down at the table again and looked at the map, choosing to exercise his mind over this difficult siege. He said, "I think this will be the hardest task he has yet faced. He has taken part in many a siege but never commanded one; it will be a crucial battle in his career. I wonder why I so often forget how young he is."

He heard a sound by the door and looked up to find that Mary was about to leave the room; her hand was already on the latch. "I am tired," she said rapidly, "and the queen has need of me early tomorrow."

He rose without a word and she left.

After a while he went back into his private chamber and slowly packed up the backgammon board in its inlaid, lacquered case. Then he sat before the table, slumped in his chair, looking at nothing. It was another hour before he lay down, and next morning he went to court exhausted, to find things much altered by the departure of Prince Rupert.

Chapter 17

IT WAS EARLY ON the morning of Wednesday, July 26, and Rupert was riding amongst one of his brigades of foot positioned to the north of Bristol, while the great guns on the ridge above him pounded over and over in their bombardment of the outer works of the city. The air crashed around him, and far below, earth and smoke plumed upward through the running figures of men amongst the fortifications at the foot of the slopes. Beyond these he could see open ground and then the handsome city, with Brandon Hill at its center, the buildings and spires and towers of pale gray stone standing as proud witnesses to the great port's commercial wealth. To the east, where the rivers came close to each other before parting to flow around the city, an old castle provided a bastion for the defenders. In the west, far to his right, lay the broad expanse of the Severn estuary, which was the color of pewter under the dawn sky, and he could see a dull gleam on the River Avon, up which the parliamentary navy sailed its ships to moor at the quays below the city.

On Monday he and Maurice had paraded their armies on Durdham Down and sent a summons to Colonel Nathaniel Fiennes to surrender, which was refused. On Tuesday Rupert had called a council of war and persuaded everyone that a prolonged siege was out of the question: Bristol must be taken at once by assault, with Maurice and his Cornishmen attacking the next morning over marshy ground to the south, and Rupert and his three brigades storming the forts and earthworks in the north and west. He got agreement, yet they all knew it was a perilous choice.

Then this morning Maurice had attacked at three a.m. without waiting for the signal they had agreed upon, forcing a beginning to the battle, which Rupert directed at first from the high ground. Maurice's troops were having a hard time of it in the south, so it was up to the brigades on the other sides to find or force a gap in

the defensive line and push through, or scale the earthworks somewhere, all the time under musket and cannon fire from the string
of enemy forts. Lord Grandison was dead, lost in the first assault,
and his acting major, Lieutenant Colonel Moyle, had taken over
Grandison's brigade, amongst which Rupert was riding as he made
his observations.

Suddenly Rupert saw his friend Will Legge, the major of his
own regiment of horse, spurring across the broken ground toward
him.

"Your Highness," shouted Will as soon as he was within hearing, "Colonel Wentworth has led a handful of his brigade along a
dip in the ground down there"—he pointed as he hauled his horse
to a stop—"along with Colonel Washington and a few officers and
men. And I'm to give you word they've made a gap in the earthworks, big enough for foot and horse!"

"Lieutenant Colonel Moyle!" Rupert shouted.

"Your Highness?" Moyle brought his horse forward.

"Get the men down there at the double and I'll support you
there with the life guard. Major Legge," he said, "I'll go for the
lads; be off with you, and the devil take the hindmost."

Rupert spurred the big stallion across the hill toward his life
guard's position, while the cannon kept pounding above and
below and musket fire from the enemy's ramparts whistled by like
swarms of wasps. Now, at last, his chance had turned up. He disliked waiting around for days when a task sat before him, tempting and challenging in its complexity. Then suddenly the hillside
tipped, his stallion's head came up with a snap, there was a puff of
blood in the air and a long shudder passed beneath him. As he felt
the horse go he leaped free and landed on his feet, and there was
a hollow thump as the great beast fell on its side. He stepped away
from the thrashing hooves, waited what seemed just a second, and
it was over. He walked to the head, put his hand on the stallion's
neck and saw at once: it had been shot through the eye.

The soldiers marching past him hesitated and then halted, and
across the field came a mounted officer, white-faced and in haste.

Rupert stood straight and began walking on, at right angles to
the ranks, toward his life guard.

"Your Highness, have you taken hurt? May I humbly—?" The
officer was about to leap from his horse.

"No, man, you'll do no such thing." He pointed. "Report to Sir Richard Crane and have them bring me a mount. Look to it."

The man sputtered something, then caught his eye and departed like an arrow. Rupert kept walking, and behind him felt some of the soldiers swerve after him and follow. He did not turn or reprimand them.

Once he was horsed again and had led the life guard downhill at the gallop, he could see that Wentworth's men had flooded into the gap between the fortifications and the town and were spreading toward the quays alongside the River Frome, where tall masts crowded together like a bare forest against the lightening sky. When he got to the breach himself, an officer came back with a request for permission to fire the ships, but he said, "Bloody hell, we want the city, not a heap of ashes!"

Thereafter it should have gone more rationally, given the fact that Belasyse's and Moyle's men were now advancing in formation toward the city, but it did not. The enemy in the forts were still firing, though timidly, for they were now isolated and must fear being put to the sword if they were taken. Meanwhile the defenders in the city raised a wall of fire at many points, Maurice and the Cornishmen had still not made their impact in the south, and there was only one way to coordinate the detachments of his men pushing in against the defenders—he must ride around them himself.

He sent Maurice's messenger back with a command for one thousand Cornish reinforcements to be sent to him, and set off at speed to the worst trouble spots. For the next two hours he had no real idea how the battle was going; he was too immersed in what needed to be done at the weakest points. Yet everywhere he went, whether he led troops into an assault or encouraged them in their endeavors and moved on, all responded with courage and alacrity. If they lost this battle, it would not be their fault: they fought like Titans.

In the end, just as Maurice himself arrived with the reinforcements, men of Grandison's regiment shot their way through the Frome gate and into the inner city. Not long afterward, Colonel Fiennes made it known that he was ready to discuss terms of surrender.

It was Thursday, and James Stuart should have been at court, but waiting for news from Bristol gave it a tense atmosphere and he felt of no use to the king at such a time. James had also decided that this was the moment for a discussion with his wife, and if it took place during the day he felt it might somehow shed a clearer light on the matters he wished to broach.

This morning, however, she had so far kept her bed; he inquired and found out that she was not ill but reading, and the queen did not require her presence at Merton that day. At about eleven o'clock, having rehearsed his opening phrases quite long enough, he decided it would be cowardly not to go in and have his talk with her. James was a skilled politician and in the natural way of things made use of his many talents when dealing with Mary, but today he both hoped and feared there might be plain speaking between them. He would prefer to hear from his wife that she was just as immune to Prince Rupert as ever. On the other hand, if she admitted to different feelings, he had no idea how he would cope with the confession.

When he knocked and was given leave to enter, he found her in bed with a book, propped up with a blue embroidered stole around her shoulders and her gleaming red-gold hair spread on gigantic bolsters behind her. At this familiar sight the careful phrases flew out of his mind and with a smile he asked his usual question, "What are you reading?"

"John Milton."

"The lady of Christ Church? Milton declares himself for Parliament."

She laughed at him over the open pages. "For an extremely intelligent man, you do make some irrelevant comments."

He was not in a playful mood, and one of his prepared phrases came back to his aid at once. "Do you have any reason not to show me the handkerchief Prince Rupert gave you in the Hague?"

She looked at him with genuine amazement, then said, "Goodness me, no. Anne!" He started when her page appeared from around the other side of the bed; he had had no idea anyone else was in the room. "Anne will show you—it's in with the others over there." As Anne Gibson went to open the dresser, Mary said, "Do you want it? Have they lost all your handkerchiefs again? I can never work out where they disappear to."

He shook his head. He could now spy the shelves out of the corner of his eye and her piles of neatly folded linen were there for any servant to see. The little woman found the right piece on the instant and came over to spread it on the counterpane in front of him. The handkerchief looked expensive and well laundered; it in no way resembled a fervently mauled sentimental relic. He tried not to feel stupid as he posed the next question. "Why did you not give it back to him?"

She shrugged. "I never knew whether it was a loan or a gift. If it was a gift, then—you know the largesse of princes—I should have offended him by handing it back. But if it was a loan, I thought it better to give him something new in return, for then it could serve at Christmas. It occurred to me that Prince Rupert might have no idea what a fuss we make at Christmas—we must be the only people in the kingdom who do—and he might bring nothing for anyone, which would embarrass him. So I could not give him a *true* gift in case we embarrassed him even more. Therefore the handkerchief was a perfect choice. Or so I thought. Do you disagree?"

Faced with this defense, James could only choose to go on the attack again. "And what about his present to you?" She raised her eyebrows, and he continued, "Was there a message in it?"

"Yes, on the first page. You read it, as did everyone else, I recall."

"And apart from that?"

"He gave me nothing beyond what you may see if you open the volume. It's in the bookcase in the great chamber, next to your Cruso and Ward."

"Do you know why I ask these questions?"

"Yes, you seem to be wondering whether Prince Rupert"—she searched for the phrase, just as he had done all morning, and came up with his identical choice—"may be paying court to me."

"And is he?"

She smiled. "If he were, I should say he would be tragically hampered by the fact that he is very fond of you."

"And I of him," he said without thinking.

"Do you have any further questions?" she said, picking up the Milton.

"No. I should much prefer something franker and more forth-coming on your part, madam."

Her page was still bloody there, folding up the handkerchief to replace it in the dresser. He was at the door when Mary's voice reached him across the room. "James." He turned, and saw that she was leaning from the bed and holding out her hand. "Come here. I have something to say to you." The page moved out of his way as he returned. Mary took his hand and looked up into his face, her gaze deep and troubled. "James, I am yours."

The words pierced him, but he just released her fingers, bent and kissed her forehead. When he was at the door again he turned and said, "I'm afraid you are too clever for at least half the world."

She gave a little laugh. "And a deal more innocent than the other half, I fear."

Standing in the great chamber, James wondered for an instant whether both might be true—and both at once. Irresistibly, he took the Shakespeare out of the shelf and flicked through it, then put it back.

Whatever the state of events, he had a right to depend on the prince's honor. And he had always believed he could depend on hers.

Alone in the bedroom, Mary closed the Milton and rested her hands on it to still them. "I am yours"—those words to James were true. Despite the turmoil that Rupert caused her, she had not broken her marriage vows to James. Nonetheless speculation had begun, and just where it would hurt most cruelly, in her husband's mind. If James ever came to believe that anything were going on between her and Rupert, it would destroy his happiness and his future. She had always been able to depend on James, and she willingly repaid his devotion with the duty he merited. But if the king and the court became convinced that she and Rupert were having an affair, James would be humiliated before everyone who now honored his lofty position and his integrity. Worse, her husband's great services to the king would be rendered useless, for the king and queen would banish Mary in fury and suspicion, and James himself would be unwelcome in the king's presence, tainted by association with his faithless wife.

Mary forced herself to think through the king's every possible reaction. They were all dire. Charles would view an illicit union between Mary and Rupert as a threatening alliance forged right under his nose. The king was a faithful and devoted husband and knew James to be equally bound to Mary; he would be horrified if he thought she was an adulterer; he would be indignant on James's behalf, shocked by her sinfulness and effrontery; and he would never trust either her or Rupert again. The queen would feel deeply injured to think that Mary was in close, secret collusion with Rupert, for she would at once look back on Mary's behavior in the Hague, decide that this was an affair of long standing, and conclude that she herself had been shamefully used.

The king and queen would look with angry hostility on such an affair, because in anyone's eyes it would stand far, far too close to the throne. Mortified and furious, Charles and Henrietta-Maria might suspect Rupert and Mary of some conspiracy. Here, to make things worse, Mary genuinely had something to hide . . . her correspondence with Essex! What if it also came to light that she had let Parliament know of the king's attempted arrest of the Five Members in London? And her second note, calling for reconciliation before Rupert reached England again, named Rupert himself. Charles might well be driven to demand Rupert's arrest and her own—for a plot by the king's nephew and his adoptive daughter, designed to betray the king into shameful capitulation to Parliament . . .

Unable to sit still, she sprang from the bed. She must set James's mind at rest, and kill suspicion wherever else it might lie. Her marriage and position—even Rupert's life and hers—might now depend upon her discretion and courage.

The news from Bristol came to Oxford while Mary was with the queen and her ladies at Merton. It was brought by Henry, Lord Jermyn, commander of the queen's life guard, a handsome gentleman of about forty who made little secret of his admiration for the queen while keeping his behavior strictly within the bounds of chivalric decorum. It was just the kind of situation that Henrietta-Maria liked—brought up in a court where sexual worship was refined to the pitch of art, she had in the past found the English court lacking in imagination and verve. She now had the king back in her bed and was relishing a time of gratification and fresh enjoyment of her womanly powers. Lord Jermyn knew just how to play up to her without hinting that he was anything but a servitor trembling beneath her heel.

Mary had already seen all this without disparaging either the queen or Jermyn, both of whom behaved blamelessly. Indeed, she had been even more inclined toward Jermyn than the queen, for he was a staunch supporter of Prince Rupert.

When Jermyn first begged an audience and was shown up to the queen's apartments, Mary, with so many other things to worry about, felt no suspicion of what he came to convey. They were all in Henrietta-Maria's favorite room, perched above Fitzjames Arch in the middle of the college buildings. It had two handsome windows on each side, looking down from one set into the Front Quad and from the other into the Fellows' Quad, and the bright day outside filled the wood-paneled room with warmth.

"We are so cozy here," the queen said, "that I have no heart to move to the reception room. We shall let Lord Jermyn see us in all our disarray."

He arrived, smooth, diligent and eager with the news, which he had begged permission to bring to the queen. Dispatches just received by the king reported that Bristol had fallen and His Majesty's forces now held the port, its cannon, fourteen merchant ships and four parliamentary ships, which had transferred themselves to the king's side.

"And treasure?" Henrietta-Maria cried, "is there treasure?" For a year, the raising of funds had taken first place in the queen's mind. But even with her new, fearful caution, Mary could scarcely prevent herself from drowning out her mistress: *And Prince Rupert?*

Jermyn looked slightly bemused at the question. "I believe there are one hundred thousand pounds in specie. And under the terms of surrender the defenders have pledged to raise a further one hundred and forty thousand in return for the city's not being sacked."

"Prince Rupert would never have sacked it," Mary said involuntarily.

"And why not?" cried the queen. "What else do they deserve?"

"At any rate," Jermyn continued, "Colonel Fiennes and his commanders were permitted to leave with their arms and possessions but the troops were required to walk out without their weapons."

"You have not told us whom we have lost," Mary said in a low, trembling voice.

He threw her a look of genuine sympathy, and she warmed to him. "Around five hundred of ours have fallen. Amongst them"— he looked nervously around the room, hoping he could begin the recital without causing cruel grief—"are a Lieutenant Colonel Moyle and one of General Belasyse's colonels named Henry Lunsford, shot through the heart. General Belasyse himself is wounded, but expected to live." There were exclamations, which interrupted Jermyn for some time, but he continued, "Prince Maurice lost two of his colonels, Slanning and Trevannion." Here he looked hesitantly at Mary and went on with gentle regret, "And I am most sorry to tell you that William Villiers, Lord Grandison, fell in the first assault."

Mary looked at him, a hand to her throat. "He was a valiant man," she managed to say, then sat down on a nearby chair and bowed her head. There never seemed to be a battle in which either she or James did not lose one of their family.

"And Prince Rupert?" the queen said at last. Crushed now by sorrow and fear, Mary turned away to the window, her hand against one of the diamond panes.

"His horse was shot from under him in one of the attacks, but he was not wounded." Mary gave a gasp but Jermyn's voice went on. "The battle was a close-run thing. Apparently the prince predicted it would be, and warned the council of war, but they supported him wholeheartedly. I believe one of Prince Maurice's officers reported: 'Rupert's very name was half a conquest.' "

The queen, who had heard of her husband's fraught council of war before Edgehill and evidently felt him slighted by the comparison, was not pleased with this. She said in her best mode as Generalissima, "To whom do we owe our thanks for making the first breach in the enemy's position?"

"I think that would be Colonel Wentworth, madam."

"His Majesty and I will ensure that he receives the honors he deserves."

"Oh!" Mary turned. "It was Prince Rupert who led your armies into Bristol!"

"And it is my husband who is captain general of them all," the queen flashed back. "If he had been there, the outcome would have been the same. If not better. How many prisoners were taken?" she said to Jermyn.

"That I cannot say, I'm afraid, madam. But a large part of the Bristol garrison has come over to us."

"Ah!" The queen clapped her hands. "So will the country. So will the country when Parliament at last learns its lesson." She thought for a moment, then said exultingly, "We do right to show force. I have been right all along in that respect, and my husband is resolutely of my opinion."

Mary bowed her head again and closed her eyes. Rupert was alive and she must thank God for his safety. To ask more of fate was surely blasphemous.

At home that night, repeating the whole report to James, Mary had the relief of mentioning the outcome at Bristol without causing the constraint that had lingered between her and her husband for days. It was banished by her account, by the further detail that James was able to give her from the dispatches that had come to the king, and by their sad talk of her cousin Grandison.

She relayed to James the queen's callous remarks about the battle for Bristol. "It was almost as though our losses meant nothing to her as long as we had victory. I am afraid of her attitude."

"I know what you mean. I noted her new belligerence the moment we met her in Stratford-upon-Avon. Before, the king was amenable to discussion on military matters. Now he seems convinced that anything but absolute firmness is beneath his dignity and courage."

"But firmness about *what*? The options change from day to day. All he seems firm about is not ever talking to Parliament."

James smiled. "Do not despair. Try for a balanced line of argument. You would be of just as much harm to him as the queen if you tried to push him down some abject road of conciliation. If he is to bargain, it must be from a position of strength."

"That is just where he now is. Bristol is a clear triumph: the king has secured a major port, the core of a new navy and safe passage for his armies to Wales, Devon and Cornwall."

"The last is perhaps a little exaggerated. But you are becoming as keen an amateur strategist as I. I wonder why," he said somewhat wistfully.

She looked at James's pale, composed face, and allowed herself to see what a change she could wreak in his expression merely by pronouncing the words "Prince Rupert." And what of James's heart, which she feared to know? She had the power to hurt this man who for all their marriage had surrounded her with warmth, protection and seamless tolerance. She held the weapons to tear his life apart. Nothing but catastrophe or exposure could ever justify her using them.

She continued in a detached, speculative tone, "And *I* wonder whether the king is not too obsessed by Parliament on this matter. He has rejected its commissioners, but could he be persuaded to talk to Parliament's Lord General?" James raised his eyebrows incredulously but she pushed on. "Parliament may not be able to assess the king's present position firsthand. But the Earl of Essex can, and he is an honorable man. Might a royal overture be made to him?" The memory of her own two overtures to Essex made her catch her breath at this point, but James was too busy considering her remarks to notice.

Finally he said, "You are aware that one was made?"

"No!"

"After the Battle of Powick Bridge, Prince Rupert sent a letter to the Earl of Essex suggesting a challenge to bring the war to a close. Either a pitched battle—between equal forces, I presume—on Dunsmore Heath, or single combat between himself and the earl." He gave a sardonic smile. "A trifle medieval, perhaps. At any rate, Essex declined the challenge."

"What is the earl's currency with Parliament just now? Do we know?"

"It seems to vary. While he was hanging about, making forays around Oxford, we heard he was being labeled an idler in London. But after he captured Reading his stakes went up. I agree with you," he said unexpectedly, "that it's a possible avenue. But nothing can be done until the king holds a council of war once the prince gets back." He paused, evidently for Mary to ask when that would be, but she did not pose the question and waited coolly for him to go on. He gave her a look almost of gratitude and concluded, "We need Prince Rupert here. Only he can convince the king that he may have peace with honor."

Chapter 18

❧

PRINCE RUPERT DID NOT immediately return to Oxford—instead King Charles decided to go to Bristol. In his dispatches after the battle he had named Rupert governor of the captured city, but the prince wrote back soon afterward with a request for advice—Prince Maurice's superior in the west, the Marquess of Hertford, had simultaneously appointed to the post Sir Ralph Hopton, another of his commanders, and both these gentlemen were very discountenanced by the king's decision.

"Rupert does not seem concerned one way or the other about his own appointment," the king confided to the Duke of Richmond before he left Oxford, "but he has very properly not refused the governorship, no doubt in case he offends me! Sir Ralph lies ill in Bristol recovering from wounds. I have written to him that although I set the greatest value on his services, I cannot cancel Rupert's appointment."

"And what about the Marquess of Hertford, Your Majesty?"

"I believe I must see him in person and make sure no rift is caused by this . . . this misunderstanding. When I arrive I shall suggest to Rupert that he appoint Sir Ralph Hopton as deputy governor; I am sure he will think that the right solution, and it should please Hertford also if I present it in the correct light. I shall then be on the spot to hold a council of war about our next dispositions. I have received a great deal of advice already from the kind councillors around me in Oxford . . . with some tactful exceptions." He smiled at Richmond at this point because he was one of the rare gentlemen at court who had not taken a vociferous side. For Charles, escaping to Bristol to lay the issues before a well-disposed set of practical men would in some ways be a relief. "As you know, there are two possible plans for the immediate future. One is to consolidate the fruits . . . the fruits of recent victory and then march on London." James Stuart dropped his gaze here, in recognition of the fact that this was the queen's ambitious idea, and the king had no chance to guess what he thought of it. "The other plan comes from what I may call my . . . my military camp, and I set equal store by their thoughts. They lean toward capturing Gloucester, to safeguard what we have achieved in the west."

"Sire, there is a third choice, which can run concurrently with either of the first two—to reopen negotiations with Parliament while they are downcast by the loss of Bristol."

The king gave him an indulgent smile. "It is like you to remind me of all sides of the question, and I thank you. I hardly think it a policy my victorious nephew will think of advocating—but I can't be sure of that until I reach him."

James seemed about to say something more, then asked a question instead. "Have we received any notice from Parliament about the attack on the men of the garrison? I am anxious to hear that Prince Rupert has been exonerated—it would be a happy piece of news to take to him."

The king shook his head. "That affair is a blot on my nephew's triumph that can only be removed by Colonel Nathaniel Fiennes in his report to Parliament." Charles had been disturbed by the news: the defenders of Bristol had been permitted to march out of the city unmolested the day after it fell, but they left earlier than Rupert had ordered, and on their way out some of his own soldiers lost control and let fly with insults and weapons in an unprovoked attack on the column. It was some time before Rupert and Maurice were told what was going on, whereupon they and some officers drew their swords and rode into the melee to beat their men off. The king could just imagine Rupert's fury at the time—and only Nathaniel Fiennes could lift this imputation of dishonor, by stating that the attack could not be blamed on Rupert.

James looked disappointed. "When he writes to us he never mentions military matters; he writes almost as though he were going on a journey of pleasure. Except for the letter of sympathy we received from him concerning Lord Grandison."

Charles interrupted, much struck. "He finds time to send you such letters? That is true friendship."

"Yes," Richmond said quietly, "and one that I truly value. But he did mention this matter in his last. To me, it indicates how much it preys on his mind."

Charles nodded, then gave him an encouraging smile. "We will hear good news about this, I am certain. No one on either side can doubt Rupert's honor."

Prince Rupert came back to Oxford in August, but only on flying visits to the garrisons, which meant he hardly ever came to his quarters in the city. The king's council of war at the beginning of the month in Bristol had decided on an attempted capture of Gloucester, for which the king planned a conventional siege. With the death of Lunsford at Bristol, Rupert had inherited a regiment of foot to add to his regiment of horse and his 150-strong life guard, and he wanted to spend time on training. He had therefore declined to conduct the siege and this responsibility was handed to Patrick Ruthven, the king's field marshal at Edgehill, now Lord Forth. But such were the calls for Rupert's expertise that he spent almost as much time at the siege works around Gloucester as he would have if he had been conducting the operation himself.

Mary's first meeting with Rupert after his return from Bristol was in the queen's chambers in Merton, where a crowd of people including Lord Digby and the queen were talking away an overcast afternoon. The relief and joy of seeing Rupert and the tension caused by concealing this from everyone would have been too great for Mary to bear, but that she happened to glance down and catch sight of him when he first entered under the gatehouse from Merton Street and walked into the grounds. Breathless, she watched him approach across Front Quad, and once he was out of sight she had a minute or two to remain in the same position, her forehead against the pane, trying to make her heart beat less fitfully.

When he was announced, she knew he must have inquired who was present, because she could see the strenuous effort he made not to look her way. The welcome he received was courteous to the point of being effusive, but she wondered whether he noticed less affection in the queen's manner: Henrietta-Maria resented his not seconding her favored option of a speedy invasion of London, even though he had not come down for the Gloucester option either. Digby was his usual urbane self, though he had supported the queen's initiative—and then Mary forgot them all when Rupert turned to her.

"Pray do not move, madam," he said as she prepared to step

forward from the window. "You appear to too much advantage in that light. Allow me to give you my humble and most affectionate greetings." She murmured something as he bowed over her hand and squeezed her fingers. "May I exercise the privilege of a friend and join you where you were sitting?"

Lady Ann Dalkeith, who had been sitting with Mary, vacated her chair at once and withdrew, the prince thanked her graciously and he and Mary sat down facing each other, their profiles to the room and their conversation audible to almost everyone in it, should the people around them care to eavesdrop.

They talked at first of the death of Lord Grandison, and Rupert repeated the condolences he had sent in his letter. She soon turned him from the subject, however, because she sensed that his loss was greater than hers, for Grandison had been his friend. She asked Rupert therefore where he was most occupied (Abingdon) and he asked her what she had been doing in the last month (very little). He said at one point, "I have been most grateful for the duke's letters." After a pause: "I have received none in your hand."

She took a breath. This was one of the issues on which she had prepared answers, and she must produce one before they all fled from her mind. "My husband is the only fit correspondent for such matters. When I write I always feel I am descending into frivolities."

"I have received but one such from you—perhaps I am not the best judge."

"Oh, I am sure you have thrown it away long since!"

"No," he said very low, "it is not far to seek, madam." And he put his fingers quickly over his heart.

She gazed at him with consternation in hers, but the people within earshot showed no reaction to this—if they heard it, they must have thought it a meaningless gallantry. "I should much rather you took care to wear something of sterner stuff! I must hope you do, for during your absence we have heard dreadful things. They say a grenade exploded close to you at Gloucester. And a stone cast down from the walls wounded you in the head."

She could see at once that this reminded him of the first night she had been able to touch him, and her voice faltered. But his did not soften; rather there was a note of bitterness in it. "That's war for you. No account is ever on the mark. I receive a minor graze at Reading and someone is supposed to have crushed my head in at Gloucester. I suppress a riot of my own men at swordpoint and I am supposed to have put villages to the torch somewhere else—men, women and children all."

"Never mind," said Digby, who had been drawing nearer during the time they were talking, "all you can be accused of at the moment is sitting idle in Oxford."

Mary saw a flash in Rupert's eyes that she had seen but once before, on a bleak afternoon in Dover, and he shifted in the chair as though to rise. She stretched out her hand to his wrist, which Digby saw but she could not avoid. "My lord," she said in a bright, carrying voice, "this is *my* conversation. Rather than standing *idle* on the edge of it, why not add your scintillating mite to someone else's?" She looked up at Digby with a real warning in her eyes, and saw his widen in response. "And I must exact due apology for the interruption."

Digby looked from her to the prince, by no means inclined toward humility, but the queen glanced over and said, "My lord, do leave the duchess to her interrogation, we have need of you here on an equestrian matter. If ponies are allowed to be horseflesh at all." The queen disliked dissension during her afternoons unless she provoked it herself.

"My profound regrets," Digby said to Mary, just including the prince in his bow, and withdrew.

The prince looked toward the window and growled, "This is intolerable."

She said, "At least the calumny at Bristol has been reversed. Nathaniel Fiennes's testimony clears you—and I assure you, Your Highness, no one in the kingdom can be in doubt about that."

"Thank you," he said, still looking toward the window.

"Have you met my husband today? He has been expecting you at court for many days."

"I did. He very kindly invited me to see you both this evening."

"Just what we hoped for. And are you free?"

"Thank you," he said again, and her heart leaped. And then fell. There was so much to be said beforehand, and she had no idea how or where to say it to him. He seemed to catch her uneasiness, and gave her a deep, inquiring look.

She tried to deflect it. "How is Prince Maurice?"

He bowed slightly. "He is now general in the southwest. And engaged in the capture of Exeter and the remaining ports in Devon and Cornwall."

She gave him her warmest smile, quite free of restraint. On this subject she cared not who heard. "You must be so proud of him. What a pattern of valor your dear brother is."

He was too moved to answer, and indeed, the conversations around them became subdued for a moment in genuine respect.

"But in order not to sink us all in gravity," Mary continued, "allow me to return to the frivolous and fanciful. How is your inimitable trickster, Boy?"

"He is downstairs, awaiting your pleasure."

"Oh, I did not see him—" She stopped in confusion, which no one noticed but the prince. She said feebly, "At the gatehouse?"

He got to his feet. "Would you wish me to have him fetched, or would you like to come down? I had very little time to spare here anyway, so if you would care to . . ."

She rose at once. "What a good idea. Madam," she said to Henrietta-Maria, "will you permit His Highness's poodle to come up here and receive my greeting?"

The queen pouted. "He may bully the new puppy; in fact I'm sure he will. No, I don't think so. However"—she waved her hand vaguely—"you might have him brought up to the landing. But leave the door open or we shall be too stuffy in here."

"Then I shall take my leave, Your Majesty," Rupert said. His aunt received his farewells with elaborate grace, and one of the queen's pages was sent running down the stairs to bring Boy up from the gatehouse. The only person who gave Mary a speculative glance as she left the room was Lord Digby, but she guessed he was just trying to think up another clever remark about the prince's animals. They were able to walk away before his wit ignited.

She could not talk to Rupert about anything important near the doorway, so she began, "How does Boy weather this war? He must have run thousands of miles with you and put his head down in a hundred billets."

They reached the space near the top of the stone staircase and Rupert said, "He has voiced no objections so far. My greatest concern is finding reliable people to keep him indoors when he is not to come with me. But so far he has never got out." They were now out of earshot of the queen's room, and he continued, "Why could you not have come downstairs with me, madam?"

"We have so little time. I must be back in the queen's room on the instant."

"Why?"

She moved until she was at the top of the stairs and facing him, so that in order to speak to her he turned his back on the room beyond.

She tried to keep her face cheerful, but had doubts about her success. "You remember I told you how important it is to me that no one should ever question my faithfulness to my husband?"

"Yes. What do you mean?" His expression began to alter.

Just then Boy came racing up the stairs and skidded to a stop by executing a circle around them both, his claws clicking and scratching on the stone. She dropped to her knees and embraced the poodle about the neck while he panted eagerly in her ear.

The prince, watching from above her, said, "What is amiss?"

Her voice was muffled in Boy's woolly coat, but then she raised her face. "I never could have guessed that my husband might be the first person to have doubts."

Rupert went pale. "What, does he . . . ?" She was staring at him, desolated by what she was about to do, to herself and him. Boy shook himself out of her arms and sat down on the top stair. Intent on her face, Rupert said, "My God, he does not think the worst of me? He cannot!"

She rose slowly and unsteadily, brushing her gown. The page reappeared on the stairs below, ducked his head as he mounted to their level, and slid by. They waited in silence until he had gone back into the room, then Mary said very quietly, "No. With your every letter he becomes fonder of you and respects you more. No, it is me he watches. Or so it seems."

Rupert's voice was hoarse with the effort not to reach those within hearing. "What has he said to you?"

She shook her head. "Nothing to the purpose. But I will not feed suspicion. I will not give him that pain. Which means"—her throat constricted and she had to take a gasping breath before she could go on—"you and I cannot see each other in private."

"*Bon Dieu,*" he said, "we have never done so! Except here." He stamped his boot on the floor, making Boy jump up. He went on in the same low, intense tone, "Once, under this place, we met by accident. By the decree of fate. And because of that, you tell me I must not see you?"

"I didn't say we could not meet as we have today—"

"Today? God spare me from another meeting like this." He moved past her and took two steps down the stairs, then twisted back to look at her.

She said, "You need not come to us tonight, if it is beyond you."

"Oh, *certes* I shall come tonight. Ten thousand devils could not keep me away. My honor is at stake in this, madam, and so is your husband's." She could not reply or move away. His desperate look paralyzed her. After a moment he said, "But I must release you. Your minute away from your friends is well gone by."

This goaded her, but when she spoke her voice faltered on one word. "It seems you forget *my* honor. But I cannot. Even if to preserve it I must break my heart." She turned and walked away from him. It was all she could do.

James Stuart, while giving a warm welcome to Prince Rupert in his home that night, had the suspicion that His Highness might be under the influence of liquor, the first time he had seen him so. But after a few minutes James decided a little inebriation added something to his guest's charm, for it relaxed him. The prince had also brought his pet monkey, which he spared James from greeting, since the animal was anonymous and thus could never be introduced. He explained that apologies were due to the Duchess of Richmond, however, because she did not like monkeys.

Having greeted her impeccably, he went on, "What can I say? She escaped and came after me. Would you like her banished to the bookcase again? Your wish is my command."

Mary shook her head. "For a whole evening? That would be cruel. Do please take her to the chimneypiece and stand there for a while so I can get used to her at a distance."

He did so, waiting with one boot on the hearthstone and one arm along a groove in the carved mantel, looking at them both with a smile made somehow more engaging by the fact that the monkey was perched on his shoulder with her little head against his hair. "Thank you. She has been neglected of late—I've had no chance to play with her. She will behave—she is always overjoyed to be back with her own kind."

James laughed as the prince was handed a wine cup. "*Her own kind?* Your Highness, if you could see yourself standing there saying that, you would catch the absurdity!"

The prince shook his head and the monkey ran down to his free wrist. "But I can. She is my mirror." He turned his head and smiled at the creature, which went quite still and stared back, its lustrous eyes intent on his. The prince took a sip of his sherry and went on, "Have you never had that sensation with an animal, especially when you have been together for an hour or two, teasing each other and playing?" He released the monkey from his gaze and it began pulling at his lace cuff with its tiny hands, its slender tail twitching where it hung below his wrist.

"I can't say I have," James said, still laughing.

"Nor I," Mary said, taking a chair at a safe distance. "You will have to explain this unique sensation more clearly."

"Very well. You must be aware of the communion you can have with an animal. This experience comes when you have been alone with one, after playing with it for hours. I first had this curious conviction when I was a boy, and since then I have only known it with this little person. Suddenly there comes a moment when you look at it and . . ." He stopped, genuinely searching for the words, and James realized that he was not in the least joking. "I can only say, you suddenly look into its face, its whole being, and think, 'This is me. And I am this.' It is my impression that she feels the same. That I am of her kind."

"At that moment of wondrous union," Mary said in her lightest, most ironical tone, "do you thus feel yourself to be a great ape?"

He grimaced at her in mock anger and laughed. "I'm sorry, but I am serious, madam. It happens with this monkey, that's all. I daresay it might happen with something else."

"So it doesn't happen with Boy? You do not feel yourself to be a ball of white wool and he a madman of six foot four?"

James protested, but the prince laughed so much the monkey abandoned him and ran down his body to the floor and thus to a bookcase where it took up a position on the top shelf, chattering at them and showing white pointed teeth within its black lips.

"No," the prince said when he could catch his breath, "with Boy it's love."

"Oh," Mary said. After a pause: "I could more easily imagine that sense of identification happening with a horse, because when one rides, one feels part of the beast. And you spend most of your life thus."

"That is true, but we don't identify, nonetheless. With horses it is also love."

"You must have hated losing that magnificent stallion at Bristol," James said, and with a pang he thought of all his own beautiful Barbary horses at Cobham Hall, now in the hands of Parliament.

The prince bowed his head and said, "But to lose men . . . there is no comparison."

During the meal the monkey remained a theme, since rather to James's surprise Mary allowed the little creature to the table. It did not snatch at the viands but stayed by the prince's plate, looking from one person to another, and would only accept food from the prince's fingers. He would murmur something, hold out a morsel, and one tiny hand would come out to snatch it while the monkey turned its white-masked face once again to each of them, then neatly devoured what it was given, its tail draped in nonchalant fashion over its shoulder.

"*Liebchen, petite tête*," the prince said to it at one point, "I think that's enough."

Mary was wearying of this, James rather thought. She said, "Do you ever run out of endearments? You must have uttered more than a score in the last five minutes."

The prince raised his eyebrows. "I cannot, one requires a battery of them. If I repeat myself, she stops responding and then sulks."

"Oh, what nonsense."

The prince sighed, put down his knife and beckoned the monkey closer by running his finger along the table toward his plate. "*Viens, mon amour.*" The animal advanced hesitantly. "*Mange, mon amour.*" He picked up a piece of fruit and held it out. "Here it is, *mon amour.*" The only response on the monkey's part was to back away a little. "*Mon amour,*" he said even more softly, and all at once the creature spun round, ran to where a table napkin lay on the board and coiled itself underneath.

James and the prince laughed at this, and at Mary's discomfiture. After a moment she smiled and said, "Do you take her with you to Gloucester?"

The prince shook his head. "Gloucester is no laughing matter."

After a moment Mary continued, "I don't know whether you are aware, but while you and the king have been absent at the siege, the queen seems to be growing uneasy. I would almost say she is a little jealous of your influence with the king."

A look of irritation passed briefly over the prince's face. "Except that I take my orders from him. So the influence is in the opposite direction."

"Precisely," Mary said with tact, though James could tell she thought the prince's remark disingenuous. "I wonder whether it might set her mind at rest if you could persuade His Majesty to take a day away from the siege and come down to see her? Then she could play the Generalissima with him to her heart's content, and have him to herself for a while."

"As a matter of fact I was thinking of just that," the prince said. "I shall try to arrange it for next week."

James said, "Her Majesty is more inclined than before to tender advice to the king and make comments on the conduct of the war. She is trying to help, but there is already a pettifogging crowd of others doing the same thing."

The prince shrugged. "That is inevitable in a war that has gone on as long as this one. It always happens so. People at every level, not just the military, begin to say, If only this had happened then, or that had not happened thus, we would be doing better. And then it becomes—If only this person had not done that, or that person had been allowed to do this, we would have won by now. If you happen to be fighting the war yourself, all you can do is not listen to such trash." Seeing that they were both slightly taken aback, he went on, "With a siege like Gloucester, the situation is very clear before you. The enemy is inside and you are outside trying to get in. If someone says to you, We should do this, you have only to point to the town and say, Go and try it; do you think you would succeed? Easy. They can work it out for themselves, and if their idea is of no use they shut up. But in a campaign, or a series of battles, or a long war, the situation is not so clear. Not only that, people's memories play tricks and they accuse each other about the past. For instance, I might say that we should have seized the opportunity to take London the moment after we punished Essex at Edgehill. But we did not, and it serves no purpose to discuss that. What I want to do is smash Essex next week and enter London the week after. *That* is talk I will listen to."

"I'm so glad," Mary murmured, "that we get to listen to it too."

He started, then grinned at her. "*Ach*, was I shouting?"

"I suppose we must forgive you; you have so little opportunity."

He laughed at this, and the rest of the evening passed very cheerfully. During it, James backed Mary up at least three times over her idea of Rupert bringing the king to Oxford the following week.

When the prince left, considerably the worse for drink than when he had arrived but still in amiable control of himself, he took a hand of each at parting. "You are my greatest friends. May nothing I do ever be unworthy of you."

Mary was alone with the queen reading poetry. Her Majesty had had the megrim for two days and was just recovering, and did not want noise around her. The college was still and quiet, basking under a blue sky, and if the queen felt better in the afternoon she planned a little drive in the pony cart, which the highly flattering Lord Jermyn had now taught her to drive, after much teasing and laughter.

"He turns himself inside out for you," Mary said as she looked up from a volume of Andrew Marvell, "to such an extent I would fain laugh at him sometimes. But I thought when he handed you down the other day, he managed to look almost as though he were genuinely in love with you."

"But of course he is! There would be no fun in it if he were not! What suggestion is this, Mall; do you think I am losing my powers?"

"No, but I wonder how long he can prolong this mighty attachment without a response of some kind."

The queen smiled. "This is wicked of you, you know, very wicked. But you are not saying anything is to be done about it? He *must* suffer in silence, after all."

"Ah, but he does not: think of the poetry he quotes on occasions. Casually, as though it has just slipped into his mind, though we know he must have conned it the night before."

The queen laughed. "The effort is commendable, I grant, but the tone does not suit him. He is too manly; I can scarce control my mirth sometimes."

"And the flowers he brings you, for nothing but a smile in return. What do you say to a poem in reply?"

The queen sat up, her headache gone. "Mall! What wickedness is *this*?"

"Left in his way anonymously and addressed to 'A Gentleman.' Or 'A Beauteous Gentleman,' if you prefer."

The queen's eyes sparkled with the scandal of it. "Beshrew me, it is too dangerous a trick. And ten to one there is not a verse that would do for him, search how we might."

"Possibly. But I might write it. And he would be bound to suspect that it came to him at your bidding. And he could never, never acknowledge it, but we should have such fun seeing whether he tries. Think if he tried to do so *in verse*! For it would have to be his own; he cannot poach others' forever."

The queen got up and began to walk about the room, twisting a ruby bracelet around her wrist, her bright gaze on the floor. "Oh no. But it's too delicious. It would have to stay between us two, we could never *possibly* . . ." Then she stopped. "It could be addressed to him by his initials."

"Or reversed, for greater mystery: 'To J.H.' "

"Oh no, still too obvious. What about J.G.?"

Mary shrugged. "Would he realize it was meant for him?"

"Anyway, we don't have the poem," the queen said. "I don't know why we tease ourselves about it."

"What would you say to this one?" Mary pulled a piece of folded paper from her copy of Marvell and handed it over.

The queen gasped, then opened it at once. "It is not in your hand!"

"No," said Mary dryly. "I rather thought it was better so."

"And you have had it all along. You wrote it especially for me— to make me laugh? What a funny, mischievous creature you are!" She held up her hand to declaim. "Let us hear the effect."

Dear object of my love! Didst thou but know
The tortures that I daily undergo
For thy dear sake, thou sure wouldst be so kind
To weep the troubles that invade my mind;
I need not tell thee that I dearly love,
No, all my actions will my passion prove:
For thee I've left the wise, the great, the good,
And on my vows, not my preferment, stood.

"Oh, this is so clever. *Not my preferment*—just so. And there is more!" The queen turned the page and her eyes sped downward. "Madam, I am constrained to say, this is *very good.* Is it even too good for sad Lord Jermyn?" She gave Mary a piercing look. "Or are you mayhap in love with him yourself?"

"I will swear on anything Your Majesty cares to name that I am not in love with Henry Jermyn."

Mary looked at the floor as the queen read on, her heart beating painfully. Alone the night before, she had at last written about Rupert, in an outpouring of love and longing that left her sleepless until dawn, whereupon she had had Anne copy the poem out as part of her collection and then burn the original. Showing it to her queen like this had but one purpose—to turn Her Majesty's sharp eyes away from anything she might have noticed on the day Rupert visited Merton. If Henrietta-Maria thought Mary secretly attracted to Henry Jermyn, she could not possibly guess her lady-in-waiting's most dangerous secret.

"I like this," the queen remarked. *"Since first thy courtship me to love inclined, Thou ne'er hath been one hour out of my mind."*

"I'm not sure it scans very well," Mary said.

"It does very well altogether. On all counts but one . . . I find I cannot bring myself to play such a jape on any gentleman—I have not your penchant for practical jokes. But will you leave it in my hands for a day or two, to enjoy at my leisure?"

Mary rose. "I regret, madam, if it is not to serve its purpose it is best hid with me, where it can do no one any harm."

With the slightest hesitation, the queen handed it back. Then she gave a teasing laugh. "But if I ever say 'J.G.' to you in company, we shall both know just what it means and no one else will guess! And I'm still not sure that those two little letters do not mean more to you than to me."

When Mary got home that evening she went to the dresser where she kept her gloves, locked the poem into the flat leather glove case and replaced it on the shelf. It had served its purpose: she had now written a love poem, after all Anne's urging; and the queen had seen it. As for herself, she could not bear to read it again. Writing had not healed her—it had made her loss deeper. And she had not written it to give secretly to Rupert; she knew now he was not a man for poetry, despite his ingenuity with the Shakespeare lines and despite his having kept her doomed, damaged poem about friendship. Even before she wrote this one, she vowed he would never see it. In any case, private communication between them was now unthinkable.

They were so different from each other, she sometimes wondered how they could be in love. But she knew Rupert believed they were—because he made distinction between love and that state which he had tried to explain, in which another being could correspond to oneself like a mirror image. Love was between unequals and required the powerful link of passion to draw them together. Whereas the identification of soul to soul happened by looking into the other's eyes and accepting: *I am this; this is me.*

She wondered, if she had ever had the chance to look deep into Rupert's eyes—for hours, he had said—whether by some otherworldly dispensation she could have become the mirror of his soul and he of hers. Would such an act mean renouncing love, or going beyond love to seek another union of perfect equals? She felt afraid when she thought about this, with an almost religious dread.

Part Three

*Fondly men say the world doth move
By love's command; for simple love,
Alas, is subject unto fate.*

—EPHELIA

Chapter 19

THE FOLLOWING WEEK, RUPERT escorted King Charles into Oxford. The king had two things to look forward to: spending time with his devoted queen, and taking the Prince of Wales and the Duke of York out with the hounds—both boys had been looking forward to a few days' hunting and he would not disappoint them. Rupert had but one aim—he hoped to persuade the king to give full audience to three prominent peers: the Earl of Holland; the Earl of Bedford, who happened to be the brother of Lord Digby's wife, Lady Ann Russell; and the Earl of Clare, the brother of Denzil Holles, one of the five members whom Charles had tried to arrest in January the year before. These three noblemen were coming to Oxford together to submit to Charles—to renounce their former allegiance to Parliament and declare loyalty to their monarch. The king seemed disinclined to listen to anything they might have to say about Parliament, its aims, or future negotiations—despite their new vows to serve him, he found it hard to see them except in the guise of enemies—and the queen's reaction was similar. Amongst the king's councillors in Oxford, Digby was scornful about any advice his brother-in-law and Bedford's friends might have to offer. Secretary of State Lord Falkland and Sir Edward Hyde on the other hand both hoped that consultation with these powerful men might further the cause of peace. Rupert dreaded that the king, if he consented to see them at all, would afford them a poor reception, but he himself gave the earls a welcome due to their dignity and integrity.

When Rupert had accorded them a fit reception at Christ Church, he forestalled any refusal on Charles's part by conducting them to the audience himself. He remained in the room, but with no intention of speaking unless the king invited him to. As with previous audiences of this kind, the king did not call upon him.

Rupert watched, listened and ground his teeth. The earls' behavior was as respectful, accommodating and considered as if this were two years ago and they had been invited into the king's presence at Whitehall. They were qualified to give knowledgeable and thoughtful views on every aspect of the conflict, including the military, for in the first months of the previous year the Earl of Bedford, a close friend of the Earl of Essex, had been Parliament's General of the Horse. But Charles received them with a stiffness that during the exchange resolved into a cold resistance against any meaningful dialogue. He was letting them know, without equivocation, that he thought them unworthy of his attention and his time.

When Rupert conducted the earls downstairs again, he had trouble concealing a disappointment that almost amounted to shame. Perhaps they guessed it, because their farewells to him were especially gracious. He walked out into the quadrangle after they had gone and strode about alone, willing himself to calmness so that he could accompany the king and his two boys on the hunt, as promised.

When he returned indoors, he headed for the apartments of the Prince of Wales, but on a staircase he came across the queen. Henrietta-Maria paused at the top of the flight, gazed down at him for a moment with a fixed expression of displeasure, then swept past with her attendants, without uttering a word. For a second he stood quite still, a foot on each tread, to let a string of curses unwind themselves in his mind. She knew what he had tried to achieve this day, and it ran directly counter to what she had wanted the king to do. In fact Rupert knew she had tried hard to forbid her husband from seeing the three earls.

Nodding to the attendants on young Charles's floor, Rupert walked slowly to the prince's reception room, realizing that Henrietta-Maria's affection for him had gone. Indeed, it might fast be turning to active dislike.

He came to young Charles's open doorway and stopped. The prince was not within. Instead the Duchess of Richmond sat at a little table, idly stacking chess pieces in a box; she and the prince must just have finished a game. In that posture and with a pensive look on her face she looked for a moment almost girlish, despite the regal appearance set by her glowing russet gown and the elaborate combs, sparkling with diamonds, that she wore in her hair. She looked up on the instant, and in her amazement her hands opened to let the polished chess pieces cascade from her fingers.

He said, "I am in search of the Prince of Wales. He is already gone down to the stables?"

She nodded and rose to her feet.

"Then I have but two minutes." He gave a sardonic smile. "Twice what you last accorded me."

He would not take into account the evening spent with Richmond, but he waited to see whether she would. If she did, he would turn on his heel and go. But she lowered her eyes without reply, so he stepped into the room and went up to her.

"This is fate, again. Will you grant me your hand, my lady?"

She did so and he held it loosely in his own so that it lay cool and white across his hard palm. With the thumb and middle finger of the other hand he made a circle around her wrist and stroked it gently along her forearm to the elbow and down again, the smoothness of her skin awakening a tenderness that swept aside every other sensation caused by this worst of days.

She was devouring him with her dark blue eyes, but he looked down and murmured, "I dream of your hands. They come to me with the lightness of butterflies. They touch me everywhere. And wherever they come to rest, it is the same frisson."

He could tell by her shuddering intake of breath that she felt it too. So he bent and kissed her, holding the hand against his midriff until she extended the other and clasped her arms around his waist. The kiss was long, deep and rapturous, as though nothing could part them. Her perfume filled his head and throat and her warm body molded itself to his, yielding and demanding at once.

He broke the kiss and bent his head again so that his temple lay against hers. He closed his eyes and pressed her body to him with one hand and her head with the other. "I will never let you go," he whispered.

Then he unwound her arms and stepped back out of her reach. She gazed at him without moving, her breath uneven and her eyes wide and full of impossible yearning.

He gestured toward the open doorway. "I must go, before someone comes to seek me. I love you."

He left before she could say anything, knowing that if she did he would stay with her, and with his ill luck on this day they would be discovered.

He descended the stairs three at a time, but before he reached the bottom he came to a stop with one hand against the wall. For the first time, he had given her no formal greeting or farewell. She set store by such things. And for her, somehow, good-bye meant indefinably more than good day. But he could not go back.

Behind him, upstairs in the room, Mary sank down onto the chair again and bowed her head. She should have walked away from him, or insisted that he leave, but the words had refused to come to her lips. She had only held herself together by staying silent—a pitiful show of weakness after all the resolution she had promised herself. Under such self-imposed torture, day by day she could feel her resources ebbing away. And what might it do to him, if she could ever find the strength to reject him completely? It might drive him to despair—to a wild recklessness in battle that would take him to his death.

It was the eighth of September, and the Earl of Essex was enjoying Gloucester. It had been held by Parliament long enough for the regulation of troops and citizens to be second nature to the garrison commanders, his own fifteen-thousand-strong army was generously welcomed, and the comforts of life had been restored with admirable speed following King Charles's lifting of the siege and removal to Painswick.

On the instigation of John Pym, who had convinced Parliament that Gloucester should be relieved, the earl had spent more than a month on the march, bringing this newly coordinated force—the best trained in his career, he believed—out of London on a wide, punishing arc to the north of Oxford and out through Brackley, Stow-on-the-Wold and Cheltenham. It was his presence at this last town that had finally prompted the king to abandon the siege of Gloucester and regroup at Painswick.

It had been in many ways an exhilarating progress for Essex. He had had to put up with some harassment on the way by royalist cavalry, led at different points by Lord Wilmot and by Prince Rupert, but he had fended them off without having to give battle. And he was close to achieving his purpose, which was to have the king realize once and for all that he had no hope of taking London without dealing with Essex himself. The earl had the luxury of feeling that it was immaterial whether the king could muster a challenge against him, or whether he himself took the chance to complete his virtually untrammeled circuit and march back within the defensive perimeter of London. The point was made, whichever way he looked at it. But the old soldier in him could not help hoping, as he prepared to march out of Gloucester, that Prince Rupert would be of a mind to put an army in his path, as he and the king had done at Edgehill. And in this case, Essex told himself, the odds had shifted in his own favor.

When James Stuart got home at the end of a chaotic day he found Mary in the great chamber, rearranging books on a shelf. She turned to smile at him and he said, "I give you good evening. I also bring a good-bye, from Prince Rupert. He had to march to join up with the king; there was no time to bid you farewell, so he asked me to convey his regrets and his very best."

She went pale as he began speaking, and with each word became paler, until her face was white. When he had finished, he was chilled to see that she had to support herself against the bookcase.

"Sit down," he said without moving.

She felt her way to a chair and obeyed. Her eyes were glassy with horror. "He didn't say good-bye."

"He did. I have just conveyed that." His voice rose. "What do you mean?"

"He—" She shook her head; she could hardly speak. "We did not say good-bye together."

"What precisely were you wanting by way of a farewell?" His voice was loud enough to bring three startled servants to the door. "Get out!" he roared and they obeyed, stricken—no one ever shouted, screamed or wept in his house.

But she was weeping, her face frozen and great tears rolling down her cheeks. "He will die. He's going to die!" The last word was a shriek, partly muffled by her hands.

He stepped forward and pulled one wrist away. "Christ Jesus, what is this? Are you mad? What are you saying?"

She shook her head violently, her hair flying over her face. "I can't tell you—it's secret, I've never told it, otherwise—"

"You'll tell *me, now!*" His face was hot but his stomach was so cold it hurt. "By God, you'll tell me everything!"

She was sobbing hard and he let go her wrist, but he remained in front of her, his body a barrier that kept her in the chair, forcing her there as though into a confessional. After a moment she managed to say with desperate defiance, "You'll tell me it's wrong. A ritual—a spell, I don't know what. I don't care, it was my way"—she gave a gasp of grief and then bent forward, her hair brushing him as she pressed her hands to her sides—"my way of keeping people alive."

She frightened him, her agony was so deep and her voice so wild. He stepped back a few inches. "Control yourself. You may tell me. You must."

She slowly sat upright again, her face wet with tears and livid. He looked away and she said, "When my father left the house I used to kiss him good-bye on the lowest step. Not in the house, not in the garden—always on the step. Once I didn't run out fast enough and he was already in the street. I waited on the bottom step but he lifted me up and put me on the top one and kissed me there. And then he left me . . . and they killed him." She gave a strangled scream and covered her face again. "They killed him!"

Appalled, he put his hands on her wrists again but she twisted them out of his grasp and rammed her hands into her lap. "You wanted to know, so hear me! Ever since, whenever anyone leaves me, there is something I do to keep them from dying. It must always be the same. And now it can't be—" She stopped on a sob and shook her head again, and in his panic he thought that she might be mad.

But he kept his voice level. "If I qualified as *anyone*, I would know this ritual. Pray tell me why I've never observed it."

"No one is supposed to! I told you, it's a secret. It is *my thing*, it is *my bargain*—"

On a surge of revulsion and rage, he pulled her up from the chair. "This is insane, woman—this is blasphemy. You are talking like a witch!" He released her and brought his face close to hers. "What is it you do?"

"When I say good-bye, I make sure that I invoke the day we will meet again. I speak of it three times. It has to be three." He tried to think whether this was true in his case, but his mind failed him. She went on, "Then I go and touch the knife. And I say—"

"The knife?" His stomach shuddered. "What knife?"

"Come, since you demand it!" She grabbed hold of his sleeve

and with manic urgency led him, almost running, through the rooms, past more gaping servants who fell back before them. Anne Gibson was in the bedchamber but Mary hissed, "Anne, you may leave," then without pause let go James's sleeve and ran to a drawer and wrenched it open. She pointed with a shaking hand. "The knife that killed my father."

The shock was so great he almost vomited. He stood looking at it, one hand against the wall. It lay in the empty drawer, a rusted blade with a dark bone handle. "How in God's name do you have this? *Why?*"

"Charles got it for me. Long after the trial. I had to have it."

"A tenpenny knife wielded by a madman?" He put his forehead against his hand and groaned. Nothing she could say to him now would make any sense.

"A madman? That's what they said when they executed him. But how do I know? So you see, when I have said good-bye and talked of the future three times, I come in here and I take this knife—"

He snatched it before she could, and she screamed and lunged so that he had to back away before she slashed her hands on it. "Mary—"

"And then," she wailed, hysterical and terrifying in her pain, "I say *I have the knife. They can't kill him! I have the knife.* They can't—" And she collapsed onto the floor, gasping and shuddering so that her whole body shook.

All the servants appeared again at the door to see him standing in the corner with the knife in his hand and Mary lying racked with sobs in front of him.

He threw the knife across the room, put his hands over his face and said, "Assist my wife, if you please."

He heard them advance and pick her up and help her onto the bed. He heard her voice weaken to a whimper, and then there was the pad of feet as they brought things into the room, and at the bed there were endearments and soft coaxing words from little Anne. Only when silence came did he drop his hands.

Mary was on the bed with her face turned toward him, lying curled up like a child. One hand was at her throat, but the other lay open at the edge of the counterpane. Her eyes were open, watching him.

The others were still in the room but he went to the bed and knelt, and took her wrist and laid his cheek on her palm. "Mary," he said, "oh, Mary; what are we going to do?"

He said no more because he was crying too hard, but after a moment her other arm came around his neck, and she moved over to embrace him, and held his face against her breasts to stem the tears.

It was the sixteenth of September when word got through to the king's army that the city of Cirencester, taken by Rupert in the previous winter, had just fallen to the Earl of Essex; the parliamentary forces had left a garrison behind and were already on the move to complete their long and successful sortie back toward London. Rupert at once asked permission from the king for the army to go in pursuit, but Charles delayed his decision. Unable to remain inactive in this crisis, Rupert led the royalist horse to Broadway Down, six miles or so south of the king's main force, and then set himself to plan the series of movements that would allow him to catch up with Essex, force the earl to turn and give battle and, if Parliament's army could be defeated, open the road to London once more.

By six o'clock in the evening, Rupert had still had no decision from the king and it was raining—both of which had been more or less the case for the past few weeks. Ordering one officer and a page to accompany him, he mounted up and called for Crane, the colonel of his life guard.

"Sir Richard, where does His Majesty lodge tonight?"

Crane, his sodden hair stuck like a dark helmet to his scalp, lifted a weary face. "Your Highness, I regret to say no word has been sent to us."

"Fichtre," said Rupert loudly, making the page jump, "you mean the king's horse has no idea where the captain general is?"

"Your Highness," Crane said, "His Majesty has not sent the usual message of—"

"Gottverdammt," Rupert snarled, "we're supposed to be hunting Essex, not the king." And without a word to his escort he wheeled his big bay horse and headed off into the dark, back the way they had all come during the day.

It was purgatory, picking their way north again in the downpour. When they came upon a group of houses Rupert would stop and, still on horseback, kick at a door with his boot until someone opened up, and shout harsh questions at the sleepy person who stood gawping at him from the doorstep. He found that at this hour the farm people were either gathered around one candle in the kitchen or abed—the chances were that if the king was in one of the hamlets in their way, he and his staff would be the only people up and awake within miles.

So Rupert stopped tormenting villagers and pushed onward in search of a light. The king was probably lodged with the two commanders who had been with him since the siege of Gloucester—Lord Forth and Lord Percy, general of artillery. What Rupert felt like saying to them flooded against his back teeth and surged in his head. Then he saw a lighted window on the edge of a field and took his escort straight up to it.

Inside the uncurtained window, sitting at a table in a humble but well-lit room, the king and Forth were playing cards with Percy looking on.

Rupert dismounted, smashed on the door, pushed past the householder and guards within and flung open the door of the king's room to stand, dripping, on the threshold.

"Sire." He bowed. "The Earl of Essex is on the high road to London. If he reaches Reading he can defend it with ease, but if we catch up with him first, he can be brought to battle. May I repeat: I request permission to pursue him with the horse, without further loss of time."

"Now? Through the night?" The king, managing to look as though this idea were new to him, gazed at Forth and Percy, who gave their views in turn. Rupert listened to their first few words then, realizing they were talking nonsense in these circumstances, simply waited until they had finished and repeated his request.

The king, with another look around the room, finally said, "Granted. I think my Lord Forth has . . . has well expressed the risks involved, however. We shall send a thousand musketeers out in front of our advance guard to support you."

Rupert bowed again, thanked him, and then asked Forth for a map so he could show the king roughly where he hoped to be by morning. When Forth could not produce one, he did a quick sketch with a pencil on a piece of paper and took his leave.

On the way back the rain eased but the horses were still slipping in the wet. He keenly missed the black stallion, friend of
more than a year and a talented night horse. He looked over at
the young page, who had shown a nervous alertness throughout.
"You've kept your eyes wide enough. Could you find your way back
in this direction again?"

The lad started, then took a moment to think. "I could, Your
Highness."

"My God," Rupert said, "you're a prodigy! We'll make a scout
of you yet." He could see that the lad, though thrilled by the first
remark, was made even more nervous by the second. "When we've
been an hour on the march I'll send you back with someone to let
His Majesty know our position. Stick by me, please, until I give you
the message."

"I shall be honored, Your Highness." The lad's eyes were shining now. After a pause he said respectfully, "Am I to return to you,
Your Highness, after that?"

"No, lad, you'll move forward with the king's forces until they
meet up with ours." He gave him a sarcastic look. "So you'll have
my permission to play piquet."

Chapter 20

⁓◎

ON THE SEVENTEENTH OF September, Mary was walking along a fine gravel path between two rows of fragrant lavender with Sir William Harvey. Harvey had attended on Mary in the last week, but had suggested that after his next visit she take the air with him and ride out westward beyond the walls to Saint Thomas's Church, where there was a pretty nursery and garden of herbs established in the fields nearby. There was a magnificent Physick Garden sheltered behind high walls right next to Christ Church, but Harvey hoped she would profit more from exploring the new one.

It drizzled in the morning and threatened the expedition, but by midday it was fine and they rode out together with Mary's attendants, chatting comfortably all the way. She suspected that Harvey was glad to leave the debates at court behind, for they usually became nastier when the king was absent, and one of the most steadfast peacemakers, Secretary of State Lord Falkland, had left with the army and was fighting in the cavalry as a volunteer.

"Nothing like what you are used to at Cobham, as you see," Harvey said as they crunched down an alley bordered with basil. He was a short man, olive-complexioned, and she often thought that he would not look out of place in a painting of the physicians of the ancient Mediterranean. "We see here a fraction of what I have known cultivated elsewhere. But I took an interest in the nursery when I first arrived and these simples have the virtue of springing up rapidly. Now here"—he bent and fondled the soft leaves of a tall plant with its little daisylike summer flowers withered upon the stalks—"is feverfew. A new strain. You may remember the queen very kindly ordered it for me from the Abbaye de Royaumont in the Vexin, and it arrived in spring, long before she did. I should like you to take an infusion of the leaves twice a week." He smiled when Mary rubbed a leaf between her fingers, sniffed at it and pulled a long face. "Have no fear, you mix it with a little warmed wine and it's quite inoffensive—which possibly means it has no effect at all."

"I know better," she said, putting a hand on his arm. "Believe me, I shall be obedient." They walked on and she said, "I'm sure my husband wondered for a moment if I am not quite mad, and I have wondered myself on occasions. What do you think?"

He became very grave. "I am not used to jesting on such matters, so I must tell you at once I do not hold that view. Let me see." After a few paces he said, "I have observed that in women, such . . . moments as you went through are often related to the blood. Your courses are regular, abundant and painful, and you were in the midst of losing blood at the time—this alone can make you vulnerable to strong emotion."

"I wish there were something we could do about those," Mary murmured.

He shook his white head. "Nature dictates them, and for every woman they are different. You can be grateful that your courses are so regular and distinct, however. If you should ever miss one, it gives you an almost certain sign of conception."

There was a pause, then she smiled sadly and said, "Do go on, Sir William."

"Very well. You understand my methods by now, your grace— or perhaps I should say my lack of them. In a case like yours, you will receive no medical strictures from me. Let me give you a picture instead. We have established that your blood has the tendency to overheat—you are subject to occasional fevers." He seemed to expect some response to this so she nodded. "I shall not bore you with my own theories about the blood—they were published over a decade ago and they have yet to sway the world! Let us be conventional: if someone were to explain yourself to you in terms of the humors, he would say you were choleric."

She laughed. "Ah, you have me trapped there, for if I contradict you, you will think me angry!"

He shook his head, and asked her to sit down on a wooden bench by the path. "I myself am choleric: when my ideas crowd my brain they will not let me sleep and I pace the floor for hours until I get the better of them." They remained on the bench while the weak autumn sun coaxed the last perfume from a bed of bergamot behind them and a clump of late-flowering absinthe on the other side of the path. The garden stretched out around them, its orderly plots and pyramids of climbers bounded by pretty fences of latticed willow saplings that divided it from the church grounds beyond. Farther off, the stone church and tower looked somber against the pale sky.

"My ideas about you," Harvey said, "and you are to think of this as a picture—a picture that may be retouched at any moment, not a statue hewn in stone—is that you are somewhat of a choleric temper, but striving to appear sanguine. You perceive I do not question *why* you might be so, if indeed you are—I merely say how you appear to me. Because of this, you have the habit of concealing some of that hot-bloodedness you wish not to show. In this you are like all of us—every natural being strives toward balance. But for you, the weight of secrets may be too much to bear—it may lead to imbalance. What have you done with the knife?"

She gasped, the question was so shocking after his mild exegesis. "My husband has it. He says I may keep it, but it stays in his chamber."

"And do you agree with him?"

"Yes, I do," she said, looking at her hands.

"Why?"

"Because I don't want to see it ever again. I cannot use it anymore. It is in the open now; it serves no purpose."

He sighed and drew circles and crosses in the fine gravel with the toe of his riding boot.

She looked at him sideways and eventually said, "You think I keep too many secrets?"

"What do you think?" His black eyes twinkled.

She considered for a while and said, "Yes, that is possible. But everyone does. As you say, the world would start from its sphere if everyone screamed their thoughts at everyone else's heads at every turn."

He laughed. "Did I say that? I must try to remember the exact phrasing." He patted her wrist. "From childhood, your life has in many ways been one of show. And there is a liking for drama in your temperament that accords, if you will permit me to say so, with your spectacular beauty. You are at home in a crowd, and the crowd feels at home with you. Few people would imagine that your ebullience and radiance are maintained at the cost of concealing many wants and hurts that only you can know. My advice, and you are as free to reject it as we are to trample these humble weeds under our feet, is to reveal those wants and hurts from time to time to people who are close to you. You may be surprised how it will relieve you. And do not fear, my dear lady, that by doing so you will rip the fabric of the world from end to end."

"You mean I should be more frank with my husband?"

With a keen look he said, "There my adumbrations must give way to yours. But may I say this: I believe you are very fortunate in the gentleman with whom you spend your life."

Rupert was at the council of war called by the king on the evening of the nineteenth of September. Having snatched only a few hours' sleep in the last three days, he was swaying on his feet, but concealed this by propping himself against the wall of the room in the riverside town of Newbury, more than twenty miles south of Oxford, where the king had gathered his commanders.

If this exhaustion was the cost of having Newbury and their present dispositions for battle, Rupert was glad to have paid it. He had moved the horse at speed from Broadway through the night of the sixteenth and in the morning, riding with his advance guard, he had come across the long column of Essex's army, strung out on its line of march. Without waiting for the king's musketeers to catch up, Rupert had attacked the rear guard with his cavalry, their repeated assaults harassing and slowing Essex to the point where the earl withdrew the parliamentary army to Hungerford for the night. With the way clear ahead, Rupert pressed on by day, then drew his brigades together during the following night and in the morning led them straight into Newbury. Essex had sent troops of horse ahead to secure the town, along with quartermasters to find billets and food for his army; Rupert's cavalry put these to flight or captured them, and the citizens of Newbury were forced to give up to him all the stores and supplies they had been collecting for the parliamentary forces.

Now the king had arrived, and the royalist army was drawn up about a mile out of town, on low ground to the south of the River Kennet, camped across Essex's path. All they had to do was wait for the earl and his tired, famished, sopping wet forces to turn up.

"We are well fed and rested, gentlemen," the king was saying with a smile, "and we have laid a sturdy bar across the road to London that Parliament's army must now do its utmost to push aside. We stand between our enemy and Newbury: the question is, should we attack him at first sighting and sweep him away; or hold to our present position and leave him to make the first move?"

"Sire," said Sir John Byron, "we have outrun and outfoxed him so far—why wait for him to dictate the way we do battle?"

"I agree," Lord Percy said. "I am confident as to artillery—our reconnaissance of Essex's train tells us that he disposes of no more cannon than we do."

"Sire, we are short of powder and shot," Rupert put in. "In all other respects we are well found. If we delay launching our attack, we can bring down what we need from Oxford and Wallingford and lose nothing by it in the meantime."

The king looked thoughtful. "We already have significant reinforcements from Oxford—our foot now numbers eight thousand."

"Exzhactly," said Lord Forth, who had been drinking deep since arriving at Newbury—his normal habit in any town. "We have possibily fewer infantry than the enemy, but we are shuperior in cavalry." He turned his ruddy face toward Rupert and gave a throaty laugh. "Your Highness, I should have thought you would be for your own policy—to horse, boyzh, and at 'em!"

Rupert said, "My lord, if I had held to one policy for all military occasions I should not be alive tonight to listen to yours."

There was a heavy silence after this remark and Rupert instantly regretted it, for Forth was in many ways a friend. The old man turned even redder and looked to the king. The king, however, was gathering other views. "Sir Henry," he said with a smile to Wilmot, one of Rupert's best commanders but not quite his best of friends, "how well prepared is your brigade to take the battle to the Earl of Essex?"

"Sire, Parliament's cavalry are but knaves on horseback, while our men are of such nobility that we fear not the face or the force of any foe."

The king looked impressed by this pronouncement, but after reflection said mildly, "Sir Henry, you will no doubt be facing Sir Philip Stapleton. I might resent his being a thorn in . . . in our side since Edgehill, but I should not go so far as to call him a knave for it."

Having said his piece, Rupert saw no point in contributing to the rest of the discussion, which labored this way and that over the same ground for another quarter of an hour. In the end the decision was to preserve the status quo. The army would not occupy Newbury, but remain drawn up in north–south position below the river. The consensus was that Essex would approach parallel to the river, and finding them across his path would probably give battle in short order.

Rupert went back to his tent with his commanders, made sure the instructions went out, then sat down on his stretcher to think. What preoccupied him was the high ground about a mile to the south of their position, which he had had reconnoitered during the day to ensure it was empty of Essex's troops. Might the earl decide to move any of his force onto that high but fairly distant area?

At last he said, "Get me Sir Richard Crane."

Soon Richard came actually running—Rupert could hear his boots thumping across the uneven field. As soon as he pushed aside the tent flap, Rupert thanked him and then said, "Richard, the high ground. Tell me about it again."

He then realized that if he looked as tired as Richard, he must be a sorry sight, so he asked him to sit down. He listened carefully, though it was the third time at least that they had talked of this issue. "From here," Richard said, "it's a gentle slope up to that round hill you can see by daylight. The hill is part of a crest that curves away from us southward like this." Richard made a horseshoe shape in the air, tracing a flatter curve on the western side.

"Beyond that, what is the terrain?"

"On the plateau . . ." Richard considered a moment. "Hard for cavalry around the edges—too many little fields and hedges. There's a stretch of open ground within that called Wash Common. Further south it's more open again—Endbourne Heath."

"But he still might bring infantry up there," Rupert muttered.

Richard stared at him. "You mean tonight? Is that his style, Your Highness? I'd have thought it was more ours."

"Christ, and I've given you every reason to think so. Go and put your head down. I'll mull it over."

When his friend had gone, Rupert lay down fully clothed and closed his eyes to think. And fell asleep.

Five seconds later, or so it felt, he opened his eyes on daylight to see Will Legge standing beside him. He said thickly, "Oh, God. They're on the fucking plateau."

As he swung his feet to the ground, Will said in astonishment, "How do you know?"

"Because I just dreamed it." He put his face in his hands, took a deep breath, then let it out in a groan. "What have they got up there?"

"We can see two light guns on the hill, and the scouts have spied infantry on Wash Common—a tidy force, at least a brigade. The rest are advancing along the river flats."

Rupert remained with his head in his hands. "All right. He's going to try to weaken us from above by turning our flank, and if he can't push through to Newbury he's going to slip by and on toward London. Well, there's the answer we wanted last night—we'll have to attack him now on both fronts." He looked up. "Have the king informed I'm on my way."

They fought all day. Richard was right—the terrain on the plateau was diabolical for cavalry; and Rupert was right—Essex had chosen mostly infantry to occupy it. The main body of the king's army remained on the low ground to face a mighty tide of foot soldiers and one dazzling wing of the parliamentary cavalry. The king sent Sir John Byron up with two regiments to sweep the enemy emplacement off the round hill, and Rupert took the rest of the horse and a thousand musketeers in a great arc onto the heights to contest Wash Common, where he found himself pitched against Sir Philip Stapleton's cavalry and Essex himself, directing a solid operation from behind a phalanx of infantry. Rupert had artillery hauled up to the common and kept them hard at work sending volleys across the broken ground into the enemy advances, after which he led assault after assault into the same bodies of men, but although he and the horse beat Stapleton's cavalry back into the bewildering patchwork of fields around the rim of the common, they could never make a gap in the hedges of pikemen, behind which the enemy horsemen managed to take refuge when the going got too hot.

Rupert had no idea what was happening down by the river or even near the round hill, from which the enemy standard still flew.

It was like a chess game where someone had thrown one dark glove down to conceal half the board.

At one stage he paused with his officers to grasp what he could about what was going on, when a lone enemy horseman shot forward, bore down on them at speed and fired a pistol shot so close to Rupert that the shoulders of their horses almost collided. There was an almighty clang in Rupert's ears, his mount shied and he swayed from the saddle, his ears ringing so that for a moment he had no idea whether he was on horseback or on the ground. Pulling himself up straight, he saw the others plunging around him and Richard Crane pursuing the horseman across the field toward a high hedge.

"Sir Richard! *Halte!*" he roared, and Crane reined in as the rider leaped the hedge with insouciant elegance and disappeared from view.

Rupert pulled off his helmet and found a dent the size of a quail's egg in the top of it. "It glanced off. Sir Richard!" He beckoned with his arm and Crane rode reluctantly back. "It could have been a trap, man!" he shouted at him as he approached.

"No, it wasn't," Crane growled. "You know who that was? Sir Philip bloody Stapleton."

"Well, aren't you glad you didn't shoot him in the back? He missed: that's punishment enough for a gentleman of his caliber."

It went on until nightfall. Again and again Rupert gathered his troops and led them into a charge across the maze of fields, but the horses, weary and hard driven, lost their footing more often in the holes and hollows in the ground, made more mistakes at the hedges, fences and ditches that divided the fields, and at last felt their strength fail them as they ran, foaming and sweating with terror, at the glittering barriers of pikes.

In the dark, having fought themselves to a standstill, the two armies drew back a little to take stock. Essex dominated the round hill. Rupert had pushed the enemy troops to the edge of the plateau. The king's men held the low ground and Newbury was untouched. The Earls of Carnarvon and Sunderland were dead. And Lord Falkland, the brave Secretary of State who had volunteered for this expedition, was missing. He was last seen amongst Sir John Byron's brigade, putting his horse through a gap in a hedge raked by musket fire from the other side. Rupert had a messenger escorted through to Essex, requesting news of Falkland, and it came back within a short time, courteously and regretfully worded: the earl had been killed in that very spot.

When the king gathered his commanders to decide on the outcome of the day, Rupert stayed on his feet to deliver his verdict: the king's army was virtually in its position of the morning and Essex had suffered just as much as they; therefore he should be engaged again at first light while they had him in a state to be brought to heel. Rupert then sat down to listen to the others, his elbows on his knees and his gaze on the ground. The thousand shocks of the day still hammered along his limbs and thudded in his veins, but his mind was in the alert and exalted state that battle wrought, and he had no trouble following the tenor of the meeting, which was for withdrawal. Back and forth the opinions went, then the decision sliced into him like a cut to the flesh that he was almost too battered to register. The king and the army would move out through Newbury and march back to Oxford.

When everyone had gone, Rupert rose and said, "May I respectfully request permission to pursue the Earl of Essex's rear guard, sire?"

The king stared at him. "Rupert, I—"

"I can bring together a few troops of horse tonight, and be after the enemy tomorrow as they move out. There is no doubt where they will be heading. Having failed to take Newbury, the next garrison on their march is Reading."

"Rupert," the king said again, then stopped. There was a long moment while his eyes filled with admiration, regret and unparalleled affection, then he said quietly, "Permission granted. And God speed."

Chapter 21

~⚬~

ON THE MORNING AFTER the battle of Newbury Rupert ambushed and defeated a party of Essex's retreating troops near Aldermaston. He sent a detachment under Sir John Boyes to garrison Donnington Castle just outside Newbury, for it was on the highway to London and provided a stronghold for communication and resistance when the parliamentary forces moved that way again, as he knew they would. Donnington would also serve as a dungeon for the prisoners he had taken in the ambush, and he sent his quartermaster back to arrange for his own lodging in the village overnight.

As evening fell, he was standing in the road watching some of his officers strip the prisoners of their arms and possessions, pile the weapons and gear into a commandeered cart, and form the men into a column to be marched into Donnington. Rupert had dismounted, since fatigue threatened to paralyze him and he found it just possible to stay awake if he was on his feet. He wanted to form some more ideas about Essex's troops by examining the prisoners.

He held out his hand to one of the foot soldiers. "Your helmet, if you please." The man relinquished it, with an incredulous look that showed he knew who Rupert was. Rupert examined it and tossed it into the cart. "You're well equipped. Which company?"

"Fourth company, Colonel Skippon's regiment, Your Highness," the man said, looking around him as if not sure which way up the world stood. "But," he added stoutly, "I've been a soldier of the Blue Trained Band for nigh on three years."

"London, that is?" There were six London trained bands, named for their colors. When the man nodded, Rupert surveyed the prisoners in a long, comprehensive glance. "You fought well yesterday. The Earl of Essex seems to have pulled you all together with a mighty hand."

"That's due to Colonel Skippon, Your Highness. At the very

beginning he said to us: 'Come, my honest brave boys, pray heartily and God will bless us.' "

Rupert bit back a piece of sarcasm and extended his hand again. "The pistol you have hidden in your sash." Handing it over, the soldier grimaced and began turning out his pockets. "Leave those alone, man, you'll want all your coins where you're going. But I'll take that"—and he pointed to a piece of paper that the soldier held bunched in his fist. "Another pamphlet, is it? Give it here. We need those to wipe our arses on."

The man stepped back and closed his hand more tightly around the dirty scrap of paper. An indefinable look crossed his face—nervousness, embarrassment, perhaps even shame. Rupert gave a rasping laugh. "Whatever you have there, I've seen worse. If it's an infant on a spit, I have a hundred of them. Hand it over." He turned his head and, seeing that the column was at last ready, nodded to his officers. "March on."

He stood in the road, the big bay's reins looped over his arm, opened the paper, and the countryside spun around him so that he had to put a hand to his horse's neck to stay upright. The pamphlet contained no pictures, for it had no need of them; the sanctimonious phrases about the lewd obscenity and lust that prevailed in the royalist high command were only too descriptive. The printed paper contained a detailed condemnation of the adulterous and blasphemous union between Prince Rupert of the Rhine and the Duchess of Richmond.

He remounted and without a word rode with his officers through the countryside to the village. There they conducted him to his billet, a cottage in the main street inhabited by a woman and two children—his bed was apparently upstairs under the thatch. He strode in to see the table in the front parlor laid with drink but no food, and walked straight into the kitchen, where he surprised the woman at a fire that had been lit but minutes before. There was not a morsel of a meal to be seen in the pots or on the filthy table. He shouted something and the children screamed and hid behind their mother's skirts. Three of his men came rushing in and the woman took the chance to bolt for the back door with her brood and escape to her neighbors'.

"What do you call this?" he roared at the stunned faces before him. "Lodging? It's as cold as the backside of hell. Who else is idling about here, perdition take them?" He drew his sword, pounded upstairs and scoured the rooms above, scaring the daylights out of an old man, who tottered squealing down the stairs with the sword-point in the small of his back.

"Get out!" Rupert yelled at the hapless group who were now tumbling out of the front door. "If you can't do better than this, ten thousand devils take you, and if any of you shows his hide here tonight I'll do the devil's work for him."

He slammed the door after them, let the sword clatter to the floor, shot one of the bolts home and stood there shuddering with fury, his forehead against the damp, slimy timber.

Then he went back to the table in the parlor, pulled up a stool and emptied the first draft of execrable liquor down his throat. But for an hour it seemed to have no effect. Exhausted beyond thought, he had equally gone beyond sleep, which refused to conquer his brain.

Mary Villiers stood pilloried before the nation. He could not bear to read the pamphlet again but the calumnies and ordure that had been thrown at her resounded in his brain. When the single candle burned down, the heaviest words came at him like missiles out of the darkness.

The enemy troops would be making up songs about her and roaring them out over the tables when they got drunk. He remembered a tavern song, from when he first came to England, that proposed an obscene toast to every great courtier in the land. One verse he remembered was about Mary's aunt, first lady to the queen, and her late husband, the Earl of Denbigh—the gentleman who had received a mortal wound at Birmingham.

> *A health to my Lady Denbigh*
> *that's groom o' the stool to her grace*
> *and to my Lord her husband*
> *whose nose has fired his face.*

And another:

> *A health to my Lady of Kent*
> *with her fat bouncing cunt*
> *and to my Lord her husband*
> *that fucks my Lady Hunt.*

Oh, God, what were they mouthing about the Duke and Duchess of Richmond? It was abominable; he could summon no perspective—he just felt himself sliding further and further under a heap of dung.

The resistance of his brain notwithstanding, the amount he had drunk finally had its effect on his stomach and he ended up doubled over in the dank little yard outside, desperate with every heave to expel the phrases that Parliament's men had hurled at him and Mary. But they stayed at the back of his throat, burning like acid.

Staggering back inside, he fumbled the step and fell in the kitchen, where blackness at last roared over him like a wave. They found him there in the morning.

Mary was in Magdalen Grove with the queen, days after the army returned to Oxford. Henrietta-Maria had organized what she called a "Mary day" and they had taken the pony cart to the grove, followed by another cart laden with necessaries for a rustic lunch, then eaten it together at a table erected under a majestic elm whose dried brown leaves drifted over the cloth on a gentle breeze. It was a fine day, and woolen cloaks protected the women against the autumn air.

They were alone, at the queen's behest. This treat, on the first day of Mary's return to Henrietta-Maria's side, was her welcome back, and during her indisposition she had received many other marks of the queen's concern. James had confided in no one but Sir William Harvey about the crisis she had undergone, and even Harvey knew nothing about the first basis of the quarrel that provoked it, but everyone on being told she was ill had responded with kind attention. Mary now felt spoiled, and not least by the queen.

When Mary lost both parents—her father to his death and her mother by her marriage to Antrim—she had somehow by natural progression been able to accept Charles as a second father, for she felt a bond with him that went beyond words. With Henrietta-Maria, even though she had grown up under her aegis, it had been different. Apart from the fact that only thirteen years divided them in age, there was something kittenish, volatile and unpredictable about the queen that disqualified her as a second mother—but this very unpredictability had endeared her to Mary as an older friend. Mary could make her laugh, in the most unlikely circumstances, whereas trying to cheer the king was by no means so successful. And very often she received from the queen genuine signs of affection that disarmed her. Henrietta-Maria was emotional and took no trouble to conceal her feelings; hence, for instance, her recent behavior toward Rupert, whom she saw as standing between her husband and herself. Mary, though desolated by this attitude, had the strongest reasons for believing it could one day change back to what it had been before—admiration for Rupert as the queen's personal hero. Mary did everything she could to hasten that day, without in the meantime betraying any dangerous partiality for him.

Today they talked and laughed in a light, fond way that restored Mary's spirits, somewhat as her walk in the herb garden with Harvey had done, though speculative thought was foreign to the queen's mind. At last, when two little cups of Canary wine glowed on the cluttered table between them, the queen said, "Mall, I have something that the king especially wished me to tell you. Now, you are not to take fright, because though it is serious enough now, the effects will pass."

Mary's heart turned to ice. "There has been another battle."

"No, no! Oh, a few skirmishes on Rupert's part, scarcely a new thing—but speaking of him, he is expected today or tomorrow and we both felt it best that you know beforehand . . ."

"He is wounded?"

"Say rather," the queen said solemnly, "that you and your dear husband . . ." She put her hands on the table and looked at them as though seeking inspiration.

Mary, knowing how confused and confusing the queen could be in difficult moments, tried for composure and waited.

Finally her friend resumed, "When the king left Newbury he brought back with him some documents printed by parliamentary supporters and handed out to townspeople and soldiers—terrible things, I have no need to describe them to you. But there is a new one he has never seen before, and that is the one I must inform you of. The king tells me that your husband has seen it—and both of them have charged me to make it known to you in private. After that, none of us need ever speak of it. It is unworthy of our notice."

A document. Authorized by Essex? Seized by dread, Mary spoke with harsh defiance, "What, are we all accused of burning chickens and goats on the altar of Christ Church? Fear not, madam, I have more things to worry about than varlets' fantasies."

"No. The accusation is against you and Prince Rupert. Parliament claims you are linked in adultery."

The blow was all the harder for the fear that had gone before it. Mary clenched her hands together and looked at Henrietta-Maria in horror. The queen's hand came out to close gently over hers. "I told them it would devastate you! Do not look so pale, my dear, or I shall castigate myself. There have been a thousand broadsides against the prince—this is just one more—but we are appalled and incensed that it should name you. I have never felt so indignant in my life. *He* may be hated and abominated by the enemy in a million ways but that *you* should be vilified—I hold it against him, I can't help it."

"Madam," Mary gasped, "how can you condemn him any more than you can condemn me?" She put one hand to her face. "And oh, James. Oh, my husband."

The queen suddenly looked frightened. "I have done this badly. Pardon me—I beg you to listen. No one will ever discuss this before you or the prince or your husband or anyone else. When Rupert arrives we shall see whether he has heard of it, and if not, he too will be informed. After that, silence and dignity will prevail on this throughout the court, Oxford and everywhere His Majesty holds sway. Which is to say," she added, straightening her back, "throughout the kingdom. Let no one imagine that *we* descend to the level of the caitiffs who write these hideous, blasphemous lies."

"Oh!" Mary said, and put her head in her hands. "I can't take it in. It is too cruel."

"None of us can believe this has happened. But you and Richmond are his friends, that is well known—so it must also be well known to the horrid little calumniators who concoct these papers and twist everything they hear to mischief, and may they rot in hell."

Mary looked up, startled and moved, as the queen crossed herself. "Madam," she said with tears in her eyes and astonished relief in her heart, "thank you for telling me and for being my friend. What should I do without you?"

They embraced across the table, scattering cups and plates onto the soft grass below.

When Prince Rupert came to Christ Church and sent a message that he would like to see the Duke of Richmond after meeting with the king, James Stuart was in his bureau within the college. It was a comfortable room furnished with bookcases and chairs, where he and the prince had often talked before. He appreciated the prince's coming to see him instead of summoning him elsewhere; it showed he felt the weight of what they were about to say to each other.

James worked steadily at his desk until he heard the familiar tread through the outer room and called on a servant to show the prince in. He rose as the door closed behind the tall, dark-clad figure and went forward. In fact he had no idea what they were to say to each other, so he shook hands with the informality they had grown used to, and then murmured some kind of welcome, gesturing toward the fire that was burning to keep the autumn dampness from the air.

Prince Rupert did not sit, but moved nearer the hearth. James would have preferred him seated, since in the small space he loomed: a sober figure in brown velvet, padded, slashed, and trimmed with falls of lace in the same color. His sword, forged long and heavy for his height and strength, hung at his hip on a baldric embroidered with gold thread. For a few seconds, James was hit by the impression that His Highness had dressed for dominance, an idea that caused a small worm of anger to curl in his stomach.

The prince said in a low voice, "I'm told you've heard."

"Yes."

"Have you read any of it?"

"No! And shall not."

In answer, the prince removed from his sleeve a folded piece of paper and threw it backhanded into the fire. "I want you to know there is no truth—"

"God's wounds, I should say not!" James's voice was wild with fury for the first few words, then he mastered it. "If I had ever believed anything of the kind, do you think I would ever have invited you across the threshold of my house?"

He watched the shock of his anger, and the repetition of "ever," cause the other to flinch and grow pale. God's blood: did this fond prince believe that on his return from Holland he had not instantly betrayed that he had fallen hard for Mary? Did he not know that James had monitored his visits after Mary arrived? James had noted to his satisfaction that after two ill-judged private calls Rupert had been discouraged from making any more by Mary herself. Did the prince not realize that there had been many such episodes in the life of the incomparable Duchess of Richmond? Or that each admirer in his turn had not been coaxed, teased, laughed or frankly mocked out of his infatuation?

James had waited in hope, but this infatuation had never died. His anger flared again. " 'I want you to know there is no truth'— How dare you utter those words? That is an imputation against my wife that I will not accept—and that you should be ashamed to pronounce. I want *you* to know, Your Highness, that I need no assurances from anyone as to the integrity and honor of my wife."

If the prince chose to be high-handed about this statement, it meant a duel. James didn't care; he had been wanting to draw a sword and kill someone ever since the king told him what they had found in Newbury.

The prince was still pale and his lips quivered. He took two paces across the hearth and away, to pause with his gaze on the floor and his hand on his sword hilt. Then he stood erect and looked at James. "Forgive me. I am driven mad by this. You are both desperately wronged and I can do nothing about it. I would rather have died in the battle than found this out after it."

"Be good enough to sit down." As the prince did so, James took a few paces back and forth across the room. "Yes," he said, his voice still laced with sarcasm, "we are wronged indeed. But although it cannot amuse me to be branded a cuckold before half of England, you will understand that I feel ten times the injury to my wife. She has been ill recently, from other causes. This has prostrated her."

The prince bowed forward in the chair and pressed his forehead to the heels of his hands. "How can I face her? I can never see her again."

James did not reply for a moment but stood looking at him. The fall of dark hair did not hide all of his face and James could see that his lips were drawn back from his teeth in a grimace of suffering, almost as though he were about to weep. Then James realized that the prince had made no complaint about the fact that he too was branded with infamy. What was it like to be a man of twenty-three, called to lead tens of thousands of men onto the battlefields of a country not his own, and to have every aspect of his life, character and high ideals dragged in the dirt for more than twelve burdensome months? "We are all wronged," James said, and sat down opposite him. "And we will face it down together. Otherwise the filthy authors of this piece of shit will achieve just what they want—they will sow division amongst those most loyal to the king."

The prince shook his head, his fingers pushed into his hair. "This is like nothing else. I would not have believed it of Essex. How can he allow such a thing into the hands of his troops?"

"How can he prevent it?" James said. "We must not suppose it originates from such gentlemen as him! It is beneath our notice and will remain so. We shall not falter or bow before the world. Which is why I must invite you to dine with us tomorrow evening in the usual way." The prince shrank back and sat up. "And I must ask you to accept." The prince looked so shaken that James felt almost sorry for him. "I humbly and affectionately beg you, Your Highness, to afford us the honor of your presence tomorrow evening."

"Is the duchess well enough?" Rupert said at last.

"She has kept to the house, with visits only from the queen. But she attests to the utmost appreciation if you will grace our home tomorrow."

The prince rose. "Thank you. I accept. You do me too much honor."

They bowed to each other and the prince strode out.

James returned to his desk and sat looking down at a blank piece of paper. The wounds in his heart were not a fraction healed by this interview but it had strengthened his assumptions. If Rupert's passion for Mary had ever needed confirmation, this was it. But James knew that the prince's code of honor would never allow him to step inside their home tomorrow if he had forced his attentions on her. As for Mary's passion for the prince, the nightmare incident with the knife had shown James how it tormented her. In the aftermath, when she had turned to him to give and receive comfort, he knew that if she had yielded to Rupert, she would have confessed to him and begged his forgiveness. He knew this as he knew his own soul. Since then, he had seen her shocked and brought low by obloquy. Whatever her feelings for Rupert now were, they must be altered in some way by such a blow.

James rested his head in his hands to thank God and call upon him for mercy and aid. Mary had never yielded to Prince Rupert. She never would. He must draw strength from this to continue a friendship, and a high mission for the king, that together gave the deepest meaning to his life.

Chapter 22

~≈

MARY TRIED TO CALM herself with feverfew and warm wine on the night that Prince Rupert was expected, but the combination seemed not to help much, so she sampled a little of the fine sherry that James had had decanted for the prince. Her husband looked at her ironically but said nothing; they were silent as they waited for Rupert to be shown in. What was there to say? What would they all say when they were together once again? In the eyes of half England, it was a curious meeting: the cuckold, his wife and her lover. The other half would be shaking their heads with pity and horror that the three of them had to go through this. And possibly, in the backs of their minds, they were relishing the whole lurid and ridiculous shame of it. If this were happening to anyone else, might she not be tempted herself into knowing and sarcastic comments, and even laughter, with someone like Digby?

Rupert arrived and the three of them greeted one another formally. James invited Rupert to sit but he remained standing, moving toward the fireplace but then turning back toward them, as if unwilling to take up his usual relaxed position with a boot on the hearthstone and an arm along one of the deep grooves in the carved mantel.

His expression was cold and remote and when he looked at Mary he allowed no sympathy to show. She was grateful; any softening in his manner would have weakened her resolve to be courteous but unmoved by anything they said to each other tonight. They were both wearing black—he in Dutch velvet, she in delicate Italian wool—which she feared James would find a telling coincidence, but which suited her mood of gravity and mourning.

James himself wore dark blue Italian velvet slashed with watered silk and splendidly embroidered, and as always he was the most composed of the three. She knew James was considered haughty by those who stood below him at court, but it was not a word she associated with her clever and lofty husband. Dignity was simply part of his temperament—and tonight she envied it.

No doubt Rupert was thinking in the darkest terms, for he said after a while, "I regret I was not back in time to attend the funeral of Lord Falkland. Of all the losses at Newbury, we may call his the most severe."

"We attended," James said. "It was a fitting service for a gentleman of his high principles."

Mary said, "There was some very sad speculation that he might have deliberately chosen death on the field rather than face the failure to bring peace between king and Parliament."

The prince said, "Sir Edward Hyde told me in tears today that it could not be so. Falkland volunteered to fight, just as he did at Edgehill, as a demonstration of his loyalty."

"I believe that too," James said. "He did not want his efforts for peace to be interpreted as a lack of fidelity to His Majesty."

"Nonetheless," Mary said, "it sounds as though he rode alone, with no apparent reason, into a hail of musket fire."

The prince's voice was patient. "The reason one rides into battle is to defeat the enemy, madam. Lord Falkland needed no other reason and looked for none. He died as a brave gentleman who will be much missed. In battle, men die. *Finis.*"

She looked at him with an inward shiver. She had heard the story of the breakneck attack on him by Sir Philip Stapleton. She knew that if Stapleton's aim had been true, Rupert would have received the bullet in the face at point-blank range. She had had to suppress a wave of nausea when she heard it, for it brought back her terror when he went on campaign without saying good-bye.

He continued talking to James about what had been happening in Oxford during his absence, and she examined him, her heart aching. At all times the skin around his eyes was of a slightly darker hue than the rest of his face, which made his open brown eyes seem larger. Tonight this shadow was more pronounced, and she recognized it as a sign of weariness. And also of defeat? This was the first time she had seen him after the king had lost a battle. Neither she nor James had said anything about Rupert's part in it; it did not seem possible tonight.

So she asked her usual question: "How is your dear brother Prince Maurice? Have you heard from Plymouth?"

"Yes, but he had to dictate the letter. He is unwell."

"What's wrong?"

He shook his head. "I can't tell."

Her anxiety grew as she looked at his face. Illness was a beset-ting curse of the king's armies and Parliament's alike; there were any number of agues and fevers that might have attacked Prince Maurice, especially while he was besieging a city and unable to es-cape from the noxious airs that could turn a siege into a hellhole. "Does he say anything about what ails him?"

"A little."

"Can you ask Sir William Harvey's advice?"

"I have my own physician, madam. But I thank you. I shall con-vey your kind concern to my brother."

Eventually they sat down at the table and ate. The meal went badly: Mary had had no appetite for days, James objected to the roast fowl and growled at the servants about it, something she had never known him to do before guests, and the prince looked as though he would prefer to be at Plymouth or points farther west. Cornwall, perhaps, or even Ireland.

"What would the king have you do now you are returned?" she ventured at one stage.

He did not look up from his plate. "More or less what I was doing before we lost this battle. Recruiting, arming and training. Holding on to and building on what we have."

"It must have been . . ." Her voice and invention failed her.

He smiled grimly. "No man can claim to be a soldier who has not gone through a defeat." She said nothing and he looked up. "Have no fear, madam, Essex has gained no strategic advantage by scattering us from the banks of the Kennet. He has marched back through Reading, but abandoned it in the process. You need not tremble for Oxford yet."

Despite all the self-mastery she had promised herself and tac-itly pledged to James, she felt herself go pale. "How can you say that to me? Do you imagine I reproach you? About anything?"

He rose, nearly tipping over the chair beneath him. "Forgive me. I beg you to forgive me. This is impossible." He turned to James. "Will you permit me to go? I thank you for your ever gener-ous and thoughtful hospitality, but . . . I'm sorry, this is beyond me. Please allow me to bid you good night."

James rose at once and extended his hand. "You are weary and we have overtaxed you. Thank you for coming—it means a great deal. God keep you until we see you again."

James motioned to the servant at the door, the prince bowed to them both and was ushered from the house.

Mary remained at the table, devastated. James returned from the door and stood behind her. "We are all weary. He cannot think that you question his ability to save this kingdom. It is a hard time for all of us—forgive him for turning on you. He did not mean to do it." He stepped away. "Come; bid me good night and go and take your rest. Have you had Anne prepare you some absinthe to help you sleep?"

She got to her feet, faced him and nodded. He leaned forward as though to kiss her forehead, but something stopped him. She shrank away, desperate to escape, and he said in a level tone, "Good night, wife."

"Good night, my lord."

Rupert went for another three weeks without seeing the Duchess of Richmond. Thus, counting his absence on campaign in September, by the third week in October he had seen her but once in two months, at the dinner to which her husband and she had summoned him. Since then, Richmond had renewed the invitation with friendly regularity but each time Rupert had turned him down. He came into Oxford only for the councils of war and strategy meetings; the rest of the time he was busy at the garrisons. It might be better so; he was too preoccupied to figure it out.

Rupert was the only person who attended both the war council, which dealt with practical military issues, and the king's Privy Council on strategy, which included Richmond and Digby. Rupert had never had any great love of Digby and now knew him to be heavily in league with the queen. As an additional irritant, the king had named Digby Secretary of State to replace Lord Falkland. Rupert could not think of a greater contrast between the two gentlemen: Falkland had been a deep thinker and frank proponent of peace, while Digby was a suave politician who seemed to relish the war. Despite Digby, when Rupert could be present at the Privy Council he found it fruitful—he always had Richmond's support, and the king continued to listen to him.

There was another group of which he was not a member, and had neither the time nor real desire to be. This council included Hyde and Culpepper and was chaired for the king at Oriel College by Lord Cottington, a seasoned diplomat. To learn about the affairs of state deliberated at these meetings, Rupert was dependent on the Duke of Richmond, who was present at each session. Rupert's liking for Richmond had not diminished—in fact it was enhanced by a new respect. For this reason, he believed he must tear himself away from Mary, at least for a while, and be sure that Richmond knew it.

It was a hellish month. The memory of her face haunted him; drawn, pale and hurt. Parliament's vicious attack had laid her low, Richmond had said, and on that disastrous evening he himself had made everything worse. But he could not comfort her without seeking her out, which would make things worse still.

At the same time he was distracted by concern for Maurice, whose condition had deteriorated so far that there were no more letters from his brother from Plymouth, just discouraging reports from his own physician, whom he had sent to the port the day after he had seen the Richmonds.

Time dragged. He filled it with a hundred tasks, was hard on himself and made things even harder for his men.

One afternoon he was at Abingdon watching troopers training their horses in maneuvers, riding one at a time, fully equipped, along a worn track in the exercise field by the river. The track was shaped like a cross with three circles—one at the tip and one at each end of the crossbar.

"Left!" he shouted. "You must make him lead with the left leg there or he cannot make a neat turn. If he cannot make a neat turn you may be on your back before the next, with your comrades treading on your balls. Come round and do it again."

The trooper managed it, but the horse was ungainly and unhappy. As the man went off the field past him, Rupert turned and ordered him to halt and dismount.

"I want you to stand close to your mount and tell me what you can smell."

"Smell, Your Highness?"

Rupert stepped forward, put his hand on the man's shoulder and wrenched him around so that his nose was an inch from his saddle. "I could smell it from over there; now tell me what *you* can smell!"

Humiliated and confused, the man could only shake his head.

"Take off the saddle." The man did so, aware of his whole troop watching, but still wondering what he was expected to find. "And the blanket. Now," Rupert grabbed him and forced his face close to the horse's back again, "what do you *see?*"

The man gasped, "Only saddle sores, Your Highness."

Rupert let him go. "Only? They are open. They are putrid and infected and they stink to high heaven, and so does your care of your mount. Horses cannot resist infection like this; in a few days yours will be useless to you, in a week it might be dead. What precisely do you expect to ride when Stapleton comes charging at you again? You will now tell your comrades, at the top of your voice so they stay awake and stay alive, just what you are supposed to do for your horse before you eat, drink or do anything else you may fancy at the end of every day."

The trooper stood to attention, his face flaming. "Unsaddle, check the blanket and the back, wash the back, dry down with bunch of straw or cloth! If there are any lesions, arrange to spell the horse the next day and report this to the horse master!"

"Thank you. Next!"

As the next rider took the field, the trooper arranged the saddle and blanket over his arm and began to lead his horse away. Rupert glanced at him sidelong. His equipment was shabby, so he was not a man of means, but the mount must have cost him at least eight pounds, probably more than he could have afforded to spend on his clothes and his weapons. And he had most likely never been recompensed for any of it; so many of the king's men funded themselves. Rupert said to him, "You'll have to spell that animal right now. Report to Sir Richard Crane and have him delegate you one of my string for a week. Yours will make a good mount in time—never fear."

The man looked back in astonishment, halted and touched his helmet with the hand that held the reins. "Thank you, Your Highness!"

"No, His Majesty's cavalry thanks you. Go."

*   *   *

James came back from court one evening with such a worried look that Mary made him sit down and tell her all the news. Usually it came out over dinner, but tonight he looked too burdened to wait. When he reached the end, however, she guessed there was more that he was not telling her. She had an instinct that it was to do with Rupert.

She said, "The queen sent today to Prince Rupert's quarters to inquire if there was any news of Prince Maurice. The page came back with a very confusing message. In fact it was no message at all—the men said some word had come from Plymouth but they would not divulge it."

James looked apprehensive. "I hate to cause you pain, but I beg you to prepare yourself. A message came to Rupert today that Maurice is dead."

She put her hands to her mouth.

He went on, "I spoke to Rupert but he refuses to believe it! He practically threw the messenger out. Apparently the information was not delivered in writing—it seems to have come across country from Plymouth, handed along by Prince Maurice's troops from garrison to garrison."

"Oh, Lord. What chance is there that it is not true? How could anyone be careless about news like that?" She felt tears coming into her eyes and blinked them back.

James shook his head. "Prince Rupert won't accept it and there's an end on it. But we all dread the fatal word from Plymouth. And so must he; he's driving himself beyond the limit. The king is very anxious and distressed about both his nephews."

"What can we do?" she whispered.

"Nothing. Wait. I feel for the prince; I know what it is like to lose a brother. His elder brother Frederick died as a youth, but that was many years ago. With Maurice it will be infinitely worse; they are so close."

Seized by the same helplessness, neither of them mentioned the subject again that evening. And next day Mary waited, as James had proposed, with no prospect of seeing Prince Rupert or of being able to bring him any comfort if she did.

Two days later she did see him again, however. She and Henrietta-Maria were walking with Lord Jermyn in Magpie Lane, accompanied by four guards. Henrietta-Maria had grown quite fond of such excursions, as long as she had to walk only the length of the lane and then only if it was market day, which afforded some amusement. The cobbled lane was wide enough for a row of stalls on each side and a navigable gap in the middle, along which purchasers and peddlers jostled their way. The guards often had to nudge aside a redolent onion seller or a gaudily dressed jackanapes offering trays of ribbons to let the queen pass. The shopkeepers and stall holders seemed charmed by her presence and she bought things like flowers or sweet confections and had them carried in her wake back to Merton.

A wintry sun shone on the upper stories of the houses down one side of the lane, making bright squares of the household linen hung over windowsills, and brilliant flags of the clothing spread along wooden balcony railings, where children or servants lingered here and there to look down on the throng. The market was a dense corridor of color between the gray stone buildings, broken by awnings and canvas partitions and vertical racks of cheap fabrics or game such as rabbits and ducks. The slope of the lane made it feel as though the best wares must be at the top end rather than down opposite the college at Merton Street, but it was at the top that the tinkers worked, sitting cross-legged on leather mats on the cobbles, and there most of the cheesemongers had their displays, so Henrietta-Maria tended to stop beforehand to avoid the din and the smell.

Mary saw Rupert just as they were about to walk back down the slope, when he turned into Magpie Lane from the High Street. He was striding along with two of his officers and he had a hand on each shoulder as he bent to listen to them. He was laughing, his teeth flashing white in his tanned face and his hair swinging forward over his shoulders. Then he looked up, saw Mary and the queen and straightened without breaking his stride. The expression on his face grew even happier, and with a quick word of excuse to his men he walked forward and made a deep, elaborate bow, taking up a deal of room in the thoroughfare as he did so, and causing passersby to smile and step aside. Boy emerged from the thicket of legs and sat down by his master, his mouth open in a wide grin.

Henrietta-Maria and Mary exchanged greetings with Rupert and he and Lord Jermyn acknowledged each other and said a few friendly words. Mary was perplexed about Rupert's manner and she could see that the queen, who was very fond of Prince Maurice, was wondering whether to say his name.

But Rupert said it for them, with a beaming smile. "I have just had a letter from Maurice. He wrote it himself! He is getting better—shaky, but much better, and my physician has no more fears."

"Oh!" cried the queen, and crossed herself. "*Que Dieu soit béni.* Oh, Rupert, what a blessing." Tears filled her eyes.

Rupert looked at her with smiling compassion. "Thank you, my dear aunt." He kissed her hand, then looked at Mary. "And thank you for your kind inquiries. I have sent word to the king, so your husband will soon know. Do thank him too."

"I shall. I can't tell you how happy I am for you and your brother."

"Your face says it," he replied, with such a look of adoration that she had to bend down and make a fuss of Boy to escape it.

"You must tell us all about Maurice," the queen said. "Otherwise it will not sink in and I shall find myself just as anxious as before. But how do you come to be here? Were you on your way to see me?"

"I must confess I sent you a message instead; you will receive it at Merton. No, I am come to buy Maurice some candied chestnuts and send him a box—he is very fond of them, and he reckons that no one makes them earlier or better than the comfit maker down the bottom there, next to the flower stall."

"So you were not going to tell me in person?" The queen looked vexed, which Mary thought unjust, since she had made it clear enough that she desired no visits from the prince.

"But you are out gallivanting, so I should have missed you!" he said cheerfully. "Instead I have met you, which is ten thousand times better. Now I can treat you to chestnuts." He gestured down the slope. "Come, will you take Lord Jermyn's arm or mine? I don't object to parading, but we can't do so four abreast."

The queen was more than happy to take Jermyn's arm, and Mary wondered whether this was to prevent her from walking with him herself—ever since Henrietta-Maria had read the poem to "J. G." the queen had been a little jealous of Jermyn's attentions, and Mary was profoundly grateful for this.

Prince Rupert offered Mary his arm and the queen turned and smiled her approval—a signal to both of them that Henrietta-Maria still viewed the scurrilous attacks by Parliament with disbelief and lofty disdain, in private and in public.

It was indeed something of a parade, and there were comments on both sides of the lane as they passed by—all of them pleasant, Mary was glad to notice. On ordinary days the lane was lined with the tables and benches of the tradesmen, who in fine weather worked outside on the cobbles rather than in their dingy shops. On fair days, stall keepers set up their displays between the craftsmen's wares and stood against the house walls, hailing the passing housewives and servants with a string of blandishments or loud praises of the goods they had for sale. With two guards walking ahead, Lord Jermyn steered the queen along and Prince Rupert and Mary walked behind, while Boy followed with the other two guards.

Once they were out of earshot of the queen amongst the noise of the street, Rupert pressed Mary's hand to his side and bent to her. "I have been thinking very earnestly this morning and I have come to a conclusion. You remember how you first offered your friendship to me?"

She nodded.

"How wise you were, and with what sweetness you proposed it to me! How ungrateful I have been, ever since. It shames me to think of it." He saw her doubtful look and smiled joyfully at her. "This morning I realized: we are alive, I love you, and I may see you whenever I like. How could I be so selfish as to demand anything else? The queen is right: life itself is a blessing. From now on, I am no longer ungrateful. We are alive, *mon amour*, and we are friends—I shall never ask for more."

She looked at him in wonder. Had he heard what he had just said? There was a contradiction in his face, too—the warmth of conviction on his cheeks, but hopeless love in his eyes. She said softly, "It is suffering over Maurice that makes you think this way."

"Yes, and if anything good has come out of the last hideous weeks, there it is. Life is a blessing. I am grateful and I will remain so. Especially to you."

She could not reply and they walked on in silence. She might have said, *All I want is your friendship, too*, but the words would not form; she would have been lying. And he was not—he was sincere about this new vision.

He did not seem to mind her silence. He went on, "I keep thinking of what you wrote: *We'll mix our souls, you shall be me, I you.* We will make that possible."

She said lightly, "Does this mean my husband and I will have the pleasure of your company once more?"

He smiled down at her. "Yes. How could I have spent all this time avoiding you? It was another sign of my ingratitude, do you see?"

"Then I shall mention it to him; he will be delighted."

The smile faltered. "Mention what?"

"That I met you today and you told me that if we invited you soon, you would be happy to come. Is there anything else you think I should tell him?"

"No!" They walked on a little farther and he gave a sigh that was not unhappy. "I see. You don't believe it is possible. But it is—and I will prove it to you."

It took some time to get to the comfit maker's stall. Boy was keen to try the wares of a sausage maker on the right side of the lane and Rupert stopped to give him a sample. Flowers were bought for the ladies at a place on the left, crammed with color and fragrance, where the young and comely flower seller clearly knew the prince. She also seemed familiar with Lord Jermyn, however, so if Mary felt a twinge of envy she was certain to be sharing it with the queen.

At the comfit maker's they found he had set up his brazier and was selling hot chestnuts as well. Rupert bought a paper cone of these for everyone, and when the queen failed to see how one could shell them without getting spiky bits under the fingernails, Rupert insisted on peeling hers and Mary's and then showing a fast-gathering group of bystanders how well Boy could jump for his own. Boy preferred the candied sort, of which an enormous box was ordered for Prince Maurice.

Rupert's officers reappeared on the fringes of the crowd looking thirsty, and Rupert finally took his leave and headed back up the lane toward the High Street and no doubt the men's favored tavern.

As the women crossed Merton Street to reenter the college,

Henrietta-Maria said thoughtfully, "He can be so bounteous when things are going well for him. I thank God he has not lost Maurice. And for all his faults, I must say, my dear"—and she leaned close so as not to hurt Jermyn's feelings—"I do believe he is the most beautiful man on earth."

Chapter 23

JAMES STUART WAS WITH the king at the end of a long day, and things were not going especially well. Word had come in from Ireland that would have implications for the northwest, and the king was uncertain what to do about it. If he decided to bring troops over from Ireland, an experienced commander must be on the spot to receive them and integrate them into his forces. James supported the appointment of Sir John Byron but the king was considering sending Prince Rupert, to either Shrewsbury or the port of Chester, since Rupert had been responsible for the northwest since his victory at Lichfield.

"Sire," James said, "while Prince Rupert is quartered in Oxford you can always call on him for advice. Have you thought what it would be like to put him at too great a distance? Dispatches are never as helpful as talking face-to-face—indeed, remember what happened over the governorship of Bristol, and all because of the distance involved."

As he waited for the king's answer, he thought how ironical it was that he should be advocating Rupert's nearness to the king; the thought of the prince at Shrewsbury or Chester caused him no personal uneasiness. But with Rupert absent, Essex might well consider a concerted attack on Oxford, and the king might find his capital difficult to defend. As far as James was concerned, military wisdom dictated that Rupert remain within reach to protect the king. It did not matter how large or powerful the royal armies were elsewhere in England—if Parliament should manage to lay hands on Charles, it would forever have the upper hand. James often wondered whether even Rupert himself was aware of that appalling risk. With Charles in its power, Parliament could put the king on trial, and with him his highest commanders and councillors. James sometimes felt he was the only person completely aware of how precarious all their lives were in this beleaguered city: barricaded into the king's pretend capital, propped up by a polyglot army, surrounded by mortal dangers. It made him fiercely possessive about the only real things that remained to him: his loyalty, his wife, his love.

The king sighed. "We will talk of this tomorrow. There is much to contemplate. I ask your opinion on these matters now because I should like to hear it fully before you go. It is in my mind to offer you a mission to France." He saw James start and looked up, smiling. "Not for long—some weeks only, provided you have good sailing."

James's heart rebelled but he swallowed and said, "What would you wish me to do, sire?"

The king waved his hand. "Let us discuss the details later. But in essence, I feel the French court may be sensing some . . . some neglect on our part. That must not continue. Your visit there will be greatly appreciated, and you will ascertain the kind of welcome my beloved wife might receive, should she elect to go there herself at some stage." He said quietly, "Only you, myself and the queen need be aware of that aim, of course. I should also like you to pay a visit to the Rohan family and bring forward the discussions about Prince Rupert's marriage. It is normal for these things to take time, but we have not been assiduous of late; there too, inattention would be most discourteous."

James's outlook improved suddenly. "Prince Rupert's marriage?"

"We have not discussed it?" the king said. Then he smiled. "Well, he is not loquacious about it himself, I suppose. For many years—when did we start this dialogue, 1636?—we and the Duc de Rohan considered a marriage between his daughter and our nephew. The duke was Huguenot, so there can be no . . . no religious objection, and her inheritance on his death is impressive— just what we could wish for my nephew, in fact. Almost seven years have passed, however, and I do think it is time to . . . to bring matters up to date. The duke's brother, the Prince de Soubise, is more than ready to discuss this with you. I am going to arrange for a miniature to be painted of Prince Rupert so you can take it with you as a gift to the young lady. I should like you to gauge her wishes and bring me back a report. If there is no . . . no prospect of a settlement in the very near future, I think we would be wise to break off negotiations."

"I shall do what I can, sire," James murmured.

The king looked at him shrewdly. "I detect a lack of enthusiasm. You do not wish to go? I hope you know you may tell me why, and I shall listen without prejudice."

James shook his head. "I am deeply honored to be your ambassador, sire. If I looked reluctant, I cry you mercy. But since you ask, I dislike to leave my wife. Not long ago, she was absent for almost a year, and though you ask mere weeks of me now, I—"

Charles put a hand on his arm. "I understand. But I have spoken to *my* wife about this and she at once came up with a suggestion. Don't fear any loneliness for Mall—if she wishes to, she will spend all the time of your absence at Merton, and no one could be more welcome at Her Majesty's side or surer of our tender care. Now, do you like my scheme better?"

James bowed. "You are both exceedingly kind."

"I have another idea!" the king said, and looked delighted. "When I commission the prince's portrait from Dick Gibson, I shall command one of Mall—and you shall take it on your journey. It seems a long time since she was painted. So sad that Van Dyck is gone, but . . . a splendid idea!"

James bowed again, gave his sincere thanks, and went home. It had been on the tip of his tongue to ask where exactly Prince Rupert would be while he was away, but he could not do that to Mary, for Charles was a sensitive listener at times and might have guessed his motive. He had been so preoccupied by this that he had not even asked when he was to leave!

The king had not authorized him to tell Mary about the embassy but he knew he could do so if he wished—she would probably hear everything from the queen the next day anyway. But he decided to wait until dinner was over and their guest was gone. Prince Rupert was dining with them, for the first time since the uncomfortable meal after Newbury, and despite James's confidence in his wife he did not relish the idea of seeing the prince's face or hers while his own absence was being spoken of.

As it happened, the subject flew from his mind almost the moment he got home. Mary was nowhere to be seen so he went in search of her and found her in her private chamber, drying her hair before the fire. As soon as she saw him, she moved her chair away from the hearth, made him place another in front of hers, and sat down again.

"Now," she said, her hair tumbling over her shoulders and her hands lightly clasped in her lap, so that she looked rather like a clever young scholar about to demonstrate her accomplishments, "you will sit down and listen without irrelevant interruption until I give you leave to speak."

He grinned and obeyed. She had something outlandish or exciting to tell him, and it must be to do with those closest to them. Had young George fielded some accolade for his studies or his military career? Neither seemed very likely, so he kept his peace.

"You know how I have been somewhat unwell lately in the mornings? And sometimes a little tired in the afternoons," she admitted with a quick smile, sensing a possible interruption. "But nothing, really. However, I asked Sir William to visit me, as you suggested, and he gave me an answer that I never could have believed. But I might have added it up for myself, if I had had the least experience in these matters! James"—she leaned forward and put her hands on his knees, and with the movement two tears slid off her eyelashes and fell, to create round cobalt spots on her aquamarine dress—"allow me to give you joy. I have felt this joy for the last three hours; I have felt it so strongly I have not moved from this room. I have been here, waiting for you, dying to tell you."

"Mary?"

She nodded, and more drops scattered, this time over their joined hands as she bent further forward to whisper, "We are going to have a child. Sir William says I must have conceived last month. All the signs are there, he says. There is no doubt. Of the baby or the date."

He bent his head so she could not see the calculation going on behind his eyes, but his mind had already sped down a shining path—the child was his. Rupert had been absent all September; it was now the end of October. In the next second he felt revulsion against himself for allowing such thoughts into his mind, for he had already seen the truth in his wife's eyes. Then it was as though there were no other emotion in life but the wonder she had just given him. He slid to his knees and kissed her hands, then put his own on each side of her waist and looked at her—at the beautiful face, glowing with innocent pride, her splendid white breasts and slender form, which felt warm beneath the slippery fabric under his fingers, and the gentle hands, one cupped as she stroked his cheek, the other curved around the back of his neck.

"Six years of wishing," she said. "Are you glad?"

He smiled into her eyes, letting her see everything. "What does it look like?"

"It looks to me as though you are even happier than I. But I don't think that's possible."

"Sir William is sure you are quite well?"

"Yes, he is. It appears I am to be a very common or garden mother."

"Bless you, wife, for you have blessed me." He leaned closer and brushed her lips with his, and she did not pull away. Instead she wound her arms around his head and held him to her fiercely.

"James, we are so lucky."

A few hours later they dined with Prince Rupert for the first time since the ill-fated meal from which he had walked out. Having told James he was to be a father, Mary was in a daze of surprise and joy. She and James had come to fear they would never have children. Now, just at a time when her husband had begun to suspect himself cheated and deprived, she brought him the greatest gift she could offer. God had blessed them after all, despite her wayward selfishness. Their child would be born legitimate, honored, cherished. She already loved it with a warmth that filled her being.

She was nowhere near as attentive as usual to Rupert; in fact, she felt almost shy with him. Meanwhile, she sensed a new bond with her husband, because they had a wondrous secret that they could share with just a glance or a smile over the table. Mary's sexual awkwardness with James had always haunted her, and she had even wondered whether this flaw in her was the reason that her virile and devoted husband had no child. But now she knew she had not failed James after all, and tonight this intimate knowledge brought them closer together. She speculated whether Rupert would notice, or feel subtly excluded, but in fact their own happiness seemed to blend with his over Prince Maurice, and it was one of the most cheerful evenings they ever spent together.

During the following week, she and James decided that people should be told their secret, mostly because Mary needed to inform the queen, and if one told the queen one almost immediately told everyone. Mary had been arriving late at Merton in the mornings, and although Henrietta-Maria was not exacting, she would feel hurt if Mary continued to do so without an explanation. She also loved news, and would feel deprived if they waited ages to tell her. In addition, Mary was eager to confide in the king, for she knew how much their happiness would please him.

Meanwhile, she and James entered another phase in their life together. He began to spend more time at home, and was more assiduous than ever about making sure she was cared for. He insisted on paying a visit to Sir William Harvey to put him through an interrogation about her health and the pregnancy, and the result of this was quite different from anything Mary could have predicted.

On the night after his visit to Sir William, James came to her bedroom. She prepared herself to receive him as usual, but his manner had changed. He took her hand as soon as he entered, led her to the bed and begged her to lie down. She was about to stretch out as usual when he pulled back the covers and said, "In the bed, Mary, for I want you to be comfortable. I have something to say."

It felt strange. She lay sideways with her legs under the sheets and her head on the bolster and watched as to her surprise he stripped off his breeches and hose and climbed in beside her wearing only his shirt. They were inches apart but were not touching—just looking at each other.

"I asked Sir William all about you today. I also asked for some husbandly advice as to how I should behave in bed. I got more than I bargained for!"

He was smiling, so she said, "Am I to hear it?"

"I may lie with you; it is perfectly safe. If I am gentle." He was still smiling, but with a kind of timidity that softened her. "I asked for more details and Sir William gave me that look he has sometimes—like a tutor disappointed in a promising pupil—and he said, 'Need I explain, your grace? Gentleness prolongs the pleasure, for both man and woman.' "

As he spoke, he had been delicately undoing the small pearl buttons down the front of her nightdress. His fingers hardly touched her—and she had the sudden strange wish that they would. But she said nothing, just lay there, confused and expectant.

When he reached the last button and drew the nightdress

softly open, he murmured, "I must say this is already doing very good things for me."

She put out her hand and slid it down his arm to his chest, seeing a change in his eyes that she could also feel in his breathing and his skin. She had never thought of giving him pleasure. She had believed that he had taken pleasure, but she had only thought of submitting, not of offering him anything. Her hands slid around his waist and she put her lips to the bare skin at the opening of his shirt. His body was not raw-boned as she had always unfairly imagined it—no, for all his leanness his skin was as white and smooth as hers.

As she pressed her body to his, she felt as though she had gained power over him, a benign power that made him tremble with anticipation in her arms. It gave her an equally tremulous sense of liberty.

The next evening, Mary looked forward to the arrival of Rupert with tension, excitement and alarm—for she had no idea how he might react to the news that she was with child. She knew that by rights it ought not to give him pain, but she could not banish the fear that it might. It was one thing for a man to be jealous of a married woman; it was another to have it explained in the most telling way possible that that woman had regular relations with her husband.

She and James had told Charles and Henrietta-Maria together, and there had been a fond and delighted reaction from the king and motherly tears from the queen. Rupert now knew: apparently he had received the news from Charles, with what reaction she did not know, and he had sought James out to congratulate him, which James said he did with great enthusiasm.

The closer the hour came for Rupert's arrival, the more fearful she was. She wondered whether his new construction on friendship would crumble before this change in her. She wondered if it might drive him away again. And she recognized that despite that very change, and the alteration it had brought in her relations with James, she had to have Rupert's love. If he chose to describe it as friendship she must allow him his self-deception, but she knew that what drew them together was too overwhelming to be so coolly defined. There was nothing she could do about her love for

Rupert—it was wound into her being and she was helpless to remove it. He said it was fate; she had never admitted it to him, but that was how it felt to her too. Fate decreed that she was James's wife, would be the mother of his child—and was in love with Prince Rupert. She could not negate any of these truths.

When Rupert arrived and was shown up, he gave them his usual affectionate greeting. He bowed low over Mary's hand, kissed it and said, "I have heard of your happiness. Believe me, I wish you every joy in this child." She murmured her thanks without quite catching his eye.

He then apologized for not having changed—he had been at Woodstock all day and his commanders there had upended a heap of problems over his head that delayed his return.

"Forgive me if you can," he said with a weary smile, "I never seem to get the better of supplies. Dan O'Neale once told me he had rather be my groom than look after my regiment, and sometimes I would rather be the king's page than his general. I've left Boy downstairs—he's even more mired than I am." He stopped pulling off his buff coat and looked at them both. "Tell me if you would rather I went away and came back looking less of a savage; I didn't want to delay your meal any longer."

"Never fear," James said, "come through with me where we can dispose of your gear; I've had some hot water brought up."

Rupert gave Mary an unreadable glance as he left the room after James, and she smiled at him to mask the suspense she felt. This was the first evening after her news had broken; could she count on another?

As it happened, it began very well. Prince Rupert seemed to conquer his tiredness with the first cup of wine, and as usual they all had much to discuss. At one stage James mentioned his mission overseas, which the king had now confirmed, and which Mary had known about since the day she discovered she was pregnant. It turned out that the prince knew of it too. He avoided looking at Mary while he and James talked about it, and there was no change in his demeanor. He even bore it very well, at first, when James brought up the question of his marriage.

"Are you still having the miniature done?" James asked. "My wife is already sitting for hers."

"Yes, I have a session tomorrow. It is the king's commission and

I can only comply." He glanced at Mary. "The two of you probably know more about this tedious business than I do. Has the king spoken of it?"

"Over a period of years it has come up once or twice," Mary said smoothly. "But of late I imagined it had dropped out of mind. I must say I was surprised to hear of it again."

He looked conscious, as well he might. She had certainly been surprised when James told her about this part of his mission, and she could not help feeling an unfair resentment that Rupert himself had never said anything about it to her.

"There is nothing in it," he said rather too firmly.

"Really?" she replied. "I wonder if that's what the young lady will think when she is given your portrait. I suppose you have received a picture of her at some time in the last seven years?"

"I have."

"And what is she like?"

"Of fairish complexion, I think. But her best feature is her disgusting wealth." They both looked shocked at this and he gave a short laugh. "Forgive the sarcasm; it's just that the whole thing has been the king's affair, not mine, and he has prosecuted it for my sake and with my welfare in mind, so I haven't had the heart to tell him to forget it. He wants to provide me with a rich marriage—how else are penniless younger princes supposed to line their coats?"

"You are not, please, going to claim penury to us?" James said dryly.

"No, but war is an expensive style of life and I never have enough for the men. Nonetheless," he said with a satisfied grin, "I issued my whole life guard with new cloaks yesterday—it took four hundred yards of cloth. They're all in scarlet; I called the guard out on parade and they looked like a field of poppies! When I said so, they threatened to hand the things back. There's gratitude for you."

"I don't think you quite finished telling us about Mademoiselle Marguerite de Rohan," Mary said sweetly.

"There is nothing more to say. I don't like to discourage you over your embassy," he said to James, "but I would be most grateful if you don't push too hard for a result. If you can let it die the death when you get back I'll be even more grateful. I could even give you a scarlet cloak—there's a few yards left over."

James did not smile. "In all conscience I cannot undertake this for the king if you have already made up your mind that it will have no issue. It would be dishonest toward His Majesty. Unless he knows your opinion on the matter?"

Rupert looked annoyed for a moment, then gave a groan. "Yes, he does. But he won't listen. He hates to be deprived of doing me a kindness." He shook his head. "Can we talk about something else? I have plenty of other dire subjects to expatiate on, if you are interested."

In the end, perhaps because Mary had been thinking of babies all week, they talked about their early childhoods—hers in the luxury of Wallingford House and York House in London, James's at the beautiful family home, Cobham Hall in Kent, and Rupert's in Leiden, Holland. Mary told James the hair-raising story of what had happened to Rupert as a baby in Prague, and they all agreed that of the three he had had the most bizarre upbringing.

"But the Prinzenhof gave me a freedom that not many can boast of," he said. "There was old Frau von Plessen, who had been our father's governess; she and her husband looked after us, and we were so many, there was always some game going on. And we could have as many tutors as we wanted. The University of Leiden was just over the road, so one could scarcely lack for knowledge; I began there when I was ten. I still do that now—if I want to know something I just find someone who is imbued with it to the hilt and is ready to teach me. I'll never forget, when I first came to England I was lucky enough to talk to Phineas Pett, that extraordinary shipwright at Woolwich. You could spend a lifetime at a port just talking to seamen. The things they have to say about the world! Maurice is fascinated by Plymouth. When he takes the city, the first thing he wants to do is go to the wharf from which the Puritan pioneers sailed for the New World. Imagine, setting off to create a new, ideal life in that strange place."

"You're not saying you would fancy doing the same!" James said.

The prince thought for a moment, then said, "I should like to see how the natives hunt bears." They both laughed at him and after a moment he did too.

"Were you able to study in prison at Linz?" Mary asked.

"I did a lot of drawing and painting. I made an instrument for drawing in perspective, because it interested me—and because I had the time! And I learned about the art of engraving. Now that is something worth knowing; I wish I had the time for it these days."

"So when you were a boy," James said, going back to what had struck him, "you derived all your education from your preceptors? Your parents seem to have had little to do with it."

"Oh, we saw our father. He came to the Prinzenhof regularly. We all worshipped him, and who can have more influence than one you worship?"

"But weren't you young when you lost him?" Mary asked.

"It was in November 1632, a month before my thirteenth birthday. He died of the plague, after a campaign." He shook his head, looking at the table, and then said in a detached way, as though he were talking of someone else, "It was the worst time I have known. I cried for three days. No one could comfort me; I became a little legend. The Russian ambassador called me Rupert *ryova*, which means Rupert crybaby. I have never forgiven him. And I have never cried since." He looked up. "So I was of no use to my mother, and for her it was terrible. For three days she did not move, speak, sleep or eat. They thought she would die too. But," he said with a sudden, incongruous smile, "here we all are, alive after all."

Mary looked at him in amazement. *Of use to his mother*—of what use had she ever been to him, except to bring him into the world? But Mary saw much of Elizabeth in him just the same, especially the resilience and strength of purpose. What had he gained from his father? A belief in the necessity of war, to begin with. She shivered.

Later, when the sweet wines, fruit and comfits had been sampled, James had to leave the room to talk for a moment to the steward. As he excused himself and walked out, Mary almost felt her courage fail her.

The prince looked startled, then gave her an apprehensive look and at once took the initiative. "Last time, I knew there was something you were not telling me. I spent all week trying to work out whether it was good or bad."

"For me it is a matter of great joy."

"Then it is so to me, too," he said. He smiled at her, and she saw with astonishment and relief that some of her own happiness had penetrated him and made his eyes glow with sympathy. He put forth his hand as though to take hers, then withdrew it. "This is good, this is wonderful news. How could you doubt that I would be happy for you?"

She shook her head. "I did not doubt that. I know your generous heart too well."

"Generous!" He put his face in his hands briefly, as though to gather his thoughts, then stood up. He was about to say more, but James reappeared, smiling, and they spoke of other things. Watching the men, Mary thought, *He knows, he accepts.* But after Rupert had gone, and James had tactfully bidden her good night and she was in her room alone, she lay in bed wondering just how sharply such news might cut a man's pride, or his trust—or his passion.

Rupert himself went not to his quarters but up the streets to the Blue Boar. The taproom was still open but at this late hour none of his men were there so he sat at a table alone and ordered a tankard of ale.

He felt defeated. He had felt it for two days, since the king told him Mary's news, all unconscious, in the midst of another conversation. He had had to turn away for a second to conceal his reaction, but after that he had managed it as well as he could. He told himself that he was happy for her sake. But they had defeated him, she and Richmond together. He smiled sardonically to himself, remembering his comment one night about soldiers and defeats. How did that translate into his situation now? *No man can call himself a lover until his beloved conceives by another.*

He had once had a huge advantage over her, yet he had not abused it. He recalled the moment when she had begged for his friendship and then said she was afraid she might need him more than he needed her. He had known why, soon after—it was because of love. She was afraid of love, because she had never known it. He had known it, and that had given him the advantage.

He knew how one fell into love and how long it took to fall out. He had not fallen out of love with Susanne von Kuffstein, his sweet jailer of Linz, until Mary Villiers took his hand in the Wassenaer Hof. He would not fall out of love with Mary until— There was no *until.* He thought of a line from the poem, the sonnet he had slaved over for days and that she had dismissed in three words. He had it by heart, just as he had her lacerating poem on friendship. Shakespeare said it for him: *Beyond all date, even to eternity.* It was like being in prison again.

The barmaid came and sat down with him; she often did that if the night was not busy. She was a comely maid, with a self-confidence that sometimes took his breath away. She knew who he was but pretended she didn't, and always addressed him as "sir," which made his men frown but tickled him. ·

"Now," she said with a wink, "you look as though you should be in bed, sir, not sitting here drinking with me."

He laughed softly as he looked at her. "Where do you sleep?"

She jerked her head toward the ceiling and wrinkled her pert nose. "Up there, under the roof. I share it with too many creatures, though, not all of them human. Still, it will do for the time being."

"You've no family to stay with? You're not from Oxford?"

"No, sir, Woodstock. Do you know Woodstock?"

"Yes, I have a lot of . . . Yes, I know it."

"Then you'll know what a grand little town it is." She smoothed down her dark hair, then ran her hands over shoulders and breasts to do the same with her blouse and bodice, which were white and red with black lacing. In the dim light she looked like someone in a Breughel painting. But softer and more approachable. ·

"Why did you leave?"

"You know what they make there? Nails. My father makes nails; my brothers make nails, my mother and sisters sort them and pack them and help sell them. Can you see me forever putting nails in little bags, sir?"

He laughed. "I can understand you dreaming of greater things. But is this what you want—the Blue Boar?"

"Yes! That is, you have hit it, sir: I should like an inn of my own. And there are but two ways for that: once I know the business—and I do boast that I know it now—I must marry an innkeeper. Either that, or someone must set me up in a place of my own. I don't aim high; a nice taproom and a few tables will do me to begin with. I'm saving, of course, but by my reckoning it would take a few hundred years on my wages just to get me started, so a generous gentleman it will have to be." She looked at him with frank ambition, her black eyes smiling. "I should be ever so grateful, sir, if you hear of one who would suit."

He grinned. "In either respect?"

"In either. I don't sell myself cheap, you see," she said, taking the words out of his mouth and making him glad he had not said them, for there was an insouciant pride about her that commanded respect. And he liked her; it was impossible not to.

"Well," he said after thinking hard, "I've but one piece of advice. Before you accept either of these arrangements, I strongly suggest you see the money on the table first. And I mean that—to the last farthing. Let no man take advantage of you."

She considered, and after a while she nodded. "Thank you. I shall keep that in my bosom, sir. It's the friendliest word anyone has ever said to me."

"I wish you good fortune." He smiled. "What's your name?"

"Mary, sir."

He ran his hand over his face and laughed, rose and put a pile of coins on the table. "Good luck, Mary." Then he went home.

On the way he made a mental note to ensure the horse master and the farrier at Woodstock were getting nails cheap on the spot instead of bringing them in. That at least salvaged something from the evening.

It was Mary's last sitting for the miniature, three days before James left for France and before she moved into Merton with the queen, and she was walking up the stairs with two attendants toward the warm, well-lit room under the eaves of Christ Church where Dick Gibson, husband to her page, Anne, was doing the portraits. She enjoyed the visits to the painter, as in the normal course of events she never saw him, and she was struck by the contrast between him and Anne. They were the same height but Anne was fair and expressive, with swift changes of light and shade in her manner, while Dick had shaggy dark hair and was calm and earnest. He was proud of his craft and meticulous in everything he did; he never smiled while he painted Mary, and the dark slanting eyes that glanced between her face and his paper as he sketched were as neutral as if he were drawing a complicated piece of statuary. But before and after the sitting he bustled about trying to make her comfortable and attend to her wants—which were few, in the end, for there was something peaceful about being at rest in his spacious, well-organized room, with nothing to do but sit and think and dream.

Today was different, however, for as she reached the door she met Prince Rupert coming out. He stopped for a second, his tall figure barring the doorway, then he stepped back, opened the door wider and bowed low to usher her in.

"Madam, this is an unexpected delight. We are giving Mr. Gibson no rest!" He raised an eyebrow at Dick Gibson as he straightened, but the painter shook his head.

"The Duchess of Richmond is exactly on time, as always. I was anticipating her with the greatest pleasure. Madam, your humble servant. Allow me to take your mantle."

"Let me," the prince said, and stepping beside her drew it gently from her shoulders. Then he folded it over his arm and stood looking at her front on, as though he were the portraitist instead of the little man who was now examining them with a doubtful frown on his face: he knew princes, and these two were about to play havoc with his working day.

"Why are you wearing green?" Rupert said.

Mary gave an apologetic look at Gibson. "The choice was Mr. Gibson's."

The painter said stiffly, "I use a viridian pigment that comes up with particular brilliance over ivory."

"Oh, do you?" the prince said. "You must show me." He was still taking in Mary. "But it should be blue, for your eyes."

Mary laughed. "It is not going to be anything, Your Highness, unless you permit me to sit down."

"Is this your last sitting?"

"Yes. Is your portrait done too?"

"It is, but I am not allowed to see it. Perhaps if you add your pleas to mine, the artist will let me?" He raised an eyebrow again at Gibson, but received a stern look in reply.

"It is still wet, Your Highness. No impression of the colors can be gained until the last layer is dry. You saw it at the beginning of the session—I made only the lightest finishing touches, but I cannot be easy showing it to anyone until the paint has settled."

"You see?" Rupert said to Mary. "If I have been depicted as Bluebeard I shan't know until tomorrow. I shall be content with watching while yours is completed. I know Mr. Gibson will not deny me that—I am too much an admirer of his technique."

Gibson sighed but could see that no protest would work against the prince, and he began to prepare for the last phase of the portrait. During the first sittings he had made sketches in pencil and watercolor, then a deft little piece in oils that the king had already laid claim to; they were all on a table at the side of the room. The prince looked them over one by one, his intent expression not unlike Gibson's when he was working, which rather amused Mary. Meanwhile, as Gibson was arranging her and the chair on the right angle, she held the almost finished miniature in her hand to review it—an oval piece of ivory on which the colors glowed as though the light were somehow coming from behind them.

The prince appeared at her elbow. "But this is exquisite. You have excelled yourself, Mr. Gibson. For the sake of this, I forgive you everything you've put in mine—even the Prussian blue."

Mary looked up, laughing. "You are to stop teasing Mr. Gibson; that is my job. You will now sit down and behave yourself while I try to compose my countenance."

His hand closed over the back of hers as he took the ivory from her fingers. "You have painted her with nothing behind the head and shoulders but a blue . . . what is that delicate tint? The sky at dawn. She is a creature of the air, an angel."

Gibson grunted as he bent to adjust Mary's skirts, though they were not in the painting. He was smiling to himself, and she knew he must like to have the prince's praise almost as much as that of the king.

Eventually they were all in position: Gibson at his preferred distance from her with his table of materials to one side and the piece of ivory clasped in a small frame on a stand before him, and Rupert sitting behind the artist's shoulder where he could see both Mary and the portrait.

But he was not looking at the miniature; he was gazing at her. She thought at first he was playing a game, trying to make her laugh and interrupt the sitting, or to see who could make the other blink the most, but his look did not make her smile or move. Instead it made her remember the miraculous moment in the tunnel under Merton, when he had stood limned by lantern light, with an even brighter glow in his eyes, and said, *I want to look at you. I never can.*

There were no barriers between them, and no watcher but the artist, whose swift glances and tiny strokes were operating with another purpose from the deep, intense gaze that she and Rupert exchanged. Time and the room around them retreated as she opened her eyes on his. Soon all she could see was his face, surrounded by a shimmer of light in white and gray. And she was able to speak into his dark eyes wordless messages that she poured out across the narrow space between his body and hers.

She opened herself to him and told him all her secrets, the greatest being her love, unending and unalterable, and made richer by every second she was with him, or thought of him, or hoped for him. In return he took all her pain and wishes into himself and let her see his own, transforming them with the same mystical gesture into blessings that he received out of his love for her. Together they accepted everything fate might provide, as long as love endured.

Then he was gone, and she did not see him leave. She was still looking at his face, suspended like an icon before her gaze, when Gibson laid down his brush and looked round, and they both realized that the chair behind him was empty. Gibson tilted his head and Mary followed his glance to see the door silently closing.

Gibson raised his eyebrows and smiled. "The prince might have stayed, he is the most discreet observer. And I have never seen you look so serene, madam. May I keep you just a little longer? We are nearly finished here."

She did not answer. She remained floating in the trance that she and Rupert had created, wishing it a boundless sea.

Chapter 24

❧

James spent some of his last morning in Oxford with the king and Digby, which he would have preferred to avoid, for given a quick, early start he might have found it less arduous to tear himself away from Mary. As it was, he would be returning home for the farewell and waiting there for his escort to turn up—Prince Rupert himself was to accompany him out of the city and provide the troopers who would travel with him to the coast.

James had a feeling Digby had contrived the meeting, for his lordship's fellow Secretary of State, Sir Edward Nicholas, was not present and it had an ad hoc and unofficial flavor. James did not mind being at his monarch's beck and call, but he resented the idea that the king might have had him summoned because Digby had thought up some trifle to be discussed at the last minute.

But the king made him feel that the meeting was simply to give him another fond farewell, and his benign and ceremonious manner softened James, who answered the usual questions of concern with patience. Yes, he carried with him the miniatures of Rupert and Mary, carefully packed: the one he would gladly relinquish to Marguerite de Rohan, and the other he cherished and was grateful for.

"I have seen it," Digby said, "and I never saw a better likeness of the inimitable duchess. It has its critics, though, she tells me—Prince Rupert objected to her choice of gown."

There was more than Digby's usual slyness in this remark, and James went cold. What did the man suspect? He felt more relieved than ever that Mary had agreed to spend the time of his absence at Merton, where Rupert was still unwelcome and where the world—Digby included—could find no fault with her manner of existence or her friends.

Meanwhile the king answered for him, saying to Digby, "Rupert is an artist, and it was a true artist's comment. I don't know if you are aware, but he has done some very fine engravings in the past, which I should be happy to show you."

Digby gave James an ironical and complicit smile at this point, then declined very courteously, and they moved on to other subjects, none of which afforded James any more peace of mind than the first. After which he was allowed to go and take leave of his wife.

They sat in the great chamber waiting for the escort to arrive and talked mainly about babies, a theme that Mary, to his amusement, could follow for hours. She was reading everything she could on it and had even borrowed books from Sir William Harvey that had drawings of homunculi that he couldn't stomach the sight of. She also had many cautions for him about traveling by sea, which were of little use to him as he was always robust—but he liked the way she gave them, with a wistful, anxious look that clouded her blue eyes.

Eventually, when he reckoned it must be about time, he said, "I am thinking I should like to institute a farewell ritual of my own. It's very simple: we exchange a kiss on this threshold and you do not accompany me below. But you may wave from the window; in fact if you do not I shall dismount and run up here and oblige you to embrace me all over again."

She laughed, for she could tell he wanted her to, and suddenly there was a commotion of hooves on the cobbles outside. James ordered his mount and sumpter horse brought round, and then kissed Mary in the doorway, to the edification of far more servants than he thought necessary. She did not open her lips on his—she still never did—but she felt very soft and pliant in his arms; it was as though there were no child within her. But he had seen now the subtle changes in her skin and her breasts, with the dark aureole about her tender nipples. He wished fiercely that he could be here to see all the other changes to come, and watch her grow into a mother. She sensed this and with her mouth to his ear she whispered, "I shall write often, and tell you everything." For that moment he believed her.

Then he stepped back out of her arms and made her an elaborate bow, and startled the household by almost running downstairs.

Rupert and the escort were all there waiting, superbly equipped and ready to ride, so with a quick word to them James mounted up and raised his eyes toward a pale oval face at a high window. He swept off his hat and waved it, and both her hands came up in fluttering response. Then his party crashed away up the street.

He and Rupert talked little as they pushed through the town, a rapid maneuver as everyone gave them thoroughfare. But he had something to say before the prince sheered off to whichever garrison he was heading for, so eventually he said, "I saw Lord Digby this morning."

Rupert grinned over at him. "That must have been a pleasure."

"Less so than usual," James said mildly. "You are quite well aware, I'm sure, that Lord Digby is occasionally malicious on your account. I should tell you that today he happened to mention your name in the same sentence as that of my wife." Rupert looked both annoyed and alarmed, and James sighed. "It was trivial and the king noticed nothing. But I did."

"Why do you tell me this?" Rupert said, so low that James could hardly hear over the thud of their horses' hooves.

"Because of something Sir Edward Hyde said to me the other day. I thought it very perceptive. It is Hyde's view that the king has a natural penchant to give more notice to the advice and opinions of people he likes and trusts. Thus, in the midst of a debate, he may sometimes be swayed more by affection and esteem for a speaker than by that person's argument. Your Highness," he went on, slightly exasperated by the prince's dark and challenging expression, "the king loves you. This gives a force to your counsel that I would not on any account wish you to lose. I am your friend—allow me to give you a friend's thoughts before I part from you. Beware of Lord Digby and anyone else who may seek to lower you in the eyes of the king. You cannot be criticized as a soldier and commander—no one could possibly do that—but as these appalling times have already shown us, even a prince's character may be impugned by people driven by the basest motives."

"Thank you," Rupert said, and looked away. After a moment he said, "Have you mentioned this to your wife?"

"Of course not. Digby is an old favorite of hers; she enjoys his company and she is perfectly capable of managing whatever his conversation may throw in her way. I mention it to you because it seems congruent with what Lord Digby has been doing of late—

persuading the king that his generalship of the armies is enough in itself to ensure outright victory. The implication is that His Majesty needs no military advice but his own. Which can be seen as a reflection on yourself."

"Digby has no idea of how one prepares for war," Rupert said, "let alone how one wages it. But I uphold his view in one respect; His Majesty is the guiding light that we all follow."

"Indeed," James said patiently. They were riding past the castle, and he looked up at its craggy walls, already counting the weeks when he would see them again. "But he seems bent on flattering the king into such a strong notion of his own powers that the idea of defeat in any shape is made foreign to his mind."

"I know what you mean," Rupert said unexpectedly. "The other day in the war council Digby tried to tell the king we had not lost at Newbury! He said Essex had abandoned Newbury and Reading and gone back home with his tail between his legs. His Majesty had a very dry rejoinder to that: he said he would have much preferred to see Essex marched under escort to the castle here. That shut Digby up." He ruminated for a while, then turned a frank face to James. "I shall take what you say to heart. I always do."

At the end of November, the Earl of Essex paid a visit to John Pym, who lay dying in a great redbrick mansion not far from the Thames. Pym had been suffering from cancer for a considerable time, but even up until a week before he had been working with the same acumen and diligence that he had manifested in his long political career.

As the earl was shown upstairs toward the sickroom, he reflected on what the man's achievements had been and on what Pym might hope for from this visit. Pym's guiding purpose as a statesman was religion, and the earl recalled a phrase that had defined that purpose for him when Pym addressed the king in Parliament, three years before: *The greatest liberty of the kingdom is religion; thereby we are freed from spiritual evils, and no impositions are so grievous as those that are laid upon the soul.* Now this high-principled man was about to meet his Maker, and only a week since, the Solemn League and Covenant, adopted by Parliament in late September, had become law. Henceforth, every English Protestant, whatever church, meeting or congregation he or she might wish to attend, was bound to worship as a Presbyterian according to the strictures of the Scottish Kirk. The Scots Covenanters had wrought this by offering Parliament an army of twenty-one thousand men in a military bargain that Essex as a soldier could only approve. As a Puritan who had fought and was still fighting for independence of religion and worship, however, it made him reluctant to discuss the question with Pym. That every churchgoer in England should have to swear an oath to keep the Covenant sorely tried Essex's conscience, but he could not wish his own kind of torment on a dying man. Whatever Pym said on the subject, therefore, he told himself to accept.

Pym had a right to die expecting that his great work for the power and privileges of Parliament would be upheld, and since he had made religion a matter for Parliament, he gloried in the Solemn League and Covenant and would not appreciate any argument upon it—in fact Pym himself had been the first in England to take the oath. But there was another question, on which Essex as a soldier had a duty to be strictly honest. He knew Pym would ask him how soon Parliament might vanquish the king in the field and bring him to London on Parliament's terms. Essex had not thought of the right answer to this one before he was shown into Pym's room.

Pym was fifty-nine, a strong, square-faced man who had once been called "the Ox" because of his appearance, which was plain to the point of being unkempt. Now the light hair was streaked with gray, his cheeks were hollow and the hands that lay on the coverlet were faded and bony, but the calm light of conviction was still in his eyes, which brightened further at the sight of the earl.

After the greetings were over, Essex sat down on a chair that had been drawn near the bedside, where Pym was propped on bolsters and surrounded by books and papers strewn on the coverlet before him. The chair was too small for Essex, and it creaked as he leaned forward and said, "I shall not stay long; I don't want to tire you."

Pym gave a gentle smile. "I shall soon have all the rest I require, my lord. How does Lord Warwick fare? And Lord Saye, and his son Fiennes?" They talked of friends and family for some time, and it happened that between them they mentioned all the brave companions whom King Charles had tried to arrest in the House in January the year before. Since then the most brilliant of them all, John Hampden, had been killed in one of Prince Rupert's raids at Chalgrove. William Strode—the gentleman who had suffered longest from the king's displeasure, having spent the eleven years of Charles's personal rule in prison for sedition—was still just as outspoken a warrior for Parliament's cause, along with cavalry commander Sir Arthur Haselrig. Meanwhile the more peaceable Denzil Holles, brother to the Earl of Clare, as a Presbyterian leader felt that the Solemn League and Covenant had brought timely ratification of his ideals and aims for the Christians of England.

Pym eventually turned to the outcome of the war, and Essex was moved to find that he still had the dying man's support for his own strategies. "I have great faith in Oliver St. John," Pym said, "and he has great faith in you. As long as his voice prevails in Parliament—and there are some who say he wears a corner of my mantle," he added with a sad smile, "your experience will count where it is most needed. And those who take a precipitate view, and who cry up commanders like Waller and Cromwell, as though these men alone can win the war, cannot sway the Committee of Safety toward recklessness and risk. We must continue to build and train the armies along the lines you have established, and mold the Scots army into brothers for our cause."

Essex could only agree, and he murmured something about the magnificent example Pym had set on the Committee of Safety, the administrative body for the military that Pym had hitherto ruled with vigor. Essex had much to regret in his going, especially since the exploits of other commanders like Sir William Waller in the western theater of war and Oliver Cromwell, a mere colonel in the midlands, were being very favorably compared with his own record as Lord General.

He could see that Pym was looking for some encouragement about the campaigns that would come once the winter was over, so he began, "The Scots army will prove a great asset in the north, for many reasons. Not the least being that it may tempt the king to send some of his best commanders there in an attempt to hold its advance. The more attention is diverted there, the weaker his position may become at Oxford." He gave his most aggressive smile. "We shall certainly exploit that to the hilt."

Pym nodded. "And in the west? Heaven forfend that he will have the iniquity to bring over a Catholic army from Ireland—but what should we do in such a case?"

It was on the tip of Essex's tongue to ask Pym where the difference lay in Parliament bringing an army from Scotland and the king recalling troops from Ireland—but in the circumstances he did not voice that thought. Instead he said, "The troops that are already being shipped to the west coast require months of preparation. Fighting the Irish Confederates is quite another challenge from the shock they will get when they face our armies. Again, the king will need to send experienced commanders to handle them—and again, we shall see Oxford weakened."

Pym closed his eyes in exhaustion or pain, and Essex decided to give him one more message of hope before he quitted the room. "Friend, let me tell you honestly that midway through this year everything seemed to point to ultimate victory for the king's men. Now, bit by bit that has altered. It may not yet be perceptible to the king—though the Scots must surely be giving him pause—but to my mind his day is going by. The sun is setting on his cause, and as it does so, we pledge ourselves to strip him of the means to prevail."

The quiet, steady voice that used to hold Parliament spellbound issued forth again, though Pym did not open his eyes. "And one day he will be brought before Parliament and tried for the evils he has committed against the commonwealth. For the second greatest liberty is justice, and Parliament is the fountain of law, the great council of the kingdom, the highest court. This duty we undertake in the name of his people."

Essex rose. "Amen," he said, as though to a prayer, and took his last leave. When he got to his house he made his secretary ransack the shelves for a copy of John Pym's speech against the king's summary dissolution of Parliament in 1640, and found the paragraph that had been haunting him all the way home.

The words of dying men are full of piercing affections; if we might be heard to speak, no doubt we should so fully express our love and faithfulness to our prince, as might take off the false suggestions and aspersions of others; at least we should in our humble supplications recommend some such things to him in the name of his people, as would make for his own honor, and the public good of his kingdom.

What would John Pym have done if King Charles had walked into the sickroom to talk with them that afternoon? Essex believed he knew. But he also believed it was too late.

It was mid-December, and Charles was spending a family evening with the queen, Mary Villiers, and Mary's stepfather, the Earl of Antrim, who had come over in secret from Ireland to Oxford. Charles was wary of Antrim but Henrietta-Maria was not, for she had already accepted his first diplomatic approaches while she was in Yorkshire, before her progress down to Oxford, and was very eager to promote what he now had to offer to their cause. To be fair, Charles thought, this was not simply because Antrim was Catholic, but because he had a voluble Irish way with him that perhaps reminded Henrietta-Maria of the rambling fashion in which they discussed things at the French court. Charles had a very good idea of how long it would take to reach a decision in the councils in Paris. He used to feel some sympathy for Cardinal Richelieu, whose method had been to cut through argument and deliver a slashing dictum, and he very often wished he could do that himself.

Mary meanwhile looked pleased to be with them, despite his guessing that she too was wary of the earl, though for different reasons. He knew that all her filial devotion was his, but it touched him to see her eyeing Antrim as though looking for protective qualities and finding none. Antrim was no doubt an excellent husband to Mall's mother, Catherine, but he was all for himself in the end, and exuded none of the sustaining warmth of the late Duke of Buckingham, who could beam like the sun on his intimates and reconcile them to him and the world with just one winning smile. Charles, who had loved Buckingham almost as much as Mall, remembered best his rich laugh, which, though loudest when he was telling his own jokes, was instantly infectious.

Mary asked many questions of the earl about her mother—her pursuits, her books and her home—but Antrim kept returning to the war. "The Cessation," he said in his agreeable voice, "was a stroke of genius that gives Your Majesty untold powers in Ireland."

Charles smiled. He thought his Lord Lieutenant, the Earl of

Ormond, would be only too happy to exercise untold powers on his behalf in Ireland, but he had had enough trouble as it was securing the Cessation in mid-September, a year-long truce between the Catholic Confederate rebels and the royal forces. "It gives us the opportunity to recall troops, certainly. And as we bring them back it is scarcely possible for Parliament to throw the usual lies at us about who they are—they are all English and all Protestant."

Henrietta-Maria put in, "Oh no, we shall still be accused of raising Catholic armies and unleashing them on innocent women and children—we always are! And those disgusting pamphlets will go on being thrust under our noses by Roundhead villains. I thought when that detestable John Pym died we might see no more of them, but they increase by the week! And if it's not about Irish atrocities it's more of—" She caught Mary's eye and broke off. The scurrilous papers about Prince Rupert and the Duchess of Richmond were still appearing, which was irksome for them and everyone else.

"In which case," Antrim put in smoothly, "if you cannot give your slanderers the lie, why not settle it with yourselves to raise still more men from Ireland, whatever their persuasion? You already have an impressive and heartening number of loyal Catholics in your armies. . . ." He caught Charles's eye and hesitated for a moment. It was an awkward issue for the king; at the beginning of the war he had sent out a decree that no Catholic could hold an officer's post under his command, but he had quickly realized he could never enforce it. The fact was that many English Catholics, despite their almost total lack of rights under his government and his merciless imposition of recusancy fines for their continuing to worship in their own way, had decided they still had more to gain by throwing their weight in with him than with Parliament; many of the wealthy Catholic nobility had thus raised considerable forces on their own account and dedicated them to his cause.

Antrim, having searched his face carefully, decided to continue. "The Earl of Ormond, for all his competence, is not as well placed as I to see the grand potential amongst my countrymen, but I assure you, Your Majesty, that given the time and power to act, I could negotiate with more gentlemen of influence than you think possible, and recruit a force that would strike a mighty blow for you the moment they stepped onto the soil of England."

Charles raised his eyebrows. As a grab for Ormond's job this was as blatant as Antrim could get, and he was not surprised to see on Mary's face the same expression that must be on his own, though Henrietta-Maria was glowing at the prospect of a gigantic army building on the western shores. He sighed inwardly; nothing in this war was easy. And the idea of Antrim as his Lord Lieutenant was ridiculous—he could never appoint a Catholic.

As the evening drew to a close he asked Mary how she was and received a grateful smile and many reassurances. In fact she looked splendid. Her gown concealed her shape but he could swear there was no change in it, for she was as slender as ever. It was still early, of course—scarce three months. And now he had an added joy in seeing the two women depart together, for his lovely queen was pregnant too, though it was too soon for anyone but Mary to have been told.

"My wife is not taxing you?" he said with a smile after he had kissed her hand in farewell.

She gave Henrietta-Maria a bright glance of gratitude. "On the contrary; I feel as though I live in a cocoon."

"We take it in turns to spin it," Henrietta-Maria said, her eyes sparkling. "It is the tenderest endeavor, keeping each other safe and well."

Chapter 25

WHILE RICHMOND WAS AWAY and Mary was at Merton, Rupert could not see her. He kept hoping to run into her at Christ Church, where she went often with the queen or sometimes alone, but it never happened. At times he would go there on the basis of something that had been said the day before, fully expecting her arrival, but he was always disappointed. It was absurd, but he felt as though there was a conspiracy to prevent their meeting. The parliamentary pamphlets about them were still turning up, causing him the same anger and her the same hurt, or so he imagined. Perhaps, for this or some other tormenting reason, she was avoiding him.

James Stuart was expected back around Christmas or the New Year. Rupert often thought of the last Christmas and remembered his vows and hers, the gifts mined with meaning, and the radiance that love and the season had lent her. Whereas this Christmas loomed chilly and mournful, for he could not shake off a presentiment that he would not be allowed to see her on the night that had been so poignant and momentous the year before.

So he made himself a present, to commemorate his birthday on the seventeenth. He was now twenty-four—not so venerable that he wanted to advertise the fact, so he mentioned it to no one. And he would never reveal to her what he made. Purchasing in secret from Dick Gibson one of the sketches done for her miniature, he obtained steel for engraving and a fine burin, and every night, late into the small hours after his return from duty, he worked away on a copy, fashioning a small rectangular plate that held her image reversed. When it was finished he slipped it into an inside pocket of his doublet so that it rested all day over his heart. He often recalled her exclamation that he should wear something sterner to protect him than a buff coat. Now she was with him wherever he rode, close against him and gazing into his heart as though into a mirror. And at any time, in order to see her he had only to draw out the steel, apply ink and press it to a sheet of paper for her true face to appear before him like magic.

Sometimes he could not resist riding past Merton. He always stopped outside the gatehouse and someone would run up and make to hold his horse so he could enter, but he would wave them away. He pretended to be interested in the weird carving in stone above the gate that showed the founder of the college, the first in Oxford—Walter de Merton, Chancellor of England and Bishop of Rochester. Rupert wondered, if Essex's men ever got into the town, whether they would climb ladders and take mallets up there and smash the kneeling bishop and the figure of Saint John. If they went on to the rest they would be slaying an astonishing array of animals—unicorn, lion, sheep, hound, wolf, and a perfect warren of rabbits peering from their burrows, while above a covey of birds looked down from a line of aggressively fruiting trees. In the center was a closed book bound with iron bands: the book of Revelation. After a minute he would ride on, his heart so tight he felt suffocated.

And then at last, still in cold December, he saw her. He was walking down Magpie Lane alone on market day, and far ahead he saw a glint of red-gold hair that could only be hers, and stopped by a stand displaying sheets of songs. She came into view by degrees, bright pieces of her appearing amongst the crowd and being snuffed out again like segments of a stained glass window lit by fitful sunlight. She was wearing dark swallowtail blue, the color she should have worn for the miniature. The mounds of her breasts shone like marble over a low bodice sewn with pearls and her neck was bare. All this he could see though she could not see him, for he never caught her eye, her head being turned this way and that, to the queen, to Jermyn who accompanied them, or to the shops on either side. It shocked him that she should be wearing nothing against the cold, but then he saw the edge of a fox-lined cloak draped across the tip of each shoulder. Was she feverish, and oblivious of the keen winter air that pinched his cheeks as he watched?

He did not want to move. If he approached, the vision of her would be even more fragmented by the grudging haste of the queen's greeting and Mary's own surprise and disarray.

Then as they drew closer the mob in the center of the lane parted and he had a better view of them all. They were paused at

a stall that displayed lace on high racks, and the queen was holding swaths of the trumpery fabric over her face and shoulders and
laughing with Jermyn while Mary stood to one side, looking at
nothing, a hand gripping a wooden upright and the other at her
throat.

Then he saw her sway and begin to sink. This time the picture
behind her was as clear and congealed as a painting, while in front
only her figure moved, as her knees gave way and she began to collapse to the ground, unseen except by him.

He ran forward, not even registering the people between, and
caught her just before her head hit the stones. He was on his knees,
his arms about Mary's neck and shoulders, when the queen turned
and screamed. Mary's head had fallen back, her eyes were closed
and her face was as white as paper.

"*Grand Dieu!*" the queen cried. She too fell on her knees, regardless of the dirt, and put a hand to Mary's cheek. "She said she
had a fever five minutes ago—how can she be so cold?" Henrietta-
Maria shuddered. "Does she breathe? Oh! I shall never forgive
myself." She put her face to Mary's for a second. "She lives." The
queen sprang to her feet and said to Jermyn, "She must be carried
back at once. At once!"

Rupert kept one arm around Mary's shoulders and put the
other beneath her knees, then stood and strode away. There was a
commotion behind him and the others followed, the high, anxious
voice of the queen pursuing him down the lane. His heart beat so
fast and loud that he could not hear Mary's, though he held her
close against him. He looked down at her still face, then bent his
lips to her neck to search for a pulse beneath her white skin. She
took a trembling breath against his cheek and he raised his head
and hurried on through the crowd that parted before him.

Just before the gate of Merton she opened her eyes and looked
up at him, lost and frightened, and he said, "Put your arms around
my neck, my darling, I am taking you upstairs."

She obeyed without a word and dropped her head on his
chest, hiding her face, and with guards and no doubt a mob of
other people in his wake he mounted the stairs, his heart thud-
ding. She was now tense and somehow lighter in his arms, and if it
were not for his terror he could have carried her on for hours, out
of everyone's lives and away, to escape at last to somewhere they

could be alone. But instead he said, "Her bedchamber?" to one of the servants scurrying by his side, and with them running before, he reached her room and walked in and laid her down on her bed. Regardless of the others he took her face between his hands, with his fingers entangled in her soft curls, and said, "*Mon amour*, are you in pain?"

A rictus crossed her face and she whimpered, "Oh!" in the voice of a child that has been struck unjustly, and at that moment the queen burst panting into the room.

Rupert rose and said to Henrietta-Maria, "She needs Sir William Harvey. Now."

The queen's hands flew to her mouth and she gave an anguished look at Mary, who was bent toward them with her eyes closed and her hands clasped over her stomach.

"I'll go myself. Look after her," he said, and ran from the room and down the stairs.

He shouted to Jermyn as he went, swung his baldric over his head and threw his sword to him. He had little more than four hundred yards to cover to Christ Church and he did it at speed, the cold air lancing his lungs. He darted left at the end of Merton Street then right past the cathedral and at last out across the great quadrangle, scarcely aware of the people along the way who stopped to stare at his charging figure. He tore across the grass to an inner doorway and raced up and through the buildings to the princes' apartments, where he knew they and Harvey would be at lessons.

The schoolroom was neat, cool and quiet when he burst in, and Harvey looked up with an annoyance that changed to alarm. Rupert's breath was sobbing in his chest as he said, "The Duchess of Richmond."

"Where?"

"Merton. I implore you to go now." He read Harvey's unspoken question. "There's pain."

Harvey turned to the boys, closed the lesson with his usual sentence in Latin and walked to the door. "I shall collect my things and be gone."

"I beg you to make all haste. I'll follow."

"Get your breath back, Your Highness," Harvey said kindly. "Nature goes at her own pace." Then he left.

Rupert leaned against the wall with his eyes shut and forced his breathing to subside. He could still feel her arms around his neck, clinging desperately as though he could save her. But he had left her in the hands of others, as he must.

When he opened his eyes the boys were still at their desks, staring at him in consternation. He took Harvey's chair and sat facing them, his arms on the desk and his head bent, and all at once his little monkey leaped down off James's shoulder and ran to nestle between his hands.

"She still likes you most," James said with a hint of jealousy.

Rupert raised his head. "But she's much better off with you. She was pining at my place; I was never there. I'm glad I gave her to you—don't worry, I shan't take her back."

James smiled happily but young Charles said in a low, solemn voice, "Is Mall going to lose the baby?"

Rupert shook his head. "I can't tell you. Sir William will do everything he can. But as he says, Nature . . ." He couldn't go on.

But Charles gave it some thought and then said, "Mam said to our father yesterday it's a pity Mall is so delicate, but even if she loses this one, at least it shows she *can*. So she may have another."

This struck Rupert as the cruelest thing he had heard that day, but he could see that Charles was looking for reassurance. So he said, "Your mother will take the greatest care of her, we can count on that."

"And it would only be very, very small, wouldn't it?" Charles said.

Rupert was stroking the little monkey. "Yes, and some people think even newborn babies are not really people for a long time, so it is best not to get fond of them. But I don't know. I'm odd or stupid, perhaps, but I can't help feeling that losing a baby, because it's so tiny, must be very like losing a pet. Only harder. And I hate losing pets."

James had come up beside him, and at this he laid a gentle hand on Rupert's arm. "Don't be sad, cousin. You'll never, ever lose Boy. He's magic."

Rupert picked up the monkey and placed it back on James's shoulder, and smiled at the boys. At that moment he had a sharp revelation that he wanted children. And he thought of Mary lying curled on her bed in her blue dress and realized that in a secret, strange and impermissible way he had wanted this one.

Chapter 26

❧

MARY WAS STROLLING IN the Physick Garden with Digby. Her body felt whole now, though fragile, but her heart was still raw. She knew that until James came home, and they could hold each other and weep, she was not healed. But her royal family and everyone at court had been kind and they were pleased to see her abroad again.

On the day of her loss, Prince Rupert had waited in the Front Quad of Merton for hours until Sir William Harvey went down. Then he had sent up his sympathies and left. Later he sent flowers—how he had found anyone to lay hands on them in mid-winter she could not imagine—and afterward, every day he was in Oxford he had called at the gatehouse to inquire after her and wait to receive her reply. He did not write, he did not visit, and she had known he could do neither, realizing how such behavior would be viewed by the queen and her court after his rescue of her in the street.

In the vast enclosed garden, both she and Digby were in furs against the cold, and he remarked that they were like a couple of bears in a nursery rhyme that had climbed over the walls to steal honey from the college. He himself had studied at Magdalen, and he had exaggerated tales to tell about what the scholars got up to in his youth. He had always had the ability to cheer her, and he did so now with amusing talk as they wandered about among the plots, some of which were bare and already furrowed for spring planting, while others held the faded fronds of autumn.

At one point he said, "When I went looking for you at Merton I put my head into the tennis court. Prince Rupert was there, play-ing a match with one of his officers. I shouldn't like to take him on—with his long arms, you'd have much more chance of being whacked about the face with his racquet than hitting the ball with your own. Did he call on you before the game?"

"No. I see nothing of him."

"So I hear," said Digby in an approving tone full of innuendo. She looked at him sidelong and he said, "Not that he didn't do you a great service not long ago. I applaud his promptitude. But—"

"But what?" she interrupted, to warn him. She wanted light conversation, not a probe about Prince Rupert. She hoped against hope that she was no longer in danger of her passion for the prince being discovered. James's confidence in her and the prince's absence from her life were plain to the whole court. Only old evidence, like her poem of friendship to Rupert or her notes to Essex, could possibly destroy her. She was giving no one any present cause for speculation about her loyalties.

Digby was sensitive to her reaction, however, and raised his eyebrows. "You don't like it when I criticize our dear and glorious prince, do you? Why is that?"

She smiled at him. "He is a friend. So are you, and if people criticize you I defend you."

"Of course you do." He patted her hand on his arm. "But he was not always your friend, and I'm somewhat intrigued that he is now. What do you value him for?"

They went on a few paces and, searching her mind, she could see no harm in Digby's being told something of it. It might surprise him into saying something frank for once. "I consider Prince Rupert to be our best hope of winning this war, and of winning it in the right way."

"*The right way?*" Digby said. "Hanging about Oxford playing tennis?"

"Don't be simplistic, it doesn't suit you." He gave a laugh at that and she continued, "I once told him, to his face, that he would be the king's agent of destruction. That was early last year, while I was trying to persuade him not to come to England."

Digby pursed his lips in a soundless whistle. "My, my, how interesting. Why?"

"I hated to think what it would be like if we were thrown into civil war. Now I know, and it's ten thousand times worse than I foresaw. We see people like Falkland dying in despair, as though by his own hand. We see brother fighting brother, son against father— husband against brother-in-law. If it goes on and on like this, think of a child . . ." Her voice faltered and he looked at her, alarmed, but she went on, "Imagine a child born tomorrow, born into war, turning to his father one day and saying, 'Father, why did you kill Cousin John at Edgehill?' "

Digby was about to interrupt, but she said, "Does the father reply, 'Because Cousin John did not believe in Jesus Christ our Savior'? No, he cannot. Does he say, 'Because he claimed there should be no king in England'? No, for Parliament's war cry is For King and Parliament! Does he reply, 'Because he came from another country, while we ourselves are one nation under God'? No, he cannot. All he can say is, 'This abomination has been visited upon us and we are tearing this country apart because we have lost the wisdom to treat one another with humanity.' "

"I'm sorry I spoke," he said. "This agitates you. Would you care to—?"

She stopped him with an ironical look. "Oh, my lord, you know me, I am quite capable of agitating myself!"

"You will sit down here, however," he said firmly, and they settled side by side on a stone bench under a skeletal rose arbor. He began, "Very well. You were afraid that Prince Rupert would thrust us all into war before we knew its horrors. Now that we are girdled by them, why do you think him the right agent to end them?"

"Because he is our finest general." Digby's eyes narrowed at this, but she went on anyway. "If Parliament is to be withstood, we depend on him to do it."

Digby gave a short laugh and tipped his head back. "*Withstood?* Parliament must be brought to its knees, my lady, in every sense of the word. There, you see, despite having the prince as your *preux chevalier*, you have hit it, the chink in the armor. As you say, this war has indeed gone on long enough—too long, for everyone's sake. And which piece of holy writ says that Rupert is the one to bring it to a resounding close?"

She shrugged and said, "The king believes in him. Why should not we?"

"Ah." Digby leaned forward, his forearms on his knees, and looked at her sidelong, past a thick lock of fair hair. The blue eyes were speculative. "Should you like to hear what the king really believes at the moment?"

"I'd as soon hear what you think."

It was a barb—and he laughed again and sat up. "Very well, I shall tell you honestly what I think." He smiled at her startled expression. "Though using the word 'honestly' is a sure sign of the simplistic, my dear." When she failed to smile at this, he went on, "The thing has gone on too long. And what do we have now? The Scots thundering down from the north, their mouths full of John Knox and their hands out for booty."

She plucked a sprig of rosemary from beside the bench and held it to her face, relishing the sharp but honeyed smell. "I don't think 'thundering' is quite the word. They will need to deal with the Marquess of Newcastle first."

"Newcastle? What has he ever done but dither about the coast where he can get away fast? Don't even mention Newcastle. The point is, now we need something decisive to be done, before the whole thing gets out of control."

"That is exactly what Prince Rupert said at the beginning—a swift victory, and everything falls into place."

"That's not how he sounds of late," Digby said, and went on with deceptive gentleness, "but perhaps he still talks like that with you?"

She held his eye and said, "Really, my friend, do you think the prince has ever wasted my time talking to me of war? We have much more pleasurable things to discuss." He gave her a careful look but made no comment. She was sure he suspected her with Rupert, and had for some time, so there was no point in being defensive; in fact her alluding to it disconcerted him somewhat. "But you may hear my view, if you care to." He gave a little mock bow. "The nature of this war has changed since the beginning of last year. I hate to use the word 'simplistic' again, but it seems to me we can no long expect to have Parliament on its knees after one great battle, no matter where it takes place. They must be worn down to the point where they realize they have no options left."

"On the contrary," Digby replied. "Whipping the Scots would collapse Parliament in a second. They have paid a huge price for that army—the Solemn League and Covenant, no less—and the architect of *that* is dead. Bring them to the sticking place, and they'll suddenly find they have nothing in the armory. The result? A settlement on our terms. Winter will soon be over—the time for flapping about here and strengthening our forces is over too. Spring should bring victory, mark my words. And unless it does, there will be disappointment of a very serious kind. And a revaluing of the high command."

"Are you hoping I shall pass this on for Prince Rupert's edification?" Mary said, rather more briskly than she had intended.

Digby's eyes widened. "Why should I? It is the king's view, as I humbly interpret it, so I imagine he has already propounded something of the sort to the prince. There is always the question, however, of whether Rupert chooses to hear it."

Mary tucked the rosemary sprig into her bodice under the furs, between her breasts. "Consider the situation, if you choose, of the commanders who have been training our armies week by week, month by month, year by year." Digby frowned briefly—he had been one of those commanders but she was ruling him out of the equation. "Are they likely to fling them into one colossal decisive battle, on one throw of the dice, winner take all? Would it make sense to risk a kingdom in that fashion? Shouldn't we be in a better posture than we now are, before—"

"So that is the prince's view?" Digby interrupted.

She gave him a brilliant smile. "I cannot tell you; I suggest you listen to him when you are next in the war council."

"Let me put it this way," Digby said in his most silky tones. "The present view is that, in fact, we could not be in a better posture. And everything must spring from that."

"Is that your considered opinion?"

"It is His Majesty's," he said softly. "What other should I have?"

Christmas came and went before the Duke of Richmond returned. The king celebrated in private with his wife and his two boys, not without recalling the warmth of yuletide the year before. He remembered, too, the expression on Rupert's face as he had looked at Mary, and reflected sadly on what that might have meant. The queen had lately suggested to him that Prince Rupert might, after all, have a penchant for the Duchess of Richmond. If so, it was in no way returned by their dear irreproachable Mall; her indifference would put a dent in the prince's touchy pride and preoccupy him with matters nonmilitary. For this and other reasons, the king wondered whether perhaps he should get over his reluctance to post Rupert away from Oxford.

James Stuart returned on a frosty January morning, having sent a herald ahead the night before to tell the king when he would ride into the city. True to his meticulous sense of duty he reported to the king at Christ Church immediately on arrival. The audience was brief, for the king had come to a compact with the queen that the news James had to hear about his wife was best conveyed in the most private, sympathetic way before he saw Mary, to spare her the extra hurt of giving him pain. How this well-meaning attention struck James, his monarch was unable to see—he bore the news with downcast eyes and a pale countenance that betrayed no emotion. The king then put off the official audience until the afternoon and begged James to go home to his wife.

After James had gracefully bowed himself out, he came across Prince Rupert in one of the reception rooms. He had been told about the prince's rescue of Mary, and when the two friends saw each other they stepped forward and embraced. "Thank you," James said.

"I'm sorry," Rupert said. Then they parted.

Mary was at home. She had moved there two days before, when her brother George, Duke of Buckingham, obtained leave to come into the city and be with her. As James reached the great chamber, George opened the door to him. They greeted each other, said a few words and George withdrew. Mary took one look at James's face from across the room and held out her hands. He went forward, kissed them, then wrapped his arms around her and they wept. They could not speak for a long time, but he knew that words could not comfort either of them—only this nearness. Finally he said into her hair, "My dearest wife, we shall trust to the future."

"I do," she said, and her arms crept up around his neck. "But don't go away again."

Not long afterward, the Richmonds gave a dinner at their home for a dozen people. Prince Rupert, Lord Digby, the Duke of Buckingham, Viscount Grandison and Lady Ann Dalkeith were of the number. It was a lavish affair and a quantity of rare foods not usually available in January graced the board. The duchess presided, in a sparkling mood that communicated itself to all the guests, especially Prince Rupert. The prince was there in the full glory of his recent honors, for the king, in order to give his nephew a seat in the House of Lords, had created him Duke of Cumberland and Earl of Holderness—titles that hinted at the possibility of his being soon sent to the north to take care of the Scots. However he had also been named President of Wales. Young Prince Charles was nominal commander of the principality, but in this way His Majesty had put Wales directly under Rupert's jurisdiction. Speculation continued about where he would be posted soon—but it must be west or northwest. Rupert meanwhile did not speculate; he awaited his orders.

The Duke of Richmond's embassy to the French court had been a success and the king was well pleased with the assurances he received about Henrietta-Maria's welcome should she wish to establish herself in Paris. The duke also returned with promising news about Prince Rupert's coming betrothal but the prince had again given the king a determined negative from his side and the issue was finally allowed to die.

On the day after the banquet, Mary was in the library at Merton, searching the shelves for things to read to the queen. At least that was the ostensible reason—the real one was solitude and contemplation. It was a tranquil space, and at this early hour it was deserted. Merton was the only college in Oxford that had not declared for the king, and all the dons and scholars had decamped to Wales, so there was only one retainer to look after the remaining books, and he seemed to spend all his time in a study downstairs. The library occupied the upper story of the south and west sides of the Little Quadrangle next to the college chapel. The ceilings were vaulted in a shape that echoed the upturned hull of a ship, pierced at starboard and port by wide, high dormer windows that gave an airy amplitude to the reading rooms, which were separated by elaborate arches.

The pride of the library, which Mary often requested to peek at, was its more than three hundred medieval manuscripts. The pride of Merton itself was its scholars, and she could never step into the hallowed space without remembering that this was the college of John Wycliffe, the man who had first fought for the Bible to be read in English.

She was in one of the wooden stalls looking at a chained, leather-bound manuscript psalter from the 1300s, when she glanced up with a start to see Prince Rupert standing at the end of the row. He did not look surprised; she had the impression he had been gazing at her for some time.

She gave an exclamation, then something about his face froze her. He was not smiling. There was none of the quick delight she might have expected on his finding her alone like this in the quietest of hidden places. She said, "What do you do here?"

"The gatehouse guards told me where the books are. I had no idea you were here: I was looking for the work of Thomas Hobbes. He is a fellow of Christ Church, so I have found him there, but—"

"What, the man himself?" she tried to smile. "I thought he had gone to France."

"He has. I meant his books. There is just one that I seek; perhaps you can point me in the right direction."

She looked at him, cut by this coolness. Yet there was something baffled and hurt in his eyes that told her he was holding back a torrent of other words. She braced herself to hear them. "Won't you sit and talk to me? I have never thanked you in person for the way you helped me on that terrible day. Will you permit me to do so now?" He did not reply, but nor did he move away, and at last she cried, "Why do you just stand there? Why not tell me what's amiss?"

"I need to look at you. To ask myself if I know you . . . if I have ever known you. But perhaps there is no answer."

"How can you doubt the answer?" she said passionately, and saw him glance over his shoulder as though afraid they might be overheard.

Then he came closer, took a piece of paper from his sleeve, opened it and standing over her placed it on the sloping desktop, above the open psalter. "Can I doubt that this is yours?"

Mary gasped. It was a slip of paper: her second and final note to the Earl of Essex, which she had had delivered from Dover to London two years before. To disguise her hand she had written it in childlike letters in fine red chalk. It began with a humorous sketch of a devil's head, and it read: *R sure to return, perhaps within months. Essential that reconciliation be sealed before then.* And it closed with a butterfly.

She could not look up at Rupert. The blow had fallen—in the last place where she could have expected it. Horror and astonishment choked her voice as she said, "How do you have this?"

He left it before her and moved away slightly but did not sit down. "Essex has just written to me. He is mortified and sickened by the slander that Parliament's pamphleteers are printing. As a gentleman of honor, he wishes to inform me that he knows there is no truth in it. Witness this message that he tells me he received from you and that exhibits sentiments the very opposite of what the vile calumniators in Parliament would have the world believe. If I authorize him to do so, he is prepared to reveal the existence of this message, declare your enmity toward me and clear my name before his compatriots. He is also prepared to forbid any further printing of such filth on pain of punishment."

She was so cold she was almost numb. She could hardly speak. "And will you do so?"

"*Gott!*" he said. "Do you think I care about that? What else could I have in my mind but that you wrote this about me? And sent it to *Essex*? How many more are there?"

He said it brutally and she shrank back; then she looked up and saw such fury on his face that her voice trembled in response. "What do you mean?"

"This . . ." He stabbed toward it with his finger and did not finish what he was about to call it. "This is too cryptic to be anything but a message between people who have corresponded before. As it stands, it is treason. You will tell me what the rest of your correspondence contains. And how long it has been going on."

Anger scoured away all the fear on this score that had haunted her for so long. "How dare you!" Her voice filled the vaulted library and she saw him flinch as she rose to her feet. "Essex was Lord Chamberlain when I wrote these words, the loyal servant of my king and knowing me to be so. What do you accuse me of, some grand conspiracy? My correspondence contains two messages, and only two, written in January and February of 1642, when I freely expressed to *you* my sentiments, as you call them, about how England was being governed. Now sit down and give me a hearing, Your Highness, or I shall leave you here to molder in your own misconceptions."

If he had not done so she would have tried to push past him. Fighting hard against tears of outrage and desolation, she sat down a yard away from him. The slip of paper with the red marks on it burned at the corner of her eye.

"What was in the first?" he ground out.

"The sketch of a butterfly and nothing more. I used it to gain entry to the Earl of Essex's house on the eve of Charles's attempt to arrest the Five Members of Parliament. When I saw Essex, I told him of the arrests so he could warn the members if he wished to. That is all that has been said and all that has been written between Lord Essex and myself. He burned my first message. I am surprised he did not burn this, but since it is in your hands you may do what you like with it."

As she spoke, he stared at her, appalled. "*Jésus*, how can anyone in this family ever trust you again?"

"You condemn me because I intervened in the king's business? I have learned to be ashamed that I went behind his back, but I have never learned to be sorry those five men were not arrested. You may not be aware but there was another lady at court who gave Essex the very same information—the Countess of Carlisle. Whether she told him before or after I did, I have no idea. She banished herself from court, you may be sure, and the queen has never spoken her name since. But I have thought much about her, and I am inclined to think we did it from the same motive and on the same principles."

"Yes, I did hear. She was a sympathizer with the Puritans: a spy!"

"She was a woman of conviction!" she burst out. "Yes, I acted secretly, and so did she, but how else are women to act in a disaster like the one that a single misguided man brought about? We women have skills, but can hold no office. We have minds, but they are not to be bent to the use of the commonwealth. We have vision, but no one will regard it."

He put his head in his hands. "*A single misguided man*. You are speaking of the king. This is treason. How can you not see it?"

She leaned toward him and leveled her voice. "Essex was Lord Chamberlain. I informed him of the king's decision, as any other servant of my sovereign might have done. As any other servant *should* have done, if they were to do their job properly." He said nothing, and after a while she went on defiantly, "If you decide to reveal this to Charles, it will hurt him to the heart and make him hate me. But when he hears my reasons, he will not believe that I am a traitor. He cannot—I know him too well and he knows me too well. My king will banish me and it will destroy my husband. Is that what you want?"

He sat forward, took the piece of paper off the desk, read it again and his mouth twisted. "How could you write this of me?"

"You know how. I explained it to you, in the Wassenaer Hof. I was afraid for the kingdom: once you were put at the head of the army, I could see no hope of reconciliation with Parliament."

His eyes were as hard as stones. "And that is what you want, above all. You will sacrifice anything to it. Including me. You once said you loved me. Why did I believe you? Why would I believe anything you say after this?" He screwed up the paper, tossed it into her lap and got to his feet. "You are a liar," he said, turning away.

"I've told no lies," she cried in despair, "except for love. Can *you* condemn me for that? Are you so pure that no man in this town could point the finger at you?"

He looked back at her. "No, I am compromised," he said bitterly. "Essex's letter filled me with shame and he will get no answer. Where you are concerned, I have no honor."

"And I see you must find something to blame," she whispered. "What shall it be? Me, or love?"

"You cannot love."

She gasped and staggered to her feet. The paper fluttered from her lap to the floor. "Rupert, I would love you if you were the devil himself."

"*Ach, Jésus,*" he said to himself, and walked off.

Chapter 27

～e

WHEN PRINCE RUPERT WALKED away from her in the library at Merton, Mary took a few steps after him, but she got only to the end of the row of desks before pain stabbed her in the chest and she doubled over, struggling to breathe and struck dumb, one hand on the desk and the other at her breast. Then she managed a gulp of air, but felt so faint for a moment that she found herself on her knees, where she remained while sobs began to shake her body. Only her fingers clamped on the edge of the desktop kept her from collapsing to the flagstones of the library floor. The pain was edged away by the flood of tears, but for a while she could not see or think.

"You cannot love." It was the most vicious thing anyone had ever said to her, and at first the cruelty and injustice of it caused a grief that shut out everything else. Then a wild fury lanced through her.

What, he pursued her for more than a year, then broke with her like this?! As the cold silence of the library settled back around her she shuddered at hearing such words from the man she had lost. She was kneeling with clasped hands at the end of the stark row of desks like a prisoner in a court that dealt only death. He was not coming back; one slip of paper had signed her fate. At that moment she glimpsed the thing on the floor and reached out to crumple it in her fingers.

He had not heard a word she said. She had seen his eyes: uncomprehending and glazed with proud resentment. The fine piece of chalk with which she had sketched his caricature as the devil was the same one with which he had drawn the plan of Bristol for her and James in July. Had he guessed that too? With his overweening pride, with his overscrupulous sense of personal honor, with his steely memory, perhaps he had, for he had at once believed that the message was hers. The moment he had laid eyes on that note to Essex, all their antagonism from the time before the Wassenaer

Hof had shut down his mind like an iron portcullis. She was court-martialed without reprieve. Her hands trembled with helpless rage as she tore the slip of paper across and across until it drifted into the chilly air like snowflakes.

Then she got up, dried her eyes and went to close the manuscript psalter, after which she doggedly searched the shelves for poets of the last fifty years, excluding Shakespeare. An hour later, composed, empty and armed with the poetry of Sir Henry Wotton, the clergyman scholar who had written so eloquently about the Winter Queen, she glided back through the buildings like a ghost to rejoin her own.

Rupert was riding through Buckinghamshire with some of the horse toward the town of Aylesbury. There was snow about, which had been falling gently for days but had now stopped. The leafless landscape was etched in white and shades of gray, and this detachment of his life guard would have created warm splashes of color along the line of approach if he had allowed them to wear their red cloaks. But they were muffled in dark colors on his orders; he wanted to traverse the countryside of Buckinghamshire as unobtrusively as possible.

The bleakness of the scene suited the cold, high plateau that formed in his mind when he thought back to the Merton library where he had last seen Mary Villiers. When he had walked away under the arch to the corner between the two wings where the stairwell began, she had not tried to stop him or call him back. She might have been paralyzed by anguish but she might have spoken, nonetheless. As he strode down the stairs he had heard sounds behind him that were perhaps muffled sobs, but neither then nor now could he think of going back. It was over. He never wanted to see her again.

When he had reached his quarters that night he had taken the engraving of her from inside his doublet and glared at it with eyes that still smarted with fury. It no longer looked like the angelic mirror to his soul—it seemed like her other face, the one he had never suspected: devious, quicksilver and mocking. He had thrown it into the back of a dresser.

At midday, riding with his party along minor lanes, he recognized they were close to Aylesbury, and the scouts came riding back to say they were near the rendezvous, which was marked on his makeshift map as a stand of yew trees. Aylesbury was held by Parliament, and a parliamentary spy had been conducted to him four days before with a message that the governor was prepared to open the town to his forces and let him take it without bloodshed at a time to be appointed by them both. It sounded too good to be true, hence his caution, but he owed it to the king to test it.

The yew trees were in a small gully hidden around the next bend in the road. The scouts had done their job well and they reported that no gatherings of men could be seen in the adjacent farmland, which they reconnoitered unseen from the top of a nearby hill. Indeed, few figures moved in the frozen landscape, not even peasants, and the only person the scouts had seen in the last hour was the promised contact in the yew glade, whom stealthy inspection had shown to be a thin young lad, alone except for the horse he had ridden out of Aylesbury and visibly nervous.

Rupert posted sentries and then swung with his party into the grove, startling the fellow almost out of his wits: he was clearly not of the military. But he was articulate enough, so Rupert dismounted and leaned against the flaky bark of the tallest tree to interrogate him. Around and above them old yews clustered, the dark spikes of their dense leaves motionless in the biting air, forming the perfect cover for the interview.

He was not used to taking towns by stealth, but he was not averse to spying if it produced results. Once, in darkness and mist during the siege of Breda, he and Maurice had crept up until they were directly outside the fortress and managed to climb up the very walls. They overheard soldiers inside talking about a sortie planned for that night, whereupon they sneaked down again and hurried to the Stadholder to tell him from which gate the sortie would be made. The enemy party were ambushed and destroyed the moment they appeared. He smiled to himself grimly—he had been eighteen, no older than this fellow, who had the soft look of a citizen about him. When asked about himself he looked uneasy, as though he had not expected the enemy general to be interested in him, and he gave evasive answers.

An unsettling factor was that the lad kept insisting that the governor was ready for them and they should enter the town at once. He seemed unaware that Rupert had stipulated that the governor's brother should be the one to escort them in. Without saying anything about this or his own purposes Rupert continued the questioning and the lad became somewhat perturbed and inconsistent.

By now Rupert had given the order for his men to dismount, except for the sentries and four other horsemen placed at gaps on the edge of the grove. Suddenly he pushed himself away from the tree, took two paces toward the nearest pair of men and jerked his head at the Aylesbury guide. "Take him." They did so without hesitation, binding the lad's hands before him and checking him for hidden weapons. "He's lying; it's a trap." The guide let out a squeal of protest and Rupert snapped, "Shut up! Your story is over." He said to the others, "Get him on his horse. Sir Richard, recall the sentries and tell me what they can see on the Aylesbury road and the way we came."

He mounted up and signaled to his men to do the same. While they waited for the sentries he swung alongside the guide, who sat with his wrists still tied and his hands wound into the horse's mane while a trooper held the reins. "Where is the ambush, in the town or on the route?" Rupert's voice was like steel and the lad took it like a blade in the stomach, suddenly bending forward and vomiting down the side of his horse's neck. Rupert gave a bark of contemptuous laughter and urged his horse to the middle of the glade where the sentries were waiting. "He's very lonely and very scared—so the ambush is probably in town. Can you see anyone on the roads?"

"Nothing, Your Highness."

"We'll go at the gallop to begin with, nonetheless. Lash that gutless whoreson to his mount so he doesn't fall off. I'll have him hanged in Oxford."

They rattled back through Buckinghamshire without incident, then crossed Oxfordshire at a sensible pace. When they got to Abingdon, Rupert sent a report in to the king containing the prisoner's full confession, which had been extracted without undue violence. He committed him to the castle and demanded that he be hanged.

In council with the king, however, Lord Digby had the sentence revoked and the lad pardoned. Rupert gave another sarcastic laugh when he was told this news. He would soon cease to be irked by what went on in Oxford, for now he had his new commission at last: he was appointed captain general of the counties of Cheshire, Lancashire, Worcestershire and Shropshire and he was posted with his own force to Shrewsbury, to raise a massive army in the west.

James was worried about Mary but he also battled with a fragile new hope. After showing her resilience by rising above the loss of their child and taking over her role as merry mistress to the court, she had sunk back into a time of unhappiness. He reassured himself, however, that this was a natural reaction to her first show of strength after such a hard physical trial. And he also detected that it had something to do with Prince Rupert, who was avoiding them as a couple although his relations with James alone did not alter. James could not help forming an idea that Mary was withdrawing her affections from Rupert. Everything pointed to it—her cool demeanor when his name came up, her languid reaction when it was mentioned that he might be present at some gathering, and above all the fact that she always gave some excuse at the last moment not to go.

James thus found himself in the ironic situation of urging her presence at the last occasion before the prince departed for Shrewsbury. "There is a banquet in the Dining Hall that everyone is expected to attend. We shall be in awful splendor and no doubt required to eat swan, which always disagrees with me, but we bear such sacrifices as we must."

She smiled. "Nothing to compare with the swans' sacrifice, husband. What makes you think I am unready to go?"

"The gleam in your eye suggesting some major literary effort that will require you to slave over a page—"

"A page! I'll have you know I can run to two when in the vein. Especially if I don't have to digest swan at the same time."

He grinned. He could almost swear she was cured. "Have I your pledge for tomorrow night, then, my lady?"

"I have nothing to wear."

"Which of the hundred garments I have lately seen paraded will do in a pinch?"

"The crimson velvet sewn all over with crocodiles, apes and pineapples?"

"If you wish," he said with a frown, then grinned at her peal of helpless laughter. "Very well, let us eschew exotica and go with the green gown you have on in your miniature. Sorry"—he held up an apologetic hand—"I should have said viridian. And the family emeralds," he said suddenly. "You never choose them. But why not tomorrow?"

"Why not indeed? If someone can be delegated to lift their weight off my breast on occasion, to allow me to breathe, I undertake to wear them."

"Permit me to fulfill that onerous duty," he said solemnly, and she laughed again.

She persuaded James that they had no need to mill about with the king and the principal guests in Christ Church before the dinner, and they thus turned up just at the moment when the people invited to sit at the high table were about to file into the hall, led by the royal couple. Since Mary and James were the last to take their places and everyone was ready to enter, they received hurried greetings only from those nearest to them and Mary had no need to avoid Rupert's eye, for he was at the front, directly behind the queen.

As they went in, she noticed that they would all be sitting in a line looking out into the hall and down the other rows of tables, so unless Prince Rupert was placed beside her she could ignore him all evening. It transpired that he would sit at the other end of the table on the king's right hand. Mary meanwhile would be flanked on the far left of it by her husband and Digby, the perfect companions for a jolly and witty meal.

The guests were on their feet, strung like brilliant jewels down the length of the sumptuous room. At the lower limit of her vision Mary could see her own green fires sparkling on her breast, and knew that she looked more than worthy to grace the king's table tonight. Charles spoke to the hall in fluent, happy tones, and as he mentioned the prince and the occasion for this rejoicing, she felt it was safe to glance down the table and observe Rupert.

He was magnificent in red brocade laced heavily with silver. She looked at his strong profile and her heart faltered, but also saw that his face displayed both determination and pride, which revived all her painful resentment. She quickly looked away. There would be more than enough said and done tonight to bolster his sense of superiority—she would not add to it by stealing glances in his direction.

The king closed his welcome, there were cheers for him and the queen, then they all sat. Because of the occasion, some of Rupert's commanders were at the high table, and more were prominently placed at others. As the first dishes were being laid on the cloth before them, Mary leaned toward James and whispered, "No swan yet; perhaps it is all reserved for the military."

James gave a doubtful shake of the head in reply and Mary turned to Digby. "I could swear half the army is here tonight. Aren't you sorry not to be marching off to Shrewsbury with them?"

Digby gave a shudder of distaste. "To teach hordes of bog Irish to tear the heads off Lancastrians? I thank my stars to be hundreds of miles from that, my lady."

James looked across. "The first shipments are all Englishmen. I don't know that any Irish are being brought across yet."

"Which troops are quitting Oxford?" Mary said, looking down at her plate, at something that resembled salsify but might have been another vegetable, overboiled.

"The prince's life guard and his regiments of horse and foot. Sir John Byron has been training Irish units in Cheshire for weeks, so the prince is supposed to take them in hand and continue receiving men as Lord Ormond ships them over."

Mary looked at him sidelong. She knew that Digby had told Ormond in a letter that the best captain general for the northwest forces would be Ormond himself, not Rupert—but Ormond had rejected the sly suggestion. There really was no end to Digby's envious efforts against Rupert, and in the past this one would have annoyed her. Now, she told herself, it was not her affair. "Is there a sauce for this, do you think? I fear I cannot eat it if I have to see it."

Digby laughed. "There is a white one you may try." He poured it himself from a gold jug, coating the salsify with care. "Though it should be green. Everything should be green tonight, to match you. You are a spring vision, a slender tree in bounteous leaf burgeoning in midwinter."

"My lord," James said dryly from her other side, "I had to haul my wife away from poetry to attend this evening—pray don't start serving it up to us here!"

"But your lady merits nothing less," Digby protested. "I may say truly with Willie Shakespeare:

"Mine eye and heart are at a mortal war
How to divide the conquest of thy sight;
Mine eye my heart thy picture's sight would bar,
My heart mine eye the freedom of that right."

"Odds blood," James said in mock exasperation, "that's rhetorical enough for our Parliament! May I suggest you insert it in your next speech? By the time they've figured it out you'll have carried the day."

Mary tapped James's wrist with her fan. "You are not to carp at praise of me! However, to please *you* I am all modesty and no reply: *My tongue-tied muse in manners holds her still.*"

James groaned. Digby laughed, then said, "I agree with you, my lord, it would fit our periphrastic Parliament like a glove. Should I ever bother attending again."

Their new Parliament—in which Digby, James and Prince Rupert all held seats in the House of Lords—was made up of members from Westminster loyal to the king who had been lately invited to abandon London and hold their own sessions in Oxford. The schism in England was thus complete: there were two capitals, two Houses of Commons and Lords, two navies, and two mighty cohorts of armed forces on land. The Oxford Parliament might have been expected to debate the issues of war and the funding of the king's armies, but so far they appeared to take only their own status and concerns to heart. And army moneys continued to be raised by commission for the king—Rupert, for instance, as captain general in the northwest, had the power to recruit forces and collect taxes in Wales and the counties under his aegis. Meanwhile a Scots royalist, the Earl of Montrose, who was also at the banquet, would travel back to Scotland within a few days and raise an army to combat the dire threat on the Scottish border. And Mary's stepfather, Antrim, also present, had at last been given leave to go back to Ireland and muster two thousand Ulster troops for a landing in Argyllshire by April.

The Oxford Parliament was too much of a bore for them to talk about for long and they moved on to other subjects. Occasionally, through the hubbub in the enormous room, Mary heard Rupert's deep voice. She could tell by his tone that he was content and cheerful, and she often heard him laugh. The queen, seated on the king's left, looked up at him over her husband's head and seemed to react very graciously—either her fondness for Rupert was returning or she was glad to think that his influence with the king was about to diminish with the distance his new role demanded.

When the most elaborate courses arrived, Mary stole morsels of swan from James's plate so he would not have to eat it, and thought with a shiver that she had not adjusted to the idea of being far away from Rupert. It should be a blessing, but she could not help taking it as another blow, as hard as the ones he had dealt her in the library at Merton. For him, she knew, this was another venture in his life as a warrior. He must be more than ready to plunge into the weeks and months of thinking about nothing but the enemy and the defeat thereof. He must be planning to forget her, to bury her image in the unfolding landscape of war.

For her it would be different, and she felt this certainty and shrank from it. She loved Rupert despite her anger and his cruelty, and the future showed her no respite from passion. On the contrary, everything pointed to her experiencing the sharpest torment while he was away. She dreaded that one day a dispatch would come to Oxford, couched in the same terms as the haphazard message that had once come to Rupert about Maurice: *Prince Rupert of the Rhine has fallen in the siege of Liverpool.* Parliament held Liverpool and the king had told her he wanted it, since the port of Chester to which the troops from Ireland came was perilous because of the silting of the River Dee. And she knew these things by heart! Her mind and her memory turned such things over day by day—because of Rupert. The tall, muscular body that she had twice encircled in her arms was now about to venture forth into regions where she could not follow and where she did not matter, to the king, to England or to him.

At the same time she hated him. The memory of his arms around her, his voice in her ear, his hands on her body, was too acute for her to accept that he had ripped apart the bond between them. The action was monstrous and as much a lie as the lies of which he had accused her.

The room was so packed it was overheated, and she cooled her face with a fan that James had brought her back from France. It was fine-ribbed, trimmed with Breton lace and painted with a hunting scene in which the riders were women and the prey was a gallant in blue coat and breeches hurdling a crowded sheep pen in his haste to get away. As she plied it, James looked up and said, "It actually works? I was worried I had bought you a mere ornament."

"It cools my brow and my intellect. What it does to my *imagination* I shall leave you to guess at."

He laughed softly and Digby glanced at her with surprise and a hint of jealousy. It was the first time the Duchess of Richmond had ever flirted with her husband in public.

With the last courses of the feast there were speeches. Prince Rupert rose just once to reply to them all and did so with grace and brevity, thus remaining the dignified but modest hub around which the splendid evening revolved. Then the king drew it to a close by rising and escorting his queen from the high table and out of the hall.

The order of going was not as well managed as the coming in, and at the doorway Mary found herself next to Prince Rupert. He drew back and bowed, and she nodded to him and summoned up congratulations on his appointments, his prospects and the celebration they had just enjoyed.

He bowed again and said, "But you eclipse me as always, my lady."

As they all walked on through the inner rooms, Digby behind her whispered, "Gallant, but a little peacock envious, perhaps?"

She looked over her shoulder and smiled. "But I am the one wearing green, my lord."

James murmured, "I wonder what he would have found to say about the crocodiles, apes and pineapples?"

She gave a whoop of mirth, which disconcerted Digby but made James clamp her hand to his side as he laughed with her. She thought ironically of a recent pamphlet that offered yet another sly speculation about her supposed relations with the prince:

> *Mary Richmond is brisk and jolly,*
> *Which makes Prince Rupert melancholy.*

No one else knew how bitterly that melancholy was shared.

Chapter 28

RUPERT HAD TO SAY good-bye to Mary, but he could not think of a way that would preserve his dignity and forbid his heart to quail when he spoke the farewells. At his banquet she had looked more dazzling and unapproachable than ever. For a moment, when she paused in front of him before exiting from the hall, he wondered how he could possibly have imagined conquering her.

He recalled Arundel's description, long ago in the forest of Rhenen: *The most beautiful woman in England, the most captivating and the most chaste.* And the Oxford court, who all admired her, considered her the sunniest. Certainly, on the night of the banquet, no jollity had been lacking at Mary Villiers's end of the table and each peal of laughter had made Rupert wince with resentment.

He could not have predicted where he would last see her: it was at a parade of his regiment of horse. As a gesture of solidarity with his cause the Duke of Richmond insisted on witnessing it, rather in the way he used to sometimes ride the rounds with Rupert during the early occupation of Oxford; and when he came to Abingdon he brought his wife.

Rupert wanted to see his troopers drawn up in all their superb toughness before they left Oxford with him. He had depended on their strength and loyalty in battle after battle and they had never let him down. Now they would be part of a new force and he wanted them to know that his trust in them would not change, whatever their future trials and chances might be. He ignored Richmond, his wife and the other bystanders as he spoke to the men, making his voice carry to each end of the files and to the farthest rank. They cheered when he finished, and in the deep tone of their response he recognized that they knew him to the hilt and believed in his uttermost affection for them, and that he and they would journey on without losing what they had forged together.

He took their salute, they dispersed, and he remained on the same spot until they were all gone. He was mounted on a gray part-Arab stallion that he had purchased for a fortune in Wallingford and that was unused to crowds: he could feel it twitching and ruminating about the unexpected experience, but he could also feel a curiosity in the beast that promised well for when he had it trained for battle. It was not as massive as the black paragon he had lost outside Bristol, but it possessed resilience and stamina, and even with him on its back it went like the wind. It also tolerated Boy, who had enjoyed the parade and was now circling around the Richmonds' horses and looking up at the duchess now and then in the hope she might have brought him a treat. A month ago she would have dropped lithely out of the saddle to embrace Boy. No. A month ago she was in the midst of pain and grief.

He looked over at her while she was laughing at Boy and talking to Richmond. She looked supple and light in a gown the color of a dove's wing, overspread with a sweeping cloak of sables that almost covered her horse's rump and descended to neat buckled shoes poised in low stirrups. They were in the exercise field by the river, and against the backdrop of the gray, slow-moving current of the Thames her hair glowed like a fireship.

Sir Richard Crane and some of his officers from the life guard and regiment of foot were also present, but as spectators—he was going to parade the others in the afternoon. Richmond, whom they all liked and respected from long association, joined their group and the duchess was momentarily alone and out of earshot of the rest. Rupert spurred over to join her; he could not put the encounter off any longer.

She watched him approach, her face a little pale in the white morning light. He brought the stallion up next to her mare and they stayed looking at the river, side by side without a word, for what seemed a long time.

Finally he said, "I may never see you again."

Her voice was as cool as her features. "Isn't that what you wanted?"

"Yes, it was. But I was unjust, perhaps."

"Perhaps?" She gave a little laugh. "And I was a fool."

"Why?" he said, trying to control his voice. "To say you loved me? Or was that a lie from the beginning?"

"I never lied to you. I lied to others where you were concerned—never to you. But you are a tyrant, Your Highness, and I thank heaven you showed your tyranny plain enough for me to break free of you."

Horrified, he exclaimed, "Can you expect me to leave you with such words between us?"

"They are not mere words, Your Highness, but the truth." She turned her dark blue eyes to him. "Please believe another truth—I pray God daily to keep you from harm." Her lips quivered. "Since in battle I know you never think of God or your loved ones, while you are gone my prayer will be, *O God, though he forget Thee, forget not him.*"

He reached over, took her gloved hand and raised it to his lips. The mare tossed its head and pranced aside because the stallion was nudged too close, and their fingers parted. The thud of hooves on the hard ground echoed the loud, rapid thumping of Rupert's heart. He wheeled away so as not to see her face and to conceal his own from the attentive watchers, and let the stallion shake the restlessness out of its legs with a short canter down to the riverside and back.

She was with Richmond when he returned and the duke took over the ceremony of parting, keeping it brief but saying all the right and well-considered things.

Rupert bowed his head and took his leave of them, repeating something that he had said some time ago, though it felt as though it had been in another century: "You are my greatest friends. May nothing I do ever be unworthy of you."

Then without waiting for them to depart or for his officers to join him, he wheeled away again and cantered down the bridle path to Abingdon with Boy at his side, a breeze off the river whistling past his ears and blowing his hair back from his cold face. All the warmth he had ever gained from Mary Villiers seemed to stream away from him into the winter air. He had turned his back on the sun.

Part Four

So strong his passion was, so far above
The common gallantries that pass for love.

—EPHELIA

THE EARL OF ESSEX, Lord General of the armies of Parliament, never received a reply to his gentlemanly letter to Prince Rupert about parliamentary propaganda, but the pamphleteers eventually ceased to wallow in court gossip from Oxford and became incensed instead about the shameless importations of Irish troops to the shores of England. Irish atrocities of the past were dredged up, and the prose and pictures chosen required little originality on the part of the pamphleteers, since rape, dismemberment, infanticide, disembowelment, the slicing off of genitalia and even cannibalism had long been ascribed to the Irish soldier in rut and rage. The troops from Ireland under Sir John Byron had not fared well at first: they and the rest of the royalist army in the northwest were put to rout outside Nantwich by one of Parliament's stalwarts in the north, Sir Thomas Fairfax. Those who were not killed or who ran away or were taken prisoner or escaped back to Ireland, fled south to join the royalist army under Hopton. Afterward, Essex received the information that Prince Rupert had taken over and was rapidly recruiting forces in the northwest. The earl had no doubt about where they would be deployed once the prince had pulled them together in his efficient fashion: they would be sent across country into Yorkshire to challenge the Scots.

Meanwhile Essex did receive a letter from Oxford—from the king's puny Parliament. Forty-four peers and 118 members of the Commons respectfully requested him to consider taking the role of middleman to negotiate peace between Charles I and the Westminster Parliament. Within the letter was another that Essex was invited to present to both houses in London. After debating with himself, he saw no reason to risk his neck in such a position and did not present the second letter. He sent a reply to Oxford, however, enclosing a promise that any member of the Oxford Parliament who signed the Solemn League and Covenant would receive an instant pardon from their counterparts in London. He was not astonished when the correspondence died out.

At the same time he had personal grievances to cope with. John Pym's protégé in Parliament, Oliver St. John, had lost his influence in the House and the war party was virtually ignoring Essex and bolstering a growing force in the Midlands, around Manchester. A recent commander was being much cried up—the second in command of the Manchester Eastern Association Army, a novice by the name of Oliver Cromwell, who before the commencement of hostilities had had no military experience whatsoever. He was now general of the horse and the allocations to his cavalry by Parliament were increasing while Essex's own were dwindling, however hard he pleaded for funds. Meanwhile Parliament's army in the west, headed by Sir William Waller, the man whom Essex seethed about in his lowest moments of apprehension and envy, had been given a force almost as strong as his own.

But the deadly game of chess in which Essex had been engaged since Charles I raised his standard in August 1642 had not changed in essentials. Because of Parliament's acquisition of the Scots army, the most sweeping moves looked likely to be carried out soon in the north; but the piece on which everything centered had not shifted. King Charles was still in Oxford, and if he did not move from there, then it would be around this elegant royal city that the endgame would be played out. Essex had proved that the king's position was within convenient striking distance of London. Let others skirmish elsewhere—in the contest for the kingdom Essex might well declare checkmate.

Mary was in the queen's private room at Christ Church, where merchants had been bidden to come and leave a welter of fabrics so that Henrietta-Maria could plan the gowns that she needed for the rest of her pregnancy, which would come to term in July. She was never content with seeing the first yard of any roll of material—it must always be spread like a sail over items of furniture or flung out across the floor in billows of color.

The room was like an ocean, through which the queen bade Mary wade like a sea nymph amongst aquamarine tissue, silk grosgrain brocaded with pale filigree, crimson satin to be embroidered with mother-of-pearl, silver tissue, coral cloth of gold, and tawny velvet tossed about the margins like seaweed on an exotic shore.

Mary lifted a length of gold lace and held it against her. "How is the effect from where you are, madam?"

Henrietta-Maria was in a wide chair by the window that had a back in flexible leather that she liked to relax into. She had dismissed everyone but Mary because she felt languid and unwell, and she had come to Christ Church to spend a few hours near the king. Henrietta-Maria could be querulous when indisposed, and miserable and testy when she was really sick, but today Mary had been able to keep her amused as the new wardrobe was being planned.

The queen said, "I think it glares too much. That's the problem with gold—it does not so much set things off as swamp them."

"Then it needs a strong contrast. What say you to the purple velvet?"

Henrietta-Maria contemplated the two swaths that Mary cast over a chair and laughed. "Oh no. I should look like the Holy Roman Empress. That would never do in our present pass." She sat up straighter. "Do you know that Rupert was named for one of the emperors—Ruprecht, who was King of Bohemia in 1400? I reminded him of that long ago while I was trying to turn him to the true church, when he first came to England. What a sweet youth he was." She sighed.

"You tried to convert Prince Rupert?"

"Yes," the queen replied without shame. "And when he left, he wrote back that if he had stayed a few days longer, I should have conquered him!"

Mary looked at her in wonderment. Rupert had afterward spent three years in an Austrian prison and repudiated conversion although it would have earned him his freedom. It amazed her that the queen could imagine victory had been just around the corner years ago because he sent her a piece of admiring banter as he went home. Perhaps this was enough to explain the queen's enmity now—Rupert used no flattery with her. Or, indeed, with anyone.

She disposed herself on the rejected velvet and gold lace and said, "What did Lord Digby say to you about Prince Rupert when he returned from the Birmingham and Lichfield campaigns, do you remember? That was when I noticed a change in your opinion of him. I have always wondered about Lord Digby's reasons for re-signing his commission. He told me at the time that it was between him and the king—but he must have confided in you; he thinks so much of you."

The queen said, "I do recall." She thought for a moment, not unwilling to search for the exact phrases. "Yes. Digby said one campaign in close contact was enough to show him the man. He said Rupert was like a bull at a gate. Utterly ruthless. And"—she held Mary's eye as though nervous of the response—"he said Rupert has never been here for us but for his own glory. There is his measure as a commander. And his danger."

Mary felt a jolt of helpless anger, then said with deceptive mildness, "Yet Digby fought with him at Powick and Edgehill and saw what he did there. Would not a gentleman intent on his own glory seek to live a little longer than twenty-two to enjoy it? Why would such a man put himself at the head of his cavalry in charges like that—full-tilt into the enemy?" Henrietta-Maria did not reply, so Mary went on, "In all this time, no body of Parliament's cavalry, however large, has ever been able to withstand his kind of charge. Madam, Prince Rupert is already a legend, to both sides. But do you really think that is what he aims for—a lace-and-tissue glory? When you see him fulfill loyally and to the last letter the orders of your husband my king, do you really believe he fights for anything but our great cause?"

Henrietta-Maria's gaze was very intent but not unsympathetic. "I must own . . ." The queen paused. "On the day when he carried you from the market into Merton I saw something in him that I had not permitted myself to see before. When he stood up from beside your bed, I verily believe he would have fainted if he had not been compelled to run and get you help. He has a tenderness that he shows only to women. No man would ever guess it." Mary went to speak but Henrietta-Maria held up her hand and continued, "And yes, I remember how kind he was to me and my little Mary on the voyage to Holland. Here, in Oxford, I thought all that kindness gone by. But before Christmas, when he lifted you and carried you into my care—"

Henrietta-Maria shook her head in confusion. "I am not qualified to judge him as a soldier." Here Mary bit back an incredulous exclamation, since that was just what the queen had been doing for months. "But I must confess to you, now that you mention it, that I miss him. When he was here, there was a cordon around Oxford that gave me a sense of protection. Perhaps it was false—but false or not I felt it. Now"—and she held out her hand to Mary, who came to sit by her side—"I sometimes feel so nervous I could burst into tears for a trifle. Do you think it is because I am with child?"

"Perhaps, madam," said Mary, patting her wrist.

"I am thirty-five," the queen said with a shaky sigh and slumped back in her chair. "What an age to be bearing again. When I've endured more pregnancies and births than I now have children living." A tear formed at the corner of each eye. "No wonder I am afraid." After a moment she saw Mary's look and closed both her hands over hers, saying mournfully, "But you know all this, my dear. It is our lot."

All this, Mary thought. To fear miscarriage. To see babies die. To dread the future. To miss Prince Rupert. But no other woman, not the queen, certainly not Rupert's mother, not his sisters nor— she would dare swear—his mistresses, could possibly feel such a wrench in her heart as she did when she thought of him. And that was every hour of every day.

Meanwhile, in his absence she was able to bring her influence to bear on the queen and the king once again—to subtly remind them of how vital Rupert had been to their cause, and how loyal and ingenious he was still proving himself to be. They listened to Digby, with all his insinuations against Rupert; but they trusted her more, because they knew her loyalty was unshakable. Whatever power she had over their hearts and convictions she would use, not just for the prince, but for the kingdom—because only he could save it.

In early March, Rupert found himself in correspondence with the Earl of Essex after all. The governor of Nantwich, either flushed with victory over Parliament's taking of the town or swayed by the virulent nonsense being printed about the Irish troops Rupert had been training for the last month at Shrewsbury and Chester, hanged thirteen royalist prisoners. His excuse was a decree given out by Parliament that any captured Irish troops were to be executed at once. Rupert retaliated by hanging thirteen of the king's prisoners and sending a fourteenth to Essex with the message that for every one of his own men hanged he would execute two of Parliament's. Essex wrote back demanding to hear his authority for this proceeding and Rupert told him his were the actions of a soldier. Parliament remained silent on the issue but the killings stopped.

At the same time Rupert also received successive letters from the king urging him to take his new army to the relief of Newark. This town in Nottinghamshire was an important point on the strategic route from Newcastle in the north to the king at Oxford, but Parliament's commander in Nottinghamshire, Sir John Meldrum, a veteran who had commanded a brigade at Edgehill, had laid siege to Newark and was settling his troops into a strong position around this important town on the River Trent.

Rupert first discussed it with his war council in Shrewsbury. "With the army we have and with that distance to cover"—he pointed to a broad map of the line of march northeast—"I don't like it."

Will Legge said a little stiffly, "You don't judge we've knocked our men into the right shape yet, Your Highness?"

Rupert shook his head. "The question is, can we take a large force like ours as far as Newark without Meldrum catching on to what we're doing long before we get there? And if he catches on they'll have time to meet us with an even larger force—they can bring men down from the north." He looked at the map again. "We have these garrisons on the way but they're small and the men there have never fought with us before." He put his finger on the jumping-off point at Bridgnorth. He said to Will Legge, "If the order comes to march, I'll need you to take musketeers up to Bridgnorth to begin with. What's the quickest way you could do that?"

Will looked at the map. "By barges up the Severn, Your Highness."

"Excellent. Then I will move horse and artillery from Chester to meet up with them . . ." He shook his head, still staring at the map. "It's still a devil of a long way to go and hope to surprise the enemy. Through Wolverhampton, Lichfield, Ashby . . . We'll have to cozen them."

The council of war ended inconclusively, with certainty on just one issue—the king's order to march on Newark would not be long in arriving.

*   *   *

On the twelfth of March, Rupert was riding back into Chester with several troops of horse and a column of prisoners. During the day he had chased a party of parliamentary troopers into a valley near Drayton, not far from where he had surrounded a few hundred the week before, killing those who resisted and taking the rest. He was not really looking forward to solving the problem of Newark, for he had enough to do training the new Shrewsbury and Chester forces and keeping the area around the old river port secure. Times like these, trotting back into town after a day of action, were moments he could snatch for thinking about strategy—but his thoughts always flew to Mary Villiers.

He had been unjust to her, and his words in the library at Merton tortured him in consequence. *You cannot love.* How could he have said it? He remembered with poignant clarity her devotion to the king and queen—even her chaste kisses on Charles's cheeks the Christmas before last had made him envious! He remembered her sisterly affection for the young princes and the intimate glow that lit up her face when she made her husband laugh. His jealousy there knew no bounds—*grand Dieu*, what else had he been yearning for over the last two years but her love! And most of all he remembered their intense, hidden encounters when her lips opened on his mouth and her arms pressed around his waist as though to mingle her supple body with his. *We'll mix our souls, you shall be me, I you.* And he had walked out of her life.

Before doing so, he had called her a liar. She had corresponded with Essex, yes—but when confronted she had owned up to it. And her secrecy there weighed as nothing in the balance against the candor that she had always shown with everyone, including him. From the very beginning, she had readily answered questions and been even readier to give her opinions on matters of little and great regard. The first words she had ever said to him were testimony to this: she had answered his inquiry at Dover and then frankly confided her hatred of being there. Thereafter she had left him in no doubt whatever about how she saw his military visions for England. And later, when he had pursued her in Oxford, she had read him gentle lectures on conjugal fidelity and her own honor. How could he call her a liar? He had lied with the very accusation.

He wished he could go back and beg her forgiveness, but that was impossible—the king showed no sign of calling him to Oxford and there was every reason to stay just where he was. So if he could not be with her, he must summon her image; and Chester somehow became the setting for impossible dreams. It was one of the most seductive towns he had ever lodged in—inland from a broad, sandy estuary and upriver where ships could navigate through deep enough waters to dock below the very walls. The handsome streets were lined with two-storied houses and shops in the old, pretty black-and-white timbered style. Outside the ancient, well-preserved walls the River Dee flowed toward the Irish Sea, and visible from the battlements were rich dales and hills, the plain of Cheshire, and the mountains of Wales.

Despite the fact that to Mary he was an abhorred tyrant, despite the insurmountable barrier that she was married, despite the fact that he could never wish harm to James Stuart, he imagined Mary and himself together forever in this tempting milieu. He and the Princess Mary would stay first in one of the handsome houses on Northgate Street while their rambling home was built just outside the walls amongst fields and orchards. It would be like the Prinzenhof, but their children would never be apart from their parents while they were brought up in their rural idyll. Although he was sure Mary would never live anywhere but at court, he pictured her walking in the grounds with him, smiling and healthy in spring sunlight. And although he knew he would never ride anywhere but to war, he imagined them cantering through the lovely town and along the riverside to the great whispering sands of Dee, to gallop along the shore beside the fast-running waves that swept upriver with the tide. Then going home to sit in wood-paneled rooms in front of the high fireplaces that she loved, before he scooped her into his arms as he had once done, and bore her—different now, and every atom his—into the dark cave of her bed.

The dreams were so potent that sometimes, when he was riding back at night, he almost believed she was there by a fireside waiting for him. But something always broke the spell before he got to the town gates. Today it was the voice of one of his attendants, a Frenchman named Mortaigne, who was leading a spare horse at the rear of the party and singing loudly. Mortaigne was a sponge for music and whichever town or hamlet they happened to occupy he always left it with a few haunting or bawdy songs. He also claimed he had not had a single good meal or a decent drop of liquor since he came to England, which gave an edge to today's ditty, sung with his atrocious accent:

> *Chester ale, Chester ale! I could ne'er get it down,*
> *'Tis made of ground-ivy, of dirt, and of bran,*
> *'Tis as thick as a river below a huge town!*
> *'Tis not lap for a dog, far less drink for a man . . .*

"Watch what you warble there!" Rupert shouted back to him. "Or I'll march you to Newark to taste what they brew in Nottinghamshire!"

The call came the next day—a letter from the king commanding Rupert to head to the other side of the country and relieve Newark.

> *. . . as for Newark, I believe before this you will have under-*
> *stood my full directions, which I hope will not be the less powerful,*
> *being the more civil: for an earnest desire to you is as much as a*
> *peremptory command to others.*
> *From your loving uncle and most faithful friend, Charles R.*

Rupert was ready and lost no time. He took with him his regiment of cavalry, commanded by Dan O'Neale, along with several more troops of horse from Chester and three pieces of artillery. He sent Will Legge down to Shrewsbury to ship 1,100 musketeers upriver. These were commanded by a veteran of the Irish wars, Colonel Henry Tillier, and would be mounted on horses that Rupert had already ordered down to Bridgnorth from Lord Loughborough, the king's commander in the Midlands.

They moved fast, as rapidly as Rupert had ever driven men before. By the seventeenth they had passed through their own strongholds of Wolverhampton and Lichfield, taking up extra troops on the way, and were at Ashby with 3,400 men. That night he talked with his officers.

"The governors of Parliament's garrisons must have picked up our passing. But they may have taken us for a detachment of Loughborough's troops on local maneuvers."

"Your Highness, where is Loughborough?" Dan O'Neale asked respectfully.

"He'll be here tomorrow with three thousand men. With a combined force like ours in movement the enemy will know we are after something major. The choices are Leicester and Newark—we must get to Newark before they make up their minds which way we're headed."

"Well, we've moved fast enough so far!"

"Indeed. That's another reason why I didn't want to take a large force out of Chester—we'd have needed a big baggage train to victual us and it would have slowed us down. As it is, we've taken food and men from the garrisons."

"Your Highness," Colonel Tillier said, "that does leave the garrisons vulnerable behind us."

"Correct. Hence the need to keep up the pace. We must get to Newark and hit Meldrum so hard no one can renew the siege after we leave. Then we must set off at speed to replenish the garrisons on our way back and reach Chester intact."

"Loughborough's men are in for smart marching orders tomorrow, then," O'Neale said with a grin.

Rupert grinned back. "Spoken like a trooper. But the foot will give a fine account of themselves on the advance; they already have. My congratulations, Colonel," he said to Tillier, who responded with a bow and a pleased look. "Now, I want you all to look at the map." He pointed toward the table in front of him. "If all goes well, we'll be more than six thousand by the time we set out tomorrow. Too large a force to move by the roads without being detected—and it will be easy to guess our direction. Whereas if we go across here"—he ran his finger straight across country from Ashby to Newark—"we stand a chance of staying pretty much unseen."

They all stared at him, baffled. The terrain between was farmland with scarcely any open heath or common, and tackling that in haste seemed insane, for there were ditches, hedges and fences to negotiate, over untold hills and valleys unmarked by any but the narrowest tracks and paths. Rupert knew he would be whistling Boy back constantly, for he would be off after rabbits at every opportunity.

After waiting a moment to see who would protest first, Rupert put them out of their misery. "The main barriers in this part of the country are the hedges. On my orders Lord Loughborough has arranged for very wide gaps to be cut in all the hedges between us and the destination. Thus we can take everything directly across country, including the artillery wagons and heavy guns. To ensure surprise, I may have to take an advance guard forward of the main force over the last stage. But I hope to get us all together at least as far as Bingham, and that's just ten miles from Newark. Any questions?"

They were all too stunned to reply, but at last someone said humbly, looking down at the map. "Newark, Your Highness—this dot. Is it on our side of the Trent River or the other?"

"You mean will we be swimming our horses into Meldrum's?" Rupert said with a grin. "The town is on our side of the Trent, to which we'll be moving roughly parallel to get to Bingham. Our governor in Newark is Sir Richard Byron. He is sure to try a sortie once we show him our colors, but I don't want to put any dependence on that. This is our task and we will perform it unsupported if necessary."

"Do we know how many we're up against?" Dan O'Neale said.

Rupert shook his head. "We'll find that out for sure when we get there. But put it this way—from information received, I'll be most surprised if they are fewer than we. And we must all be prepared to face more."

Three days later they were at Bingham, reports had come in, and before he put his head down that night Rupert drew a picture of Newark in his mind. It lay on the southern bank of the Trent, and beyond it in the river was a large island formed by a parting of the waters that he knew Meldrum had occupied. Upstream of the town, to the northeast, the besiegers had built a bridge of boats to give them access to the island and there was an old hospital there called the Spittal that no doubt they also occupied. From that position the besiegers might have time to withdraw in the direction of Lincoln if they decided not to give battle. This would not do—they had to be soundly beaten, which meant he must approach in a sweep to their south that would prevent their retreat.

At two a.m. Rupert was woken to be told that Meldrum was concentrating his forces near the bridge of boats. They could not be allowed to get away, so he left Boy safe at his billet, formed an advance guard of troopers, took Loughborough and rattled out of town in the dark. He joked to the older man as he went, "I dreamed of the battle this night. Do you want to know the result?" He could see by the flashing whites of Loughborough's eyes that he was too superstitious to say anything. Rupert laughed. "Ask Will Legge if my dreams come true or not! Take heart: we win this one."

"Provided my boys catch up with us fast enough," Loughborough muttered, forcing his horse's pace to keep up with Rupert's white Arab, which served as a ghostly guide in the night.

It was dawn when they neared a prominence called Beacon Hill and the scouts rode back to tell Rupert that some of Meldrum's men occupied it. From the top, they would be able to see right down to the hastily concentrated position by the river.

"We'll have no delay," Rupert said to Loughborough. "The rest will come up soon enough. Let the boys put on their sashes and we'll scatter the first lot off the hill."

He could almost feel sorry for Meldrum's men isolated on Beacon Hill as he and his cavalry swept out of the dawn light and rushed upon them, their red sashes streaming in the cool breeze of that March morning. When the hill was clear he took a long look at the troops in the distance below and saw enemy foot and guns milling about by the river, flanked by a body of troopers quite clearly superior in numbers to his own advance guard. He noticed Loughborough giving him a glance, but he had no intention of allowing Meldrum time to prepare for the onslaught. Forming his troops into lines and leading the first himself, Rupert brought his men down the slopes of the Beacon toward the river. They were in full view, the horses descending at a hard trot despite the steep ground, the troopers looking very dark and very grim in the pale morning light. As soon as the footing leveled out, Rupert drew his sword and pointed it forward, then roared "For King and Queen!" and all his horse swept into a gallop.

The sight and sound of their coming was too terrible and swift for the enemy to make any reaction to counter it; as Rupert's cavalry thundered across the ground it seemed to him that they had ceased moving in a kind of frieze along the bank—helmeted heads turned this way and that, horses rigid in a variety of statuesque poses and the enemy foot behind clutching their weapons at odd angles with only their pale faces turned his way.

Then his horse were upon them with an impact that crushed bone into bone and iron into flesh and sent steeds and men cartwheeling into the mass of cavalry beyond, while here and there squads of his men galloped on for many yards with Meldrum's troopers parting before them, until they embedded themselves in the enemy ranks like jagged spearheads.

Rupert, hurtling untouched into the first melee, used his sword to cut his way to the center, the gray Arab stepping nimbly under his weight to take him through the gaps between enemy horses, and a sixth sense between rider and mount driving him far into the horsemen ahead. Those of the parliamentary horse who had not crashed to the ground in the first seconds of the assault or been beaten down in the next few minutes began to turn and fall back and to the sides, parting like grass before a scythe. Rupert's men were no longer in full career but their push continued, forcing the enemy cavalry out and away.

But someone pulled two bodies of troopers together on the flanks and they tried to close in again. Rupert, still in the middle, could see and feel the movement and was determined it could be checked even though his guard had been outnumbered from the start, but as his men fought on he found himself hemmed in by three of Meldrum's horsemen. His gray Arab twisted under him to find a way out of the deadly triangle but Rupert felt a hand grab tight on the collar of his buff coat and begin to haul him backward. Three against one . . . He brought his sword down with a swinging blow and half-severed the neck of one attacker, Mortaigne suddenly reared up at his side and shot the second point-blank with his pistol, and at the same moment Rupert felt a warm spray of blood across the back of his neck—someone had sliced off the hand that had been dragging on his collar. He thanked Mortaigne, looked around to thank his other man, Sir William Neale, and then fought his way to a spot where he could rally a big enough body of men to mount another headlong charge into the resisters and disperse them.

Rupert's contingent was at the Spittal and Meldrum was fast withdrawing the remnants of his horse across the bridge of boats to the island when the rest of Rupert's force arrived, after which Rupert concentrated on directing Tillier to attack the boat-bridge with his musketeers and making sure another detachment of men could contain the defenders in the Spittal. As the battle raged on, he went downstream and swam five hundred of the horse onto the island—not without a sardonic grin at the officer who had asked the question about crossing the river. Then Sir Richard Byron managed a sortie from the town to occupy a fort on the north side, and by late in the afternoon it was clear that Meldrum had no more cards to play and no prospect of retreat. He sent to Rupert to negotiate terms of surrender and it was over.

Late that night Rupert rode out of the city with Dan O'Neale, Mortaigne and a few others and headed upriver with Boy running at their heels. "I've been wanting all day to have a ride along that boat-bridge," he said, "so who's coming with me?"

They clattered across to the middle as the linked vessels swayed and clooped under them, and the Trent rippled in the darkness like oiled muscles striving to set them adrift. Ahead on the island were the distant cooking fires of Meldrum's host preparing their last meal before they were escorted away toward Lincoln in the morning, and downstream the lights of Newark danced on the Trent. The dead were buried and the sounds of war had ceased—on this tranquil spring night it was almost as though the battle had never happened.

Rupert had lost a hundred men—one hundred in a victory over superior odds—and the captured weapons included eleven cannon and three thousand muskets. He stayed on the bridge, talking quietly to the others as the night breeze on the river fingered his matted hair. Newark and the road to the north were safe—he had done what he set out to do.

Boy took to the river and paddled around the boats, his wiry strength a good match for the current. All at once Rupert said, "I'm covered in filth. I'm damned if I don't find that water tempting."

"You're not serious!" cried O'Neale.

"Why not?" said Rupert cheerfully and, dismounting, began to throw things off. "Here, give me a hand to unbuckle if you're too gutless for a dip."

"*Nom d'un nom d'un nom de Dieu!*" Mortaigne groaned, but suddenly laughed and dismounted.

"Last one in has to tell the governor to bring out his best sherry," Rupert said.

They all stripped; he made sure he was the last, and with a shout plunged in and thrust upstream under the water. It was pitch-black and fastened like ice around his head, chest and vitals, but the shock was a fitting end to the day, like a door slamming shut on a courtroom in which he had just won a resounding case. When he came up, by contrast to the frigid water the night air felt warm on his face as the current tugged him toward the boats amongst the splashing group of men. Boy swam happily with them and Mortaigne whistled another drinking song.

Rupert thought of the news going down to Oxford and of Mary knowing he had come this far unscathed. One day soon he might be called there by the king, and in between he would plan a campaign to win her back. Floating with spread limbs he looked up and dedicated this victory to her, and then he twisted upright, trod water and shook his head before tipping it back to laugh up at the stars.

Chapter 30

On a fresh April night the Duke of Richmond came home late to his wife, too weary to talk and almost too tired to eat, and he sat at the table thinking while Mary, anxious but silent, served him with her own hands.

Freed from the physical exertions of the day, he let the situation in Oxford slip into his unwilling mind and tried once more to assess how bad it was and how much worse it might become. Which still largely depended on what happened elsewhere.

The king's cause in the west and the Midlands was secure because of Prince Rupert. Following the relief of Newark—which was bruited on all sides as the prince's most stunning achievement—Parliament had in consequence abandoned Lincoln, Gainsborough and Sleaford. Meanwhile the prince was beating about Wales and the western counties building his army still further. In the southwest, Prince Maurice held Exeter and, if he succeeded in taking Lyme, would soon command a string of royalist garrisons running from Bristol to the English Channel.

In the north, however, things looked ominous for the Marquess of Newcastle, who was battling to hold on to Yorkshire against the combined efforts of the Fairfaxes, father and son, and Sir John Meldrum, while his greatest concern continued to be the approach of the Scots army.

South of the king's beleaguered capital, Parliament's Sir William Waller had beaten Sir Ralph Hopton and the Earl of Forth in Hampshire at the end of March, forcing the two royalist commanders to withdraw to the Oxford area—so all the territory below the Thames was now in the hands of Parliament.

Eventually Mary said to him with soft concern, "Husband, where have you been this day?"

He smiled at her. "To the Thames mill to harrass William Baber about gunpowder."

She stared at him. "But that is the job of Ordnance. Why should you be worried over it? You need only go as far as New College!"

He shook his head. "Our supply problems are getting worse. The administrators hand responsibilities back and forth amongst themselves like playing cards—each one names someone else who is supposed to be doing the job, so often it is half done or not done at all."

"Then who *used* to do it? We were not always in this pass."

"Everywhere I go I hear the name of Prince Rupert. He must have bullied, forced, shamed, coaxed and bribed people to get the jobs done and the supplies and arms in. How he managed it with everything else he had to do, I cannot imagine. No wonder he looked like death sometimes when he walked into this room; he was doing the work of five men. And now that he's gone no one can take his place." He watched her face. "The king is so concerned, he sent the prince a letter not long ago commanding him home." Mary looked startled and he went on sarcastically, "And in His Majesty's usual decisive way he sent another letter next day revoking the order."

Mary looked at the table for a moment, then said, "The king should not burden you with such things when others are perfectly capable of it if they would only act! I have never seen you like this: you are worn out. And no doubt there is some urgent thing you must do tomorrow at the ends of the earth?"

"Yes. But only at Woodstock."

"Oh, James," she said in sorrow. "Come to bed, do."

He rose, then halted with his hand on the back of his chair, suddenly dizzy. She sprang up and put her hands under his elbows. "Good God. Sit down, quickly."

When he did so, to let the dizziness pass, she knelt before him and put her hands on his knees. "You see?" she said. "You are so tired. How I hate what is happening!"

He shook the haze from his head. "The king is also desperately anxious about the queen. If she comes too near her term and we need to abandon Oxford, she cannot be moved. It is too dangerous to think of. Before it is too late he intends to send her elsewhere—to safety in the southwest, to Prince Maurice." He took Mary's face between his hands. "If she goes, my dearest wife, I wish you to go with her. I won't have you here in danger."

She looked at him in consternation. He knew why: if she left with the queen, she would be abandoning home—and whatever her feelings for him, he knew she would hate to do that. Moreover, if she turned her back on Oxford she might not see Prince Rupert again. James repeated fiercely, "Promise me. If you have any love for me at all, swear you will go."

Her eyes opened on his, misted with tears. "I do love you!"

It was the only time she had ever said it. With a broken exclamation he leaned forward to put his arms around her, and for a while he could not speak as his tears fell into her soft hair.

"I promise," she said, her voice muffled against him, and he gave an enormous sigh.

When he rose and she led him to the bedchamber, she stayed with him all night. It was the first time she had done so. It was late when he left for Woodstock next morning.

Early in April Rupert sent Will Legge down with dispatches to the king, and he was in Wales when Will returned with all the news from Oxford and the other theaters of war. Will had been received with honors and was now the king's Gentleman of the Bedchamber, which pleased Rupert just as much as him. The king's letter was as usual in Digby's hand, for Digby normally drafted the king's letters after discussion with him and wrote them out when they were approved, after which they were signed by Charles.

From the north had come word of disaster: the Marquess of Newcastle had been trounced by the Fairfaxes and Meldrum at Selby and had retreated into York. Not wanting to bind up all his forces in a siege, he had sent his horse, five thousand of them, down to Newark to be taken over by Lord Goring, a fiery cavalry commander well known to Rupert. Goring had just been released after ten months as a prisoner of Parliament.

On the tenth of April a review of the king's army in and around Oxford established that it consisted of four thousand horse and not much more than five thousand foot. In the king's most recent letter, which Will Legge had just brought to him, Rupert was ordered back to Oxford to attend a war council at the end of the month.

He was also informed that the queen was being moved to Exeter, where she could remain in safety until she gave birth to the new child in July. The Duchess of Richmond would accompany her when they left in a few days' time.

Rupert stopped reading. By whose courtesy did he receive the last piece of information, he wondered—Digby's or the king's? Whoever had thought to include it, it meant the same thing: when he reached Oxford, Mary would be gone. He looked up at Will Legge, who was standing by the windows of the inn chamber that Rupert had made his quarters for the day. He had to force himself not to ask questions: *Is it true she's leaving, and so soon? How does she seem? Is she willing to go? How can Richmond bear to let her?*

He bowed his head again. If he could take horse now and gallop across Herefordshire . . . but his orders and his command gave him no shred of excuse for it. Will turned from the window and Rupert could feel himself being examined, so he looked up again.

Will said, "I trust it is all complete and clear, Your Highness?"

"Yes, thank you. I have no more questions."

"Then may I take the liberty to congratulate you?"

"On what?"

"On your appointment as Master of the Horse! I have been as pleased as Punch all the way—forgive me for mentioning it but I was told His Majesty had informed you of it in the dispatch. We shall all rejoice, if I may be permitted to say so."

Rupert shuffled the pages until he came to the paragraph. He was indeed named Master of the Horse. All the king's cavalry, in whatever part of the country, already came under his command as General of the Horse; this new honor made him responsible for managing the monarch's horses and stables and thereby gave him a great office that meant he would ride directly behind the king on all state occasions. "Ah. I see. I thank you."

Will was beaming. "May I request leave to go forth and announce the good news, Your Highness?"

Rupert nodded. "And call everyone to a meeting here in an hour. I'm summoned to Oxford for a war council shortly and I must give you your orders for the time I'm away."

Will bowed and left, and Rupert put down the letter and rested his forehead on the edge of the table. A sick feeling of anger, rebellion and despair overcame him. No matter how hard he labored or fought, this war went on forever. And it forever drove him apart from Mary. She could not refuse to leave Oxford with the queen any more than he could take horse this moment and rush pell-mell to intercept her. Love did nothing for him in these straits except add to the torture of separation.

It was the sixteenth of April. Mary's effects were packed and had been carried down to Abingdon to stand ready for her departure on the morrow. The queen's party, led by Lord Jermyn, would take to the road and the king would bid them farewell at the garrison town where Mary had last seen Rupert. This was a very different good-bye, enforced by the queen's condition and the king's fears, but it spelled the same to Mary—yet more distance set between her and Prince Rupert. She could not even write to him, nor he to her—it was not only court etiquette that forbade this, but her mortal uncertainty as to what he felt about her.

Meanwhile there was no doubt in her heart about him. She could not banish him from her thoughts or prayers and the slightest news of him sent her blood thumping in her veins with terror and exultant pride. She had a deep longing to see him come home, however briefly—to give him the welcome back to Oxford that he deserved and that he could receive only from her and James. Who else, even the king, understood his true value? Caught between the yearning of friend and confidante, of lover and wife, she ached for his return, but she was sentenced to go, before he could walk into her presence and before she could read on his face what had changed and what was the same after three months of separation.

She spent the night beforehand with James, in a physical pledge of her own claims—that she loved him and that she belonged with him. They were man and wife now in a fashion that they never had been before. If her deep passion for Rupert had not changed her, if the war and the king's danger had not wrenched all their lives into a completely different shape, perhaps she would never have found this new, more tender union with James. But she had, and it brought a new fear also. Would God allow her to love two men, albeit in different ways?

She clung to James and he to her in a tangle of limbs, in a bed that seemed too warm and disordered to allow either of them to sleep. But sleep she did, waking unrefreshed and hot. James lay with his back to her, the sheet over his head and not awake yet—unheard of at that hour. There was something languid and wrong about the household as she got dressed and bustled about, putting off the moment when she must rouse James so they could both prepare for the ride to Abingdon.

At last she entered his bedchamber again and kneeling beside the bed she said softly: "Husband, it is time."

He stirred, but she had to take the cover from over his head to see his face. He opened his eyes and said thickly, "No. I love you. Stay." She put a hand to his cheek and found it burning hot.

"James!" He did not react. Alarmed, she tried to pull the sheet back, but he held it fast and began to shiver. His hands trembled and his eyelids fluttered closed, and all at once she was aware that his breathing was painful and beads of sweat were starting from his forehead.

"Oh God!" she cried and sprang to her feet. Servants appeared at the doorway and she put up a hand for them to keep their distance. "Fetch Sir William Harvey. At once!"

When King Charles said good-bye to his queen at Abingdon, the leave-taking was worse than he had feared. His sense of foreboding was deeper than it had been at Dover two years before, though he tried to tell himself that from Holland, after all, she had eventually returned triumphant. The boys were miserable to see her leave, but they were older and more resilient now and would cope better with her absence, especially since it was to keep her and the coming baby safe. No, it was the loss of Mall Villiers that threatened to ruin his last hours and minutes with his beloved wife.

"She should be taking care of *me*, not your cousin!" Henrietta-Maria said to him plaintively as they stood alone together beside the comfortable coach that would take her away.

"She said more or less that herself, my dear, in her letter to me this morning. Everything she writes is of the utmost elegance, but I'm sure you noticed this time the unsteadiness of her hand—she is overwhelmed with regret and anxiety. And would you have her join you when Harvey has said that the fever may be catching? She does not even let the servants near—she is caring for my cousin alone."

He cringed inwardly as he said the words. The Duke of Richmond had taken a tremendous load upon himself recently, and one of the many places he had visited in the last few days was Port

Meadow, where a virulent marsh fever was raging amongst the troops. The onset was swift and it killed within days, leaving few survivors. Tents had been set up as a fever ward to isolate the sufferers, and Richmond had not been near it as far as Charles knew, but he might have been exposed to the malady in other ways.

Charles also felt the greatest fear for Mary, but did not voice it. "She will follow you, under the best guard I can muster, as soon as my cousin is well and she is fit to travel herself. It may only be a matter of days."

"I shall not be secure until she does. Think how much care she took over Merton when I came here. Not to have her making me comfortable in Exeter will be so sad. I cannot bear these partings unless Mall is by!" and she burst into tears.

Charles held her. "Ann Dalkeith and your ladies will cosset you until she comes to you," he said, and kissed her forehead. Despite her rounded shape she still seemed small and fragile, for she was several inches shorter than he and her pretty form was light and delicate. Thank God he could be sure of her safety under the tough protection of Lord Jermyn. There was a route to Exeter that would avoid any parliamentary forces and beyond that the country was secure in the hands of Prince Maurice.

When they had discussed where she should go, Henrietta-Maria herself had said that she might entrust herself to Rupert in Chester. This and other clues indicated to Charles that she was letting her resentment of Rupert slide into the past. It gladdened him, for her antagonism had caused him much unease and hidden annoyance over the last few months. It had been his decision to send her to the west; she was ready to settle anywhere that gave her months of shelter in which to prepare for and give birth to their child, attended by a practiced French midwife sent over by the kind Regent of France.

When she had stopped crying he beckoned the boys. "Come now and say good-bye to Mam. When you meet again there will be a little brother or sister to play with."

She hugged young Charles and James tightly and shed no more tears in front of them—in this she was braver than he.

He would not mount up to escort the vehicle or ride back and forth by the water waving as he had done in Dover—if he were on a horse he would find himself going with her all the way. He said this to her, in a whisper, and they embraced and kissed for the last time before he handed her up. The attendants fussed around until everything was ready, and then through a torrent of tears he watched her go.

The warm April sun glimmered on the Thames as the cavalcade and guards drew away, but he felt as though he would never see the bright sparkle in his wife's eyes again.

Chapter 31

IN NORMAL CIRCUMSTANCES, JAMES Stuart would not have been a difficult patient, or so at least Mary believed. He had never had a serious illness and did not complain when minor ones assailed him, brushing off any concern of Mary's and relying on his servants to tend to his wants. He was the most considerate man she knew; the only maladies he paid any attention to were hers and he had always surrounded her with devoted care.

In this crisis, however, he would not accept her concern and even tried to resist it, though she was the only one allowed near his bedside. The fever was rising steadily, she could hardly get him to drink and he refused food. Every time she tried to make him less uncomfortable in the untidy bed, he scolded her and told her to leave him alone.

He seemed furious with her for not leaving Oxford, and when she said Harvey had ordered her to stay he gave her a contemptuous look and turned his face to the wall. She could not possibly tell him how dangerous Harvey considered his fever to be, nor that she was with him because she was the only one who could save him, since others could not come near. So she tended him almost in silence.

"What do you do here?" he said to her once, so wide-eyed that she could not tell whether it was the fever or himself talking. "What do you know of sickrooms but the ones you lie in yourself?"

This cut so much she gasped and turned away, and he said no more.

The worse he became, the more helpless she felt. When night came she was exhausted, but no more than he, for he could not sleep—he was half-conscious, racked by the fever, and though in his prostration he let her sponge his upper body, he often tried to push her hands away.

Each night she brought her mattress right up to his bed and

lay there, terrified to go to sleep in case even with this closeness she would fail to hear if he needed help. She dozed in snatches, feeling desperate and alone.

On the third morning James's illness went into another phase. He alternately shivered and burned, and each time he burned he was delirious—he seemed not to know her and often called on other people, some of them dead, like his brother George. With all his careful barriers of ironical intellect and seamless civility removed, Mary could see to her sorrow how much anxiety and anger haunted her husband's mind. He was in a continual nightmare and the enemies he fought off changed from minute to minute—nameless figures, perhaps from his childhood, perhaps not human at all, for it was impossible for her to tell what he saw during these incoherent outbursts.

On the evening of the third day, she was bending over him as she replaced the top sheet of his bedding—she could not change the drenched bottom sheet without help. She did not call in the house servants, though she knew they were nearly all within earshot, poised and ready for her slightest request. They brought her what she needed by placing it on a table at the door of the room, and she only opened the door once they had withdrawn to a safe distance.

James took the sheet from her hands and glared at her, his eyes glittering and his skin blotched with red and white. He seemed to recognize her. "So you have not gone! You will seize on any excuse to stay."

"James!" she said in anguish, and her tears came so fast they fell on the crisp linen.

He muttered, "You may go. I cannot look at you."

It was unbearable. She turned away, took her mattress from the side of his bed, threw it on the floor by the doorway and flung herself on it, sobbing. She cried for an hour. Her husband hated having her near—and she was the only one who could save him. Because she had been constant neither to her marriage nor to her secret, guilty passion, two men abhorred her. She was now most loathed exactly where she most loved. And she had no one to blame but herself.

Where could she ask forgiveness? James could not listen—she would add to his torment by trying to confess to him. And Rupert was far away. Even when he came to Oxford within the next few days she could not see him. Sometimes in her desperation she wished that she might resort to the comforts of Henrietta-Maria's religion and summon a priest to hear that which lay like lead on her heart. But everything was against it: her Protestant upbringing, James's stern principles and Rupert's even sterner beliefs all shut out that abject escape route from guilt. She must bear this along with her greatest suffering, which was terror for James's very life.

James meanwhile lay silent but restless, and now and then she crept over to observe him. At one point, when she was beside the door weeping, little Anne, who slept every night on the other side of it, got up from her pallet to knock gently. Mary flung open the door and hissed, "Move away!" When Anne had jumped back and scuttled out of reach she said more loudly, "Why do you disturb us? He is not dying! I will not let him, do you hear me?" Then she closed the door and leaned against it, sobbing.

At last, after one more look at James, she stretched herself out on the mattress and sleep took her, sweeping her into a darkness that was like a great flood in which all hope was washed away.

In the morning she woke to the same pain and guilt, opened her eyes and looked at once over to James. He was so still that she started up in horror and stumbled to the bedside, her eyes fixed on his face, which was turned toward the room. His eyes were closed and his golden hair, darkened with sweat, lay damp on the pillow. She dared not touch his face. Instead with her right hand she took his, which dangled over the edge of the bed, and felt his pulse with the fingers of her left. He was alive, but in her panic she could not tell whether the pulse was weaker or stronger than before.

"Oh, God!" she whispered.

At that he opened his eyes and his hand closed on hers. "It's you," he said in surprise, striving to lift his head so that he could look at her. She dropped to the floor, still holding his hand, and when her eyes were on a level with his he smiled. "I thought you had gone. Why are you still home?"

"To care for you. Will you let me? You have not been well."

He frowned slightly. "How long?"

"Never mind. First you must drink. Then we shall see what else you can manage."

He submitted to everything she suggested and made no protest when she sponged his chest, neck and face. He did not see her tears as she gently set the bed to rights and rejoiced in the touch of his skin under her light fingers—the fever had gone.

When he had drunk some water and lay looking up at her with a dreamy expression, he said, "Now, my good angel, I shall sleep as you tell me. But you won't go away?"

"No." She leaned over and kissed his forehead.

"Why not the lips? I am not so feeble as I may look."

She transferred her lips to his and felt them smile beneath hers, and a minute later he slept.

When Harvey came on his daily call and stood talking from the other side of the outer room, she told him what had happened. She could hardly stand, she knew she looked disheveled almost beyond recognition and her face was haggard, but relief and joy were bursting out of her and she only wanted Harvey's quiet reassurances to help her breathe again.

He gave them, with gravity, and advised her on the care James needed for the day. After much consideration he also made an admission. "The signs you have described in the duke are not those of the fever at Port Meadow. I was wrong to suppose that was what he had contracted. There the patients suffer vomiting, dysentery and many other things that the duke has been spared. This fever is different and not in my view contagious. It is quite safe to approach him. You must recall your servants to their duties and get some rest."

"Oh no. I shall stay with him. I have a mattress in the corner— it is perfectly comfortable."

He looked at her with an admiring smile. "I shall believe in your comfort when I see you looking less like a ghost, madam. And if your husband is not asleep, I shall now examine him."

"He is resting." She was at attention, barring the door like a demented guard.

Harvey stepped forward and put his hands under her elbows. "So will you, madam, for you richly deserve it. That is a medical stricture from me."

When Rupert reached Oxford on the day before the council of war he was looking forward to nothing but seeing the king. The courtiers, the king's Parliament and the colleges full of military officials were bound to be at their usual squabbles and did not need him to add to them. As for the garrisons he had put in place to protect the city, he had had hints in letters from Richmond that there was a degree of slackness that would only anger him. For that reason he was less than keen to see Richmond himself and have it all confirmed. And to approach the city and know that Mary Villiers had ridden out of it the week before made it a desolate place.

His audience with the king was affectionate and protracted. Charles was most unhappy about the queen's departure and very mournful on the subject. Rupert made sympathetic remarks but asked no questions about the leave-taking, which he preferred not to picture. They had been talking for an hour before the king, who was enumerating who would be present at the war council on the morrow, mentioned the Duke of Richmond.

"Fortunately he is well enough to attend, but only just. We were all in fear of his life; it was most distressing."

"I beg your pardon, sire—what, he is wounded, or ill? No one told me about this!"

The king gave a tired, apologetic smile. "With so many disasters heaped upon our heads, we hesitate to pass on new ones, otherwise you should have been told. My cousin was attacked by a dangerous fever and is barely recovered. Harvey tells me only James's dear wife could have saved him. We thank heaven she stayed behind instead of leaving with the queen."

Rupert's heart jolted and he looked away. "She is here?"

"Until the day after tomorrow. The duke is determined that she go to safety and my wife eagerly awaits her. We all hate to part with her, but it is for the best."

"No doubt," Rupert said dutifully, then tried to focus his mind. "But how is Richmond? Is he truly recovered?"

"Harvey has no fears for him. My cousin has sent me a note assuring me of his presence at the council tomorrow. I could ill do without him—I always hear sense from him."

"Amen to that," Rupert said, then changed the subject.

When the audience was over he begged leave to return to his former lodgings and the king urged him to do so and take some rest.

Irresistibly, Rupert called at the Richmonds' first. He was met with joyful smiles by the servants, who opened the doors, ushered him in downstairs and made ready to announce him to the duke.

"No," he said, "I am here to inquire about his health, not on any account to disturb him. Please convey my greetings and compliments and my concern for his well-being. I shall wait here for his reply."

The man went out, then returned within minutes with a specific message that he voiced rather timidly—it appeared that the duke was quite healthy enough to receive the prince, and if the prince would not accept his warmest invitation to come up, the duke would be forced to run down to greet him.

Even then, Rupert knew quite well that he should refuse, leave his compliments again and go. Instead he asked, "Is her grace also at home?"

"She is, Your Highness."

"I shall step up for a few minutes."

As he was ushered up the familiar stairs, Rupert had never had such need of self-control. She would be prepared for him if she had been in the same room as James when his inquiry was taken up, and for all he knew would look at him as coolly as she had on that diabolical day at Abingdon. Whereas he was shaking with tension. Richmond had faced death in the last few days and deserved a friend's heartiest affection. Nothing should pass between himself and Mary, not a word or a glance that had to do with their own feelings except as they related to Richmond. They had no right to show anything but their devotion to her husband.

As it happened, it was easier to manage than he had feared. Mary was at the window when he was shown in, half turned away, and though courtesy demanded that she face him she did not do so immediately. This gave him the chance to greet Richmond, who was on his feet, smiling and frankly glad to see him.

"My dear friend," Rupert said, clasping his hands, and his voice roughened as he said it. "I have only just been told how ill you have been. I can't believe no one got word to me. How are you?"

Richmond grinned. "As you see. Upright and ready to make a nuisance of myself in whatever field you care to name."

"The king tells me how much you have done for the garrisons since I have been away. I wish to God there were more gentlemen to make such nuisances of themselves."

Mary advanced then, and he was able to include her in the same smile he gave James, without revealing the happiness it brought

him just to look at her. Her face was not cool, but calm and serene. Her voice as they greeted each other was lower than usual, as
though she were tired, but there was no weariness in her graceful
movements after he accepted the invitation to sit with them.

Despite his assurances, Richmond still showed signs of his
ordeal. He was pale and unsteady, and weakness made him look
drawn. It would be very draining for him to attend the council the
next day but he was determined to come, which made Rupert feel
indebted, for it was Richmond above all who had made his efforts
in Oxford feasible and who was still his strongest ally with the king.
Looking at his fine, determined face, Rupert was overwhelmed by
how much he owed this man.

"I must not tax you," he said to James, sitting with his gloves
and his hat on his knee—he had not relinquished them to a servant because he needed them as reminders that he was to be up
and away. "I am lodged in the old quarters but I haven't seen them
yet—no doubt there are things to organize. I can stay a minute
only."

"Whom did you bring with you?" James asked.

"Apart from Boy," his wife put in with a little laugh.

They talked for longer than he had intended but they all recognized when he rose to leave that this was the briefest visit he had
ever paid. The three of them were here in the same place and in
the same company that had made up their evenings of good cheer,
laughter and friendly alliance in the past—but that era was over.
There could never be another intimate dinner at the Richmonds',
for too many changes had occurred for it to be bearable to any of
them.

When he bowed and left, he realized he had hardly dared to
look at Mary, and except for their initial greeting every word he'd
spoken had been directed at Richmond. Yet her features were en-
graved even deeper on his heart. She was more slender—caring
for Richmond must have told on her—and although he knew it
was impossible, her eyes seemed a deeper blue. And considering
the effects that her low, soft voice had had on him, she might as
well have been speaking words of eternal love.

On the next day the war council went on for hours, as Mary had
known it would, and late in the afternoon she paid a visit to Sir Wil-

liam Harvey, who had promised to give her some medicines and advice that might be useful while she and the queen awaited the birth of the child in Exeter.

In the schoolroom at Christ Church she was able to catch the princes at the end of their lessons, and thus bid them farewell and receive their messages to relate when she caught up with their Mam.

When the boys were gone, Harvey took her through the things he had collected for her, then put them in a linen bag and offered to have them delivered to her that evening. She had just thanked him and was getting ready to leave when they heard someone striding toward the open door. Mary stopped speaking and waited, her heart lifting and then plummeting in hope and apprehension.

The footsteps came to a halt and she looked over to see Prince Rupert in the doorway. She feared that the look of amazement and ecstasy on her face might be instantly reflected on his, but he hid it with a bow.

"Excuse me for interrupting. I was told you were here, your grace, and I hope to give you a few verbal messages that you will be obliging enough to carry to Her Majesty for me."

She took a deep breath. He had sought this; it was not fate that threw them together again. "By all means, Your Highness."

"Thank you. I had no other opportunity—I ride out early with His Majesty tomorrow to review the garrisons. Which will take more than a week, I predict."

"Then I shall leave you," Harvey said quietly. "Pray remain here if you wish; provided you can stand the discomforts of a schoolroom, your grace." He bowed and collected up Mary's linen bag and some papers from his desk.

"You are very good," Prince Rupert said, and Harvey bowed once more and left, closing the door behind him.

Rupert was beside it, on the opposite side of the room from her, looking at her with such naked longing in his eyes that she ran to him, cannoning into his chest. He took the shock, put his arms around her at once, held her tight and leaned back against the wall.

She pressed her cheek against his chest and felt the pounding of his heart. "Don't let me go," she said. "I can't bear it; I can't bear any of it. Hold me."

He did so for a long time, silent, his chest rising and falling deeply.

She moved to put her forehead against him and with her eyes closed she said, "Forgive me."

"Forgive you?" His voice shook with surprise. "What have you done? Nothing. It is I. You must forgive me, for everything I said before I went away." He took her face between his hands and tipped it toward his. "Erase all those words, or I can't go on. I hurt you because I loved you, that is my only excuse. Tell me you don't hate me."

"I love you," she said passionately, then with her hands clutching the front of his doublet she pulled herself closer to him and kissed him with a fierceness that left her breathless and caused a deep sound in his throat that aroused her at once, sending a soft, sweet pulse up through her body.

It was he who broke the kiss, pulling his head back and crushing her waist between his hands as he looked down at her. "Oh, God," he said, "what are we to do? You leave tomorrow." He sounded angry, but she knew it was not anger that made his voice hoarse.

She put up her face to kiss him again but he held her as before, his hands on her waist maintaining a few inches of distance between them, and suddenly said, "Come, sit with me." He clasped one of her hands tightly and led her to Harvey's desk, where he sat on the big armless chair and drew her down so she was sitting across his thighs.

Bereft while she could not touch him with her whole body, she wound her arms around his waist and put her cheek to his shoulder. He was wearing his sword as usual and she could feel the hilt cold against her forearm. She shivered and he embraced her more closely.

"I'm not going to say good-bye this time," he said. "When we walk out this door we do so as though we shall meet tomorrow, or the day after. If you hear I am dead you are never to believe it." She gave a cry but he put the fingers of one hand over her lips. "If I hear you have left England with the queen I shall never accept it. Everywhere I go I shall expect to see you just around the next corner. Promise me you will do the same."

She shook her head. "I won't go! I won't go with the queen."

"Sshhh," he said and stroked her hair. "That is not a permissible subject. I am a tyrant and you will obey. Promise me."

"I hate the things I said about you. I hate myself."

"You cannot—I love you too much. I love you enough for both of us."

"Oh, Rupert." She freed herself enough to raise her head and press her lips to his cheek. "I don't think that makes any sense."

"Very well, I am a senseless tyrant."

With a despairing laugh she kissed his face—his forehead, his eyes, his nose, his chin. He kept trying to meet her lips and kiss her back but she was too quick for him, even to the last when she buried her face in the crook of his shoulder and gave a dry sob that communicated itself from her chest to his.

His face against her neck rasped a little with the beginnings of stubble that had grown since he shaved that morning. His thick hair smelled fresh and clean. The lace over his shoulder prickled against her lips and carried the faint scents of camphor and sandalwood.

She gave a shuddering sigh. "I would do anything for you," she said. "I promise."

He stirred, put his hands to her waist again, kissed her long and deeply and then with one swift movement spun her off his lap and onto her feet. "Go, then," he said as though the words caused him mortal pain. His eyes shot a command into hers. "Go without looking back. And I shall not regard you as you leave."

Even before she grasped the words, his hands parted and she swayed back just out of his reach. She gazed at him, horrified, and he put his long fingers over his face.

"Go!" he said between his teeth, and shifted so that he was bent over the desk with his elbows on the top.

She took a gasping breath, divided between anguish and a wild fury against him and the world. She had to turn away in order not to see him broken by the same despair. Then she ran from the room.

On the following day there were two departures from the city that were much talked about. Prince Rupert, whose advice had dominated the war council the day before, held that the king's best strategy was to make his position in Oxford stronger than ever. To this end, the prince would not go back to his northwestern command until a full assessment had been made of the fortifications, strongholds and garrison towns surrounding the capital and until the most solid of defensive policies had been laid down. He and the king therefore left on a tour of inspection that would take ten days.

The Duchess of Richmond said her good-byes to her husband within her own home while her escort drew up in the street outside.

The servants said that when the duke and duchess stood at the threshold of the great chamber, the duchess lightly and cheerfully evoked the future and spoke much of the day when she and the duke would be reunited. In the end, however, she could not disguise her distress; she was torn by emotion and did not want to let her husband go. The servants heard her when she clung to him and cried with the deepest feeling, "James, never forget. I am yours." His reply was muffled in her close embrace.

As she went downstairs he crossed to the window, waited until she appeared below and waved until he could no longer see her. Then to everyone's horror he collapsed onto the coffer beneath the window and wept as though he would never be able to stop, with his forehead on the sill and his hair falling over his face.

They could not know that in the midst of his grief was an unexpected spark that illuminated this parting. When they had kissed, his wife's lips had parted under his for the first time. It thrilled and prostrated him to believe that after all his years of hopeless love she might at last respond, for all their unknown future, to his impossible desire.

Chapter 32

☙

THE MERRY MONTH OF May smiled with particular kindness on the Earl of Essex. The demonic Prince Rupert made his decisive presence felt in the fortified circle around Oxford during the first few days of the month, but then took himself off again. He was scarcely over the horizon before the king's councillors fell out amongst themselves and someone decided the royalists could do without Reading, which they had held ever since Rupert had snatched it back in September of the year before.

It seemed too good to be true, but Essex exploited the windfall by moving up the Thames valley at once while Parliament ordered Sir William Waller and his army to join him in a new campaign. He and Waller got on no better than some of King Charles's bickering courtiers, so after some acrimonious discussion they agreed to act independently: Essex as Lord General was in command, but in practice they followed their own loosely linked strategies, with Waller circling Oxford from the west and Essex crossing the Thames at Sandford to march around to the east.

It seemed magical. The closer they drew their pincer movement about the city, the less eager the king appeared to put up a fight. Their greatest prize was Abingdon, headquarters of the royalist horse, from which the king's men one day withdrew their thousands of troopers and wagonloads of equipment, leaving the handsome riverside town to Parliament's approaching troops without firing a shot in resistance.

It seemed like perfect timing, for Rupert could not come charging down to the king's rescue—the prince was far too occupied in the northwest. There, one had to admit, things were not going Parliament's way. Rupert was on the march, having gathered up an army in Shrewsbury, left one of his majors, Will Legge, behind as governor of Chester and proceeded to maraud through the northwestern counties at his usual terrifying speed. He first wiped out a parliamentary detachment at Knutsford, next took Stockport in a vicious assault and then descended upon Bolton, the defenders of which made the mistake of declaring a royalist prisoner an Irish Papist and hanging him from the walls.

Essex winced when he heard this and had no trouble believing the sequel: in a towering rage Rupert dismounted, strode to the front line of his foot soldiers and led them in repeated attacks until they took the town. No quarter was given—any man, woman or youngster seen holding a weapon was slaughtered and Bolton was sacked. Rupert then marched to Liverpool and took it in four days, leaving it in secure hands before leading his victorious and now dizzyingly experienced army back to Chester.

That was in the first week of June, and by then the king had fled. Glimpsing a loophole in Essex's careful maneuvers, Charles managed to slip out of Oxford by the Banbury Road, sneak past Essex himself, not far from Woodstock, and make good time with his forces to Worcester.

It was humiliating, and it caused Essex hidden fury and a certain amount of public recrimination. But in other ways it opened up interesting new possibilities for the Lord General. He need no longer worry about taking Oxford, which would need too much time and a skillful siege to make it fall. The king had flown and was, if not exactly in the open, at least on the run. The question was, who should continue the pursuit: Essex or Waller?

The Lord General called Waller to a council of war at Chipping Norton. It pleased him to see Parliament's much lauded favorite this far from his usual haunts, the western counties in which he had long waged punishing campaigns against Hopton and Prince Maurice. Waller was in his forties and had been the member of Parliament for Andover when he became colonel of a regiment of horse in Essex's army. His military background was the same as Essex's, for he had fought for Prince Rupert's father, the Elector Palatine, in Europe, but as Essex eyed him across the room in which he conducted the council of war, he reflected that despite Parliament's plaudits the bluff, competent-looking man opposite him had suffered as many reversals as victories during the difficult conflict in the southwest.

"Sir William," he said amiably, "we have had much need of you to contain the threat that Hopton and Prince Maurice pose in the territory from which you have joined us. But there comes a time when containment is not enough."

Waller's alert eyes widened at this as he decided to swallow the affront and wait to see where Essex was leading.

The earl went on, "We must rejoice that you and your forces are at hand for such an opportunity as this. I have decided to entrust to you the high task of closing with the king and either soundly defeating him or forcing him into an untenable position, whether that happens to be in Worcester or elsewhere. I shall meanwhile march on Lyme, raise the siege there and put a stop to the depradations that Hopton and Prince Maurice have for too long inflicted on Devon and Cornwall."

Waller reddened, opened his mouth and shut it again. If he objected and strenuously defended his record in the southwest, he risked being deprived of the chance to close in on King Charles. Which was the greater sacrifice—to let Essex march off and wring some tinsel victory out of the morass Waller had been battling with for ages, or to pass up the potential glory of collaring the King of England?

Waller accepted the command, as he must, and Essex congratulated himself on the chance to show up his younger general in the southwest. He would thus avoid the thankless task of chasing Charles about Worcestershire and be free to explore the possibilities offered by another piece in the chess game of this war—the queen, tantalizingly stranded at Exeter.

So it was that the Earl of Essex marched southwest with vengeance and hope in his heart while Waller marched north on the trail of the errant king.

It was the sixteenth of June and Mary was in Exeter Cathedral. She had come there on her own, refusing any escort in a ploy to be alone for half an hour. The beautiful red stone cathedral was within walking distance of the converted priory inside Exeter's stout city walls that formed the mansion, Bedford House, in which Henrietta-Maria now awaited the birth of her child. Thus Mary was in as little danger treading the cobbles to the cathedral square as she had ever been in Oxford's Magpie Lane.

In contrast to its ruddy exterior the cathedral inside was pale, bathed by light that flooded through high windows into the nave and drew Mary's gaze aloft, up the pillars of bluish Dorset marble to the intricate tracery of the vaulting that was fashioned in warmer Devon stone. Somehow the cathedral raised her into an airy realm of clarity and hope.

From one point of view, Henrietta-Maria and her little group of ladies could feel safe in Exeter. The city had fallen to Prince Maurice in September of the previous year and the governor was Sir John Berkeley, a Bruton relative of the great Berkeley family of Gloucestershire, an experienced commander admired for his victorious campaigns in Devon and fiercely loyal to the king. Exeter on its steep and heavily fortified hill was well garrisoned and Sir John held it with an iron hand. In addition he had pledged that after the birth of the child, if the situation demanded he would personally escort the queen through Cornwall to Falmouth Havens, where his relative the Earl of Falmouth would shelter her in Pendennis Castle while a ship was made ready to take her to France.

All this should have felt like a comfort to Henrietta-Maria, for she was snug in an ample house of Rougemont stone and had reached it without hindrance. Mary often thought of their march from Oxford in terms of a military withdrawal: they had chosen a safe route, ensured adequate escort and supply, and a feasible line of escape lay open to the sea, thanks to Prince Maurice's domination of Cornwall. She felt that if Prince Rupert had been called to judge their retreat, he would have approved of it.

But the journey had been arduous and the queen's time in Exeter was haunted by anxiety and pain. Mary, having left Oxford on horseback rather than in a coach, had made good time to catch up with the queen on the way—but she had found her exhausted and ailing, and by the time they trailed their way to Exeter, Henrietta-Maria was seriously ill. She had muscular spasms that terrified everyone with regard to the baby, and pains in the chest that caught her so forcibly she sometimes seemed to be suffocating. The queen's letters to the king, sent to Oxford and then to Worcestershire, caused him such anguish that he wrote to the former royal physician in London, Sir Theodore Mayerne, "Mayerne, for the love of me go to my wife." Mayerne, a skilled French doctor who had stayed in London to tend other illustrious clients when the court left Whitehall, lost no time in making his way through to Exeter.

It should have given Mary some repose to know that two experts—the midwife from the French royal court and Mayerne himself, whom she knew and trusted—were tending the queen, but in these last weeks before the birth, Henrietta-Maria turned to Mary in her worst fears and tribulations. And Mary felt helpless— as bereft as she had when James had been ill. To sit beside the bed where another lay in pain was so hard to bear that if she could have taken the queen's torments upon herself she would have done so—and for a secret reason, since she could not help envying the queen her condition, however harrowing it appeared to be.

So it was with a mixture of fear and sorrow that Mary came sometimes to the Lady Chapel, a sanctuary of finely carved stone that closed around her like a blessing as she entered and knelt before its delicately gilded altarpiece. This cool, quiet space beyond the high altar at the eastern end of the cathedral was decorated with a mixture of sculptures and images that had come to it over the centuries. Today she sat gazing for a while at a wooden carving of shepherds at Bethlehem crowded in with their sheep and listening to one of their number playing a pipe. It brought her as much succor as paying a visit to Bishop Lacy, whose plain fifteenth-century tomb nearby was said to offer healing to those who approached it with reverence.

In the Lady Chapel, dedicated to the Virgin, Mary prayed for the king, who to the best of their knowledge had left Worcester and was either in or heading for Bewdley. She prayed for James, with a fervent plea that God would go on granting him the strength that his every letter offered her. She prayed for the health of Henrietta-Maria and her child. She begged forgiveness for the guilt of loving Rupert. And she dared to pray for him, not as a warrior but as a young man called into dangers from which only miracles could continue to deliver him.

On this day, she had long finished her prayers and was still kneeling with closed eyes and clasped hands when there was a sound beside her and she looked up to see Lord Jermyn standing in the aisle. He had tracked her down from Bedford House.

He bowed and said, "I cry you mercy, my lady, but Her Majesty has sent me to say she has urgent need of you. You must know—her travail has begun."

*   *   *

On the same day, Rupert received a letter from the king. It was deciphered and handed to him while he was conferring with his officers, and excusing himself he unfolded it while they were still in the room—any message from the king inspired anxious curiosity in anyone who knew of it, and he never delayed opening dispatches.

It was not overlong, but momentous enough to make him sit down heavily and read it twice before looking up and saying, "Gentlemen, you are dismissed. His Majesty lives and is safe. Be assured I shall give you any news that you would wish to hear when I've had the liberty to digest this."

They left and he bent his head to read the carefully written pages again. The black script flickered before his eyes and he closed them and tried to concentrate. He had just been given a clear road to follow, but the king's demands, as they were set out, filled him with dread. He could not help the feeling that this letter spelled out the way either to his most glorious battle or to his doom.

That same evening, James Stuart was in his lodgings in Bewdley, near the king, when a visitor was announced. Sir John Culpepper had been Lord Keeper of the Great Seal and Chancellor of the Exchequer from the beginning of the war when he joined the king at York, and since then a faithful adviser at Oxford. He was an intelligent and thoughtful man whom James had always been glad to see in the king's councils, and no more so than at the council of war of two days before, when the king's next moves had been debated.

Culpepper sat down in the chamber where James had so far received very little company—scuttling about the countryside with Charles and the army was his least favorite style of existence, and after the trials of the day he preferred to bury himself in the most comfortable environment he could find and shut out the world until morning. Culpepper looked distressed, and with an inward sigh James made him welcome, offered refreshment and tried to find some positive things to talk about.

But the old man had come with a single purpose. He sat pulling his neatly trimmed gray beard for a while and then said, "Did you see the letter His Majesty dispatched to Prince Rupert two days ago?"

James shook his head. "No, but we all understood and agreed upon its contents in the council of war. Why, did you?"

"No, Digby's draft came to my notice. It has preyed on my mind ever since."

James felt a twinge of apprehension. "What, was the message different from what we settled on?"

"In respect to the king, no. His intention of moving back down to Oxford to collect the foot is confirmed in the letter. And he does not as yet tell Prince Rupert whether our forces can be combined."

"So he is not giving the prince permission to come to his aid?" James sighed. "I confess sometimes I wish he would. How else are we to fend off Waller?"

"No, His Majesty is not calling Prince Rupert to us. It's the opposite—he has ordered him to march to York and defeat the Scots and Parliament's armies together!"

James looked at Culpepper in consternation. "That is not what the council decided. At least, it was not to happen definitively or immediately. It was an *option*, to be discussed with Rupert. The armies sitting outside York are of a size and posture that godlike Achilles himself would hesitate to confront. What is going on?"

"Prince Rupert has been given the order, with no room for question or maneuver. He must march to York. When I saw the draft and read it through, I went straight to the king. I asked him whether the letter had been sent to Prince Rupert as it was, and he said yes."

"Damnation. What did you reply?"

"I said, 'Why then, before God you are undone, for upon this peremptory order he will fight, whatever comes of it.' "

Chapter 33

≈

ON THE FIRST DAY of July, Mary was in the queen's bedchamber, sitting by the window with her cousin Lady Dalkeith. Strong-minded, handsome and resilient, Lady Dalkeith was the competent gentlewoman chosen by Henrietta-Maria to look after everything to do with the new princess, Henrietta-Anne—her care and needs, the provision of an excellent nurse and attendants, and the baby's daily routine, for nothing of the kind could be supervised by her mother, who was still recovering from the birth and her illness.

Sitting with Lady Dalkeith near the window but out of the rays of the summer sun, Mary was holding the fortnight-old baby in her lap and playing with her fingers as they curled themselves around the tips of her own. Henrietta-Anne was a treasure of a baby—round-limbed and comely, with eyes that were still as blue as a kitten's and amusing in their eagerness to focus on the world beyond her tiny reach. Mary bent low, knowing that the surest way to engage the little thing was with her voice, and she softly told the baby princess stories of where she was and how she was loved and protected, while Lady Dalkeith looked on with an indulgent smile, and the queen lay resting fully clothed on her bed, too far away to hear Mary's murmured endearments.

It was a strange tale that Mary had to tell Henrietta-Anne on that sunny afternoon, and she left out more than she put in. The very place where the child was housed was the Exeter home of the Russells, the noble Puritan family to which Lord Digby's wife, Ann, belonged—and for almost two years of the war the Russells had supported Parliament, before the Earl of Bedford made his submission to the king at Oxford. And as soon as the queen was well enough, she and a tiny group of her devoted entourage would be sneaking out of this shelter, for the Earl of Essex was on the move toward them and if he surrounded Exeter the queen would be trapped. Essex had driven Prince Maurice from the port of

Lyme and raised the siege there, had occupied Weymouth and was marching inland. The queen had decided to slip away: she refused to leave herself in danger of capture, for she was convinced the king would do anything to rescue her and thereby put himself and all his plans in jeopardy.

Before the birth, and at the worst point of her illness, Henrietta-Maria had sent a message to Essex asking for a safe-conduct to Bath, in the hope that the waters there would revive her. But the earl sent a brutal letter back, stating that the only place he would escort her to was London, for trial before Parliament. Essex's response chilled Mary, for it showed her how far this bitter war had carried him from mercy and understanding. Only flight could now save the queen and her child.

"Your mother takes the greatest care of you, you see," Mary said to the baby, and brushed a fingertip lightly across one silky cheek. "And no wonder, for you are so beautiful. Do you know what the French agent Monsieur de Sabran said of you when he came to see you the other day? He said, *'une très belle princesse.'* Yes, he did." She looked up. "I could swear she understands me!"

Henrietta-Maria did hear this. She stirred, sat up and lifted her feet over the edge of the bed to the floor. Her eyes were moist as she looked across at Mary. "Mall, it touches me to see you dandling my daughter with such affection. But I beg you, do not get too fond. I must make the sacrifice of tearing myself away from her—it will be all the harder for me if you suffer too."

Mary lifted the baby and held her in the crook of her arm, glancing down with a look of tender alarm at the small head beneath her breast. "Madam, you don't mean this!"

Lady Dalkeith held out her hands. "Let me take her for a while. She must soon go to the nurse—isn't she a hungry little piece of mischief?"

Mary relinquished the baby but could not smile back at her cousin.

Henrietta-Maria continued, "She will be safe here, for Exeter will withstand any siege by Parliament—I have Sir John's assurance on that; indeed, he swears it on his life. And my wonderful Lady Dalkeith has pledged herself to Henrietta-Anne's care and protection."

"For as long as you wish, madam, be it months or years," Lady Dalkeith said, avoiding Mary's eye.

Mary rose and walked away from the window, then stopped before she reached the queen. She was in the center of the room, halted by conflicting emotions. She had never wanted to quit Oxford, but she had not been able to shirk her duty to the queen. She owed Henrietta-Maria her support and allegiance, but she could not believe the queen would leave this new creature, her helpless baby daughter, in a beleaguered city.

"Mary," Henrietta-Maria pleaded, "don't make me weep for this necessity too! I must leave my husband and England; I am by no means better yet, but as soon as I am, I shall hasten away. I must summon the courage to make sacrifices for his life and his throne!"

"But why this, madam?" Mary burst out.

Henrietta-Maria shook her head mournfully. "For the same reason that my little Elizabeth and Henry are still in London. I have already had to hide in hedgerows and ditches! I will not subject small children to the perils of hard travel and of this . . . this vagabond life that I am forced into. When I am established in France, the dear protectors who look after them will bring them to rejoin me. I promise you, madam, that is the best way to keep them out of danger. One day I *will* see *all* my babies with me in sanctuary."

Mary looked at her in silence, her lips trembling.

With a tragic sigh, Henrietta-Maria reached out and took a folded piece of paper from under the bolster of the bed. She held it out to Mary, who came forward reluctantly and took it, then waited.

Henrietta-Maria said, "I must leave in secret within the next few days and set sail from Falmouth Havens. We will wait at Pendennis Castle for the right weather. You know how terribly I fear the sea! Yet go we must, and before we sail I intend to send this letter to the king. Pray read it—I believe my husband will understand my heart, my principles and my actions; I would have you do the same before we part from here."

Mary retreated to the window, sat down and bent her head over the page. The words swam, but she made some out clearly enough.

I am giving the strongest proof of love that I can give; I am hazarding my life that I may not incommode your affairs. Adieu my dear

*heart. If I die, believe that you will lose a person who has never
been other than entirely yours.*

Lady Dalkeith, seeing a tear slide down Mary's cheek, said
kindly, "I think it is time I took this child to her nurse." She rose,
holding the baby to her shoulder so the little head was close to her
glossy dark ringlets as she turned to go.

Henrietta-Maria smiled over and said, "Thank you, my dear
friend. And now, Mall, I want you to fold that paper up, and come
and sit by me on the bed and give me your sweetest attention. For
I have a favor to ask and an idea to discuss that needs all your love
and intrepidity."

As Lady Dalkeith went out with her tiny charge and closed the
door, Mary got slowly to her feet and crossed the room to rejoin
the queen.

On that same day, Rupert was approaching York and thinking of
the enemy. In the rapid march during which he had brought his
army across the north of England, he had gathered in much intelligence about the forces that he would meet outside the great cathedral city. The three generals besieging York were the leader of
the Scots army, the Earl of Leven, who was the senior commander;
Ferdinando, Lord Fairfax, head of Parliament's Northern Army, in
which his son Sir Thomas Fairfax served as a cavalry commander;
and the Earl of Manchester, formerly Viscount Mandeville, whom
King Charles had once sought to arrest for treason at the same
time as the Five Members of the Commons in January 1642. As
far as Rupert could calculate from informants, simply confronting
Leven, Fairfax and Manchester would pit him against odds of two
to one—his fourteen thousand against the enemies' twenty-eight
thousand.

When he found that afternoon that they had temporarily raised
the siege and were waiting for him south of the rivers protecting
York, directly in his path, he sent a small force at them as a feint,
then took his army over the rivers and in a giant arc to fetch up outside the city, capturing the parliamentary armies' bridge of boats.
This surprise march of twenty-two miles delivered the enemy siege
works into his hands, and his men hunted the remaining soldiers
out of the trenches to liberate York in a frenzy of triumph.

It took him until past midnight to prepare all his dispositions for the battle the next day. He had received a fulsome message of thanks and praise from the Marquess of Newcastle by the time he briefed the gentleman he sent into the city to meet with him—the firebrand cavalry commander Lord Goring.

He and Goring held their conference deep in the forest of Galtres under a black grove of trees, while the warm summer night breathed around them and lights glowed from amongst the trunks that ringed the clearing. In the peaceful environs Rupert's men were preparing for the morrow, either curled up asleep beside their stacks of weapons, cooking a late meal or still moving into their allotted bivouacs.

Rupert leaned against a tall elm, attuned to the rustle, clang, thump and murmur of his army as he said to Goring, "You'll explain why I can't ride into York to meet the marquess myself; there are more than enough tasks for me to perform tonight and he will understand that. We move out before dawn and I rejoice to know his six thousand foot will be with us. You will give him my compliments, express my gratitude and my confidence in him and you will bring me back his assurance that his foot will join us, here and here"—he showed Goring his sketch of the morrow's concentration of troops—"at four a.m."

Goring nodded and asked a few questions. Rupert gave the answers and then said, "You will also be speaking to Lord Eythin. Eythin of course knows me from the past in Europe—we fought the Austrians together, but at the time he was less than complimentary about my youth and what he was good enough to call my foolhardiness." He gave a sardonic smile. "I remind you of this because I don't want you to feel you have to react if Eythin says anything disobliging. Ignore it; it will be trash anyway." He saw Goring grin at this and knew he had picked the right man for the job. "Leave him to me: I'll be seeing him soon enough. And his attitude is unimportant—what we want is his men and he will not delay marching them out to us when we have just liberated York. I am of course hoping he will be courtesy and appreciation personified."

Goring departed, Rupert held a council with his officers to give the directives for the morrow and at two o'clock he stretched out on a couple of cloaks with Boy at his back and slept until Mortaigne woke him as arranged just after three.

*   *   *

Five hours later Rupert was still expecting Eythin and the foot brigades from York. The predawn maneuvers over the water had gone as planned but without any sign of the forces from the city. But Goring had received Newcastle's and Eythin's promise of support and in consequence, though exasperated by their lateness, Rupert did not delay moving his regiments. In fact it was imperative that he did so, for the enemy had also begun moving before dawn—away from York and southward, withdrawing in good order in the direction of the town of Tadcaster. At least half the enemy horse, who formed the rear guard, were visible on high ground, known as Marston Moor, that stretched between two villages named Tockwith and Long Marston. As Rupert kept his army in a steady advance the horsemen gradually fell away, continuing to shield their army.

Rupert was still on the road to the moorland when Newcastle finally caught up with him on horseback, surrounded by his life guard and followed by his coach and a group of officers. He explained the absence of his troops—during the night they had surged out from the city to loot the abandoned enemy trenches; they had enjoyed the booty they picked up by getting riotously drunk and were now proving very difficult to round up and re-form.

"Lord Eythin will have them in hand very shortly," Newcastle said as they topped the ridge together.

"Not before time," Rupert said coldly. "I expected them at four: it is now nine." Newcastle remained silent beside him. Rupert then received reports from his scouts and rode up to a knoll to see what the enemy were doing. The horse still formed a screen over the heathland in the distance, but beyond them the retreating infantrymen had moved off the moor and were stringing out along the lanes and defiles that led down toward Tadcaster.

Rupert gave a muttered exclamation and the gray Arab shifted his footing beneath him. He was sorely tempted to take his cavalry, smash through the enemy horse and subject the divided enemy foot to a running battle along the lanes, where they would have no chance of turning to fight a solid engagement. But the devil of it was that if he went careering about on the farther ground he would have no hope of controlling what went on elsewhere. He had an army to command and he must do it with the best view of how it was deployed. He hated exaggerated caution, but he told himself a running battle was irresponsible.

While directing his men into position on the moor, he found that Newcastle was by no means convinced they should fight at all that day. The marquess said, "If you had done me the honor of consulting with me yester eve, Your Highness, I could have told you that we daily expect reinforcements to come to York under Colonel Clavering—I venture to hope they number as many as three thousand."

Rupert's lip curled: "On the way here I ventured to hope the same from the Earl of Montrose, but in the event he has not been able to break through to us. My lord, I have waited hours for your infantry—that is no encouragement to hang around for days for Clavering."

"Then may I ask why you are eager to take on a superior force that appears at the moment to be most unwilling to engage you? Should we not allow them to withdraw?"

"They're not withdrawing now," Rupert said. "They can see just what we're doing and they're turning to fight." He sighed. "My lord, the king has commanded me to bring Leven to battle and I must do so."

"For what reasons?" Newcastle asked.

"I received His Majesty's letter a fortnight ago and as you may imagine I have it by heart. He told me: 'If York be lost I consider my crown little less.' " Newcastle drew in a breath at this and Rupert went on, "The king explicitly commanded me to march here and relieve York by beating the Scots. Only three things were to prevent me: if the city was already lost, if you had broken the siege yourself, or if I couldn't lay hands on enough powder to bring it off. Neither of the first applied and I obtained the powder—so here I am." He quoted with acid emphasis, " 'Wherefore in this case, I can no ways doubt of your punctual compliance with your most loving and faithful friend, Charles Rex.' "

"Your Highness," Newcastle said in subdued tones, "please accept my assurance that I shall follow your instructions in all respects as if His Majesty were present in person. I have no ambition but to live and die his loyal subject."

"Thank you, my lord," Rupert said, then galloped away with his officers to direct the positioning of the infantry regiments on the ground sloping toward the two-mile-long road between Tockwith and Long Marston.

It was late in the afternoon of that very laborious, very hot day when Lord Eythin eventually hauled his foot regiments up to Marston Moor. The Earl of Leven had meanwhile recalled his men from the low country that led to Tadcaster and both great armies were drawing up in battle formation. Rupert placed most of the York regiments behind the middle of the first line and some companies of their Whitecoats—so called because of their undyed wool uniforms—behind these. He placed his cavalry on the wings and kept a large reserve; essential if he was to have flexibility against his numerous opponents.

At five o'clock in the afternoon Lord Eythin was riding with Rupert and the officers through the lines and offering his opinions rather more often than Rupert had time for. "You have disposed your troops uncomfortably close to the enemy, Your Highness. I remember years ago you made the same mistake when you rushed at the Austrians at Vlotho."

Rupert gritted his teeth, exchanged a sarcastic glance with Goring, who looked over at him with fellow-feeling, then replied, "Being close ensures that they will engage us, my lord. I intend them to attack first."

Eythin said testily. "They also have the higher ground!"

"Very slightly. But we have the better. The ditch you see down there on our side of the road will break up their infantry advance in the center. On our right wing, Sir John Byron's cavalry is in a handy position behind a field pockmarked with rabbit warrens—he has my orders to draw the enemy cavalry over that field before retaliating, which will seriously hinder them also." He turned to Eythin and said with studied politeness, "But please feel free to tell me if you think any of the regiments could be disposed differently."

Eythin waved his hand vaguely. Rupert concluded his inspection of the battle lines and held a meeting with his officers. Leven showed no sign of attacking and Rupert concluded that it was now too late in the day for him to do so. Newcastle accordingly withdrew to his coach to smoke a pipe and Rupert left Eythin to mind his own business. He ordered the wagons to be brought forward for the troops to take their meal, and had an officer take Boy back and make him fast to a tree in a safe spot on the other side of Wilstrop Wood, a quarter of a mile behind the reserves. Rupert gave the poodle a pat before he went. "I'll take you for a swim in the river tomorrow. *Patience, mon petit.*"

Chapter 34

AT SEVEN O'CLOCK THAT evening, Rupert was sitting on the ground to the rear of his army eating supper when a violent storm began and Leven launched the attack. A salvo of big guns from the high ground behind the enemy lines joined itself to the thunder from the sky and Rupert leaped to his feet, sprang to the saddle and rode forward to see the massed infantry of Scots foot and Lord Fairfax's regiments in the center of the enemy line march out from their uncomfortable positions in wet standing corn. They had eight hundred yards to cover before they reached the ditch below Rupert's infantry but the rain could dampen his men's powder and the great phalanx of enemy foot was a forbidding sight—he calculated they had close to eleven thousand men in their center.

Rupert gave the order for his own ordnance, sixteen guns placed within his front lines, to begin firing. At the same moment both wings of the enemy cavalry swept across the heathland to engage his own. Sir Thomas Fairfax, advancing against the royalist left wing, had Goring's horsemen to contend with plus musketeers placed in the gaps between the regiments, and after a bitter tussle they proved too strong for him. Before long Fairfax's horse were streaming from the field with Goring in hot pursuit, while Goring's second line of horse swung in to batter the startled enemy foot, who now had to contend with Newcastle's infantry. Newcastle himself joined the fray with his guard, pushing beyond the ditch and across the road to carry his men well into Leven's center.

Darkness was falling as Rupert dashed from one vantage point and trouble spot to another to judge what was happening. To his silent astonishment, the whole of the enemy's right wing and center seemed to be in deep difficulty. He could see no cohesion being applied from the opposite high command, and the incredible report came in that Lords Leven and Fairfax had both been seen leaving the field and bolting to the rear. Whatever the truth of this preposterous piece of news, as the light failed he began worrying about what was happening on the right of his army. Sir John Byron was supposed to have stayed put if the enemy charged—but Rupert found that whatever had gone on there, enemy cavalry were pounding across the road and the ditch and plunging into a deadly tangle with his men, who were well forward. He had never faced the first of the two enemy commanders on that wing but he knew his reputation—it was Oliver Cromwell who led the Eastern Association into the field and now Byron was desperately fighting to rally his men against him.

Rupert could watch no longer—with his life guard and the other regiment of horse that formed his reserve he charged down the slope and burst with shattering force into Cromwell's horse, flailing at them again and again to try to force them from the field. It came to close combat with the sword as stubborn lines of men and horses swayed back and forth in the gathering darkness. He never saw Cromwell himself and someone shouted that he had retired wounded. The storm passed and the sounds were now the ring of steel, the rapid concussion of hooves on the stones and mud of the moorland ground and the boom of enemy artillery that was still sending shot up and over into Newcastle's rear lines of infantry. Swinging endlessly at the armored and helmeted men before him and feeling the growing panic of the gray Arab beneath him, Rupert sometimes had the impression that he was hewing at a fortress that could never be breached.

He had used all his reserves for this rescue bid and he had no more horsemen to cast at Cromwell's wall of steel. He could only stand and fight—and suddenly this too became impossible. The second commander on that wing took action and a full regiment of horse thundered in with such massive force that Rupert felt the tide of his men turn and rush away. He joined them, determined to help and regroup them when the first impact was over and they could spin around and give fight again, but it never happened. His whole right wing was in flight and the enemy was turning his flank, skewing his battle line round at right angles to its original orientation and transforming an army that had just tasted victory into divided, muddled and terrified groups of men fighting in the dark.

Thenceforth it was a night of horrors. With his own men dispersed up the slope and far beyond Wilstrop Wood, Rupert could not scramble together a large enough body of his horse to turn toward the enemy, and Sir Richard Crane was nowhere to be seen, though he was probably attempting the very same elsewhere. Fighting through skirmishers to try to get to the center and see what was happening there, Rupert held on to the hope that Goring might have by now returned after chasing Fairfax from the field and would be helping to rally a charge against the flanks of Scots infantry massed across the road. In fact someone told him Goring's second in command had swung troopers into that area, but Rupert could not get through and in searching for them became separated from the remnants of the horse that had been with him, until he realized that he had galloped blindly over so much ground and in such desperate fury that he had lost his sense of direction.

He hauled his horse to a stop in a rutted lane that he thought might lead to a place called White Sike Close. A small stand of trees grew behind the fence above him and in their shadow he and the beast waited, panting and sweating, for some clarity to return. Taking a long, ragged breath, Rupert looked up through the summer leaves in search of the moon that had risen as the thunder clouds dispersed. *You are lost*, the moon said. And a whisper of a breeze through the trees said, *It is lost*. But he banished the sound and at that instant, looking up the lane he saw Sir Richard Crane riding down with five troopers.

He spurred out into view.

Crane cantered up to him, followed by the others. "Your Highness!"

"What the fuck is happening?" Rupert said. "I've lost contact with everyone—tell me."

Crane looked exhausted and grim. He hesitated a moment, then said, "I was looking for you, Your Highness. First there's something . . ." He looked behind him at the black skyline. "It's Boy. He must have broken free."

Rupert looked up the lane for a white shape bounding toward him. Then he realized. "Did he, the devil." After a moment he managed to ask, "Shot or trampled?"

"I believe shot, Your Highness."

He was looking for me. Rupert took another breath. "Thank you. Do you know where Newcastle's Whitecoats are? Someone shouted to me that they're the worst hit, but I can't find them."

Crane said, "We can try this way." They galloped off together toward the sounds of battle.

But everywhere they encountered hordes of their own leaving the field and Rupert began another furious phase of trying to rally them. It took him another hour to realize there was nothing he could do; his surviving men were retreating of their own accord from a battlefield strewn with his broken regiments.

For the rest of the night the enemy occupied Marston Moor and Rupert worked at the bridge of boats and back and forth around the edges of York to regroup his men. News came in to him at punishing intervals: Colonel Henry Tillier was captured; officer after officer was dead, including his friend Viscount Grandison, younger brother of the colonel he had lost at Bristol; the White-coats had refused to surrender and had been cut down to a man.

It was still before dawn and Rupert was preparing to go and confer with Newcastle and Eythin, last seen fleeing to the city, when Sir Richard Crane appeared beside him.

"Your Highness, two of Tillier's foot have been good enough to bring Boy in for you. They picked him up from where I saw him—near Wilstrop Wood."

"Where are they?"

"Not far."

He nodded and said, "I'll follow you."

They headed back in the direction of the river. Standing guard on a little knoll on farmland that stretched away toward the River Ouse were two soldiers. As Rupert rode up he could see Boy at their feet amongst some bushes, a flat white shape that looked like a long, thin sheep. He and Crane dismounted and Crane held their horses while Rupert went up alone and nodded to the men.

He looked down at Boy. He lay unnaturally with his fore and hind legs spread out—the men had arranged him on his side where the bullet had gone in, so no blood would show. Rupert squatted on his haunches and touched the soft white wool at the shoulder, which was surprisingly clean. He did not caress the curly head; Boy's lips were drawn back in an uncharacteristic snarl.

Rupert looked up and said, "You know, he never bit a soul in his life. What do you think of that?" He looked down again and said in his mind, *Adieu, petit diable,* but he swallowed the words. He was not going to mourn an animal in front of his men on this night.

As he rose to his feet one of the men said, "Would you like him buried, Your Highness?"

"Thank you. Thank you both, very much." He looked blankly around. "Somewhere here amongst the bushes where he . . ." He began to unwind his scarlet sash from his waist and one of the men at once stepped forward to help him. "Thank you," he said again and handed it to him. "You'll put this around him, if you please. After I've gone." He patted the men on the shoulder and said, "You're good fellows. You all did your best tonight and there's not a jot of shame in that, for the living or the dead."

When he walked back to the horses, Crane was about to mount up, but Rupert took his arm and spun him round so violently that he saw a rictus of apprehension cross his friend's face. "Richard," he said without relaxing his grip, "promise me you won't die."

Crane looked at him in bewilderment and Rupert put up the other hand and shook him by the shoulders. "As long as we fight together, you won't die! Promise me!"

"Oh, God, Your Highness," Crane said, then gave a helpless laugh and a shrug under Rupert's hands. "If you say so, I promise you I'll not give up the ghost if I can help it. But I can't swear to live to a hundred."

Rupert gave a sound that should have been laughter and released him. Then they mounted up again and rode back to York.

On the seventeenth of July, James Stuart was in Bath, looking out a window into a precipitous street of houses while on the other side of the room the king and Digby were at a large table poring over maps and papers.

The panic that had prompted Charles's mid-June letter to Prince Rupert demanding victory at York had gone by almost as soon as the letter was dispatched. Far from being hunted to earth by Waller, Charles had stayed on the move and knocked him savagely back from the town of Cropredy at the end of that month. Since then the king had left trouble behind him, had reinforced his army with some of the foot from Oxford and had marched unhindered to Bath. It was here at last that Charles received on this day the full report from Rupert of what had happened outside York during the first two days of July.

At dusk on the day of battle it had looked like a great royalist victory, and two of the parliamentary high commanders, Lord Leven and Lord Fairfax, had fled the field and disappeared— Fairfax to Hull and Leven to Leeds. The townspeople of York, convinced of a triumph, had rung the cathedral bells in exultation. But Rupert's letter left no doubt about the speed with which it had turned overnight into crushing defeat. He starkly described the action and with meticulous detail gave numbers on each side before and after the battle, officers and men killed and wounded and men and equipment captured. He blamed no one else for the outcome and made no special reference to having been outnumbered from the start; in fact his only remark was that on the day the devil had taken care of his own.

It hurt James to read his friend's clear, measured phrasing and to imagine the brutal shocks that he must have suffered before the letter was written, and what he had had to endure since. More than four thousand of his men were killed and over a thousand prisoners taken. Newcastle's Whitecoats had been wiped out, having refused quarter and not ceased fighting until they were all either dead or wounded. All Rupert's ordnance, gunpowder and the baggage train were captured. Mary's young Irish cousin Viscount Grandison, who had held the title for only a few months since his brother's death at Bristol, was one of the long list of friends and officers whom Rupert had lost.

A small force was left behind in York to hold it while Rupert got the remnants of his army away from the allies, but neither of the former noble defenders of York had waited for this—the Marquess of Newcastle and Lord Eythin at once set off for Holland with several high-ranking officers. York had since fallen and the holding party had made their agreed exit. During his long march back, Rupert had met up with Clavering and with Montrose's forces, which had come down—too late—from Scotland, and he was making rapid progress to the west. He calculated on reaching Chester by the end of the month and proceeding at once to Shrewsbury.

So the king had lost the entire north of England. Watching from the other side of the room as Charles conferred with Digby, James saw with wonder that no one who had not felt to the bone this dreadful news could form the slightest idea of what it meant from the demeanor of the two people at the table.

The king, thrilled by having just beaten Waller, was deep in plans for a campaign that would bring him up onto the heels of Essex, trap the earl's army between his own forces and those of Prince Maurice in Cornwall, and grind it to pieces. The king did not as yet know whether the queen had sailed away from Falmouth Havens, but it cheered him to be making all speed toward the place where his beloved wife had last been heard from, and he looked forward to meeting his new baby daughter at Exeter. As soon as he arrived he intended to have her christened at Exeter Cathedral.

Digby meanwhile wallowed in a dream of raising two new armies to build on and extend the conclusive royal victories that were to be won in Devon and Cornwall. The first army would be formed of fresh recruits from Ireland—whether they were Catholic or Protestant had ceased to matter to the king, so he now talked of fresh manpower flooding across the Irish Sea.

The second army was to come from Wales, where Prince Rupert had only to step up his efforts to inveigle Welshmen from the green hills and valleys into a gigantic new force.

As James stood looking across the room, Digby spread his fingers out from Bristol to Shrewsbury to encompass Wales. "We shall gather an army for Your Majesty such that England has never seen."

James said without raising his voice, "I notice you have overlooked some part of Prince Rupert's recent correspondence. I recall it—he predicts that not long after his return, the whole of Wales is likely to rise up in revolt. If we winkle even a few hundred men out of there in the future it will be a miracle."

Digby looked up, annoyed. "What gloomy ideas you come up with today, your grace! Prince Rupert has been recruiting to the tune of thousands there. All he has to do is make all speed to return and raise some more."

"He has already given us his best assessment, my lord, and if it does not render *you* gloomy I fail to see what would. To make matters worse, the prince is returning from a massive defeat—do you imagine that will bring an eager horde of Welshmen to his banner? They are a stubborn, independent race and show every sign of washing their hands of us."

Digby gave a complacent smile, which he directed first at James and then, almost with a wink, at the king. "Well, we are far from ready to wash our hands of them!" The witticism received a look of amusement from the king and James had to turn aside to hide his disgust at such an exchange of flattery, false courage and self-endearment.

He could take no more. "Your Majesty. May I be permitted to withdraw?" He named no reason—his temper and his imagination were too far stretched to provide one—but the king looked over with a kind smile and gave him leave to go. James bowed, meeting the king's eye but not trusting himself to look at Digby, swept up his sword and hat from a table by the door and went out.

Once outside he waved his attendants away and strode through the streets alone, looking neither to right nor left, his mind seething with frustrated anger. The tendency of the cobbled lanes was downward and he soon found himself at the river, against a stone wall perched above the strong, dark current of the Avon. He glanced back at the handsome town stacked artfully up the hill behind him, then across at the steep, rugged hillside opposite. The king held Bath. What a triumph. And he would leave it behind shortly for whichever friend or foe had a fancy to occupy it next. To go where? James's mind stopped against another wall, but the words "the wilderness" rang faintly on the other side of it.

He closed his eyes. "Mary," he said aloud, "where shall I see you again?"

He forced himself to do what she would have him do in such a pass. Behind his tight eyelids he painted a picture of them both walking hand in hand down the avenue of pleached apple trees at Cobham with sun slanting through the thick branches and children and hounds playing in the unkempt grass beyond. It lasted until he opened his eyes on the deep-cloven valley that housed this ancient, tired town.

Then he took off his hat and with a flick of the wrist spun it out over the river in a crazy piece of divination and watched to see how it hit the water—crown up or down. It landed the right way up but was instantly caught in an eddy, to spin like a fat waterfowl with its long white feathers trailing and dipping in the water until it hit greater turbulence and bobbed downstream, looking once more like a good felt hat, but stuck on top of a swimmer frantic to get his head above water.

Not having Mary's superstitious gifts, he had no chance of reading any significance into the phenomenon he had created, but he leaned on the wall for a while as passersby gave him curious glances and he watched the thing drift until it was almost out of sight.

He saw himself from the outside: a finely dressed man with tousled hair laughing at a drowning hat. He saved the image for Mary and then turned before the hat vanished and made his way back up the long, uninviting hill.

Chapter 35

MARY WAS IN HER cabin on board ship, lying in the warm, narrow space while the timbers creaked around her. In contrast to her voyage from Dover to the Hague two and a half years before, this one was proving gentle and without storms. And although the ship was smaller, she had a more comfortable cabin, where she slept alone while her two attendants were quartered elsewhere.

Tonight she had retired early to lie down, but sleep had not come. At home she could have called in Anne—but Anne was in Oxford with Dick Gibson and her children, philosophically waiting out the war. Mary had left her glove case of poems in the little woman's care as a secret pledge of her own return someday, and until that time she would write no more. Her next work, however many years she must wait, would be penned in England. But whether she would go home to Oxford, to London or to Cobham, her imagination no longer seemed able to tell her.

Leaving the shores of England felt like a chilling defeat, and it had destroyed her power to dream. From now on it was all hard realities: the queen was on the way to France and the king was on the run; the royal family and household were in fragments; and Rupert, who might have held them all together, was dispatched to the north on a venture that sounded nothing less than suicide, judging by the letters Mary and the queen had received before the departure from Falmouth Havens.

With a shudder of pain and regret she recalled the fervent, idealistic conversation she and Rupert had had in the Wassenaer Hof, on the day when she made the fatal gesture of taking his hand. She had told him then that if he went to England he would be Charles's agent of destruction. It had never occurred to her that Charles might destroy Rupert.

But it was happening. Where now was the bright vision of a swift victory and an honorable compact with Parliament? Long,

long swept away by the king's unrelenting war on his subjects and his botched conspiracies behind their backs and the military bargains he had said he would never make and yet were being patched together wherever possible throughout his kingdom. And all the while the man Mary desperately loved was called upon for the impossible tasks, and carried them out with a bitter fatalism he never shared, even with her. When Mary had read of his brutal campaign in Lancashire, even though she already knew the vigor and fury of which he was capable, it had almost been like hearing of another man. The carnage at Bolton had made her sick with horror. It was like thinking of crowded Magpie Lane in Oxford invaded by his troopers; she saw them smashing their way down the street, slaughtering the street sellers, pulling children from the balconies and running them through, shooting the shopkeepers and the stall women point-blank and then thundering on, leaving behind piles of broken bodies on stones that ran with blood under the smashed stalls.

For some time, all she had prayed for was Rupert's release from such a war. Yet with her new, clear sense of reality, it was like praying for his death—for it seemed the only outcome that could free him. And so after a while even prayers, like dreams, became impossible.

It was partly to the queen that Mary owed a deeper knowledge of the situation into which Rupert had been forced. In the time since she had left the king, Henrietta-Maria had developed new fears that were based not on fancies caused by her own suffering but by memories of the months before she left. She had begun to give Mary a hint of her change of attitude toward Rupert even before they left Oxford. Finally, at Bedford House after the announcement that they were leaving for France, she had beckoned Mary aside and poured out her troubles.

The queen's direst fears were now to do with Digby—the very gentleman on whom she had relied for so long. Looking back, she now convinced herself that Digby possessed an ambition far greater and more dangerous than she or anyone else could have suspected. "But, my dear," she said with her fingers on Mary's arm, "I was the very one who should have seen it—how can I have been so blind? I have thought long and hard—too late—and now I tremble to think that I have left my husband alone with that man. I see it plain now—he thinks of nothing but himself and his own power. He is no servant to the king, for he has all the ambition of a *maker* of kings. He wants to be the sole architect of ultimate victory. He will claim that glory for himself and go down in history for it if he can. Anyone else, including even"—she put her hands over her face—"*que Dieu le prévienne*, even my husband, becomes his instrument to that end."

"Madam," Mary had protested, "this is your anxiety speaking. You exaggerate Digby's influence!"

Henrietta-Maria shook her head and went on, "And if any of those instruments should prove difficult to handle, or get in his way, then he will have no compunction . . . oh, how do I express his villainy? You must believe me! If any one of those instruments looks like being a danger to him, or does not suit his plans, Digby will do everything he can to sheathe it. Or smash it to splinters." She fixed Mary with a stare that turned her cold. "I am certain: Digby has reached such a point that if he should hear that Rupert has been killed at York he will feel it as a personal triumph."

The conversation had ended only when neither woman could go on: when Mary felt too sick to speak and the queen was in tears.

Now Mary lay staring into the close, hot darkness of the cabin, trying to think of how Rupert might be spared the worst in her king's dishonorable war: the end of his ideals; the inexorable warping of his purpose; defeat; death. But he was a warrior and would always be so: therefore, if he were to abandon this war he must also abandon her, to seek another country that needed him. Grief crushed her whenever she admitted the harshest truth: for Rupert to be saved meant separation from him forever. But she would sacrifice anything to save him. Even love.

On July 25 Rupert completed the long journey from York to Chester in a four-day march via Preston and Liverpool. He would take his battered forces straight on toward their headquarters in Shrewsbury next day. Chester was the place where the last fragile shreds of his hopes and dreams had lain locked up, but today, as he rode into town with his officers and guard, it felt empty. It held nothing that he wanted to see or hear or touch again, and he entered his quarters with no sense of homecoming—they were as bleak as the barest of poor billets.

The big room where he held his councils filled with officers, for he wanted to give them their dispositions for the next day. While they gathered he was handed a pile of correspondence and he saw without surprise or pleasure that there was more than one letter from the king. Somehow he could not bring himself to do the usual for his men's sake: open the most recent to scan it and give them any reassuring news. But there was one superscribed in Richmond's firm, familiar hand and as the officers assembled around him he opened and read it quickly.

It did not deserve such haste, being in the duke's tactful, friendly style. The friends often used a cipher between them for sensitive or private messages, but this one was uncoded: Richmond sent Rupert sympathy over what had happened at York, encouragement for whatever could be achieved in the aftermath, and warm personal support. He also gave the latest news concerning the queen, who was known to have sailed from Cornwall. Richmond concluded with words obviously chosen to give Rupert courage and added the remark that as a friend he would be relieved to know that the Duchess of Richmond had left peril behind her and was with the queen on her voyage to safety.

Rupert folded the letter and remained standing behind the large desk.

"Gentlemen, the king is well and expects to make Exeter in the next few days. In fact"—he took up Richmond's letter again and looked at the date—"His Majesty is probably there as we speak. We also have confirmation that the queen has left Cornwall for France. She aims to make landfall in Brittany."

He put the letter down again and observed his patient, travel-weary companions as they exchanged looks of relief and resignation. Then he said, "Gentlemen, you are all . . . You look . . . I am surprised at myself for calling you to this meeting. Especially when I cannot summon a sensible idea for the life of me. You are dismissed and I shall see you at nine tomorrow morning. Have you any questions in the meantime?"

There was a short, startled silence until Sir Richard Crane spoke up. "May I request one word of confirmation, Your Highness? That you are about to spend that time in the repose that we all beg you to take?"

Rupert hesitated a moment, then said, "Yes. Now get you all

gone. I don't want to see hair or hide of you until tomorrow. Monsieur Mortaigne will be holding the door downstairs and it stays locked until nine."

When they had all left the room, including Mortaigne, he went to the window and looked down into the street. He watched his officers rattle away while the Chester citizens stepped out of their path or peered at them from the shelter of the rows of shops. The rows were built with upper stories projecting out over the pavements and thus provided protection from rain, a refuge from the troops when they marched through, and somewhere to stand to let the farmers go by on market days or to avoid cows driven along the central thoroughfare from their grazing fields on one side of town to milking on another. He observed the women bustling down the colonnades with baskets on their arms and children in tow. He watched a young clerk leave upper-floor premises by one of the steep staircases between the shops, and duck into a baker's and set off for his lodgings with his supper under his arm.

In his mind Rupert tried to follow these people home, around corners and into the back lanes of the town where their families were waiting for them to come through the door. He tried to imagine walking around one of those hundreds of corners and catching sight of Mary Villiers stepping lightly toward him with her golden head bent and her hands holding a purple gown above the cobbles. But he couldn't. It was an image from the past and he could not project it into the future. Chester was not his future. Where he was headed was a wasteland.

The light grew dim but he did not call for candles and Mortaigne knew better than to come up and disturb him. He stayed on his feet and moved about the room, fearing that if he succumbed to stillness a new kind of despair would emerge out of the gathering dark and slam into him without mercy.

Eventually, however, the sound of his ceaseless footsteps on the creaky floor grew too much even for Mortaigne and the Frenchman appeared in the open doorway with a candlestick, a severe expression that masked his apprehension of being kicked downstairs, and a piece of folded paper in the other hand.

"I said no messages," Rupert snarled.

Mortaigne put the candle on the desk and stood his ground. "This is not from your commanders, Your Highness. It comes from a lady, or so the messenger said. A groom, I would say he was. He said, 'From a lady, for His Highness.' Then he ran off down the street."

Rupert hesitated, annoyed by Mortaigne's speculative look. His men were always trying to figure out his private life and so far he had thwarted them at every turn—it was beneath his dignity to do otherwise. "Leave it on the table," he said coldly.

When Mortaigne had gone he picked it up. It was a white piece of paper no bigger than a playing card, folded twice. Nothing on the outside, and the inside hardly big enough to contain a signature, let alone a message. But there was one, scratched in fine red chalk. First, the sketch of a butterfly. And underneath, the words: *I am just around the next corner. The White Lion, Northgate Street. Your identity is Monsieur Papillon.*

He put a hand on the desk and sank onto it, one boot on the floor to steady himself. The red butterfly jumped before his eyes. He remembered where he had last seen it. *Essex.* Mary's note to Essex. No. Impossible.

He folded the paper, tried to think, opened it again. A wave of weakness surged over him and he bent forward to support himself on the desktop, his eyes blurring and his mind struggling with improbable hope. It was a trap, to be sprung by an enemy detachment concealed in the White Lion: the only possibility. If he let himself think anything else he was lost.

He spread it out and brought it nearer the candle. *I am just around the next corner.* How could Essex or anyone else write that line and expect him to believe it? It was his own, said to her in the worst moment of his life.

He thrust the piece of paper inside his doublet, strode to the door, opened it and ran down the stairs, every ancient tread squealing in protest beneath his boots. At the door to the street Mortaigne wheeled around, his eyes wide. Rupert swept the Frenchman's hat and cloak off the rack and opened the door himself.

"You don't know where I've gone," he said to Mortaigne. "And if I don't come back, bugger off home, wherever that is, and God keep you." Then he strode away into the summer night.

Chapter 36

MARY WAS WAITING. SHE had been waiting three days, but now that Rupert had returned and she had sent the message, this waiting was different.

Henrietta-Maria, because of her old mistakes and new fears and her eternal love for her husband, had sent Mary to warn Rupert about Digby and the disasters that he must prevent, for his own sake and that of the king. The queen did not say so, but Mary knew some of Rupert's feelings about her had been guessed—so Henrietta-Maria must believe she had chosen the most welcome ambassador to the prince. Which made Henrietta-Maria feel clever and resourceful, and made Mary tremble with suspense.

Sir John Berkeley's troopers had discreetly escorted her north from Exeter to Bideford and on the queen's orders had commandeered a ship to take her along the coast of Wales and then up the estuary of the Dee to Chester. The captain of the vessel did not know her name but his orders were explicit: he was to remain three days in port, and whether the lady was able to fulfill her mission or not in that time, he was to sail with her on the high tide of the fourth day.

The waiting now was different for myriad reasons, none of which Mary could quite register or put in order of impact. From the inn staff, who knew her as Madame Papillon, she had heard about the nightmare of York—the largest battle ever fought on English soil; the deaths of thousands; the loss of her cousin Grandison; the shooting of Boy; the flight of four high commanders, two from each side, leaving a single leader from each to pick up the pieces—Prince Rupert and the Earl of Manchester.

She had not quitted the large, luxurious bedchamber where she now waited, and she had ordered her attendants to remain on the ship. For the three days, only the inn staff tended to her meager wishes. All her other wants were beyond thought or explanation.

But Rupert was in Chester at last and she had sent the message.

She had commanded small things—her only realm. Though it was July she had had a fire built to give light to the room, in which there were few candles. Brocade hangings concealed the high bed. Food and wine stood on a table—the inn was expensive but the landlord's sherry was below standard and she had canceled the order as soon as they brought it up for her to sample. She had called a chambermaid in to fasten her into a gown and catch her hair up with combs. All this in a vivid dream, from which she feared and yearned to awaken.

It was far into dusk; she had drawn the window curtains across and gone to sit by the hearth before he came. She heard his footsteps outside the door and rose to her feet as it opened. He was a tall, dark shape in the doorway, then he pushed it to behind him and leaned against it.

Rupert took in the shadowy room and the still figure by the fire where her hair formed a flaming aureole about her pale face. He took his hand off his sword hilt and his breath came in gasps. All the reasons why she might be here crowded into his head like demons but he shook it to drive them off, without unlocking his gaze. She was in virginal blue and white like a painted statue.

"Rupert!" she said in a voice that did not sound like her own, for it came from the depths of her being, like a cry to another spirit lost in the wilderness. She held out her hands and he cast down sword, hat and cloak and crossed the room.

He threw his arms around her and his mouth descended on hers with crushing force. Imprisoned against him, she was bent in an arc by his hard body and he leaned over her on an angle that drove her head far back, as the kiss banished every thought and every other sensation from her but that of his possession. It punished her for all the time they had had to spend apart, for the power to torture him that she had had at her command from the day he said he loved her. It banished the world and spun everything around them out into nothing so that they were the universe. It filled her with a desire so long dammed up and twisted into shameful channels that now it was like a gigantic wave that threw her against him panting for release.

Her knees buckled and in an instant they were kneeling,

pressed against each other so closely that she could feel every contour of his body while her fingers tore at his clothing to reveal it. But she could hardly move: his mouth was riveted to hers and his arms fastened around her so powerfully that she almost believed he had forgotten his great strength and would keep hauling her into him until her breath stopped in her lungs. In her frenzy and hunger this seemed the place to end her journey—to die in his embrace, to go beyond fears and doubts and wishes into blackness from which she would never return. She struggled until she could get her arms around his neck and then clung to him with a convulsive force that would have strangled her and him if she could have made it mighty enough to match her annihilating desire.

But he released her lips, took her hands from around his neck and put them behind her waist and held them there. She could not see his face—with his knees pressed to hers he was bent with his forehead on her shoulder, so that she could not touch him or move. His breathing was ragged and for a while he said nothing. Shattered and overwhelmed, she closed her eyes and saw behind her eyelids a golden light that washed over her whole being in brilliant ripples, as though there were nothing between her and the sun, not even air.

"You are here," he said. "You are here and I have you. I have you at last."

Then he stood again and raised her, and together they tore off her clothes. His hands were expert but hers shook so much with impatience that they tangled in her hair as she wrenched out the combs and broke her tight necklace so that it cascaded around her, and when at last she stood naked her feet were caught in a billow of blue and white satin scattered with pearls. He took one hot look at her, his gaze traveling over her skin like a caress that warmed her more radiantly than the fire and more deeply than his hands. Then she struggled to help him undress and he laughed low in his throat at her clumsy haste, and stripped all his things from him as sleekly as a sea god emerging through foam.

He pulled her to him and kissed her until he felt her sinking again, then he put one arm around her and the other beneath her knees, scooped her up and carried her to the bed where they fell down together without breaking the kiss.

*   *   *

A long time later she was lying in his arms with her mouth against his chest when he said softly, "Why are you here?"

"You know why," she murmured. She leaned her head back a little to meet his eyes. "It amazes me," she said, "how I used to look at you and think I was discovering you. I used to choose one part of you and learn it by heart." She put up one hand and moved his hair away from his face. "Your eyebrows." She traced one. "They are very arched, like mine. Except when you frown."

He obliged her by snapping them together and she laughed. Her hands drifted down over his face, under his chin and onto his chest again. "By heart," she whispered, and with both hands over his breastbone created an imperfect triangle with joined forefingers and thumbs through which she kissed him solemnly, as though imprinting a mark on his skin that would stay there forever. "But it's now that I know you. At last." She ran one hand between them, down his body to hold him, and he shivered.

Much later again she said in a muffled voice, "I feel so small under you. How can you tell whom you're making love to?"

He laughed, propped himself over her again and looked down between his elbows to where her head lay tilted toward him and her eyes glowed like fireflies in his long shadow.

He said nothing, thinking suddenly that she and Richmond would fit like hand and glove. He slipped his palm beneath her waist and drew her to him and watched the fireflies flicker and then hide themselves beneath her hair.

Later again he pulled one side of the bed curtains back to admit light from the fire, then lay down again on the rumpled sheets to gaze into her eyes. He imprisoned her fingers inside his and said, "Tell me why you are here."

She took a deep breath. "The queen sends me with messages for you. She would not take the risk of writing or dictating them; she trusts and commands me to tell them to you in person. No one else must ever know. I sailed alone from Devon and the captain has orders to leave at dawn."

He closed his eyes and put his forehead against their clasped hands. Finally he said with false calm, "I never did give you my messages to the queen at Oxford. What did you do when you got to her, make some up?"

"No, I told her the truth: that the court had never seen you in more devoted love and duty to the king. It was the best message I could have conveyed to her, and she wept when she heard it."

He turned onto his back and she propped herself beside him with one hand still in his, lightly held on his chest. He said, "Then you had better give me hers."

It was more difficult than she had thought it would be. She said everything the queen had wanted to tell him about Digby and the king's present course, and gave it all with conviction, but sometimes her words sounded feeble, or so she felt. It was partly because he remained silent and partly because of the way he looked at her, making her suspect there were thoughts and impressions running through his mind that had nothing to do with what she was saying. His gaze devoured her, moving over her face and body as though he were waiting to swallow her up. Then in a second his expression would change and she could tell he was listening to every nuance, which made her feel his life might depend on one misdirected sentence, one ill-placed syllable.

At last when her voice was still he put up a hand to touch her cheek and said, "Thank you. I know about Digby and I do all I can to counter him. He has always hated me, of course." He shrugged. "And why not—I abominate him. But I've seen him as personally vindictive. A malicious meddler, with all his quirks and practices. Now I have the queen's judgment of him, it explains a great deal more. I think she is right: where he stands now, he is everyone's enemy. She has allowed me to see him clearly; you must give her my thanks and love in return."

"And will it help you?" she said. "Does it give you enough to evade the wrong turns the king keeps asking you to make?"

He frowned, sat up and thought for a while, the firelight behind him faintly illumining the smooth tips of his wide shoulders and the muscles along his lean sides. He looked down at her. "*Mon amour*, I am the king's general, not his slave. I have always been free to give him my counsel. If a planned engagement is unwise or will result in senseless loss of men, or if a more urgent task is waiting to be performed, I can respectfully ask for the command to pass to someone else. As I did over Gloucester. In an extreme case I can agree to fight but refuse overall command, as Lindsay did at Edgehill. You must not think of me as a pawn in the hands of His Majesty and Lord Digby. I accepted the York campaign and exercised my freedom in doing so."

"I wish you *could* be free," she burst out. "I wish you could be free of it all!"

"What do you mean?" His eyes narrowed. She did not answer and he went on, "Do you mean because His Majesty listens to other people's counsel I should throw my commissions in his face? Do you mean because I lost at York I should scuttle back to Holland like Charles-Louis?"

"Don't look at me like that," she whispered. "All I want is for you to live, and be what you are. Not what others want you to be."

"*Ma vie*, I am a soldier. I cannot exist on dreams; I must have action. I do not possess you, and beyond that nothing matters to me. But I do possess one thing in life and that is my purpose for this kingdom. I will fulfill it, whatever happens."

Tears sprang to her eyes. "Oh, God."

He quickly bent and kissed her eyelids, then ran his hand down her flanks, his gaze following his hand until it lay on her thigh. He said, "A gentleman told me once that when the queen used to put on masques at Whitehall you often performed dressed as a boy. He said you had the best legs at court. Now I know—you have the most beautiful in England."

She wound them around his. "And you the longest." She sighed as she pressed her cheek to his chest. "There is still too much of you, even when I have you trapped in bed. I never thought I should get an ache in my neck making love!"

He shifted so that his face was level with hers again. "There are ways of solving that," he murmured, and his lips began a slow journey down her body.

In the early hours before dawn, he was lying on his back and she had her head on his shoulder and one arm flung across him. She said, "I did not come to talk of loss. But in case you hesitate to speak of Viscount Grandison to me, I know he is gone. And allow me to say Boy's name and tell you I loved him."

He stroked her hair. "Thank you. I knew you would feel it."

Suddenly her fingers dug into his chest. "I'm afraid."

"So am I."

She was so shocked she reared up and looked at his face. Her heart went cold; his lips were trembling. She said, "Afraid! You! Of what?"

"Of the dawn."

She flung herself over him and kissed him avidly, then reached aside and pulled the sheet up and over them both. She stretched her body out along his, buried her arms under his neck and leaned down to put her face against his temple and say into his hair, "I am here and I have you. I have you at last."

Chapter 37

PRINCE RUPERT'S MEN DID not see him at all the next morning. He returned before dawn to his quarters, said nothing to Mortaigne, who assumed that the meeting would still be held, and went upstairs to sit in the council room alone. But at seven he ran downstairs again and demanded his horse, and when it was brought rode off without a word.

Rupert had promised to let Mary leave without going to the docks to say good-bye, and she had told him she would not allow him on board, or come ashore or even appear on deck herself when the ship caught the rising tide and began its slow escape from the long, winding estuary of the Dee. So he had shut himself away and willed himself to obey her, until the hands of the clock in the empty room showed him that the ship would have cast off, raised her sails and gone beyond the great curve of the river and out of reach.

"You see," he said to her in his mind, "how *I, my sovereign, watch the clock for you.*"

And then suddenly it became unbearable and he thundered through the town and out from the walls at the Watergate where the ancient water tower stood overlooking the docks. He asked the first sailor he saw and the answer was simple—the ship had sailed with the tide. It was nowhere to be seen on the flood so he spurred down across the green acres of the Roodee below, a vast area where they held horse races and fairs and where cows grazed sometimes on the margins before being driven downriver to meadows by the sands.

When he reached the riverside on the shores of the Roodee he knew he should go no farther. He pulled the Arab to a stop and bent over to try to get a stitch out of his side, caused by the idiotic way he had been breathing—as though holding the air in would change the wind and tide and bring her ship miraculously back.

Everything hurt—his mind, his heart, his body—but he must

face the truth. Wherever Mary believed she was headed, whatever the queen's orders were, wherever the ship was going, in the end it was toward her life with Richmond.

He leaned on the pommel of the saddle and looked out over the field toward a mound in the center topped by a stone cross. Under the mound was a statue of the Virgin. Seven hundred years before, the statue had been downstream at Hawarden Castle, where one day it had committed a great crime—it fell onto a noblewoman praying before it, and killed her. The Hawarden people put the statue on trial for murder, condemned her to death by drowning and threw her in the Dee. But she was washed upstream with the tides to Chester, where the townspeople took pity on her and buried her, putting up the stone rood to mark her grave. Ever since hearing the story Rupert had been haunted by the image of the Virgin Mary's drowned corpse drifting in the Dee, and sometimes in his mind she took the shape of a tender human body with bright hair waving in the current.

He could not go back yet; he must force his mind to take in the meaning of Mary's voyage. She had come to try to free him from the follies and demands of the king—but she had not freed herself, for she was obeying the queen to the letter by leaving.

Only once during the night had she said that she loved him— in her ecstasy, when the words were torn from her as though by force. And once again before daybreak when she embraced him on the threshold of the room. *Ah, but I love you!* A cry of agony.

She had come to Chester to persuade him into a different path. To save his life, or so she thought. To show him she was brave enough to go one way while he went another. This was her choice, out of love, and she would not change it.

Nonetheless, with the pain still in his side he wheeled the stallion and sent it flying along the shore and beyond the curve to where he could see the river flowing on between its sandbanks and into the distance amongst broad screens of trees in summer leaf. He pulled the Arab to a halt and looked downstream. A breeze scudded here and there across the surface of the Dee and the sun gilded the edges of the ripples with warm morning light. There were shallops bobbing on the margins and fishermen in small boats dipping nets and lines in the tide. Nothing else moved on the dun-colored surface.

He slipped from the saddle, dropped to his knees and covered his face. The sobs that shook him seemed to come from outside, as though someone were striking his chest with hammer blows. He wept for so long that a kind of exhaustion took over and he collapsed onto the sand, until the stallion standing over him became anxious and nudged his cheek with its nose, blowing softly into his hair.

He sat up then, but could not raise his head to look at the empty stretch of water that was carrying Mary to the sea. He took the piece of steel out of his doublet and gazed at her face, then pressed it to his forehead until it hurt, and told himself he should throw it in the tide. He should cast her image away, for she was gone in truth, and truths were now the only things he must be prepared to contemplate.

But at last he stood up and placed it over his heart again and looked downriver. Nothing moved on the water save the languid fishing boats, and far off over the sands he could see a woman walking, carrying a long willow wand and calling faintly to cattle in the meadows beyond.

Then he mounted up, and the man who never cried rode back along the waterside and let his horse find the way into the town, for he could see neither river nor land nor any path through his tears.

Historical Note

ALMOST FROM THE MOMENT I knew I wanted to write books, I wished to write a novel about the English Civil War—or, as I phrased it in childhood, about the Cavaliers and the Roundheads. The occasion for this one finally occurred when I was in England on a private tour of the Civil War battlefields, and in General Sir Frank Kitson's masterly *Prince Rupert: Portrait of a Soldier* I came upon this decorous sentence referring to events in late 1643: "It would seem that at about this time Rupert added to his personal difficulties by falling in love with the Duchess of Richmond."

Nothing of what I subsequently wrote should be blamed on Sir Frank Kitson, but this focus of interest did furnish three things for *The Winter Prince*: the time frame, which charts the beginning of King Charles the First's struggle with Parliament; the military context, which resolves itself into the protracted duel between Prince Rupert and the Earl of Essex; and a triangle of characters—Prince Rupert of the Rhine; James Stuart, Duke of Richmond; and Mary Villiers, Duchess of Richmond. I have concentrated here on what was happening, to the best of our knowledge, among and around these people from the beginning of 1642 until mid-1644.

Whether there was an intimate relationship between Rupert and Mary was their business and has remained so for more than three and a half centuries; certain of their exchanges in this novel are thus inventions. But I wish the reader to have no doubt that the origins, personal attributes, allegiances and crucial events in the lives of these three people are part of voluminous historical record. Otherwise anyone unfamiliar with the history of Prince Rupert, especially, might be tempted to think it all fiction: his family; his powerful intelligence and skills; his singular education and early mastery of war; the continuous victories he won for Charles I; his loyalty and sense of honor. These plus his personal beauty and strength, right down to his tastes, his sardonic humor and even his pets, are all authentic.

Portraits of these three people and of their contemporaries are to be found in art galleries worldwide, the most splendid and revealing being those by Honthorst and Van Dyck. From a portrait of James Stuart one may read in his alert, narrow face and thoughtful gaze the man of many qualities who was King Charles's not too distant cousin, and his close and valued adviser throughout the war. Mary Villiers was one of Van Dyck's favorite subjects and it is easy to see why, for she combined dramatic beauty with keen wit, and one detects in her also a subtle intellect and sense of purpose. Since the groundbreaking research of Maureen E. Mulvihill, scholars have come to believe that she might have been "Ephelia," a published poet of the Stuart court whose identity was carefully concealed.

All the personages named in this book are on historical record except the barmaid of the Blue Boar Inn (sited where the Museum of Oxford now stands). The poems, prayers, and propaganda quoted are all by the authors named. Of the letters quoted, all are on record except Mary's to Rupert, her notes to the Earl of Essex and Digby's to her in the Hague. All the characters' movements are strictly in accord with history, except for two liberties I have taken with Mary's: the date and manner of her journey from Holland to Yorkshire and of her departure from England.

The tide of the Civil War changed after the events we see in this novel. Following the royalist defeat at the Battle of Naseby in June 1645, Rupert supported proposals to conclude a peace with Parliament. When he surrendered Bristol in the same year the king stripped him of his commissions, but Rupert demanded a court-martial and was exonerated of disloyalty. In 1646 he went to fight for France; while commanding a brigade in the Spanish Netherlands he received a bullet wound to the head, the only time he was seriously wounded in his career, and was evacuated to Paris, where he gradually recovered. There in 1647 he challenged Lord Digby to a duel over the latter's actions in England, but the duel was prevented by Henrietta-Maria.

Rupert's next commission was at sea, as commander of King Charles's fleet. On land, however, Parliament's armies proved victorious and caused Charles to flee; the Prince of Wales escaped abroad, Charles gave himself up to the Scots, who handed him to Parliament, and the king was beheaded in 1649. Thenceforth Parliament ruled England, eventually naming Oliver Cromwell Lord Protector of the Commonwealth.

Rupert turned freebooter and with Prince Maurice operated mainly in the West Indies, where to Rupert's grief Maurice's ship was lost in a hurricane—although, as with his brother's supposed death at Plymouth, Rupert refused at first to believe Maurice was gone. In 1654 Rupert went to live in the German states but he returned to England in 1660 after the restoration of Charles II (the young Prince Charles of this novel) to the throne. In 1668 Rupert was appointed governor and captain of Windsor Castle, which became his principal residence. Rupert sat on the Privy Council, was created admiral and played an important part in the Dutch Wars. Meanwhile he continued his energetic interest in the arts and sciences, helped found the Royal Society, and is credited amongst other achievements with the invention of the mezzotint. He was the first governor of the Hudson's Bay Company, and Rupert's Land in Canada was named after him, as is the town of Prince Rupert in British Columbia.

Rupert is known to have fallen in love with Mary Villiers in late 1643, when parliamentary propaganda of the time scurrilously linked their names. The Richmonds, however, continued throughout to treat him as a close friend—an unsigned letter to Rupert in 1645, when he was at odds with the king, is believed to have been from Mary. In it she said she valued him "more than all the world besides." If Mary Villiers was Ephelia and if the poem "To Phylocles, inviting him to Friendship" was written on Rupert's account, it is plausible to imagine Mary penning it in 1643.

Rupert never married, but he did have children. Dudley, his son by Lady Francesca Bard, was born in 1666; though estranged from Lady Bard within a few years, Rupert acknowledged and supported his son, sent him to Eton and provided him with a military education. Dudley was killed in Hungary in 1686, fighting with English volunteers against a Turkish army. Rupert also had a daughter, Ruperta, by the mistress who was devoted to him until his last days, dramatic actress Margaret Hughes. Ruperta married a British army officer in 1671 and her granddaughter married into the Bromley family; the present baronet is a direct descendant.

Prince Rupert died at his London home in 1682 and was buried in Westminster Abbey. "A Pindaric Ode on Prince Rupert's Death" began:

> *Tell me, ye skillful men, if ye have read*
> *In all the fair memorials of the dead*
> *A name so formidably great,*
> *So full of wonder and unenvied love,*
> *In which all virtues and all graces strove—*
> *So terrible and yet so sweet?*

Mary Villiers joined Queen Henrietta-Maria in France for a time and was staunchly faithful to the royal family in exile. After Parliament's victories and the execution of Charles I, Mary worked with her charismatic brother George, Duke of Buckingham, as an undercover courier for the royalists. Mary and James had two children who survived, and she was known to have had other pregnancies. Their children were Esmé, born in 1649, who became fifth Duke of Richmond and Lennox but died in 1660, and Mary, Baroness Clifton de Leighton Bromswold (1651–1668).

Two more of James Stuart's brothers, John and Bernard, were to die in battle during the Civil War. James himself died of an illness in 1655, before the monarchy for which he had made so many sacrifices was restored. Under the Restoration, Mary retained her title and took up her former place at court, where she continued to exercise her wit and talents, often in a satirical vein since the licentiousness of Charles II's household was in distinct contrast to the sobriety of his late father's court. The works of Ephelia, dramatic poems of love and biting political comment, were first published in 1678. Mary married a third time in secret in 1664, her husband being Colonel Thomas Howard, brother to the Earl of Carlisle. Howard was a Roman Catholic and Mary herself converted, dying a Catholic in 1685, three years after Rupert. Rupert and Mary thus happened to live to the same age, sixty-three. Mary Villiers lies buried in Westminster Abbey.

I conclude with a few glimpses of other characters. The Earl of Essex, who suffered a string of losses in Devon and Cornwall, resigned his commission in 1645 and lived in honorable retirement until his death from a sudden illness in 1646. Sadly, Rupert did lose his friend Sir Richard Crane, who was killed in an engagement outside Bristol in August 1645. Lady Ann Dalkeith, after many setbacks, restored Henrietta-Anne to her mother in France, where the queen was also reunited at different times with the princes Charles, James and Henry (Princess Elizabeth died of lung disease in England in 1650). Henrietta-Maria never saw Charles I again and after his execution wore black for the rest of her life. Sir William Harvey did receive in his lifetime great acclaim for his theory of the circulation of blood. The Gibsons lived peacefully in England while Jeffrey Hudson accompanied the queen to France; a year later he had to flee Paris, however, after killing in a duel a French gentleman who had made the mistake of insulting him. The poet Edmund Waller was not executed by Parliament—after a year in the Tower he got off with a ten-thousand-pound fine and banishment from England. Richard Baxter, the clergyman from Inkborough, eventually became a chaplain to the parliamentary forces and he served with them until the end of the war. The stone cross in the Roodee at Chester was moved southward at some time over the last two hundred years, so no one can now be sure where the drowned Virgin Mary lies.

Acknowledgments

FIRST I WANT TO pay tribute to my dear husband, Bert: for months in Costa Rica we were both writing historical novels and reading them to each other in progress—thus every night during the creation of this book we sailed from our tropical home to the England of the past. Thank you, my love, for those magical journeys.

In chronological order of influence I would like to thank again Jocelyn Banks, schoolfriend in Cambridge, New Zealand, who when I was eight years old gave me a book I still possess: *The Children of the New Forest* by Captain Marryat. And my brother David, who invented many games based on a painting called *The New Blade* that we have since lost.

Next, very special thanks go to my agent, Kristin Nelson, and editor, Anne Bohner, for giving me the impetus to realize a long-held wish to write a novel in which every character is drawn from history.

To our friends Eric and Patricia Tracey, thank you again for the car in which we drove to the battlefields of the Civil War and the wellies in which I tramped across them. . . .

Amongst the many biographies of Prince Rupert and the histories that treat of him at length I find myself most indebted to Sir Frank Kitson, whose *Prince Rupert: Portrait of a Soldier* inspired me to choose the prince as the hero of this novel, and also to follow closely the remarkable events of his life from 1642 to 1644. The sequel biography is *Prince Rupert: Admiral and General-at-Sea*. Sir Frank very generously consented to read the manuscript of this novel for military accuracy.

No one interested in the royalist command during the Civil War can dispense with the nineteenth-century classic *Memoirs of Prince Rupert and the Cavaliers* by Eliot Warburton, whose three volumes contain much firsthand material.

For a general account of the Civil War it is impossible for me to imagine a more luminously structured or more elegant work than Austin Woolrych's *Britain in Revolution 1625–1660*. This masterpiece helped me understand the factors during the reign of Charles I that drew the three kingdoms into war, and illumined for me the choices made by the real people who became the focus of this novel. (I have followed Professor Woolrych's spellings for names.)

I wish to express great thanks to Maureen Mulvihill, author and scholar at the Princeton Research Forum, New Jersey, who helped restore the poems of Ephelia to the canon of seventeenth-century English poetry and whose research into and commentary on Mary Villiers fostered my curiosity about her character. The figure of Mary Villiers in this novel is of course fictional, and I make no claim that it would correspond exactly with the judgment of any student of the Duchess of Richmond's early life. I appreciate Maureen's kind correspondence with me on matters relating to Mary Villiers and the Restoration Stuart court, and I recommend that anyone wishing to see the Ephelia poems within a scholarly framework should read Maureen E. Mulvihill's edition, *Ephelia*, Volume 8 in *The Early Modern Englishwoman: a Facsimile Library of Essential Works*, Series II. Her multimedia archive, "Thumbprints of Ephelia," can be seen at www.millersville.edu/~resound/ephelia.

Alison Plowden's *The Stuart Princesses* and John Barratt's *Cavaliers: The Royalist Army at War 1642–1646* gave me valuable insights into the lives of the women, children and men involved at a high level in the Civil War.

My thanks also to Charles, Earl Spencer, for replying to an inquiry I sent him concerning Prince Rupert's actions during the battle of Marston Moor. Earl Spencer's coming military biography is *Prince Rupert: The Last Cavalier*.

I thank freelance writer Victoria Hill for drawing my attention to details concerning Anne and Richard Gibson. Readers interested in them and in Jeffrey Hudson may refer to *Lord Minimus: The Extraordinary Life of Britain's Smallest Man* by Nick Page.

The map of Rupert and Mary's England is by Map Illustrations: www.mapillustrations.com.au.

The Winter Prince is **Cheryl Sawyer's** sixth published novel, and her first in which every character is drawn from the historical record. She says, "Rupert and Mary were the superstars of their era. It was irrisistable to uncover the wellsprings of their turbulent lives." Sawyer has two master's degrees, in English and French literature; her subsequent publishing career brought her to Australia from New Zealand and at present she is editorial manager for an international company in Sydney. In 2005 she took a twelve-month sabbatical to research and write in Europe, the USA and Central America. While in England she made a private tour of the Civil War battlefields and spent time in the handsome city of Oxford, which was King Charles I's capital in the 1640s; in Sawyer's novel it becomes one of the rich settings for the drama between Prince Rupert of the Rhine and Mary Villiers, Duchess of Richmond.